DA BIG DAKKA

DA BIG DAKKA

AN UFTHAK BLACKHAWK NOVEL

MIKE BROOKS

BLACK LIBRARY

A BLACK LIBRARY PUBLICATION

First published in 2024.
This edition published in Great Britain in 2024 by
Black Library, Games Workshop Ltd., Willow Road,
Nottingham, NG7 2WS, UK.

Represented by: Games Workshop Limited – Irish branch,
Unit 3, Lower Liffey Street, Dublin 1,
D01 K199, Ireland.

10 9 8 7 6 5 4 3 2 1

Produced by Games Workshop in Nottingham.
Cover illustration by Chris Campbell.

See Black Library on the internet at

blacklibrary.com

Find out more about Games Workshop
and the worlds of Warhammer at

warhammer.com

Printed and bound in the UK.

They said I couldn't dedicate a book to myself, and I said
WHY ARE YOU IN MY HOUSE?!

For more than a hundred centuries the Emperor
has sat immobile on the Golden Throne of Earth.
He is the Master of Mankind. By the might of his
inexhaustible armies a million worlds stand
against the dark.

Yet, he is a rotting carcass, the Carrion Lord of
the Imperium held in life by marvels from the
Dark Age of Technology and the thousand souls
sacrificed each day so his may continue to burn.

To be a man in such times is to be one amongst
untold billions. It is to live in the cruelest and
most bloody regime imaginable. It is to suffer an
eternity of carnage and slaughter. It is to have cries
of anguish and sorrow drowned by the thirsting
laughter of dark gods.

This is a dark and terrible era where you will
find little comfort or hope. Forget the power of
technology and science. Forget the promise of
progress and advancement. Forget any notion of
common humanity or compassion.

There is no peace amongst the stars, for in the grim
darkness of the far future, there is only war.

'OO'Z 'OO

ORKS

UFTHAK BLACKHAWK	Big boss of Da Tekwaaagh!
MOGROT REDTOOF	Ufthak's right-hand ork
DA BOFFIN	Chief Mekboy
DOK DROZFANG	Chief Painboy
DA MEKLORD	Da Biggest Big Mek, Warboss of the Tekwaaagh!
NAZLUG	Spanner
DEFFROW	Nob
UZKOP	Weirdboy
DREGGIT	Spanner
WAZZOCK	Nob

GROTS

NIZKWIK	Ufthak's squigsbody
SNAGGI LITTLETOOF	Da Grotboss, Prophet of Gork an' Mork
GEKKI SHORTNOSE	A grot
GIP	A grot
SWIPE	A grot
NIB	A grot
MOZZ	A grot
BEEZ	A grot
LONGTOOF	A grot
SQUEEZA	A Disorderly
SNEEZA	A Disorderly

SQUIGS

PRINCESS   Ufthak's pet squig

DRUKHARI

DHAEMIRA THRAEX   Master Archon of the Kabal
                            of the Hollow Heart

ENZALE OZREIH   Seneschal to Dhaemira Thraex

ILYONITH ZESK   Dracon of the Kabal of the
                            Hollow Heart, commander
                            of the Trueborn

ZOTHAR ORIDRAED   Archon of the Kabal of the
                            Wounding Wind

MACULATIX   Master Haemonculus of the
                            Red Harvest

CISTRIAL VIRN   Master Archon of the Kabal of
                            the Falling Night

DHALGAR THRAEX   Archon of the Kabal of the
                            Hollow Heart, Dhaemira's
                            younger brother

XURZULI MINDREX   Grand Succubus of the Cult of
                            the Deathly Sorrow

KARFYND   Beastmaster of the Cult of
                            the Deathly Sorrow

PROLOGUE

Like a swamp made of knives, Port Tavarr squatted beneath the un-light of its captured sun. The slender, crooked shape of Fahrrul's Needle towered above all, but it was a hollow and ruined place. Broken windows pockmarked its surface like open sores, and sub-spires and offshoot towers were truncated or shorn clean off. Lord Fahrrul had not openly celebrated the death of Asdrubael Vect, supreme overlord of the Dark City of Commorragh, but the civil war that erupted in the wake of Vect's reincarnation by the blood of friend and foe had claimed Fahrrul and his territories. Now Port Tavarr, like many other sub-realms of Commorragh, was permanently on the edge of even more bloodshed than usual, as rival archons sought to claim pre-eminence without exposing their throats to another's blades.

The Venom transport came in fast and high, then rolled and plunged downwards towards Dhaemira Thraex like an aerial predator that had seen a plump avian fluttering obliviously below. She watched it approach, observing the skill of the pilot even as she prepared herself for combat. This meeting was pre-arranged, the terms pre-agreed, but nothing was certain in Commorragh, least of all now. It would be foolish indeed for the Kabal of the Wounding Wind to declare war on her Kabal of the Hollow Heart by attempting to assassinate her – her forces far outnumbered and outmatched theirs. Yet, this was a time of fools.

And that was without taking into consideration the possibility that another element had gained access to a Wounding Wind Venom and was using it to get close to her. Uklail Ghendrieth's Kabal of the Burning Red, perhaps? He would clothe his warriors in Wounding Wind colours, so that even if his attempt on her life failed, she might blame the wrong party. Or maybe the Cult of the Silver Shards – the wyches of the narrowdowns had hated Dhaemira since she annihilated their allies in the Kabal of Twelve Wounds. Sulmu Khevrein wouldn't bother with further deception; her fighters would simply emerge screaming their hatred, pupils like pinpricks as cocktails of combat drugs such as adrenalight or grave lotus thundered through their veins.

All things considered, it might seem foolish for Dhaemira Thraex to be standing so openly atop the tallest tower of Heartpoint, her home and citadel, but all was calculated risk. The Kabal of the Wounding Wind was small and weak, so cowering in her throne room and making them pass through her guarded halls showed them too much respect. She would meet them on this rooftop with the wind in her hair, as though the mere thought of betrayal was an impossibility, and they were little more than underlings coming to receive routine instruction. Which, in fairness, they more or less were.

Besides which, receiving her visitors within would expose them to many eyes, and although many eyes within Heartpoint no longer had tongues capable of forming words, not all her servants could be silenced, and there were other methods of communication. A servant without hands was of limited use, and hands could form script for others to read. Better to keep this meeting brief, so casual observers might not notice it.

Her bodyguard brought their weapons up to cover the Venom as it screamed in on its final approach. They were kabalite warriors, trueborn like her, each one gestated within a parent's womb and expunged into the world in pain and blood – a fitting birth for a drukhari – and amongst the finest fighters under her command. Dhaemira herself stood casually, as though their vigilance was of no concern to her, but her shadow field was ready to activate on a hair-trigger and turn her into a bewildering smudge of darkness in which weapons would struggle to find her. It was important not to look paranoid, but actually *being* paranoid was one of the most important survival skills in the Dark City. Beside her, Enzale Ozreih was more obviously tense; but then, her seneschal lacked the same protections as her.

The Venom pulled out of its dive without opening fire, and came to a hovering halt at her eye level. Five shards of midnight disembarked, flowing with the grace of true predators, like black ink with edges of razors. Incubi: arguably the greatest hand-to-hand warriors of all the drukhari, and some of the most feared in the entire galaxy. They were followed by the red-and-silver-armoured form of Zothar Oridraed, lord of the Kabal of the Wounding Wind. His cloak swirled around him as his boots landed on the dark stone of Heartpoint, and the bow he gave Dhaemira was shallow, his smile not without a hint of mockery.

Dhaemira's own smile was knowing. A bodyguard of five warriors from the Shrine of the Last Breath made Oridraed look well resourced... unless, like Dhaemira, you knew that this was the extent of his contract with them. Five incubi only:

that was all this so-called archon could afford to retain, with his other commitments. The Kabal of the Wounding Wind was barely large enough to bear the title, and other kabals might have taken exception to its impudence at adopting such airs had Port Tavarr's instability not concentrated their minds on other matters. Oridraed was trying to expand and secure his power base quickly, before his ambition irritated anyone enough for them to wipe him out while it was still easy to do so. That made him ruthless, but ruthlessness was not in short supply in Commorragh.

It also made him desperate, and that was something Dhaemira could use.

'Lady Thraex,' Oridraed said. He managed to look and sound haughty even when offering an honorific, but that was as much a ploy as Dhaemira's studied nonchalance. Appearances were crucial in the Dark City; the perceptions others had of you could quite literally dictate whether you lived or died. Zothar Oridraed sought to be an archon and so, lacking the power or influence to secure that title outright, he had to present himself as an archon unequivocally so that the minds of others filled in the gaps. He had to do so even if it risked angering those to whom he claimed to be a peer, because nothing came easily in Commorragh. Even death could be remarkably difficult to achieve if you crossed the wrong person, no matter how you screamed and begged for it.

'You're late,' Dhaemira said, inspecting the finish of her right gauntlet. She could feel Oridraed bristle, but her snub was not as damaging as it might have been. Another reason to be accompanied by incubi to a meeting such as this was that they were loyal only to coin. An ambitious warrior might see his archon mocked and take it as a sign of weakness – one that could open the way to a knife in the back – but incubi cared nothing for such things.

'Your message spoke of a realspace raid,' Oridraed said, ignoring her jibe. He feigned an air of unconcern, placing his hands behind his back and looking around as though admiring the view while they spoke of trifles, but Dhaemira could feel the urgency that beat within him. He was not naive enough to think that an alliance between their kabals would make him her equal, but it was far from unheard of for small groups like his to enter into an arrangement with a larger one. Serving as an auxiliary force – inevitably viewed as disposable – in exchange for the chance of greater plunder than they could have managed on their own was a good deal, so long as Oridraed himself could stay alive.

'A realspace raid, *Lady Thraex*,' Enzale snapped, but Dhaemira waved a hand idly to dismiss her seneschal's correction. That was what he was for, in this context: to remind others of how she was their better, in order for her to appear magnanimous by then ignoring him. (Also, as a tempting secondary target for an assassin if they missed their first strike at her, to discourage them from pursuing.)

'Indeed,' she said to Oridraed, as though Enzale had never spoken. 'The world of Shau-Har.'

A true smile split Oridraed's face, narrow lips parting to reveal sharp teeth. 'The maiden world? You seek sport with our rustic cousins?'

'Not exactly,' Dhaemira said. 'Shau-Har is under attack from the *arakhia*, now. The ork brutes have rampaged over it, and our kin have been unable to stop them. I believe the world spirit remains undamaged, but it nonetheless angers me to think of the Children of Destruction despoiling such a place.'

Zothar Oridraed's dark eyes regarded her steadily. 'I did not know you cared so much about the lands of our cousins. Have you not hunted them yourself before now?'

'Many times,' Dhaemira said. She recalled one time in particular, when she had used a lance to impale one of the so-called dragon knights and lift him from his saddle as her Venom passed by. The Exodites were not fundamentally different from those who dwelled in Commorragh, or their kin from the craftworlds – indeed, on occasion, individuals would move from one way of life to another – but for the most part, Dhaemira thought of them as prey. 'That world belongs to the aeldari, and I will not countenance the arakhia taking it from us. They make poor sport, after all. Their pain receptors are crude, and their emotions are blunt – it's barely possible to inflict proper suffering on one before it dies. I would rather keep Shau-Har as a more bountiful hunting ground. However,' she added, 'for various reasons, I cannot commit my own forces to this endeavour.'

Oridraed's face slid into a knowing expression. 'And what of your brother? I hear Lord Dhalgar has a particular interest in hunting vermin.'

'That is not your concern,' Enzale said, his tone one of warning. Dhaemira kept her own expression studiously neutral. Dhalgar was her junior in all respects, but he was ambitious. He did indeed relish hunting non-aeldari sentient life, but he had also been flattened by the arakhia chieftain, and was currently in the process of having his body regrown in the lairs of the Coven of the Red Harvest. This was not something the Kabal of the Hollow Heart had made public – there was face to be saved, after all – but it seemed Oridraed had heard enough whispers to fish for more information.

'My brother will not be joining you either,' Dhaemira said. 'If you and your forces were to undertake this cleansing mission for me, you would not find me ungrateful.'

She trusted Oridraed to read her intent. When Dhalgar recovered himself, he would want to find the ork in question and exact revenge, as much to reclaim his own honour as anything. If the beast that had so embarrassed him was already skinned then he could not do so, which would lower his standing. If Dhaemira did it herself, she was obviously interfering and it would be seen as a direct slight. If the ork happened to fall to an unrelated raid from a different kabal, there was nothing to be done; and if that kabal happened to be a minor one, barely worthy of the name, it would make Dhalgar's ignominy burn all the brighter. Secrets never stayed buried for long in Commorragh, and this could go some way to tempering her younger brother's ambitions for a while.

Oridraed had wit enough to see that, at least. Taking Dhalgar's kill would earn him an enemy, but one unable to pursue his vendetta openly without admitting to his own shame. And to be sure, there were plenty of ways of pursuing vendettas through covert means, but that was simply how life went in Commorragh – and indeed, often how life ended. In addition, Oridraed would gain a more powerful ally in Dhaemira, which was the sort of legitimacy his would-be kabal badly needed.

'The gratitude of one such as yourself is never to be shunned,' Oridraed said, with a sweeping bow whose purpose was more to display his armour, cloak, and grace than to honour her. Dhaemira suppressed an amused smile; if Zothar Oridraed thought he could impress her into making their alliance one bonded through marriage, then his judgement was worse than she had envisaged. It would serve no purpose to turn him down directly at this juncture, though, so she contented herself with raising an eyebrow.

'However,' Oridraed said as he straightened, 'there are certain practical matters that must be discussed before we may proceed...'

Bargaining, of course. Dhaemira humoured him well enough,

conceding the use of three of her Raider transports, and passing no comment on the fact that some of the warriors under his command apparently had no vehicles of their own. She haggled hard enough over the division of spoils that their transaction seemed genuine, but not so long that she came across as miserly; he was the desperate one, after all, whereas she was playing the role of the master archon with near-infinite resources. When Oridraed leapt back up onto his Venom with another swirl of his cape, flanked by his black-clad bodyguard, he wore the smile of someone who felt he could see a promising future unfolding.

'He will seek to use the details of this arrangement against you, my lady,' Enzale said into her ear as they left the roof, his voice pitched so low that even her kabalite warriors would not hear him. *You lack subtlety,* Dhaemira heard the old retainer's voice echo back through the years from her childhood, from when he could phrase his criticism more harshly, *and that will be your death.* Enzale's spoken words were true. Oridraed might value his alliance with her, but if he felt it would benefit him then he would sow seeds of internal conflict in the Kabal of the Hollow Heart with rumours of what he had done and why, and at whose bidding. Indeed, at the right moment, he might try to buy his way into Dhalgar's favour with the truth of how he had come to be hunting ork on Shau-Har.

'That is only a problem if he survives,' Dhaemira whispered back.

ONE

Ufthak Blackhawk's head hurt, and he blamed the finkin'.

He'd never put much faith in finkin' before; it was the sort of thing mekboyz did, or warbosses. He'd never had much time for it. He'd never needed to. He'd been a regular ork in Badgit Snazzhammer's mob, going where his boss told him and stompin' anyone who got in their way. Then he'd lost most of his body and Badgit had lost all of his head, and Dok Drozfang had stuck one on top of the other to give Ufthak a bigger body than he'd had before, and also the Snazzhammer which had given Badgit his name. Ufthak took over as boss, and then that scrap on Hephaesto happened and Da Meklord made Ufthak a big boss.

Ufthak had led his boyz through all sorts of fights since then, and they'd got bigger and tougher as they went. That was only natural – one of the weird things about humies and the like was that you couldn't always tell which one was in charge, because most of them were about the same size – but as he'd got bigger, Ufthak had begun to notice other changes.

It was the finkin'. It was happening more often, sometimes when he didn't even mean to do it. Snuck up on him, it did, like a sniffer squig stalking a grot. What was even worse was when he realised that he was finkin' about finkin'. That was pure unnerving.

Right now, he was finkin' about the planet he and his ladz were on. His part of the Tekwaaagh! had landed on it merrily enough, but they hadn't found much. There were a bunch of scrawniez here, those skinny gits with pointy ears what stuck you with sharp things and then skipped away before you could get 'em a good walloping back, but these ones were unlike those Ufthak had encountered before. Their guns were less zippy, and they rode around on massive beasts the size of squiggoths instead of hovering whatnots. That had made for a few interesting fights, but there were nowhere near enough scrawniez to go round. The Waaagh! hadn't explored the whole planet yet, but Ufthak had little hope of finding anything other than what they'd encountered so far – isolated communities of scrawniez that fought gamely enough in their weird way, but just got overwhelmed by weight of numbers. It wasn't *satisfying*. The ladz were itching for a good scrap, but Ufthak was increasingly doubtful that they were going to find it here.

However, there was something intriguing about the planet. A small group of spikiez – which were like scrawniez but with, like, knives on their armour and more hooks and stuff – had shown up one day. Ufthak and his ladz clobbered 'em well enough, but the boyz in orbit swore to Gork and Mork that no ship had come or gone. Somehow, a whole mob of spikiez appeared on the planet for a scrap, then the ones the boyz didn't manage to properly squish legged it again, all without a ship.

And then there was the grot. What was its name again…?

'Boss!'

Ufthak looked up from where he'd been idly fiddling with the worky bits of the Snazzhammer while he did his finkin'. Nizkwik was practically vibrating with excitement, which presumably meant the grot had something important to tell him, or at least something it thought was important. Lurking behind Nizkwik was the other grot, the one they'd found... Snaggi! That was its name. Snaggi had been convinced that it arrived on this planet through a giant pale archway of *something* which looked a lot like scrawniez had made it, and that they only worked when a scrawnie was nearby. Unfortunately, Ufthak had not yet been able to keep a scrawnie alive long enough to get it to the archway and see for himself. He'd considered setting a bunch of ladz to watch the damned thing in case anything else came out of it – there was that finkin' again, taking him by surprise – but orks would get bored and wander off, and grots couldn't be trusted.

'Wot?' he demanded, hefting the Snazzhammer to remind Nizkwik of how readily a clobbering could be heading its way if he felt it was wasting his time. Or, to be fair, if he just felt like it.

'Da Meklord's shouty box is shouting, boss!' Nizkwik reported, hopping from one foot to the other with excitement. 'Da Boffin said so! Ya gotta come at once!'

Ufthak grunted, and stood up to his full height. There was quite a lot of that, now. The top of his head nearly brushed the ceiling of the old Gargant head he'd taken as his personal living space, and he'd outgrown the fancy beakie armour he'd nicked on Hephaesto to the point that it was more of a collection of plates strewn around his body these days. He couldn't help but wonder if he was as big as Da Meklord now, but Da Biggest Big Mek had sent Ufthak and his ladz over to this bit of the galaxy to do a bit of stompin' and find some shiny loot, so Ufthak hadn't laid eyes on his warboss in a while.

He got to the doorway and lashed out with a steel-capped

boot, connecting solidly with Nizkwik's ribs. The grot flew backwards and then tumbled down the side of the hill on which Ufthak's bunker sat, emitting amusing noises of pain as it did so.

'I don't "gotta" do anyfing!' Ufthak shouted after it. 'Yoo just remember dat!' He squinted down at Snaggi, who had the sharp-toothed grin of any grot that had just seen punishment dealt out to someone or something else. 'Oi. Is it true?'

'Yes, boss,' Snaggi said, its grin disappearing as it looked up at him. Ufthak grunted. Snaggi bothered him, but he couldn't quite put his finger on why. It was tempting to smash the little git anyway, just to be sure, but if Ufthak were to smash every grot that bothered him then they soon wouldn't have any grots left, and then who would do all the boring stuff?

He whistled instead, and a high-pitched squeal that rapidly descended, in height if not in tone, announced the arrival of his pet squig, Princess, as it hopped down from where it had been sunning itself on top of the bunker. Snaggi – a fast learner in at least some respects – immediately took off as fast as its little legs would carry it, with Princess bounding along behind making the happy noises of a squig that had a friend to play with, or possibly lunch. Ufthak picked up his shokk rifle, clamped the Snazzhammer to the sticky-metal backplate Da Boffin had made for him and sauntered along behind, covering the same distance with one casual stride as Snaggi did with half a dozen panicked ones.

Da Boffin was buzzing around on the single wheel with which he'd replaced his legs, and tinkering with a trukk of some sort amidst the piles of scrap and apparent junk that served as his workshop. Ufthak recognised the glyph that denoted the trukk as belonging to Skumdreg, and without him even asking, his brain threw up how many boyz Skumdreg bossed and what weapons they'd had the last time Ufthak had seen them. He grunted in irritation at the unwanted cranial intrusion, and the mekboy looked up.

'Boss!' he said excitedly, throwing the still-whirling handheld buzzsaw casually over his shoulder. One of his grots ran desperately to catch it with the despairing expression of one who had taken too many kickings for being insufficiently attentive, and lost an arm as the blade sliced through flesh and bone with ease. The grot stifled a high-pitched squeal of agony, managed to shut the saw down and place it within easy reach of its master, then fainted.

'Da shouty box is shoutin'?' Ufthak asked.

'Dat's right,' Da Boffin said eagerly. 'C'mon, I'll show ya.' He buzzed away, leaving Ufthak to follow him deeper into the mess of his workshop. They passed what had once been – or possibly was going to be – a Killa Kan, heaps of old shootas, and what looked to Ufthak suspiciously like the head of a tinhead. He glared at it distrustfully, but it showed no sign of either fading away or regrowing its body and trying to kill him, so he reluctantly assumed that Da Boffin knew what he was doing.

Da Meklord's shouty box was right at the back. Ufthak had always wondered whether he should have kept it with him, since he was the big boss after all, but the thing made him uncomfortable in a way that little else did. Anyway, at the end of the day it was a mekboy's invention, so it seemed only right that a mekboy should look after it.

It was a metal effigy of an ork's head, hooked up to all manner of wires and things that bubbled and went *blip* at irregular intervals. That in itself wasn't too disturbing; what bothered him was the fact that inside the metal skull was half a weirdboy brain. The other half was still in what was left of the weirdboy, who was kicking around on Da Meklord's ship – Da Meklord having learned about the humie practice of talking across the galaxy by having one of their weirdboyz shout with its brain to another one in a different place, and figuring that having one weirdboy in two places was more efficient. After all, that way it was the same brain just talking to itself, wasn't it?

Da Boffin flicked a switch, and the speaker that took up the metal mouth crackled into life and began disgorging a familiar deep voice.

'Ufthak! Get yer ladz togevva an' get back 'ere! We've found a proppa good scrap – we're near a star wot's all big an' red wiv a smaller one dat's a bit more yellowy, ya can't miss it. Also,' Da Meklord's voice continued, in a slightly more menacing tone, 'make sure yoo bring all da loot yoo've nicked wiv ya. Yoo've been away for a long time, I wanna see wotcha got.'

The speaker crackled again, and fell silent. Ufthak looked at Da Boffin. 'Dat's it?'

'Dat's it,' Da Boffin confirmed. 'I can make it say it again, but it don't say nuffin' else.'

Ufthak grunted. Something about this wasn't sitting quite right with him, and although he distrusted finkin', it had its benefits on occasion. Da Meklord had sent him out here – pointed him at a patch of sky and told him to find out what was there – and he'd barely discovered anything worth fighting, let alone anything worth nicking. Scrawniez usually had quite fancy tech, although it tended to be a bit flimsy, but these ones were like the Snakebites of their kind – all monsters and sharp sticks, and not a lot of zoomy dakka. Da Meklord was one of the smartest orks around, and he'd always been good at leading the Tekwaaagh! to the right places for good fights *and* good loot, but for some reason he'd sent Ufthak off to a nearly empty part of the galaxy. Now he was calling Ufthak back and making a big deal about the loot he was expecting as a result, even though there was none to be had. It was almost as if Da Meklord wanted to make Ufthak look bad...

'So, we goin'?' Da Boffin asked. Ufthak opened his mouth to give an affirmative, because of *course* they were goin', Da Meklord was the warboss and he was calling them back for an almighty scrap, but he was interrupted by a new and far more interesting sound.

Ork camps didn't have sirens like humie ones did, which started blaring as soon as they saw an ork to make sure that the humies inside were all properly panicking by the time the boyz arrived. For an ork, anything worthy of note was greeted with dakka – either shooting at it, or just shooting into the air on the reasonable assumption that other orks would come over to find out what was going on – and it was this that erupted from outside Da Boffin's workshop. Ufthak raced out into the open, with Da Boffin keeping pace with him on his wheel.

Overhead, the sun was blotted out, not by one of the mighty storms that rolled across the camp from time to time, but by sleek, narrow shapes screaming from the sky. Ufthak recognised them even before they started spitting flecks of toxic crystal, even before the rappelling lines rained down and lithe, sharp-edged shapes in red and silver began to descend with notably un-orkish grace.

Ufthak grinned. The spikiez were back.

He flicked the whirly bits of his shokk rifle with his finger to make sure they still whirled properly, then activated it. The weapon powered up with a pleasing whine, and Ufthak fired it upwards. He didn't aim it as such, but quite a lot of the sky was filled with spikiez, and a pointy-helmeted figure disintegrated very entertainingly, along with the line it had been holding on to. The four figures that had been dangling beneath it suddenly found themselves dropping unexpectedly to the ground; being spikiez, they landed on their feet with sickening agility, but Ufthak had already stowed the shokk rifle and started moving.

It was the only way to deal with them, really. Many an ork had tried to out-dakka a spikie, but the gits were good at shooting and although their guns were disgustingly quiet and the ammunition didn't even explode when it hit something, they could still bring an ork down in short order. Spikiez didn't like to hang out miles and miles away and drop enormous shells on you, like humies did. Nor did they want to get close up and in your face, like the bugeyes. Spikiez liked to move fast and hit hard, staying just out of range of retaliation, because they really didn't like it when you hit back.

Ufthak crashed into these four like a smasha squig that had just been zapped by an electro-prod, and began laying about him with the Snazzhammer.

He broke one in half with his first swing, and sent it flying. The others drew long thin knives, but Ufthak could practically smell their panic; they'd intended to dangle from their lines and dakka his ladz from above, and now they were on the ground facing an angry ork. Scrawniez in general always seemed to think they were so much better than everyone and everything else, but that usually only lasted until you could lay a hand on them. He grabbed one by the head; it tried unsuccessfully to twist away from his grasp, and did manage to stab him in the arm. Ufthak hurled it into a third one, and they both went down in a heap. The last one turned to run, but Ufthak clobbered it from behind with the Snazzhammer, then set about pasting the other two.

Spikiez were annoyingly fragile, and Ufthak's little scrap was over in seconds, but battle had been joined in earnest around him now. One of the floating trukks abruptly lurched downwards and crashed as a traktor kannon's beam latched on to it and hauled it groundwards, and another one began to veer as a couple of rokkits from a mob of tankbustas struck it more or less centrally (most of the rokkits in the fusillade missed, naturally, but given there were many more floating trukks beyond the initial target, it was fairer to say that they were only *temporary* misses). His ladz weren't having it all their own way, of course – he caught sight of half a mob getting raked with fire from the spikiez' pointy rifles, then falling over foaming at the mouth within seconds – but neither were the spikiez.

Ufthak grinned. He'd been dying for a proper scrap, and at last it seemed as though the galaxy was going to oblige him.

TWO

The spikiez were gone. Or at least, they were working on it.

Dropping down into the middle of the camp with knives out and guns blazing was a bold tactic, Ufthak would give them that. It was also a highly successful one, if 'successful' meant starting a massive fight leading to a lot of casualties, which was certainly Ufthak's definition. However, he thought it likely that the spikiez hadn't meant so many of those casualties to be on their side.

It had probably been intended as a shock assault, a plan to break the Waaagh!'s will and send them scattering, then pick them off. Ufthak wasn't an expert on spikiez, but he knew they were a bit weird and liked to stick their knives into things that weren't fighting back, which always seemed pointless to him – you might as well just go and shoot rocks. Which, fine, could be amusing for a while, but the point of a fight was the *fight*, where your blood was pumping and Gork and Mork were roaring in your ears. It wasn't fun unless the other git was looking to take your head off in return.

Anyway, the spikiez' plan had backfired. Instead of shaking the ladz up and sending them running, the gits had been swarmed and stomped from all sides. There hadn't been enough of them for their plan to work, and they hadn't hit hard enough. All types of scrawnie seemed to approach the galaxy as though it should automatically behave as they wanted it to, and got very miffed when it didn't. What was left of these ones had finally worked out that things weren't going their way, and were making a break for it in their silly floating trukks.

'After 'em!' Ufthak roared, shaking the Snazzhammer to dislodge the limp spikie still stuck on the axe blade. This one seemed to be the boss, in that it had been very stabby and had a fancy red rag flapping around behind it. It'd left a fair few ladz missing a limb, or their guts, or a head; its sword had even gone right through Ufthak's armour and into his shoulder, but it wasn't a wound that was going to put him down, and the spikie hadn't got the chance for a second go. The strange, skinny little thing slithered off the Snazzhammer and landed wetly on the ground, its insides on show for all to see, just as Ufthak's kustomised trukk careered to a halt beside him.

'Mornin', boss!' Mogrot Redtoof beamed from behind the wheel. 'Fort you might need dis!' Mogrot was a good driver, deadly in combat, and boasted the intelligence of a concussed brick. He wasn't Ufthak's second-in-command so much as an ambulatory accident-in-waiting who could easily be persuaded to happen to someone else. He was all brutal, no kunnin', and as a result was one of the boyz Ufthak trusted the most.

'Good work, Mogrot,' Ufthak grunted, pulling an arm off the spikie and climbing up onto the open rear of the vehicle. Normally he might have a few of his best ladz in here with him, some of the nobs who liked to hang around with their own kind, but at the moment the only other occupant was

Nizkwik, who waved nervously at him and then shrank into a corner in case the reaction was another kick. A high-pitched wail, increasing in volume, announced the arrival of Snaggi; the little grot made a running jump for the rear of the flatbed and pulled itself desperately aboard, just before Princess landed behind it with jaws wide open.

'Princess, down!' Ufthak barked, and threw the spikie arm into the squig's mouth. Princess began crunching joyously, its jaws apparently powerful enough to get at the meat even through the armour surrounding it, and lost interest in Snaggi.

'Uh… fanks?' the grot stammered, although it looked as if it had swallowed a soursquig. Ufthak banged on the panel dividing the flatbed from the cab, and Mogrot accelerated away, following the rest of the Waaagh!'s vehicles that were already in pursuit of the fleeing spikiez.

'D'ya know where dese gits are goin'?' Ufthak demanded, pointing a finger at Snaggi.

The grot shrank back from the digit while still clinging to the handhold preventing it from being shaken loose by Mogrot's driving, and shook its head. 'No, boss.'

'I reckon I do,' Ufthak said. 'Reckon dey're headin' for dat arch fing wot yoo said yoo came froo. Dat's why Princess ain't eatin' yoo yet. Ya might come in useful.'

'Good finkin', boss!' Nizkwik piped up, then subsided again as both Ufthak and Snaggi glowered at it.

Mogrot was gunning the trukk's engine fiercely, keeping pace with the various speed freeks giving chase to the fleeing spikiez with whoops and indiscriminate dakka. The whole camp was in motion now: the flyboyz had taken off and were screaming overhead in their snub-nosed aircraft, the Stompas were grumbling into life and starting to thud forwards with ground-shaking steps, and every footslogger was flinging themselves aboard whatever trukk or battlewagon they could find in order to keep up. Having been denied a proper fight for so long, Ufthak's ladz were not intending to let this one get away from them that easily. The spikiez were like grots who had prodded a giant nest of buzzer squigs, and were now desperately running for the water.

The only difference was, Ufthak intended to see if buzzer squigs could swim. Or something like that, anyway; he still wasn't properly used to this finkin' stuff.

'Ya said da gates only work when dere's a scrawnie nearby,' he said, directing the words at Snaggi.

'Fink so, boss,' the grot replied.

'How long do dey take to start workin' once da scrawniez are near 'em?'

'Dunno,' Snaggi said. It edged a little bit farther away from Princess, which had finished its snack and was eyeing the grot hungrily. 'Fings was a bit weird in dere, an' I was concentratin' on gettin' out...'

'Grots,' Ufthak grunted. 'Never any zoggin' use.' Still, at least his hunch about the spikiez seemed to be correct: they were heading directly for where he knew the archway to be. If it was just like a doorway to them, then there might not be much hope of catching them; they could probably keep their lead and be through. If it took a while, though, then it might be possible to pin 'em down and finish 'em off before they got through the gate and back to wherever they–

Ufthak's train of thought veered off suddenly as his finkin' rapidly diverted it in a different direction. *Back to wherever they came from.* Where was that, exactly? Wherever it was, it would probably have a lot more of the gits, and that smelled like a cracking fight. Even better, spikiez had all those fancy gubbinz, and while Ufthak had limited interest in them himself, it was the sort of stuff that fascinated Da Meklord. A half-smashed floaty-trukk probably wouldn't count as decent loot to haul back to the rest of the Tekwaaagh!, but who knew what the spikiez had in *their* camp?

He took a decision. Da Meklord had said that Ufthak and his boyz should come and find him, but he hadn't said how quickly. Now, you could certainly *infer* that he'd meant 'as soon as possible', that was definitely an interpretation you could make from his words and tone of voice, but he hadn't actually *said* it, had he? And Ufthak owed his ladz at least one decent scrap before they headed back, otherwise they'd all think that only Da Meklord could be trusted to get them a good fight, and that would never do; that would undermine all Ufthak's hard work to become a big boss. Besides, if Da Meklord wanted good loot then Ufthak pretty much *had* to try to follow the spikiez and nick something impressive from them, because there weren't many other options around.

All in all, Ufthak decided, in order to *properly* obey his warboss' order, he'd have to do something else first. Take the ladz on a trip so they could let off steam by trashing a new place and stompin' whoever took issue with that, and swipe a few interesting-looking gadgets or shooty weapons while he was there.

Now he just had to hope that his ladz didn't manage to completely clobber the remaining spikiez before they opened that gate…

'Mogrot!' he bellowed. 'Hit da button!'

'Yes, boss!' Mogrot shouted back gleefully, and hammered the big red button Da Boffin had installed for just such a purpose. The trukk's boosta rokkits, scavenged by Da Boffin and his spannerz from a fighta-bommer that a flyboy had foolishly left unattended, spluttered once and then roared into full power. The trukk shot forward like a scalded squighog, and the ride got so rough that even Ufthak's teef were clashing together in his head. Snaggi and Nizkwik wailed as they desperately tried to keep themselves from being bounced over the side, and Princess clamped its jaws around one of the roll bars and held on grimly while its legs and tail waggled around in the wind.

Say what you liked about Mogrot – and Ufthak frequently did – but he knew how to handle a vehicle. He managed to weave the trukk's substantial bulk between the other buggies and traks, albeit out of a desire not to reduce his speed by colliding with anything rather than consideration for the other drivers, until they were right in amongst the leaders of the chasing pack. Now Ufthak could see the spikiez' floaty-trukks again: three of the ones that carried their boyz into the scrap, one with some of those guns what spat out bolts of darkness – skinny weapons that looked as though you could break them over your knee, but Ufthak had seen what they could do, and you had to respect something that killy even if it was weird – and two of the little nippy flyers that zipped around so fast you could barely hit them even if you aimed, and which left strange after-images on your vision so you couldn't be sure where they were at any given moment.

A buggy to Ufthak's right looked set to test that theory through sheer volume of firepower: Uzdreg, one of Da Boffin's spannerz, was swivelling a multi-barrelled monstrosity of a gun back and forth, trying to draw a bead on the fleeing gits. He pulled the trigger with a cry of equal parts joy and bloodlust, and red-hot ballistic death flashed out towards the spikiez with an impressively thunderous roar and a truly stunning lack of accuracy. The nearest little nippy craft escaped the hail of ordnance entirely, although one of the larger floating trukks got clipped by the very end of the fusillade, just before Uzdreg's magazines ran dry and clicked empty, one after another.

Ufthak pointed his shokk rifle in the general direction of the floaty-trukk and pulled the trigger, just as Mogrot hit a particularly insistent bump. The impact jolted his arm wildly and the blast of shokka energy flew well high and wide of his intended target... and blasted right through the smaller git, which suddenly found an entire section of its core snatched away into the warp, possibly along with a few limbs of the crew. That was clearly enough to overcome its strange resistance to gravity, and it arrowed downwards to smash into the dirt with a definite finality.

'Stomp 'em good an' proppa!' Ufthak yelled back over his shoulder, and a fair few of the vehicles in his wake veered off to give whatever remained of the spikiez a right good kicking. It wouldn't take the boyz long to finish and catch up, but that was a few less to concentrate on the ones still getting away. Telling his ladz not to try and kill the gits didn't even occur to him – he wasn't a Blood Axe – but getting them to focus on killing ones that didn't matter to his overall plan was fine, that was just *sense*.

The spikiez weren't going to take this lying down, though. Two of the weapons on their floaty-gunwagon swivelled around to face backwards, and two beams of darkness stabbed out to converge on Uzdreg's buggy. It disintegrated instantly, the edges clattering to the ground or rolling away, and the middle – including Uzdreg and whichever poor sod had been driving him – blasted into utter nothingness. Ufthak fired back, on the basis that the gunwagon was the only thing doing anything except running away, but Gork and Mork weren't prepared to grant him good fortune a second time in a row, and his shokk-rifle shot missed everything.

The spikiez veered off to the left suddenly, pulling the sort of sharp turn that should have been impossible without friction between ground and wheels. They were heading for a raised area of broken rock over which their strange technology would carry them with ease, but which would serve as an effective barrier to the orks following in their wake.

Time for finkin' to earn its keep.

'Leave 'em!' Ufthak roared, throwing all the volume he could into his voice and pointing forward. 'Dey're tryin' to lose us, but I know where dey're goin'! Follow me, ladz!' He leaned down. 'Mogrot, you remember where dat weird arch fing is?'

'Yes, boss!' Mogrot replied, although his eyes were fixed on the fleeing spikiez and every muscle in his body was tense with the effort of not turning the trukk to follow them.

'Get us dere, fast as ya can,' Ufthak said smugly.

It was a risk, Ufthak knew that. If he was wrong, the ladz were going to be furious with him. However, he trusted both his own kunnin' and Mogrot's driving skills, and it was borne out when they rounded a grassy ridge and saw not only the pale curves of the strange scrawnie architecture reaching up into the cloudless sky, but also the red-and-silver shapes of the spikiez' vehicles heading for it as fast as they could. They'd taken an indirect route in order to shake their pursuers, but they'd reckoned without Ufthak Blackhawk, and now their lead was slenderer than a starved grot.

'Wot now, boss?' Mogrot asked, as they tore across the ground.

'Dey're gonna go froo dere,' Ufthak told him. 'An' we're gonna go froo it behind 'em.'

'Wot's on da uvver side?' Mogrot asked, his brow wrinkling as he tried to come to terms with the concept of something he couldn't see.

'Somefing we wanna fight or steal,' Ufthak said confidently. 'Or fight *and* steal.'

The remaining smaller craft, the floaty-buggy, made it to the archway first. The empty air within the structure's outline shimmered, and became a surface of glowing light into which the spikie vehicles disappeared, one after another. Ufthak suddenly realised that he had no idea how long the gateway would remain active after a scrawnie went through it, but there was nothing to be gained by slowing down to find out. He raised the Snazzhammer for all behind him to see, lifted his head to the sky, and roared out his praise to Gork and Mork for the adventure on which he and his ladz were about to embark.

'WAAAAAGH!'

The gateway got closer and closer, and larger and larger, and then–

THREE

Dhaemira had always been fascinated by why the haemonculus covens tended to choose underground locations for their lairs. This was Commorragh, after all; it was hardly short on space, and its alternative name of the Dark City indicated that it was not overly afflicted with intrusive light. Perhaps it was down to justifiable paranoia, a desire to absolutely know where the entrances and exits were, and to minimise lines of sight for long-range assassination by hexrifle.

Then again, Dhaemira's own paranoia much preferred multiple exits to being stuck behind a bottleneck, and assassination should be low down on the list of concerns for drukhari whose mastery of flesh – both others' and their own – was so complete as a haemonculus'. It was a mystery, although not one which she currently had the leisure to interrogate.

The Coven of the Red Harvest's underspire was a bewildering labyrinth of strange angles and distorting mirrors. Dhaemira had a fine-boned face, and her eyes were lined with dark kohl made from the ashes of defeated enemies, but she walked past some reflective walls that made her appear skeletal, with sunken cheeks and eyes no more than empty pools of shadow. Others twisted her posture so that she looked as hunched and malformed as the masters of this place, while still others over-laid a sheen of decay on her image as though her living flesh was the victim of some hideous disease.

It was all designed to unnerve and intimidate the outsider – be they guest or intruder – and not-so-subtly remind them of the power wielded by the coven in whose domain they were treading. Dhaemira had no doubt that the Red Harvest could, if given free rein over her body and immunity from reprisal, alter her flesh to resemble any of the images she saw as she walked through these halls, or indeed many other even more disturbing visages. What gave the whole thing a slightly different note of concern was that the reflection of her guide – a nameless, multi-armed wrack with the swollen musculature and enlarged, protruding spine typical of its kind – appeared no different in any of the walls they passed, no matter how her own image was altered.

After many disorienting changes of route, including at least two occasions when Dhaemira's sense of direction insisted that they had doubled back or crossed over their own tracks, the ever-present background of screaming grew louder, and they passed into a small theatre. The mirrors were gone, although that did not mean reflective surfaces were absent: Dhaemira's face was all around her, in a glimpse from the door of an ominous-looking cabinet, or the momentary stare of her own eyes peering out from the flat of a blade. More important, how-ever, was what was in front of her.

'Master Maculatix,' Dhaemira said, ensuring her tone was loud enough to carry over the moans of agony but still contained nothing but respect. Nothing more than respect – it did not do to let any haemonculus detect servility in one's voice – but respect itself was key, here in the heart of this creature's power.

Maculatix turned, as though her presence was a surprise to him, instead of something of which he had been aware from the moment she arrived at the entrance to his realm. 'Lady Dhaemira. How delightful to lay eyes upon your flesh once more.'

Maculatix had three eyes, in fact – two more or less where you would expect them to be, in that they were either side of his nose and beneath his brow. One was no longer the dark, beady stare of his natural orbs, though, and was instead something larger, with a golden iris slashed with a pupil of narrow, ragged darkness. His other original eye – at least, Dhaemira suspected it was his, although little was certain with a haemonculus – now resided in his forehead, but not centrally: it was off to the left, above the golden eye, and was constantly in motion, independent of the other two.

Nor did the master of the Red Harvest's modifications of his own body stop there. He had no fewer than four arms, and Dhaemira was not entirely certain that any of them were the ones he'd been born with, however many millennia ago that was. One was relatively normally proportioned until the fingers, the tips of which had been replaced with injector syringes to subdue his subjects, or indeed any enemy who strayed too close. Another ended in a nest of razor-sharp blades, suitable for amputation, vivisection, disembowelling, or dismemberment, as the occasion demanded. The other two were more normal, with long, thin, delicate fingers that Dhaemira suspected would nevertheless possess a fearsome strength.

It was these that Maculatix steepled in front of his chest as he looked down at her. He was not naturally the taller of the two of them, but like many haemonculi, Maculatix did not debase himself by letting his feet touch the ground. Instead, he was borne aloft by suspensor technology that let him float imperiously around, like the sinister god Dhaemira imagined he considered himself to be.

'If you have come to check on the progress of your brother, he has nearly recovered,' Maculatix said smoothly, floating to one side and letting Dhaemira get a proper look at the interior of his theatre. There were several operating slabs, but only one was currently occupied. Upon it, a purple-skinned biped of a species unfamiliar to Dhaemira writhed and wailed in agony as the menacing, glossy-shelled shape of a Talos pain engine hung over it with its limbs extended. Dhaemira caught the edge of the being's suffering, that delicious thrill which reinvigorated a drukhari's spirit and let them keep the fangs of She Who Thirsts at bay for just a little while longer. However, she was not the intended recipient of this feast.

Suspended in the nurturing fluid of the reanimation pod that hung in the centre of the ceiling, her brother Dhalgar twitched and spasmed as his body absorbed the life-giving agony from below. His body was properly formed again, Dhaemira observed, with its bones reset and flesh and muscle in place, and the last few pieces of skin growing back. There had been no shortage of raw material to work with – what remained of Dhalgar's retainers had managed to retrieve most of his body from the wreckage in the aftermath of that disastrous encounter – but none of it had been in any condition to support life.

Still, despite her brother's rashness, at least he'd had the sense to make his bargains with a haemonculus of high renown before he was so careless as to allow the arakhia to render him into paste. In times of war the haemonculus workshops might be full of reanimation pods, each one housing a fallen warrior who had paid their own price to be snatched back from the jaws of violent death to fight again, but Maculatix did not deal in such crass volumes. That was the role of his subordinates, haemonculi of lesser craft who might resurrect a hundred half-born kabalite warriors at a time into forms that were merely functional. Maculatix was an artist who specialised in return-ing his clients into a perfect recreation of their original body, or indeed an improvement upon it.

The price, of course, was high. Dhaemira did not know what Dhalgar had given up to the master of the Red Harvest in order to ensure such assistance. Her own contract with Maculatix was one she would hesitate to call in except in the direst need; only at the moment of her death, or indeed immediately after it, were her retainers instructed to follow the resurrection protocols that would see her end up here.

'Abrasion is the key, in this case,' Maculatix observed, two of his three eyes straying to the slab on which the torture was progressing. 'This species has proven relatively resistant to the sharp pain of piercing, or even flensing. However, low-grade abrasion of their dermal covering provides a far more satisfy-ing result. Your brother should be whole again within another day-cycle.'

'Your work is, as ever, exceptional,' Dhaemira said politely. It galled her to speak in such a manner to this floating corpse-master, but such was the delicate balance of life – and death – in Port Tavarr. Asdrubael Vect might speak as he please, and slay whom he wanted, but Dhaemira Thraex was no Living Muse. Not yet. 'But I did not come here merely to discuss my broth-er's progress. After all, I would have no insight to offer that you did not already possess. I wished to speak of matters con-cerning power.'

All three of Maculatix's eyes narrowed, and he flicked one finger in a dismissive gesture. The wrack who had led Dhaemira

here withdrew, leaving the two of them alone apart from Dhalgar, locked behind the walls of his reanimation pod, the Talos,
and its victim who, Dhaemira suspected, had more immediate
concerns than eavesdropping on such a conversation.

'Power is a heady draught,' Maculatix said, 'and definitions
of it can vary wildly.'

*He is going to give me a self-aggrandising speech about his power
over death,* Dhaemira thought wearily, and immediately decided
that she had no patience for it.

'Then allow me to make my definition clear, master haemonculus,' she said, quickly but smoothly. 'The political power of
Port Tavarr, and our places within it.'

'The power of kabals, in other words,' Maculatix replied with
a snort, but his eyes still held a flicker of attention. His disin-
terest was an affectation.

'You know as well as I that the kabals provide the structure
upon which our society operates,' Dhaemira said firmly. 'And
you also know, I am sure, that the current situation in Port Tavarr
advantages no one. The kabals are at each other's throats, clawing for dominance, and so all are suffering.'

'Spoken like someone who does not trade in the flesh of the
dead and wounded,' Maculatix said, smiling. It was a thoroughly
unnatural expression on his face, and twisted his old, leathery
flesh into a disturbing rictus.

'I do not doubt that such conflict benefits you,' Dhaemira
admitted, 'but what of the other impacts? Our realspace raids are
sparse, for we hesitate to weaken ourselves when our rivals are
poised with blades bared. That limits the sport of the wych cults,
for we have fewer prizes to trade with them for their gladiatorial
games, and it reduces the number of interesting specimens for your
collections. Where did you come by that wretch, for example?'
she asked, nodding casually in the direction of the Talos' subject.

42

'I am not without my own resources,' Maculatix said, a little defensively, and Dhaemira allowed herself a small smile.

'Of course, Master Maculatix. You have your own vehicles, and your own warriors who can sally forth into realspace and do your bidding. But I think we both know that no matter how ferocious and resilient they are, your minions are limited to relatively small operations – surgical strikes, one might say, which I have no doubt they perform with great ability. However, sometimes the greater prize requires a larger venture.' Flesh was the area of the haemonculus covens' expertise, not hardware; Maculatix might possess Raiders and Venoms, but he had little access to larger craft like Voidravens or Razorwings, let alone ships capable of void travel. That limited him to predating on worlds which had their own webway gates, and that left a great deal of the galaxy out of his reach.

'I presume you have a point, master archon,' Maculatix said, his tone sharpening a little. Dhaemira was unconcerned: this was a dance in which she had to demonstrate that she knew her own worth to him before any bargains could be struck.

'Port Tavarr needs authority,' she said bluntly. 'It needs someone to rise up and take the position once occupied by Lord Fahr-rul – a lieutenant to Lord Vect, albeit with a greater degree of loyalty. I could take that role by force,' she continued, inject-ing her voice with an easy casualness, 'but I would be opposed by those unwilling to concede what they might perceive as a closely matched war, and the price would be high on all sides. If the kabals of Port Tavarr were to be too greatly weakened,' she added, sensing another scornful dismissal on the haemonculus' lips, 'then who is to say that forces from a neighbouring realm might not intrude? Forces that would have no ties to the other entities within Port Tavarr, and no qualms about eliminating those they found here?'

'You seek a closer alliance, then?' Maculatix said. 'You wish for my open support in order to become Lady of Port Tavarr?'

'I can become Lady of Port Tavarr whenever I please,' Dhaemira countered, substituting confidence for strict truthfulness. 'I am suggesting this alliance to make it quicker and easier, and allow us to return our attention to the realspace vermin. If my Kabal of the Hollow Heart comes to prominence, why should your Coven of the Red Harvest not rise along with us?'

Maculatix tapped his index fingers together. 'Let us speak plainly, then. Even combined, our forces would be insufficient to guarantee the capitulation of all other interested parties. There are other alliances within Port Tavarr – some of which you will know, some of which I know, and some, I have no doubt, that are unknown to us both. We would need the assistance of at least one wych cult, for example.'

'I concur,' Dhaemira said, nodding as though Maculatix had said something insightful as opposed to blindingly obvious. 'The Cult of the Silver Shards is thought to be the largest, but there is little prospect of them joining us. I would propose–'

'One moment, please,' Maculatix said, holding up one of his more natural hands, while the other went to his ear. 'I mean no disrespect, Lady Dhaemira, but…'

Dhaemira schooled her face to neutrality, then added in the faintest hint of displeasure: the very image of an archon annoyed by this gross rudeness, but willing to tolerate it – for now – in the name of their common interest. Her own ear-pearl was silent; she was far beyond the reach of her kabal's carrier waves here, in the depth of the Red Harvest's domain. Nonetheless, she had a suspicion as to what urgent news had caused Maculatix to risk insulting her so.

'There are arakhia within the boundaries,' Maculatix said a few moments later, his voice balanced exactly halfway between disgust and fascination. 'A sizeable force. They appear to have pursued the so-called Kabal of the Wounding Wind.'

'In what district have they arrived?' Dhaemira queried.

'Sabregate,' Maculatix replied, his expression stern. 'Pardon the interruption, archon, but I believe this situation must take precedence.'

'Of course,' Dhaemira agreed. They both made for the door that led back into the labyrinth and, eventually, to the surface. 'But the arakhia have pursued the Wounding Wind back to Port Tavarr? How can a webway gate have admitted them?'

'That is, unfortunately, beyond my ability to answer at present,' Maculatix replied. His scissorhand opened and closed its blades, which Dhaemira took as a sign of agitation. She herself was not agitated, although she made sure to tighten the corners of her eyes slightly in order to give that impression.

After all, it would not do to let anyone know that the reason the webway gate had remained open for the orks was because she had arranged for it to do so.

FOUR

For a while, Ufthak was not convinced that what had at first seemed like an excellent idea was, in fact, an excellent idea. His trukk plunged into the strange light that filled the scrawniez' archway, and then there was… Well, he wasn't entirely sure.

White. Featureless. Sort of… misty? They appeared to be in a tunnel of sorts, but it felt as though the walls were pressing in and yet a long way away at the same time. Ufthak was unable to gain any real insight from the reactions of those around him, either: the two grots were cowering in generalised fear, and Princess was happily chasing its own tail. Meanwhile, Mogrot wasn't paying attention to anything other than what was directly in front of him – specifically, the receding shapes of the spikie vehicles. On the basis that it wouldn't do for a big boss to seem at all uncertain about either his decisions or the surroundings, Ufthak settled for staring belligerently ahead and seeing what happened. The spikiez had to be going *somewhere*, after all…

'Dey're cheatin', boss!' Mogrot declared in outraged tones,

pointing at their quarry. 'Dere's definitely somefing funny goin' on. Dey shouldn't be dat far ahead of us!'

Ufthak glared at the walls again, then back at the spikiez. Hoots, hollers, and the roar of engines from behind him announced the arrival of more ork vehicles, but when he turned his head to look it was just as hard to pin an exact location on any of them. One moment his ladz seemed bunched up, the next spread out, and the noise reaching his ears appeared to bear little resemblance to either their proximity or direction.

'It's just scrawnie nonsense,' he said in reply to Mogrot's complaint. 'It's a weird place, built by weird gits. Keep goin' fast, and dat'll be good enuff.'

'Yoo got it, boss!' Mogrot replied, content enough that his grievance had been heard and dealt with. It was certainly a smoother ride in here, Ufthak noted, which meant the skimmers ahead of them had actually lost some of their advantage. Being able to ignore terrain was great when your pursuers were hitting bumps all over the place, but was less of a benefit when the trukks and buggies in question were driving over something as smooth and even as any humie road.

Distance blurred, and one of the fleeing spikie trucks abruptly seemed closer than it had been. Ufthak opened fire with the shokk rifle, but the tunnel was playing other tricks and his shot flew wide; that was definitely the explanation, rather than he'd actually missed. Still, Ufthak consoled himself, that was fine. The object was to chase the spikiez back to wherever they came from, rather than blow them up before they got there.

The spikie gunwagon still seemed to want to have a go, and it sent two beams of crackling darkness back at them, but they flew wide as well. Given how accurate scrawniez usually were, that suggested to Ufthak that it wasn't just him who was having trouble with calculating distances. That didn't make much sense:

why would scrawniez build something which was weird even to *them?* Did it mean they hadn't built this place at all?

He shook his head before his thoughts could run away with him. Finkin' was a hard habit to break once you'd got into it. Spend too long finkin', and you'd eventually realise that some git had taken your head off while it was busy doing something else. Ufthak had survived having his head stitched onto another body, and the dok's work had healed up so proper that you couldn't even really see the scar now, but that didn't mean he wanted to risk it a second time. He had no intention of falling victim to some sneaky Blood Axe type creeping up on him while he was wondering what stars ate, or something. If it was a straight-up fight then that was different – you went into those knowing you might not come out again in one piece, or at all, and that was all part of the fun…

As quick as blinking, things changed. What had been an almost featureless tunnel ahead of them for as far as the eye could see suddenly turned into a massive portal, or an archway, or a gateway – something like that, anyway – and the spikie vehicles flew through it without slowing. Ufthak braced himself, holding on to the trukk's roll cage with one hand and the other clutching the shokk rifle, with the Snazzhammer slung across his shoulders. This was when they would see whether they could still follow the spikiez, or whether the kunnin' little gits had some way of turning this portal off that they hadn't used on the previous one.

The front of the trukk came into contact with the shimmering light, which swept backwards over the vehicle and its passengers with a cool tingling on Ufthak's skin…

…and they were through.

The tunnel and its ethereal whiteness had disappeared. There was sky above them, of a sort, but Ufthak's eyes could tell at once that this wasn't proper sky. Not like you found on a planet, where you might get clouds, and flying gits that you could bring down and eat or which might, depending on the size of them, try to eat you. There was no shape to a sky, it was just *there*, and sometimes you could see all the way up to the stars.

This was different. It was a dome of almost unimaginable proportions and constructed of something that looked more like a force field than anything solid, but still, Ufthak could tell, a dome. He could just make out strange patterns across its surface, but then his eyes seemed to shift and suddenly it was the other bits that were the patterns and the former pattern that was actually the surface – and then there were whole new bits that suddenly stood out in different ways that he hadn't noticed before. It was positively confusing. Ufthak dealt with it the way he dealt with most things that confused him – or at least most things that confused him which he couldn't easily smash – and ignored it. The spikiez had a strange force field for a sky, good for them; it wasn't relevant to him, or what he was doing here.

'Wow,' Mogrot opined solemnly. 'Dis place is *weird.*'

Although Mogrot's assessment of things was usually about as valuable as a grot's toof, Ufthak had to admit that he was right on this occasion. Mighty spires rose up around them beneath the force-field sky, great dark daggers that looked like little so much as malignant, inverted icicles. They seemed almost fragile in their slenderness, but Ufthak was disinclined to believe that assessment for two reasons. Firstly, although spikiez weren't exactly *tuff*, they, their armour, and the things they built were surprisingly resilient for their size – spikie armour thinner than Ufthak's finger could stand up to a blow as well as a bit of metal as thick as his fist. Secondly, although distances were still a little difficult to judge, he was reasonably sure that a lot of the spires only looked thin because they were so zoggin' *tall.*

They weren't the only strange thing. The portal had spat his trukk out onto a wide plaza tiled in pale stone slabs, the surfaces of which were either naturally shaped, or had been carved, in a manner that suggested an endless tessellation of skulls and bones. Ufthak wasn't sure which option was weirder. Some way off to his left ran a wide, dark strip of viscous filth that could only be called a river because it was moving at a slow walking pace, on which sat a variety of characteristically thin, sharp-edged vessels that had to have reinforced hulls given the amount of caustic chemicals Ufthak could smell, even at this distance.

And there were spikiez *everywhere*. On the river, scattered here and there across the plaza, clustered about the stalls that ringed it, and even zipping around in the sky on those weird floaty-planks or – Ufthak squinted to make sure he was seeing this right – with wings, actual wings, coming out of their backs.

Most of these spikiez weren't armed and armoured, not like the ones Ufthak was chasing. He saw eyes turn towards his trukk and weapons emerge from beneath clothing, but they weren't tooled up for a proper fight; this was just like wandering down to the brewboyz' with your favourite choppa tucked in your belt. All the same, there were enough of the gits to make problems for one trukk containing two orks, two grots and a squig.

Then the rest of the Waaagh! began to roar out of the portal behind him, and the mood around the plaza changed from murderously curious to panic.

Spikiez were sort of like grots, apparently. They relished the chance to stick a stabba into someone if they thought there was enough of them to get away with it, but had no interest in a fight for the fight's sake. Ufthak saw blades that had just been drawn in anticipation of being applied to his flesh now used on whoever was standing beside the wielder, in order to better facilitate their own getaway. Fellow spikiez were shoved aside or trampled underfoot, stalls were smashed apart and their contents left scattered, and safety was sought through doors and down through hatches or grates.

'Alright, ladz!' Ufthak bellowed. 'Let's give 'em a zoggin' good kickin'!'

The Waaagh! opened up with everything it had, and raked the plaza with firepower that made up in brutal exuberance for what it lacked in accuracy. Chips of stone filled the air as kannons and shootas of every conceivable sort unloaded solid slugs and high-explosive rounds, and blew chunks out of the slabs on which their targets stood. Spikiez disintegrated as zappas and megablastas unleashed bolts of ravening energy, and explosions shook the ground as stikkbomb after stikkbomb was hurled at anything that looked as if it might be vaguely amusing to blow up.

Some of the spikiez fought back, of course. A few were braver or more bloodthirsty than others, or – in the case of some of those on the boats – maybe thought they were far enough away to be able to retaliate with some measure of safety. Boyz fell out of vehicles, suddenly missing part of their head, or with dark purplish threads criss-crossing their skin as the spikiez' poison needles hit home and did their deadly work.

A chorus of piercing screams heralded the arrival of the floaty-plank riders, arrowing down out of the sky with their underslung weapons spitting toxic death and huge, double-bladed glaives glinting in the weak light cast by the strange, sickly-looking sun-thing that floated somewhere high above. There was a large mob of them, but their ambition and aggression outweighed their ability. A handful of orks fell to their guns, but the sheer volume of dakka sent back at the spikiez shredded over half of them before they got close enough to use their glaives. The flying attackers decapitated or bisected a few more orks with lightning-swift blows as they reached the convoy, then they were dragged down and hammered flat by boots, dismembered by choppas, or simply plucked from their planks and hurled under the wheels or tracks of whatever vehicle was closest.

'Where to, boss?' Mogrot asked.

'Keep followin' 'em!' Ufthak told him, pointing at the vehicles they'd chased through the portal in the first place. 'Dey're da best chance of findin' more spikiez who actually wanna scrap!'

The spikie vehicles abruptly began to pull upwards; instead of floating at roughly head height, they rose into the sky to leave the ground behind entirely. Ufthak took a speculative shot at them with the shokk rifle, out of annoyance more than anything else, but only succeeded in blasting a chunk out of the lower part of a spire. The spikiez banked around it and then were gone, lost in the maze of narrow turrets, spindly walkways, and gravity-defying platforms that clogged the space between the spires like the threads of some giant, demented arachnid's web.

'Don't fink I can get us up dere, boss,' Mogrot reported with some regret.

'Nah,' Ufthak said. 'Alright, stop da trukk.'

'Boss?' Mogrot asked, sounding the closest to outraged that Ufthak had ever heard him.

'Just do it!' he snapped, and Mogrot obliged with his usual directness: he hammered on what passed for brakes, and the vehicle skidded to a halt with an ear-rending screech of abused tyres and a cessation of forward momentum that threw Nizkwik and Snaggi against the flatbed's front in a confused tangle of limbs and high-pitched swearing. Other buggies and battlewagons roared past them as the Waaagh! continued to spread out and push farther into this strange place, like a green flood released from behind a dam finding old watercourses and making new ones.

Ufthak turned on the spot, surveying his surroundings. Part of him – a large part of him – had the urge to push on with his ladz, knocking seven shades of squig dung out of any spikie he encountered, and generally have a good time, but that treacherous finkin' had raised its ugly head again. Spikiez couldn't take a punch, but they hit hard – or sharp – and almost never came from where you'd expect them to. This was Spikie City, so there were going to be a lot more of the gits somewhere, and they weren't going to take kindly to the Waaagh!'s intrusion. Ufthak knew that if his boyz lined up and charged an equal line of spikiez then there was only going to be one outcome, but the spikiez weren't going to make war like that. They'd set traps, and draw a couple of mobs off at a time, then pin them down and thin them out before anyone else could turn up to join the scrap.

That wasn't so bad, since no ork really objected to the idea of dying: it was just something that happened, and then either there was nothing – in which case you wouldn't care – or you eventually came back into a new body and got to do it all over again. Still, Ufthak was quite pleased with where he'd ended up in this life, and intended to make the most of it rather than starting again from scratch. He wanted to have a really good fight, then nick a bunch of prize loot and head back to the rest of the Tekwaaagh! to show off what an awesome boss he was. In order to do that he needed this to go well, which meant he needed to be ready to outfink the spikiez, who were undoubtedly going to have their own ideas about how many of them should die, and who should end up holding their loot.

'Nizkwik, Snaggi,' he said, looking around at the various buildings and spires and trying to decide which looked the most promising. 'Go an' get Da Boffin.'

FIVE

Snaggi Littletoof followed Nizkwik, and he *seethed*.

None of this was fair! None of this was how it was supposed to go! He'd been granted a vision by Gork and Mork where he'd been shown how it was his destiny to become Da Grotboss, and raise grots up above their brutish and dimwitted so-called masters (with Snaggi raised above the other grots, naturally, as was only proper). He'd done everything right, too; he'd single-handedly killed his old warboss! Okay, the falling Gargant head had helped, but who'd caused it to fall? He'd amassed a loyal following; he'd done what Old Morgrub the warphead had said and led his supporters to find the scrawniez' gate under the humie city. They got there *first*, Morgrub had said that the first ork to reach it was the gods' choice to become warboss. So it stood to reason that if a grot got there first then he would become Da Grotboss.

But of course, it hadn't panned out that way. Morgrub had betrayed his own prophecy and the will of the very gods he claimed to serve, and Snaggi had been cheated of his destiny. He'd been first through the gate, oh yes, but only because Genrul Uzbrag, that Blood Axe git, had kicked him through it. It had been Da Genrul who proclaimed himself warboss, and all the orks just... *went along with it*. As though it was *right*. As though *Gork and Mork hadn't definitely said it should be Snaggi*.

Then there'd been an awful lot of unpleasantness inside those weird misty tunnels, which Snaggi had avoided by clinging to the underside of a trukk. He'd had an argument with himself about it, because that was hardly the act of a great and noble grotboss, but he won said argument by pointing out to himself that if that particular Waaagh! was going to ignore the will of the gods, they didn't deserve his help. As a result, he didn't know exactly what happened, other than there was a lot of fighting at some point, and whoever was driving his trukk ended up either chasing or running away from the scrawniez, right out of another gate and onto the planet where Snaggi was found by what he'd learned was a branch of the Tekwaaagh!

And then, after everything he'd been through, after his glorious triumphs and being brought low by the most heinous of treacheries, he was right back where he zoggin' started. Just a grot, to be bullied, kicked around, sat on, and threatened with death or dismemberment by any ork that felt like it. It was as though Gork and Mork didn't even *care* that their will had been thwarted!

However, what made it even worse was that this time he had to put up with Nizkwik.

Nizkwik was, to Snaggi, everything a grot shouldn't be. He was a walking insult to grotdom – a living, breathing, arguably not-thinking example of why orks felt they were justified in pushing grots around and making their lives a misery. In Nizkwik's case, Snaggi was prepared to concede that they had a point.

It wasn't just that the other grot was stupid. It was that he was *painfully* stupid. Nizkwik lived, so far as Snaggi could lower his intelligence to understand it, in some fantasy world where everything was as it should be, and his continual abuse and humiliation at Ufthak's hands was just a part of life. The fact that Ufthak sometimes – but only sometimes – called that monster Princess off from trying to eat Nizkwik was seen as an act of favour. The designation to him of menial tasks like fetching and carrying became, in Nizkwik's head, statements of trust in his capabilities and reliability. He had no concept of the fact that Ufthak clearly only kept him around so that he definitely knew the name of someone to blame for anything that went wrong. The fact that Ufthak booted him around as he pleased but didn't actually *kill* him got filed, with a cheery and imbecilic grin, under 'could be worse'.

Even more infuriatingly, Nizkwik's stunning lack of intellect not only inured him against treatment that should have led him down the road of bitterness and hatred, but also made him almost impossible to insult. Oh, Snaggi had tried: he'd slipped delicate knives of sarcasm or disparagement into his remarks, determined to needle Nizkwik and make him realise how unpleasant his life was, but Nizkwik never noticed. Sarcasm was taken at face value, and led to Nizkwik patiently explaining to a fuming Snaggi whatever it was he thought Snaggi had misunderstood, or accepting it as a compliment and beaming, depending on the nature of the conversation. Snaggi had considered grabbing Nizkwik by the shoulders and yelling into his face exactly what he thought of him, but, well… When it came down to it, Nizkwik was possibly just a little bit *bigger* than Snaggi, and certainly not intelligent enough to realise that he was faced by the saviour of grotkind and the divinely ordained ruler of all orkdom. A direct confrontation was not strategically wise, and it wouldn't benefit grotdom as a whole if its grotboss ended up folded over and loaded into Mek Zagnit's Speshul Bommlauncha, or similar.

To cap it all off, the final loogie of insult on the steaming squig-dung pile of injury, was that Snaggi was realising he actually resented Nizkwik, was *envious* of him, when he should have been viewing the other grot with nothing more than contempt. Ufthak hardly ever called Princess off from trying to eat *him*; Snaggi had to escape the ravening ball of teeth and hatred on his own. Nizkwik might be abused and kicked and blamed by his master, but he was still 'da big boss' grot', and that gave him a bit of standing with the other grots, who were hesitant to shank him just in case Ufthak decided to splat them for it. Snaggi had no illusions that such retaliation would be out of any fondness for Nizkwik, simply outrage that someone else had decided to end a life which the big boss viewed as his to do with as he pleased, but the protection existed nonetheless. Snaggi might be back to being just a grot, but he found himself hanging around Ufthak and Nizkwik in the desperate, self-loathing hope that he could claw some similar dregs of status for himself.

Why was he cursed with greatness? Why was he doomed to live a life of misery and suffering thanks to realising the unfairness of his lot, when his companion – for lack of a better, more acerbic term – existed in a state of comparatively blissful ignorance? Why had Gork and Mork chosen Snaggi to rule if they were going to make it so zoggin' hard for him to do so?

Snaggi scurried along, glaring at Nizkwik's back as they dodged this way and that to avoid the onrushing vehicles of the Waaagh! in full flow, and envisaging scenarios that began with his stabba and ended in the other grot's gizzards.

They got most of the way back to the portal before the oncoming traffic began to slow a little. The front-runners of the warband, the fast-moving bikes and buggies, were through and already causing chaos in their new surroundings. However, the portal hadn't shut, and now the rest of the force was emerging: mob after mob of boyz with no trukk or battlewagon on which to hitch a ride, and the larger mechanical walkers – the Killa Kans, Deff Dreads and the like. Snaggi stared up at the huge arch in shock as the light filling it rippled once more, then parted to admit a massive, horizontal hollow pipe far, far above. A moment later this was revealed to be the deffkannon of an immense Stompa, as the massive monstrosity's other weapons breached the surface, followed by the curving shape of its body and the baleful, red-eyed gaze of its head. Snaggi looked up at it and had a momentary happy memory of pulling the lever that dropped the head of a Mega-Gargant (even bigger and stompier) onto his old warboss, before being abruptly shaken out of his reverie by the Stompa's first titanic footstep on this side of the portal.

'It's comin' dis way!' Nizkwik wailed. 'Leg it!' He tore off in a sprint at a right angle, big feet flapping. Snaggi growled under his breath, but headed after his fellow grot as fast as his own legs could carry him – not because he felt that Nizkwik was likely to have any particular ability to avoid trouble, but so that if they ran into something a bit more personal than the Stompa, a small group of angry spikiez, for example, he would have someone nearby to shove into their path while he made his getaway.

The Stompa didn't look as if it should be able to do much more by way of locomotion than shuffle along, but the thing's sheer size was deceptive, and although its legs were short in comparison to its body, they were still long enough to carry it leisurely forward as fast as a grot could run. It was a somewhat hairy handful of seconds before Snaggi finally managed to get out of the massive war machine's path, and he flopped down into a relieved heap as it cruised by him in a cloud of smoke, sounding an assortment of bells, whistles, and aggressive horns. One of its supa-rokkits, a gigantic cylindrical munition that was itself at least the size of an ork, ignited and thundered off to detonate somewhere in the distance. The explosion was followed by a hollow cracking sound that carried to Snaggi's ears even over the noise of the Waaagh! around him, and the top half of one of the dark spires began to list before falling with what seemed like languid slowness. The crash of *that* hitting shook the ground just as much as the Stompa's footsteps, despite being much farther away, and everyone cheered in general approval of the wanton destruction.

'Boffin!' Nizkwik piped up, jumping up and down and waving. 'Boffin!'

Amazingly, and certainly more by luck than judgement, the git had found the very ork they'd been sent in search of. Snaggi got back to his feet and surreptitiously brushed himself down. Da Boffin was pretty smart as orks went, which could go two ways: either he was smart enough to recognise Snaggi's divine leadership abilities, when Snaggi deigned to demonstrate them to him, or if not *that* smart, he was still potentially smart enough to spot a coup before it was quite ready to be enacted. Either way, Snaggi didn't want Ufthak's favourite mek to have any reason to dislike or distrust him more than was the norm for an ork where a grot was concerned. He stood straight, and tried to look generally useful whilst letting just enough of his natural aura of greatness shine through to subliminally suggest that this was a grot who would be wasted by being sent to crawl inside a large machine to unstick a cog, or deal with badly shielded cables carrying uncertain amounts of voltage.

Da Boffin rolled to a halt and glowered down at them. 'Oh. S'you. Wot?'

The good thing about Da Boffin was that, given he lacked legs, his ability to casually kick a grot who was annoying him was markedly lower than most other orks. All the same, it didn't pay to antagonise him, unless you wanted to become the test subject for his latest invention.

'Da big boss is lookin' for ya!' Snaggi said quickly, just before Nizkwik could get the words out. He pointed behind them, in the general direction of where they'd left Ufthak. 'He's over dere, said we should come an' tell ya!'

Nizkwik was staring at Snaggi with an expression of wounded betrayal. Snaggi ignored him, looking straight at Da Boffin and desperately trying to keep control of the grin that was threatening to burst forward and spread all across his face.

'Hnh,' Da Boffin grunted, which was as close to acknowledgement as an ork was likely to give a grot if no further information was required. The mekboy pivoted around on his wheel and raised his voice to bellow at his spannerz, lesser meks, and grot assistants, all of whom were currently busying themselves with what Snaggi realised was Da Boffin's workshop, hastily disassembled and brought along. 'Yoo lot! Get dat set up while I see wot da boss wants! Oi, Nazlug! Careful wiv dat, dat's da *speshul* junk!'

Da Boffin whirled about again and zoomed off, skirting around a large mob of grots who had just emerged from the portal and were cowering and blinking in the strange, empty light of their new surroundings. Snaggi saw the mekboy bend low on a turn to scoop up a now ownerless floaty-plank and place it over his shoulder as he straightened up, and then he was gone.

'I'm gonna head back to find da boss,' Nizkwik said, his voice still full of hurt.

'Nice,' Snaggi said. 'Off ya go, den.'

Nizkwik's face screwed up as he tried to process his next thought. 'Yoo ain't comin'?'

Snaggi shook his head. 'Nah, got somefing speshul to do. Somefing *secret.*' He leaned closer and lowered his voice to a hoarse whisper. 'Somefing da boss told me to do!'

Nizkwik jerked backwards in surprise, his eyes wide and mouth open in shock and disbelief. Then he gave a sharp, shuddering sniff, turned on the spot, and marched off with his arms held stiff and his ears flat back against the side of his skull, leaving Snaggi giggling at having finally found a way to annoy his companion. Nizkwik wouldn't dare question Ufthak about whether Snaggi's story was true – imagine a grot wanting to know if a big boss had given another grot a secret mission? Just the concept made Snaggi laugh so much his stomach started to hurt – but even if he did, he'd just get booted for his impudence, which would be all the funnier. Snaggi didn't have to actually be Ufthak's favourite to infuriate Nizkwik; he just had to make the other grot *think* he was, which was going to be almost embarrassingly easy.

However, that was just an amusing little side effect of the real reason Snaggi wanted Nizkwik to zog off. He'd already seen one or two of the grots pointing at them, recognising the big boss' 'helpers'. Snaggi could smell an opportunity like most grots could smell deep-fried squig legs (Snaggi could also smell deep-fried squig legs), and one was tickling his nostrils now.

He threw his shoulders back, placed one hand on the grip of his sheathed stabba in an imposing manner, checked his blasta was ready to be drawn at a moment's notice if anyone gave him some lip, and sauntered towards the group with exaggerated casualness.

'Alright, ladz?' he opened. 'Dis is a strange old place, innit?'

'It's weird,' one of the grots said, looking around him and shivering. '*Freeky.* Don't like it.'

'Yeah,' Snaggi said, nodding sympathetically. 'Shame we had

to come. Dis is more of an ork place really, innit? Nuffin' much here for yer average grot.'

This statement was met with a few nods, but only a few. Even in the midst of a Waaagh!'s invasion of someone else's dimension, grots were always going to be hesitant about voicing criticism or dissatisfaction with orks. A grot's lot might be a lowly and miserable one, but it was still usually better than getting stomped underfoot for 'bloody cheek', or similar.

'Lucky for yoo lot, I can already tell yoo ain't average!' Snaggi continued cheerfully, and a few heads came up. 'I've seen a lot of average in me life, an' yoo ain't it!'

A few more heads turned towards him. Grots were looking at each other uncertainly, trying to work out where he was going with this. Compliments were not a common currency amongst grots, but the nasty little hollow at the heart of every one of them began to seize on Snaggi's words and drink them down like an ork submerged in a vat of fungus beer. Eyes brightened, and ears perked up.

Snaggi didn't tell them that there were two ways to deviate from average, and he'd privately meant the other sort. Sometimes your audience did the hard work for you.

'Tell me,' he said, sliding his way into the middle of them like a knife between the ribs, 'have you ladz ever heard of... Da Grotboss?'

SIX

There was a common belief in Commorragh that power could not be given, only taken. This was not a view to which Dhaemira Thraex subscribed.

Power – the sort of power in which most drukhari were interested, not the everyday matter of energy harnessed from the *Illmaea*, the stolen suns that powered the Dark City – was intangible, unquantifiable. A glass might be full, or empty, or anything in between, and that state could be determined by a cursory glance. Such was the case with a splinter rifle's supply of ammunition, or even, with the correct expertise, the blood remaining in the body of an enemy undergoing exsanguination. These were mundane things, and so they could be measured in a mundane manner. Not so with power.

Power, Dhaemira implicitly believed, came from the spirit. You could hold someone immobile with crude strength; simple manacles of steel could keep them imprisoned; and a weapon could strike an enemy down so they could no longer disobey your will, but none of that conferred power. Power could not be achieved over the body, only over the spirit. When another being wished to disobey you, to harm you, but did not do so because they *feared* your strength, or your chains, or the death your weapons could deal; when they made the calculation of action versus consequence and consequence triumphed... *That* was power. Similarly, when they looked to you for leadership, when they allowed your vision of what should happen to supersede theirs because they trusted that you were more knowledgeable, or wiser, or would deal swiftly with those who defied you, or they wished to reap the benefits of being your supporter, that was also power.

None of those things could be achieved by an outside force, no matter how strong. The deadliest warrior might be able to slay any enemy who set themselves against her, but she could not compel any one of them to lay down arms. Power was *given;* more specifically, it was *given up.*

Taking control of Port Tavarr through bloodshed was possible, but it would be time-consuming, and complicated, and wasteful. Taking control through being the best option for the majority of its occupants was the easier way. Since this was Commorragh, others would only consider Dhaemira's authority as being the best option for themselves until they could overthrow her, but anyone scared of a knife in the back had no business being near power in the first place. Dhaemira would seize control and eradicate her true enemies, then embark upon the delicate balancing act of keeping her new underlings so occupied with each other's schemes that they never had time to turn their attention to toppling her.

First, however, she had to seize control; and the best way to do that, she had decided some time ago, was to show leadership in the face of a crisis. Since it was inefficient to wait for a crisis to occur, she'd had to manufacture one. Her brother had stumbled across the orks and, through his arrogant near demise, provided her with the perfect opportunity. A vicious but easily manipulated foe, a desperate would-be archon who thought he saw her duplicity and so never looked for a deeper motive, a small amount of webway sabotage, and her scheme was complete.

Now she just had to capitalise.

'Seal off Sabregate,' she ordered, as soon as she reached a part of the Red Harvest's lair where her carrier waves could be sent and received once more. Maculatix turned to look at her, but she was not addressing him.

'Yes, my lady,' replied Ilyonith Zesk, her dracon. As commander of her trueborn, Zesk served as the Kabal of the Hollow Heart's master-of-arms, and Dhaemira trusted him to act in her name – at least, so far as she trusted anyone.

'Seal off Sabregate?' Maculatix repeated, a curious yet delighted smile troubling the pale worms of his lips. 'How *decisive*. You would sacrifice the district?'

'It is small, and of little value,' Dhaemira replied. Little value to her, of course, and – so far as she was aware – the same went for the Coven of the Red Harvest. That might not be true for other factions, but that would just mean they had all the more reason to support her efforts to eliminate the threat. After all, sealing off the district to prevent the ork filth from spreading any further was the logical course of action. 'We corral them there, gather forces, then move in and slaughter them. If we are swift, the damage they can do will be limited. I will make approaches to all those I believe will listen to a proposal of joint action. Will you do the same?'

Maculatix drummed his fingertips together. 'Arakhia are of limited use and interest to me. They are blunt beings, barely sentient. My dungeons are better served hosting creatures that have a more refined appreciation of pain.'

Dhaemira waited, refusing to be drawn. She was convinced that the haemonculus saw the opportunity in being amongst the first to respond decisively to this threat, and she was not going to beg him for assistance. The Coven of the Red Harvest would be powerful allies, but if Maculatix decided to spurn her after all, she would cast her net wider.

She had no need to do so. After a couple more seconds, Maculatix tilted his head slightly into a position more closely linked with unity and accordance. 'However, certain useful elixirs can be distilled from their vital fluids, and although the beasts have a disagreeably high tolerance for suffering, both physical and spiritual, I would still be intrigued to see exactly how far their notorious robustness can be stretched. A few subjects for such purposes would not go amiss.'

'Then sharpen your blades, and gather what allies you can,' Dhaemira told him. 'We will lead the cleansing operation, and Port Tavarr will look to us for guidance.' She activated her carrier wave again. 'Zesk. Did any of the Wounding Wind make it out?'

'Yes, my lady.'

'Kill them,' Dhaemira said, ignoring Maculatix's look. The haemonculus could speculate all he wanted in that twisted, paranoid mind of his, but no witnesses meant no proof. 'They brought this plague down upon us, so they should be the first to pay for it with their lives.'

'Yes, my lady.'

'Master haemonculus,' Dhaemira said, bowing to her host. 'I will take my leave of you now.'

'Of course, master archon,' Maculatix replied. His return bow matched her obeisance to the minutest fraction of a degree, but his eyes never left her face.

Good. Let him remember it.

* * *

The corpses of the Wounding Wind lay strewn in the burning wreckage of their vehicles, not far from the now-sealed portal that led to the sub-realm of Sabregate. There were many other such portals, since Sabregate had been subsumed into Port Tavarr some time ago, and now had sufficient links for drukhari to move between the two relatively freely. It had links to a few other areas of Commorragh as well, but it was to Port Tavarr that it had the greatest connection, and to which it owed fealty. It was a minor area in truth, little more than a slum that was, insofar as such things could be determined in somewhere like Commorragh, on the outskirts of the Dark City. Sabregate might see raiding parties pass through, or return from realspace bearing spoils, but such ventures usually moved on to grander locations before disposing of their trophies.

Sabregate was unquestionably part of the drukhari realm, but insignificant enough that its infestation was an offence rather than a disaster. As such, it made the perfect location for the orks to despoil, provided they were not allowed to spread. Still, no drukhari could countenance the insult of even the lowliest district of the Dark City being overrun by such filth. The orks must be slaughtered and driven out, and the Kabal of the Hollow Heart would be at the forefront of such an attack. Dhaemira had already seized the initiative by ordering the portals out of Sabregate sealed; now she had to ensure that none of her so-called peers who might seek sport or vengeance in the district could do so without fitting into her plans. By so doing, she would guarantee that others thought of her as a leader, and so ease her path to assuming the role of Port Tavarr's ruler.

She eyed the remains of her unwitting dupes from the platform of her personal Venom. 'Did Archon Oridraed make it out?'

'We did not observe his armour, mistress,' Zesk replied, which was as good as a 'no'. No archon as desperate for recognition as Oridraed would stoop to dressing themselves in the raiment of one of their retainers; his very rank was a fiction he had to maintain at all times, precisely so that his few followers would continue to surrender their power to him.

'There are no reports of him having exited through any of the other portals?' That might be feasible – taking his chances alone if he suspected that consequences awaited for leading the orks back into Commorragh. However, Zesk shook his head, his helmet's impressive crest whipping from side to side.

'No, mistress. Some few fled the district before it was secured, but we have no indication that the archon was amongst them.'

'No loose ends, then,' Dhaemira said with satisfaction. 'Good.' She began to turn away from the spectacle, then froze as something caught her eye. It was a piece of midnight-black armour that protruded from beneath the rear of a destroyed Raider transport.

'Zesk,' she said, in a carefully controlled whisper. 'What is *that*?'

'One incubus was aboard,' Zesk replied. 'He died with the others.'

Dhaemira clenched her teeth. 'You killed an *incubus*?'

This was a concern. She had hoped that Oridraed's bodyguards would have fallen protecting him; after all, incubi were devoted warriors who sought little more than to prove their supremacy by slaying as many foes as possible. His incubi would have heard their conversation when she sent him on his doomed hunt, and although the reasoning of her approach to him had been sound and no one could blame her if a smaller kabal gravely underestimated the strength of their quarry, it was still one more connection to her than she would have liked. More seriously, there was a difference between the incubi having fallen in battle against the orks – something which would garner the support of the Shrine of the Last Breath for any attack on the invaders – and being gunned down on his return by her warriors. That was a slight that the Last Breath might not forgive.

'Have that corpse disposed of in a manner that none will see,' she ordered quietly. 'Utterly destroy the armour. No one must know that this warrior died by our weapons.'

'Mistress,' Zesk said, his tone and stance carefully balanced to avoid offence. 'Incubi armour is superior–'

'And recognisable!' Dhaemira hissed, rounding on him. She understood what her dracon was saying – the war suits of the incubus shrines offered better protection than the armour of her trueborn, better even than her own – but to wear the armour of an incubus when one was not an incubus was to bring down destruction on one's own head. The entire shrine to which the armour belonged would respond to such an insult, and there was no guarantee that any other shrine would honour a contract to defend the wearer's life in such a situation. 'It must go,' she said. 'We cannot even risk returning it to the shrine, for they will realise that the weapons which pierced it were drukhari. That warrior never made it through the portal. See to it that this becomes reality.'

'Yes, mistress,' Zesk said, inclining his head. He snapped his fingers, and two of his trueborn leaped down from the Venom to deal with the corpses.

The societal chaff which existed near this portal had fled as the first fugitives from the ork invasion began spilling through, and although all were watching from a distance, none dared approach while an archon such as Dhaemira Thraex of the Hollow Heart was making her inspections. However, others with more steel in their spines were approaching; Dhaemira could see the dark specks of transports. Her own household would be among them, Raider after Raider packed out with warriors in her kabal's distinctive yellow-and-purple plate, but there would be others. Word of the ork incursion had spread – partly due to her efforts and those of Maculatix, and partly through the organic spread of drukhari whispers.

'Take us to meet them,' she ordered her pilot, and her Venom swung up higher into the air, facing the oncoming flotilla like the single target of a swarm of arrows. Dhaemira schooled her face and steeled her nerve, and deliberately altered her own perceptions. These were *not* arrows, not projectiles aimed at her with the intent to harm; they were supplicants, coming to her for leadership and wisdom. She raised her chin and prepared to greet them as such.

The largest of the approaching shapes resolved itself into the double-hulled form of a Tantalus, a skimmer significantly larger than a standard Raider. Such craft were rare, and a mark of wealth and status. Dhaemira recognised it as belonging to the Kabal of the Falling Night even before she saw its colours, which meant the figure standing tall on the command deck could only be Master Archon Cistrial Virn.

'The arakhia are within our walls, and the Kabal of the Hollow Heart slays our own warriors,' Virn announced with macabre relish as his craft slowed to a halt, just outside of easy boarding range. Dhaemira was none too comfortable about facing down the Tantalus' pulse-disintegrator armament, but Virn's opening line suggested that he was out for blood in a metaphorical rather than literal sense, at least at the moment, lest he show himself up as a hypocritical fool in front of others. Archons were *supposed* to be duplicitous, of course, but the art lay in maintaining your façade until your final triumph was assured.

Also, at least Virn had stopped, rather than continuing past Dhaemira as though she weren't there.

'Are you here to assist, or merely to give your pleasure craft an airing?' Dhaemira enquired. That was not the subtlest of insults, since a Tantalus was a mighty weapon of war rather than a luxury barge, but neither was it sufficient to justify Virn opening hostilities. What was more, Dhaemira's Raiders were here now, cruising past and taking up position behind her, while the other craft – plenty from the Kabal of the Falling Night, but also smaller kabals like the Moon Legion, the Silver Shadows, and Blood's Gift – were stopping on the other side of the imaginary divide.

This was not her kabal facing down all the others, Dhaemira reminded herself. This was the other archons awaiting her leadership.

'What assistance do you require?' Virn asked lazily. He was a true beauty, with an artificial tint of the faintest glacial blue to his pale skin, which gave him the appearance of an ice sculpture. His hair was a shock of purest white, tied up and decorated with crescent blades and shot through with shards of bone taken from his enemies, while his armour was a deep greenish grey.

'I have sealed Sabregate off,' Dhaemira announced, watching to see who looked impressed with her quick thinking, who looked angered, who looked thoughtful. 'The arakhia are contained, but must still be eliminated.' She surveyed the assembled force: a sizeable one, to be sure, but enough to convincingly defeat the invaders? She was unconvinced. 'Things would go more smoothly if the wych cults wished to bloody their blades.'

'I'm sure they would,' Virn replied. 'And what of the covens?'

'I cannot speak for all, but the Coven of the Red Harvest is here,' a sibilant voice called.

The Red Harvest's vessels were rising up, and leading them was Maculatix on his own Raider, with ten of his most ferocious wracks. The haemonculus' craft swivelled lazily around, and he and his followers settled into position.

Alongside the Raiders and Venoms of the Kabal of the Hollow Heart.

The statement was clear and obvious. One of Port Tavarr's largest kabals and one of its largest covens were united, at least for now. It was a front, naturally, because Dhaemira had no love for Maculatix and he had none for her, but the leverage of their position was important. The other kabals were faced with a stark choice: attempt to form an immediate conglomerate of their own with the backstabbing and clawing for power that would accompany it, and risk losing all their standing; openly oppose this new alliance alone, and risk destruction; or fall into line.

It would be temporary. It would always be temporary. But for beings as long-lived as drukhari, 'temporary' could end up being a very long time indeed, and while that allowed underlings to hone their plans to dispose of their betters, it also encouraged them to wait for precisely the right moment rather than give in to the impatience that cursed lesser, briefer species. All Dhaemira had to do was ensure that the one perfect moment to overthrow her never materialised.

'Very well,' Cistrial Virn said casually, as though his question had been an innocent one, rather than an implication that Dhaemira stood alone with no allies. 'What do you propose?'

'We would be best served by the wych cults' speed,' Dhaemira said. 'The arakhia are ferocious and resilient, as we well know, but lumbering and cumbersome. We must avoid a direct engagement. Hellions and reavers should strike and disorientate them, doing damage and enraging them while keeping their distance. Our firepower will be most effective when they are truly disorganised. The kabals can then provide the support needed for the wyches themselves, and the foot troops of the covens' – she gestured to Maculatix – 'to close the distance and carve them apart.'

'We should move quickly,' Virn said. He was all business

now, at least on the surface. 'The arakhia possess little ability at constructing true fortifications, but their crude structures still play to their strengths, and could disrupt hit and run tactics. Better to strike before they begin adapting their surroundings to suit themselves.'

'I have already sent out communiques to the cults,' Dhaemira said. 'However, I believe we will have greater success if my fellow archons did the–'

She broke off as something exploded to her right. It was not the pulsing flash of a disintegration cannon, or the sputtering darkness of a dark lance. It was a loud detonation and a cloud of smoke, such as might be caused by primitive explosives launched by a solid fuel propellant.

Ork weapons, for example.

'What is happening?' she queried by carrier wave, pitching the signal wide for all her troops in the area. 'Answer me!'

The first response was the chatter of gunfire, this time to her left. Not the near-silent spitting of splinter weapons, but the full-throated roar of simple projectiles. Then the shouting reached them: the distinctive, one-note war cry of the arakhia. It was crude, and it was brutish, but it also reached into the hindbrain and caressed it with blunt, rough fingers. This, it said to the drukhari, was the voice of beings who were very unlikely to be afraid. Beings that would not stop until they were dead, which was harder to achieve than might be convenient. Beings that would never, ever give up their power.

And it was a voice that *should not be here*.

'Have any portals been missed?' Dhaemira demanded.

'All portals were sealed,' Zesk replied immediately. 'None have been reopened.'

Something else exploded, a little farther away, and that sound was immediately followed by loud and raucous cheering. Dhaemira looked around in frustration, taking little comfort from the fact that her rivals seemed just as confused as she was.

'Then *how are they doing this?*'

SEVEN

Ufthak looked at the portal, which was almost the mirror of the ones through which they'd already come. This one, however, was different, in that the mysterious shimmering lights which had characterised the others were absent. It was inert. Inoperative. *'Not zoggin' workin', boss,'* as Da Boffin had put it.

The Waaagh! had chased the spikiez through one portal into the weird tunnel place, and then through another portal into wherever they were now – the spikiez' home, or at least part of it. All around him, Ufthak could hear the noise of the spikiez who lived here doing their best to drive his ladz away, and the boyz giving 'em what-for in no uncertain terms. Spikiez always loved to show up, shank a few gits and disappear again; Ufthak thought it was highly appropriate that someone had finally dropped into *their* camp and set about violently rearranging the scenery.

But something was bothering him. Try as he might, he couldn't stop finkin' about how weird it was that he and his ladz had got through two of those portals what normally needed a scrawnie to open them, but were now stuck at this one.

'Mogrot,' he said thoughtfully, 'yoo ever get da feelin' dat someone finks dey're smarter'n yoo?'

'All da time, boss,' Mogrot said, nodding. Ufthak looked sideways at him, then grunted.

'Yeah, fair point.' He gestured towards the portal. 'Wot I'm gettin' at is, dis don't make no sense.'

'It's a scrawnie fing, boss,' Mogrot said, puzzled. 'Does it hafta make sense?'

Ufthak gritted his teef in irritation. On the one hand, no it didn't. Scrawniez and spikiez were weird gits, and that was an end to it. Even humies made a sort of sense, in a kind of weak and pathetic way; they were a bit like orks, just generally really really bad at it. Scrawniez and spikiez, on the other hand... Well, who knew what was going on in their heads? They were obviously finkin' – it wasn't like they were bugeyes, which were basically like squigs in terms of their determination to get a meal at all costs, and gave little indication of being aware of anything else. No, scrawniez and spikiez were kind of smart in their own way, but it was a zoggin' strange way. There was absolutely no reason why what they did, and why they did it, should make any sense to an ork.

But on the other hand, Ufthak was increasingly sure that it *should* make sense. That was the problem with finkin': it was difficult to work out where to stop. Once upon a time, when confronted by an obstacle like this, he'd have tried to blow it up to get through. If that didn't work – which he was sure it wouldn't, because he was increasingly suspicious that the spaces linked by these gates weren't exactly *next to each other* as he would understand it – then he would have just turned around and got to work stompin' all the spikiez he could reach. He'd wanted a fight, he'd found a fight, and the old Ufthak would have been happy with that.

This Ufthak, though, couldn't settle for it. Something was bothering him, like a splinter in his mind that not even Dok Drozfang could have removed. If it took a scrawnie or a spikie to open a gate, then there had to be a *reason* why the others had opened and this one wouldn't. It angered Ufthak that his brain was betraying him like this, refusing to let him be happy with what was, on the face of it, a perfectly good fight. There was nothing for it, though. He tried punching himself in the head to see if it shook the thoughts loose, but nothing happened other than he bruised his knuckles.

'Yoo alright, boss?' Mogrot asked, sounding a little concerned. It was hardly as though Ufthak's welfare was going to be high on Mogrot's list of priorities, since if Ufthak got blown up then Mogrot Redtoof would probably laugh at him, then set about scrappin' to try to become the next big boss, in which case might Gork and Mork help any ladz who ended up under his command. Still, any ork was going to be a bit worried if they thought their boss wasn't in his right mind.

That was the problem: Ufthak was in too much of his right mind. He had more mind than he knew what to do with, and right now it was insisting to him that his presence here, and that of his boyz, was not just the result of fortuitous chance, or Gork and Mork sending them on their way to have a good old scrap. Someone *wanted* him here, someone more immediate than a pair of mighty green deities in wherever it was that gods lived. Given that only scrawniez or spikiez could normally tell the gates what to do, that led to a fairly obvious conclusion about the nature of said someone.

As to *why* a spikie might want a massive load of orks to turn up in their home, that was something Ufthak couldn't yet puzzle out. Maybe it was as simple as setting two of your rivals up to have a scrap because you wanted a laugh. Maybe the spikie in question thought they'd laid some sort of fancy trap. Maybe…

No, wait. Go back to the 'trap' one.

Ufthak looked around again. One way in, no ways out. Well, other than possibly the way in, but no self-respecting ork boss was going to turn everyone around to go back the way they came. Go into a place, wreck it, come out the other side: that was the ork way. So, given that the spikiez knew this place better than Ufthak's ladz did, this might actually not be a half-bad trap after all.

Ufthak was in no mood to be caught in someone else's trap, no matter how nasty a surprise his would-be captor was going to get when they came to check on what they'd caught. He turned around, took a deep breath, and bellowed.

'Boffin!'

There was a gratifyingly short delay before Ufthak's chief mekboy appeared, zooming through the crowd of orks and grots who were milling back and forth, shouting and ignoring orders. However, Da Boffin's method of transportation seemed a little different to usual, and Ufthak furrowed his brow in confusion as the mek pulled up in front of him.

'Dat's… not touchin' da ground,' he said, pointing at Da Boffin's monowheel. It was indeed floating a hand's breadth above what passed for the ground here, rotating very slightly.

'Yeah, found some of dose spikie floaty-generators.' Da Boffin grinned happily, pointing to some new glowy bits on his lower half. 'Fort it might be a larf.'

'But yoo're keepin' da wheel?'

'Obviously,' Da Boffin said, looking hurt at the very suggestion. 'Dunno how long dese fings are gonna last for, it's only spikie tek after all. Can't beat a good wheel for reliability, when all's said an' done. Also, I can't find a way to turn da floaty off again, but I'm sure dat's just temp'rary. Anyway, boss,' he continued, as Ufthak's expression started to shift towards the boredom which might lead to remedial violence, 'I been takin' readings of da buildings round about, an' I reckon dat one' – he pointed towards a particularly jagged tower – 'is gonna be da best bet for findin' somefing snazzy inside it. It's got da highest power consumption, an' dere's gotta be a reason for dat.'

Ufthak nodded. The normal thing to do would be to order everyone nearby to attack the tower in question, but finkin' was taking place again.

'D'ya reckon yoo could use dere power?' he asked, causing Da Boffin's forehead to wrinkle.

'Reckon so, boss. It's all jus' energy, innit? Might need a bit of tamperin' wiv wotever we're hookin' it up to, but dat shouldn't be a problem.' His expression brightened, the face of a mekboy who could see an immediate future consisting of mucking around with wires, tools, and electrocuted grots. 'Wot's da plan?'

Ufthak told him the plan, and Da Boffin's grin widened until it nearly reached from ear to ear. 'I *like* it, boss! Yeah, dat should work. I'll get my spannerz to bring da bits up.' He turned to zoom away, but Ufthak caught him by the shoulder.

'How high does dat fing go?' he asked, nodding towards Da Boffin's newly floating lower half.

'Uh, dunno, boss. Da fings I nicked it from zipped about quite high, so it should be fine.'

'Right, den before ya go, get up *dere*,' Ufthak said, pointing to the head of a Stompa that was thumping around a short distance way, 'an' tell da kaptin dat I want 'im to give us a way into *dat*.' He pointed again, this time at the base of the spire Da Boffin had highlighted as being the one with the greatest power consumption.

'You got it, boss!' Da Boffin said gleefully. His new additions glowed brighter and whined louder, and he cackled in glee as he rose up into the air and headed off, a little unsteadily, towards the giant war machine in question. Ufthak watched him for long enough to be reasonably sure that he was going to make it, then unslung the Snazzhammer, ignited the power field around it, and raised it into the air.

Even amidst the generalised chaos that was an orkish invasion in full swing, the big boss standing tall and holding his weapon up was enough to garner attention. Nearby orks stopped what they were doing and turned to look, and their mates turned to see what they were looking at, and then *their* mates turned around, and so on and so on.

'Alright, lissen up!' Ufthak roared. He levelled the Snazz-hammer to point at the spire that was his target, nearly splitting a nearby beast snagga in two in the process. 'We're about to go an' give everyfing in dere a zoggin' good kickin'. Only one fing I want yoo lot to remember – if dere's anyfing wot looks like it's all teknologickal, leave it in one piece cos I want Da Boffin lookin' at it.'

The surrounding orks nodded. They were the Tekwaaagh!, after all: while most of them had no particular interest in shiny gizmos and gubbinz that didn't directly kill anything, they were familiar with Da Meklord's particular interests, and knew that orks who wrecked something he wanted didn't last long.

'Oh, one uvver fing,' Ufthak added with a grin, as the Stompa began to ponderously rotate and decline its guns. 'Stand back for a second, cos it's about to get a bit loud...'

The spikie leaped at Ufthak with a high-pitched scream, and a knife so thin it seemed almost non-existent. Ufthak simply shoved the top of the Snazzhammer straight at its chest, not bothering with either hammer surface or choppa blade, and the spikie practically impaled its own ribcage with the pathetic snapping noise of thin bones giving way. It fell to the floor, its face wracked with pain, but also a sort of infuriated betrayal, as though it was shocked and outraged that Ufthak had been quick enough to foil its attack. Ufthak stamped on its head, and annoyingly resilient though the things were given their gangly build, he was sufficiently heavy to crush its skull under-foot without difficulty.

That was the problem with fights these days, you just didn't get 'em like you used to. Most gits had slowed down since Ufthak was a yoof, to the point that he barely had to try any more. Back in the day, when he was just a boy in Badgit Snazz-hammer's mob, he'd have been sluggin' and choppin' away, narrowly avoiding death every other second and feeling incre-dibly alive as a result. It wasn't that fighting was *boring* now, far from it, but it was difficult to find the same rush of adventure and fulfilment from it when most enemies seemed to lack any ability to get close to you.

This did not, of course, mean that Ufthak had any intention of deliberately giving the gits a chance just to make things a bit more interesting. If they couldn't be bothered to be any good at fighting, he certainly wasn't going to make it easy for them.

'Anyone else want some?' he roared, waving the Snazzhammer, but the last spikie apparently decided that it did not, in fact, want some, and turned to flee. Ufthak hurled the Snazzhammer at its fast-retreating back, and the powered-blade side nearly bisected the luckless creature. It fell to the floor, instantly dead, and Ufthak clenched his fist to trigger the button built into the palm of his armoured gauntlet.

Throwing the Snazzhammer was fun, and often effective, but it did lead to the problem of Ufthak being over *here* and his weapon being over *there*, which was just inconvenient and down-right disrespectful. He'd had a word with Da Boffin about it, and the mek had rigged up a new device that should solve the problem, calling the weapon back to Ufthak's hand via a miniature tellyport homer.

In theory.

What happened this time was that the weapon reappeared a few feet to his right and behind him, coincidentally right in the middle of one of his ladz. There was a brief and unpleasant moment when both objects tried to occupy the same space, and then the ork in question – Zoddrag, Ufthak thought – exploded wetly. Ufthak reached out and grabbed the Snazzhammer before it fell to the ground, but there was nothing to be done for Zoddrag, who was now mainly just limbs without anything really left to which they could be reattached. Everyone laughed, including Ufthak; if you had to die, then it might as well be funny.

'Anyone else?' he shouted after the laughter had died down a bit, but only silence replied. The spikie tower was just as sleek and polished and confusing as its residents, somehow combining shiny surfaces and shadowy darkness, not to mention a layout that defied anything Ufthak considered logical.

They were less than a third of the way up, but if he'd been actually trying to get anywhere in particular then Ufthak was certain he would be hopelessly lost, thanks to switchback staircases, dead-end corridors, and secret doors. His ladz had been ambushed from behind twice, by spikie fighters slipping out of concealed entrances and burying their blades into orkish flesh before their presence had been registered, but each time the gits had overestimated the psychological impact of their appearance. A lot of species, Ufthak supposed, would be shaken by an enemy suddenly showing up next to them; for orks, it just meant your attempt to find a fight had been even more successful than you'd anticipated.

There was still no response to his challenge. Whoever was left in this tower was showing no signs of coming out and fighting for it, and Ufthak was fed up of hunting spikiez down just to kill a few of them at a time. He waved one hand dismissively. 'Alright, ladz, go get 'em. I'm goin' back to talk to Da Boffin.'

The boyz with him, who'd been hanging back so as not to get clobbered by their big boss for running into the enemy before him, surged forward with whoops of glee and indiscriminate firing of assorted weaponry. Ufthak shoved his way through them, passing scenes of slaughter and random destruction, until he found himself back on the lower levels again, where Da Boffin and his spannerz were busy hooking a bunch of thick cables up to several strange stones. These glowed with a sickly light, and the meks were convinced they held whatever the spikiez used as energy.

'Wotcha, boss,' Da Boffin greeted him. 'How's it– Nazlug! Don't touch da–'

There was an extremely loud fizzling noise, and an ork caught fire and flew backwards across the room. Everyone had a good old laugh while he rolled around slapping at the flames, then got back to work again when they caught sight of Ufthak's glower.

'Anyway, boss, how's it goin' up dere?' Da Boffin asked genially, absent-mindedly scratching his head with a tool that seemed to have at least three different points on it.

'Spikiez, innit,' Ufthak said with a shrug. 'Dey jump at ya, someone gets stabbed, ya stomp 'em and move on to find da next lot. But dey're not da proppa fighters, an' I don't wanna be waitin' around for 'em to come an' get us when dey're nice an' ready.'

'Well, I fink we've got it all sorted now,' Da Boffin said, smacking his hands together in a satisfied manner. 'Let's go outside an' see wot's wot.'

Ufthak followed him back out to where some more of Da Boffin's assistants had set up a series of large metal plates that were bolted together into a sort of second floor, and to which the cables snaking out of the spikiez' tower were attached. Two menacing-looking pylons towered over the plates, pointing downwards and inwards towards whatever might be standing on them. At the moment, a mob of thirty or so boyz fidgeted around with the restlessness of orks who weren't doing anything exciting *right now* but had been told that if they could just stand still for a bit, they could shortly be doing something *really* exciting.

'Fire it up!' Da Boffin yelled, and a particularly oily grot leaped onto a lever and dragged it downwards with its bodyweight. Lights ignited all over the device, and power began to crackle around the tips of the pylons.

'Yes!' Da Boffin shouted gleefully, and zoomed over to inspect the dials. 'Power levels are holdin' steady! Good finkin', boss. Da spikiez are givin' us da juice to make it work!'

'Make it work, den!' Ufthak ordered. Da Boffin grinned at him, and twisted a large dial.

A pulsing, throbbing noise began, deep enough at first to cause intestinal discomfort, then rapidly rising to a pitch beyond hearing, and at which ear wax began to dissolve. Then, just as Ufthak was starting to feel as though his head were being clamped between the forks of a power klaw, there was an exceptionally loud *pop!* and all of the boyz on the plate disappeared.

Ufthak looked at Da Boffin. 'Did it work?'

'Put a detektor on one of 'em,' Da Boffin said smugly, pulling out a device and consulting it. 'Didn't know exactly where I was sending 'em, but if I get a signal back den dey ended up more or less in da right place.'

'An' wot if ya don't get a signal back?' Ufthak asked.

Da Boffin shrugged. 'Den dey're probably in da realm of da gods, fightin' dose weird gribbly fings wot hang around wiv da Chaos gits.' Something lit up on his device, and he cackled. 'Dere we go! Dey got to wherever dey're goin' okay!' Another light came on. 'An' da nob pushed da button, which means dey've found somefing to fight, an' all!'

Ufthak nodded, satisfied. Finkin' was sometimes a pain, but it also had its benefits. His ladz weren't just going to sit around and wait for the spikiez to come to them, oh no.

'Get yer arses over 'ere!' he bellowed. 'Anyone who ain't fightin' a spikie *right now*, get on da tellyport pad! Yoo're goin' on a trip!'

EIGHT

Dhaemira had had a *plan*.

Lure the orks in by sacrificing a proud, desperate self-proclaimed archon and his so-called kabal, trap them in Sabregate (a location which had little value to her), then rally the other factions of Port Tavarr behind her to eradicate the brutes. Everyone got a fresh supply of slaves and victims, and the strife that had so damaged this district of Commorragh was ended as a new leader emerged: her. With that stability recovered, everyone could turn their attention back to raiding realspace and predating on the galaxy's lesser species, and give only the usual amount of thought to betrayal and deception rather than being prepared for full-blown conflict to erupt at any moment. By taking command, she would actually be doing everyone a favour.

However, despite her warriors' assurances that the webway portals out of Sabregate were deactivated and there was no way that the orks could be getting through them, the wretched creatures were somehow not remaining trapped. Dhaemira knew well enough that orks sometimes refused to recognise that they were dead until long after the time when their bodies should have given up; she had not previously been aware that they could apparently also refuse to recognise the laws of physics.

'Find out what is happening!' she hissed at Zesk, as Raiders and Venoms split off from the assembled flotilla to head towards the disturbances around them. 'Get the artisans here to inspect the portals! I want to know how the arakhia are getting out, and how far this is spreading!'

'Yes, mistress,' Zesk said obediently, although Dhaemira could tell that her dracon was resentful of being the first recipient of her rage and frustration. No matter. He would either remind himself of how privileged his existence was, or she would publicly flay the skin from his flesh as an object lesson to all those whom she had rewarded for their service. However, even if it was required, such an extravagance might have to wait until after the immediate challenges facing them had been resolved.

'Are you certain you are up for this, Dhaemira?' Virn called mockingly. It appeared that the archon of the Kabal of the Falling Night was not concerned by these developments – or at any rate, not concerned enough to let it prevent him from undermining Dhaemira's shaky authority. At least, Dhaemira reminded herself, no one could laugh at the failure of her plan, since no one else knew that she had intended for the orks to come here in the first place. It was perfectly natural for her to be angry about the arakhia further sullying Commorragh with their presence.

Paranoia lanced in, sharp and sudden. Why was Virn so unconcerned? Was this part of *his* scheme, a scheme Dhaemira had not even considered until now? Had Virn somehow arranged for the orks to break out of Sabregate in order to make Dhaemira's victory less assured, and so then take power for himself? In fact, had everything – Dhalgar's near death, Dhaemira's own scheme, and now the unexpected appearance of orks within Port Tavarr proper – merely come about from the labyrinthine puppeteering of Cistrial Virn?

No. No, Dhaemira refused to believe it. The archon of the Kabal of the Falling Night was formidable, but he lacked that sort of long-term subtlety. This was the arakhia refusing to play their part, that was all – an aggravating stubbornness that Dhaemira should have foreseen. No matter: she would adapt her scheme accordingly, find the nature and location of the breaches, and seal them off before leading the forces of Port Tavarr to–

'Mistress!' Ilyonith Zesk shouted, as a flare of green energy erupted overhead. Dhaemira just had time to feel her skin tingle in a manner she had never before experienced, and then the sky opened and began to disgorge orks.

They fell in a bellowing storm, at least two dozen hulking monstrosities in crude black-and-yellow clothing and armour. Dhaemira realised after half a second that the creatures weren't yelling in panic as they fell; they were roaring war cries, or even laughing exuberantly. The arakhia were the Children of Destruction, after all, and they lived only for warfare. It appeared that they had very little concern about how they reached a fight, or where the fight actually *was*, so long as they got there.

Drukhari reflexes were more than equal to the appearance of these enemies, and splinter rifles were raised and firing before the first orks had fallen more than a few feet. However, it swiftly became apparent to Dhaemira that even an already poisoned ork could cause a great deal of problems in such a situation. They were massive creatures, each one perhaps three times the weight of a drukhari even without their armour and weaponry, and they were falling directly onto Port Tavarr's fleet of skimmers.

One such body, already limp and with the light fading from its eyes as drukhari toxins took effect, landed on the very front of her Venom's nose. The vehicle's internal stabilising systems were tuned to hair-fine settings in order for the pilot to best jink and dodge enemy weapons fire, but could do nothing about the sudden impact of several hundred pounds of orkish muscle and wargear arriving at a decent fraction of its terminal velocity.

The Venom's nose went down and backwards, violently. The craft's rear end, in accordance with physics, was propelled upwards and forwards by the same degree. Dhaemira could have made a desperate grab for a rail and be left hanging like some desperate slave while her pilot tried to right the vehicle, but in the split second in which she made her decision, she instead opted to boost herself off.

Drukhari might be slight compared to many of the galaxy's other species, but they were almost unmatched in terms of the strength-to-weight ratio of their bodies. Dhaemira could run fast enough and jump high enough to outpace and outmanoeuvre most of her potential enemies, and she put the power in her frame to good use now. Her legs combined with the momentum of her flipping Venom to propel her through the air, and she somersaulted across the gap between her craft and that of the Tantalus of the Kabal of the Falling Night. She landed lightly on one of its twin prows, her own weight barely registering on the far larger vehicle, but then it shuddered as a handful of orks crashed down onto it.

Kabalite warriors were skilled combatants, but they were equipped to engage the enemy at range and bring them down under a withering hail of toxic splinters and other, more exotic weaponry. They focused on highly mobile firepower, striking and fading while mounted on their Raiders, and never letting the enemy close with them. It was the durable monsters of the haemonculus covens, the blademasters of the incubus shrines, or the quicksilver gladiators of the wych cults who fought foes blade to blade and brought them down with obscene power, impeccable technique or blinding speed. Against a human, a t'au, or any number of other species, a drukhari could hold their own even without access to melee weapons, but orks were another matter entirely. Their brute strength made even their crude blades deadly, and they ignored blows that would stun or incapacitate lesser foes.

Orks cared nothing for the artistry of the blade, for the dance of blows or the subtle kiss of toxins. They were not privy to the *Sula'daeth*, the Language of Cuts, whereby a skilled warrior demonstrated their disdain – or indeed, grudging respect – for an adversary through the placement and depth of the wounds they inflicted. Orks just killed. There was no finesse, and little technique.

But by the Living Muse himself, Dhaemira reflected as five orks tore apart their own number of kabalite warriors within a second or so, they were terrifying.

The drukhari's way of war was based around their mobility; in fact, the idea was never to wage war at all, as lesser species would understand it. The denizens of the Dark City did not embark on crusades of conquest such as those undertaken by the wretched *mon-keigh* (whichever foul gods they worshipped), the t'au and their deluded lackeys, or even the orks themselves. Drukhari struck hard, took what they wanted, and departed while their enemies lay bleeding. They sought no territory in realspace; they merely predated on those that did, and their vehicles were key to their success.

Now, however, those vehicles were no refuge. While some of the orks fell past with limbs flailing, plummeting towards the ground below, the crew of those craft unlucky enough to have one or more of the brutes land on them found that they now had very little room in which to manoeuvre. An ork took up a lot of space on a narrow drukhari vessel, and were hard to shift: Dhaemira saw a crewer of the Tantalus swing acrobatically around the ethersail mast and slam feet first into one of the boarders, only to bounce off and land on the deck while the ork in question did little more than rock slightly to one side. Then the foul creature levelled its massive sidearm, a weapon shaped like a pistol but nearly the size of a drukhari's chest, and fired a slug as thick as Dhaemira's arm into its attacker.

Not even an ork could miss at that range. The warrior's breastplate shattered and most of their upper body disintegrated, and the ork let out a grotesque snickering laugh, which only ended when Cistrial Virn lopped its head off with a sweep of his powered blade.

The archon of the Kabal of the Falling Night flowed into combat like a warrior god of ancient times, his power sword shimmering and his hair fanning out like snow spray. His weapon carved up a second ork with a trio of slashes nearly too swift for the eye to follow – two crossways, alternating direction, and then a third up the middle of the enemy's torso: the Rising Star, an indication that the galaxy would spin on without noticing the death of this insignificant life form – then sheared through the descending blade of a third, despite the fact that Virn's power sword looked like a mere sliver in comparison to the massive wedge of sharp metal against which it was pitted. The ork paused for a moment to gape at the failure of its strike and the remaining stub of the weapon in its hand, and Virn took its left leg off at the knee, then thrust his blade straight through its face. That was the Lance: a gesture of derision not towards the blademaster's victim so much as the victim's companions, the implication being that they were so slow and unskilled that the drukhari warrior could take the time to embed their blade in their enemy's flesh and withdraw it again without endangering themselves.

One of the remaining three orks apparently decided that enough was enough, and pulled the trigger on an ugly, elongated lump of a weapon which belched flame that stank of chemicals. The blast engulfed the ork directly in front of the firer, which howled in pain, but Virn flipped up and over the fire, then vaulted lightly off the burning ork's head before landing and bringing his power sword down to bisect the flame-wielder cleanly down its centre line. Not even an ork could survive such a blow, and Virn flipped his sword up, caught it in a reversed grip, and stabbed out backwards, without looking, to sever the spine of the burning hulk behind him, which collapsed. It had been a performance of deadly, balletic grace, and Virn brought his blade up and around almost casually to dispatch his final opponent.

But his sword was caught between the massive prongs of a massive claw-prosthetic which also crackled with the energy of a power field, and the huge ork that wielded it – a 'boss' or 'nob', as Dhaemira understood their crude dialect – lashed out with the butt of its enormous rifle-type weapon to club Virn square in his shocked face.

The archon of the Kabal of the Falling Night was knocked bodily into the boom of the ethersails, leaving his powerblade behind in his enemy's grasp as he slumped to the deck. The ork closed its claw and shattered the weapon in its grip, then drew its arm back to impale Virn on its talons.

Dhaemira could have let it happen. She could have watched the ork dispatch her stunned rival, then slain the brute herself and taken command of the Tantalus. These massive craft were rare and expensive, and it would be a boost to her authority if she were to procure one, no matter the manner in which she came into possession of it. The few remaining crew would be unlikely to give her trouble; indeed, with their archon gone, they might well seek to get into her good graces.

However, something spurred her into action from the other half of the Tantalus' twin hull. She drew her blast pistol, and fired it.

The darklight energy coursed out of her weapon and struck the ork, not with physical force, but with pure destructive power. The ork paused for a moment to assess this new threat, and Dhaemira drew her own blade and moved to attack.

Her blast pistol had done little more than singe the ork, but that was because it had first burned away a large chunk of the crude – but thick – armour plating with which the creature had covered itself. Now Dhaemira's blade flicked out, searching for the green flesh that had been exposed, or the soft and vulnerable cloth that lay beneath and between its remaining armour. Her weapon was not empowered like Cistrial Virn's had been, but it held a danger all its own: this was a venom blade, and the micropores in its surface constantly wept lightly with hypertoxins distilled from venabrous ghottiels, dusky slinkworms, and other foul creatures of Commorragh's shadows.

The ork roared in rage at being denied its prey, and lashed out with its powered claw in a ferocious backswing. Dhaemira made no attempt to block or parry the blow; she knew she could not match the brute for strength, and her blade would simply shatter from the force with which the ork had swung its weapon, let alone the power field that enveloped it. She stepped back instead, her nostrils filling with the stench of ozone as the tips of the claw passed just beneath her nose and ionised the air on their way past. Vileth's blood, but the beast was fast!

Still, startlingly quick though the ork was for its size, and despite the formidable combination that made with its massive strength, Dhaemira was quicker still. She rocked back off her heels and sprang forwards, darting across the ork's front and cutting at its thigh with the tip of her venom blade. The point of her weapon pierced the rough black cloth and bit into the flesh beneath, and then she was rolling underneath the clubbing swing of its gun barrel to end up on its far side.

The hypertoxins would be in the beast's bloodstream now, which meant its death was inevitable, but 'inevitable' was not the same thing as 'imminent'. Most enemies would succumb to even a mild scratch within a few seconds, but Dhaemira had seen Virn underestimate this brute and come undone as a result, and was determined not to do the same. Instead of posing triumphantly and waiting for her prey to fall at her feet with bulging eyes and choking on bloody froth, she stabbed again and again, sending her blade darting into the creature's back and slipping between its ribs where there were gaps in its haphazardly affixed armour. The ork bellowed in pain and rage as the organs she punctured began to fail and shut down, and its furious circling to bring her within its reach got more desperate and uncoordinated as the moments dragged on. Finally, its exertions overtaxed its ailing nervous system, and it collapsed with a sound like an avalanche in a foundry.

Cistrial Virn had pushed himself up to his knees, but froze as the tip of Dhaemira's venom blade caressed the underside of his chin. Dhaemira applied the very slightest upward pressure, just enough to force her rival to tilt his chin and look her in the eye.

The merest breath of additional force, the slightest twitch of Dhaemira's wrist, and the fate of the archon of the Kabal of the Falling Night would be sealed. And yet, Virn met Dhaemira's gaze without blinking or flinching. There was no fear of the envenomed blade there, despite the fact that he could surely feel the point pricking against his skin. He mouthed no plea for mercy, did not shrink uselessly back from the weapon as though a few inches of space could save him if Dhaemira decided to take his life. *Do it, if you dare,* his glare seemed to say, *but for your own sake, you had best not miss.*

Cistrial Virn did not give up his power. And, Dhaemira realised, this was a prospect that excited her.

'A formidable showing,' she said, withdrawing her blade and sheathing it. 'A shame the big brute caught you off-guard.' She turned away, her skin prickling with anticipation. Would Virn now come flying at her from behind, eager to redress his failure by slaying the only witness to it over whom he did not wield authority?

She heard the slight scrape of Virn's armour on the deck as the other archon rose to his feet, but this was not followed by any hiss of rage, or the sound of a weapon being recovered from a fallen warrior to strike Dhaemira down while her back was turned. Dhaemira was not naive enough to believe Virn would consider himself beholden to her for intervening to save his life, but perhaps he was content to let things stand for now, rather than risk attacking a warrior armed with blast pistol and venom blade.

The rush and exhilaration of battle began to fade, and Dhaemira looked out over her surroundings. The orks had been culled, although they had exacted a high price for it. It was a sobering reminder that no matter how inferior the arakhia were in many ways, they were still capable of doing appalling damage when allowed to fight in the manner of their choosing. As to the manner of their arrival…

Dhaemira looked up at where the orks had emerged. There was nothing there now, merely the dark skies of Commorragh rising to meet the mighty curve of the membrane that separated

Port Tavarr from the murderous warp itself. The Portgate was up there, Port Tavarr's largest and primary entrance and exit. Dhaemira could see the jagged shapes of the docking spires, and even make out the tiny shapes of starships tethered in gravity-free anchorage far above. One of them was the *Heart's End*, her personal flagship on which was mounted Voidbreaker, the largest dark lance ever created by a drukhari artisan.

The orks had not fallen from the Portgate; they had emerged far closer. Nor had they jumped from any form of sky-craft, not even a captured drukhari one. There was only one explanation for how they had come to be here, and so suddenly at that.

Little inspired terror in the drukhari, for their souls were jaded and hardened by the millennia of pain and suffering they inflicted on others in their own quests to satisfy the pull of She Who Thirsts and keep their mortality at bay, but something closed a cold fist around Dhaemira's heart now. A movement beside her alerted her to the presence of Cistrial Virn, coming up to stand next to her at the Tantalus' rail. The other archon made no mention of how close he had come to death, nor of Dhaemira's involvement in it, and did not even pass comment on her presence on his craft. Instead, Virn's face was drawn and his eyes haunted, for he recognised the truth just as Dhaemira did.

'They are teleporting,' Virn said, in a voice that was only flat because of the work being done to keep it under control. An archon could not let weakness be seen, lest their rivals seek to capitalise and the ambitious traitors within their own ranks become emboldened, and yet Cistrial Virn was teetering on the edge of it.

'They are,' Dhaemira agreed, and her own throat nearly betrayed her, because the enormity of what she had brought down upon them was starting to sink in.

Commorragh was a bastion against the malice and hunger of

the warp, a shelter in which the drukhari lived out their lives and from which they only emerged for short periods, so the drain upon their souls from She Who Thirsts did not grow too great. The Dark City had endured for over ten thousand years, but that did not mean that it was inviolable. If a portion of the webway was breached then attackers could reach Commorragh's gates, and although a webway portal could only be operated by an aeldari, the minions of Chaos had many tricks by which they could gain entry. Even the structure of the city was not fully safe, for during a disjunction the boundaries themselves could become breached. Entire sub-realms could be lost, and have to be sealed off with those left inside abandoned to their doom, simply in order to prevent the contagion from spreading any further.

Teleportation was one of the most foolhardy practices undertaken by the younger species of the galaxy, for it involved literally throwing oneself through the warp with imperfect guidance and little protection. Only the Warp Spiders Aspect Warriors of the craftworlds practised it amongst all the aeldari, and even they took great risks in doing so due to how their souls stood out like beacons in the warp. The mon-keigh of the Imperium did their miserable best to insulate themselves from the warp's predators with the pathetic emblems of their shackled god, but no aeldari would risk such an imprecise method: the odds were good that daemons would swarm to the light of an individual's soul and consume them – or worse – before they emerged again.

And then there were the orks, the arakhia, who lacked even the humans' stumbling, flawed sense of self-preservation in such matters. Only the most heavily armoured, iron-willed mon-keigh stood a chance of surviving teleportation, but orks happily threw themselves through the warp with no concern, content in the knowledge that they would end up fighting *something*. Their methods were unshielded, haphazard and chaotic.

And now they were teleporting *inside* Commorragh.

This was no longer just an insult but a real threat, far greater than that posed by the orks themselves, or their crude but dangerous weapons. The orkish army might destroy buildings and slaughter drukhari, but those were losses that Dhaemira was content to risk, so long as it was not *her* buildings or *her* life. The arakhia's teleportation, however, might open the way into Commorragh for the daemons that lurked in the warp, forever pawing at the walls separating them from the delicious morsels within. That could be ruinous: if a breach occurred, Dhaemira would not be safe even if she managed to escape into another sub-realm of the Dark City. Asdrubael Vect would brook no threat to his domain, and his warriors would be given orders to isolate and execute any refugees from such a tragedy, just in case they had unknowingly brought the faintest seed of Chaos out with them.

'We cannot wait for the wych cults,' Dhaemira heard herself say. 'We must exterminate this threat ourselves, immediately.'

'Agreed,' Cistrial Virn declared. He glanced sideways at Dhaemira, and gave the faintest nod. It appeared that a genuine truce was being offered, rather than the traditional lip service. Dhaemira could not count on Virn and the Kabal of the Falling Night for a moment longer than it would take to wipe the orks out, but until that moment, they could work together.

Dhaemira vaulted up onto the rail of the Tantalus, balancing fearlessly above the gulf below, and gestured to the pilot of her Venom to approach. The cold terror in her gut was already twisting into anger. How dare the arakhia threaten the very substance of her domain? How dare they overreach themselves in such a manner? They were her tools, but they had turned in her hand.

Well, now she would exact her revenge, and carve fear of her kind into their carcasses until the survivors were no more than whimpering hunks of broken flesh.

She set her carrier waves to broadcast as far and wide as she could. Let her voice be heard by all those assembled here, and let them know that she was in command.

'Sharpen your blades, and open the portals,' Dhaemira Thraex commanded. 'We ride to the death of our enemies!'

NINE

Snaggi had chosen just the right moment to make his move, if he said so himself. Which he did. Although quietly, to make sure no one overheard.

Some grots – fools like Nizkwik – were deluded enough to believe that a grot's natural place in the galaxy was as a servant to an ork. Nizkwik didn't *like* being kicked around, yelled at, and generally abused, but he was incapable of imagining anything else. Snaggi had never even tried to talk to the other grot about the possibility of a life not at the mercy of orkish oppression, because he knew a lost cause when he saw one.

Then there were the few grots, like Snaggi – although no one was actually *like* Snaggi, the gods had broken the mould when they created him – who recognised their condition for what it was. Intolerable. Unacceptable. The endlessly repeating tragedy of what happened when strength was allowed to win out over intelligence. The gods embodied the dual nature of the orkish species – both brutal *and* kunnin', in different amounts – but orks themselves were essentially just squigs with the ability to use language and weapons. It was grots who were the true chosen of Gork and Mork, because they were not only willing to stick the other git, but capable of choosing the best time to do so. This was why Snaggi was a prophet of Gork and Mork, although he kept quiet about that around orks, because they tended to be unable to handle the truth of it.

However, most grots sat in the middle. They didn't live in the unquestioning ignorance of those like Nizkwik, who were only content with their lot because they couldn't conceive of anything better, but nor did they have the vision, the courage, or the sheer moral fibre to actively envisage change. Most grots lived lives of sulky misery and casual spite, spreading their own suffering out to as many other life forms as they could get away with. Their directionless resentment was like a reservoir, released in little dribbles with a shanking here, or the application of an oversized wrench to the shins of another grot there, but there was still a massive amount of potential energy just waiting to be tapped by a grot with the ingenuity to harness it.

In a normal situation, that reservoir was sluggish and immobile. This, though, was far from a normal situation. The orks had dragged them all through into wherever in the gods' names this was, a completely unnatural spikie city that was dark, and smelled of dust and blood and death (but not in a fun, invigorating way), and everyone's nerves were on edge. Spikiez were just plain old *nasty*, and that was an end to it. Every grot knew that beakies were rock 'ard and deadly, and bugeyes had too many arms and too many claws, and tinheadz had guns what could blast you into the smallest bits of small that you could imagine before you could say 'Oi!', and every grot was sensibly and justifiably terrified of these things. However, if there was one good thing about those possible deaths – and

Snaggi wasn't convinced that there was, but *if* there was – it was that they would be quick.

Spikiez didn't make it quick. Spikiez, in fact, seemed to rather enjoy dragging it out. Information was a bit scarce on *exactly* what they did, because no one really got away, and no grot with any sense hung around close enough to get a proper view, but it was generally known to all that spikiez and their knives were to be avoided at all costs.

So that was where they were now. An awful lot of grots who'd been dragged, kicked, and herded through alarming portals into a place with few obvious exits, and where the shadows into which they might normally flee quite conceivably harboured spikiez with blades that thirsted for grot blood. The orks were having a great time of it, of course, stompin' anyone they came across and blowing up whatever they pleased, but the spikiez who lived here kept appearing and attacking, then running away again before too many of them could be killed. Snaggi knew it was only a matter of time before the gits decided that the orks were a bit too tough, and that they wanted to have a go at the grots instead. Typical spikie cowardice, wanting to fight grots just because they were easier to kill.

This was exactly the sort of situation in which a skilled orator could reach out and take a listener's fears to give them just the right nudge; to turn that churning mass of guileless resentment and bile into something useful.

'Dis can't go on,' he said to his twitching and flinching audience, as they huddled together in the wreckage of a battlewagon that had been the victim of either spikie heavy weaponry or poor mekboy engineering. 'Da orks've gone too far dis time. Dis ain't a place for da likes of us! We're bovverin' da spikiez in dere own holes, and dey're not gonna rest until we're all sliced up an'–' He broke off, scowling at a scuffle at the back. 'Wot's goin' on over dere?'

Gip, whom Snaggi had identified as large but lazy, and therefore the perfect sort of henchgrot, smacked the two smaller grots causing the disruption around the head. 'Dey were fightin' about da sky. Couldn't agree if it's white an' gold, or black an' blue.'

Snaggi peered upwards through a jagged hole in the thick metal, and snorted. The sky was strange, that was true enough, with the weird glyphs that seemed to be burned on it but were only visible when you weren't looking directly at them. However, the colour was obvious: it was definitely… Well… You know actually, now he came to look at it…

'Honestly, dunno wot yoo're squabblin' about,' he said with a dismissive snort. 'It's *obvious* wot colour it is. But dat's just me point,' he continued hastily, before anyone could ask him to express an actual opinion on the subject. 'Dis place is *weird*. Causes sensible grots to doubt da evidence of dere own eyes. Dis ain't where da gods want us to be.'

'How do *yoo* know wot da gods want?' someone sneered from the middle of the crowd. Snaggi's eyes found him almost immediately: scrawny even by grot standards, with the tip of his nose missing.

'Cos dey talk to me,' Snaggi said with simple pride, and awaited his acclamation.

A couple of his audience scoffed loudly. Most just sort of looked at him a bit funny. A few grots, the ones Snaggi had already identified as likely to lose to a squig in a counting competition, made impressed oohing noises. This infuriated him, because it ran counter to everything that was supposed to happen. It should be the *smart* ones who realised the truth of his divine right, while the fools rejected him! It was hardly going to impress anyone if his most devoted followers struggled to walk and talk at the same time.

Still, no one had actually left. And maybe that was partly

because they were already in the best bit of cover available while the orks tried to prosecute a war against an enemy that refused to stand and fight them, but so what? That just meant Snaggi was a genius for choosing this as the location for his first move. And there were a few, Gip amongst them, who were eyeing him as close to thoughtfully as their brains would allow. They could tell that he was something special; that if they stuck close to him, they might be able to bask in his reflected glory. That was all he needed.

'Sounds to *me* like a few of you ladz ain't convinced,' Snaggi said knowingly. Only 'a few', it wouldn't do him good to acknowledge anything more than that. Grots always sought safety in numbers anyway, so if he could make his doubters think that there weren't many of them then his job would be easier. 'Now, I ain't sayin' I'm a weirdboy wot's gonna start spittin' out propha-sees, or anyfing like dat. But I get glimpses of da gods' intentions.'

'Wot does it look like?' asked a tubby grot, whose eyes were hidden behind overlarge goggles. His voice held an appropriate tone of wonder, and Snaggi smiled beatifically.

'It's *green.*'

That was met with a few more nods, although some of the nodders then paused and looked dubious again, because *obviously* any visions sent by Gork and Mork would be green, what else would they be? Snaggi could tell he hadn't won many over – tough crowd, this one – and decided to risk one of his genuine bits of knowledge.

'Da gods,' he said, 'have shown me *how we can get out of 'ere.*'

That caught his audience's attention. Grots pressed in closer, whispering excitedly amongst themselves. It was a lie, of course: Snaggi had seen actual visions from Gork and Mork, but this was something he'd picked up on his own. Still, if he wanted to gain followers then he was better off making them believe that he was guided by the gods, which in this case meant giving the gods credit for something they'd had no hand in. Snaggi doubted that they'd mind.

'Wot we're gonna need,' he said in a hushed, conspiratorial tone, 'is a spikie. It's gonna need to be alive, I reckon, but it don't need to be healthy. Dey're da ones wot can open da gates. So long as we've got one of 'em, we can get a gate to open and zog off, an' leave da orks to have dere fun wivout us.'

'Leave da orks?!' exclaimed the grot without the tip of his nose, looking around in horror as though a runtherd was about to emerge from the shadows, bellowing with rage and swinging a grot lash. 'But how're we gonna survive?'

Snaggi took two steps forward and dealt his doubter a ringing slap around the ear.

'Dat's negative finkin'!' he barked, before the slappee could gather his wits enough to object. 'Yoo ain't gonna get far like dat! All of ya know wot's gonna happen here! Da orks are gonna frow us in da way of anyfing wot's comin' at 'em, and a lot of us are gonna die anyway! Whereas if we disappear first, maybe nickin' a few tanks an' wotnot along da way...' He waggled his brow suggestively. 'Look, all I'm sayin' is dat dere's gotta be a whole lotta different worlds wot are less stabby dan dis place. Places where a buncha grots wiv a bit of dere own dakka could live like *warbosses*.'

He could see the idea take hold, just like it had when he'd floated it before. *What if there weren't any orks tellin' us wot to do?* The words of a true visionary.

'Da gods never meant for us to be stuck fetchin' and carryin', and takin' a kickin' from dese gits,' he said, warming to his subject. 'Dey want da grots to be free! Dey want da grots to be *in charge!* I'm da one who can getcha dere! I'm Da Grotboss!'

This wasn't exactly met with rapturous applause and immediate declarations of undying allegiance, but Snaggi reckoned that more than half now looked hopeful or interested in what he had to say. 'Dis offer ain't gonna be here for long,' he said, 'an' ya wanna get in on da ground floor, so to speak, before word spreads an' everyone wants a piece of it. Get in now an' get da good positions, cos Da Grotboss is gonna need uvver bosses to keep everyone organised. Ya know, some ladz wot can do good finkin', or can knock a few heads togevver an' keep order.' He looked pointedly at Gip, who showed his sharp little teeth in a knowing grin.

'So... yoo're gonna lead us?' asked the grot he'd slapped.

'Dat's right,' Snaggi replied, puffing his chest out. 'Woss ya name?'

'Gekki Shortnose.'

'Well, Gekki,' Snaggi said expansively, throwing one arm around the other grot's shoulders and squeezing just hard enough to hint that another slap might be on the way if he got any cheek, 'dis is a great day for ya! Yoo can say dat yoo were dere at da start of da Great Rebellion!'

'So yoo're gonna get us a spikie?' Gekki asked, his eyes wide. Far too wide, in fact; Snaggi knew deliberate innocence when it sidled up and stabbed him, and his own eyes narrowed in displeasure.

'Yoo wot?'

'A spikie!' Gekki repeated. 'Ya said we need one to get froo da gates, right? An' if yoo're leadin' us, yoo're gonna get us a spikie, right?'

Snaggi laughed derisively. 'Look, just cos I said we need to get one, don't mean it's gonna be *me* wot–'

'SPI-KIE!' the other grots began to chant. 'SPI-KIE!'

'Now look,' Snaggi said, trying to keep the desperation out of his voice, 'dat's not–'

'SPI-KIE!'

'SPI-KIE!'

'I really don't fink dat's–'

'SPI-KIE!'

'SPI-KIE!'

'Alright!' Snaggi bellowed, with visions of his new authority fading away in a cloud of his own desperate excuses. 'I'll get da zoggin' spikie! But I'm gonna need help to carry it,' he continued, looking around furiously. 'So anyone who wants to be a direct underboss, no questions asked, yoo step forward right now an' say yoo're comin' wiv me.'

There was no movement for a moment. Then another moment. Then a whole handful of moments, which scurried past in a group as though trying to evade a predator. Snaggi glowered at his potential followers, wondering how long this standoff could last. He really *couldn't* get a spikie all on his own, he wouldn't be able to shift one quickly enough, even if he found one dead enough to drag but not alive enough to shank him, which was going to be a tall order in and of itself. Was this it? Was this just his peers' method of denying him, by damning the greatest mind in all Grotdom to failure simply because they couldn't be bothered to help?

Then Gip stepped forward. 'Underboss sounds good. I'm in.'

'Nice one.' Snaggi grinned at him, and turned to look at the crowd again with slightly more expectation. 'Who's next?'

He got five more, in the end: Swipe, Nib, Longtoof (whom Snaggi immediately distrusted), Mozz, and Beez. Gekki Shortnose very obviously didn't volunteer, and just stared challengingly at Snaggi. That was his mistake: Snaggi Littletoof didn't back down from any challenge, or at least not one thrown down by a grot he could spank with one arm tied behind his back.

'C'mon, ladz,' he said, addressing his new cronies and soon-to-be underbosses. 'Let's go get us a spikie.'

They stepped out of the battlewagon's ruin, and he looked around cautiously. The immediate threat was unlikely to come from the spikiez themselves: rather, it was probably going to be from a runtherd. They hated to see a grot go unwhipped, and the last thing Snaggi wanted was to be drubbed into a massed group of his supposed fellows and herded off to fight something. He had killed a runtherd before, of course, but best not to trust that he could do it again.

'Right, keep yer eyes peeled,' he advised as they scurried from cover to cover, taking shelter behind wrecked ork vehicles, shot-up spikie walls and barricades, and on one occasion even the bodies of a couple of orks who'd clearly ended up on the wrong end of some of the spikiez' poison shards. He pointed at where a bloody chunk of spikie lay – slippery zoggers that they were, by the time an ork actually managed to land a weapon on one of them they weren't taking any chances about it getting away. 'It ain't gonna be easy to find one of dese gits in one piece.'

'Uh, actually, boss,' Mozz said, tapping him on the shoulder and pointing ahead of them, 'I don't fink dat's gonna be a problem *as such…*'

Snaggi looked up, and a chill ran straight through him. There was another massive portal over there.

It was opening.

And it was disgorging death.

TEN

Dhaemira led the attack, riding on her Venom. She did not do this out of any sense of nobility, or from a notion that an archon's place was at the front – simply in the knowledge that her craft was swift and orkish reactions often sluggish, and she wanted to be at the front before her enemies filled the sky with so much ordnance that even their woeful inaccuracy became irrelevant.

Nor was this how she had planned it. She had envisaged leading – from a withdrawn, strategic position – a more numerous, more powerful force consisting of not only the Port Tavarr kabals and the Coven of the Red Harvest, but also the wych cults. That could have cut right into the core of the horde, as reavers and hellions slaughtered them at speed and the wyches' foot soldiers, pumped high on combat drugs, flipped acrobatically off their Raider transports to land like thunderbolts in the orks' midst. That would have been a joyous bloodletting, a crimson symphony of the drukhari's superiority offered up to Kaela Mensha Khaine, the god of war.

Now, however, things would be much more difficult. The forces of Port Tavarr were still deadly in the extreme, but without the wyches' additional numbers and superlative speed, they were at far greater risk of being drawn into the sort of attritional battle that would greatly favour their foe. Still, there was nothing for it. Succubi were mercurial, arrogant creatures, and any approach to them that they felt lacked the appropriate amount of respect would do more harm than good. Dhaemira could not spare the time to wait for honeyed words and reason to sway them to her side.

Not when the orks were teleporting, and jeopardising the survival of her entire realm.

Three portals connected Port Tavarr to Sabregate, and the drukhari swarmed out of all of them at once. No sooner had her craft crossed the threshold than Dhaemira caught the scent of her enemy: a thick, choking reek that plunged into her nostrils and stayed there, and which felt as though it was coating her airways. There were other smells, too: the stink of their crude fuel and its fumes, and the pervasive, pungent odour of the combustible charges that powered their ballistic weaponry.

And, by all the void, the *noise*.

Drukhari knew torture. They were the galaxy's pre-eminent experts in the subtlest torments, the most creative excruciations, in prolonging and wringing out the very last dregs of pain and suffering before a victim's body and mind finally succumbed and they gleefully embraced the release of death. Dhaemira could still remember the first time she had seen her mother flay something alive in front of her. She had screamed too, at first, not knowing why this creature was being hurt. She had wanted it to stop, for not even drukhari were born with the innate impulse to inflict such pain on other living beings. That came later, as a child grew to understand their culture. Soon, the necessity of others' suffering in order to stave off death became pleasurable in and of itself, and cause and effect merged into one. Those that could not accept such reality left Commorragh, to seek solace with the rustics on the maiden worlds or with the spineless ascetics on the craftworlds, to wither and die and have their souls trapped forever, rather than constantly replenish them from the agony of others.

Yes, drukhari knew torture, to the point where the blunt methods used by other species were akin to a warm bath and a massage. Nonetheless, Dhaemira winced as the sheer volume of the orkish horde crashed into her ears, all jagged noise and brutality, painful in its discordant simplicity and volume. There was no sense to which these creatures were not offensive!

The orks had already done a great deal of damage, but as ever with them, there was nothing strategic about it. It was destruction for destruction's sake, obeying a wanton glee that in many other circumstances Dhaemira would have considered quite admirable. Mighty spires now stood with ragged holes blasted in them, colonnades had been brought down, and bridges lay broken and ruined far below the spaces they had once spanned. Wreckage was everywhere: chunks of masonry, immobilised vehicles, and the bloody ruin of butchery, with both orkish and drukhari bodies strewn about. Even the mighty statue of Asdrubael Vect himself, Dhaemira was horrified to see, lay smashed and headless.

'Find the leader!' she snapped, despite the fact that this had already been the instruction issued to her pilot before they came through the gate. 'Find it, and kill it!'

Her Venom banked, and screamed through the sky with a dozen Raiders behind it. Most were hers, but two were from Falling Night, and one from Blood's Gift – ancestral enemies come together to bring death to what was, at the moment at least, a greater threat to them all. The warriors on the transports fired almost indiscriminately into the horde below them, the combined hiss of their splinter rifles rising into a sharp susurration that became audible even through the din of the orks' war-making. Other weapons spoke as well – the black, spitting energy of blasters and dark lances searing out to bring down the orks' blocky, lumbering war walkers, their ramshackle vehicles, or particularly large and imposing orkish leaders; and shredders, near silent other than the faint whistle of their barbed, monomolecular nets as they flowed outwards to envelop and eviscerate the lightly armoured brutes beneath.

The orks registered their presence less quickly than Dhaemira had feared, but sooner than she'd hoped. She had a few precious seconds of almost unchallenged death-dealing, cutting a swathe through the green mass, and then things changed. There was no gradual wave of realisation that spread through her foes: one moment her force was flying through clear skies, the next the thunder of orkish weaponry was redirected upwards, almost as one.

Her Venom's flickerfield was active, breaking up the craft's outline and making it harder to target, but such measures did little when the volume of fire was so great and so indiscriminate. The massed roar of the orks' clumsy but rapid-firing assault weaponry filled the air along with their projectiles, which were largely shrugged off by the skimmers' hulls even if their force fields failed to stop the incoming shots, but orkish weaponry was the epitome of idiosyncratic. Something blew a hole the size of Dhaemira's head in the Venom's right wing-vane, and something else struck one of the engines and sent the craft sputtering unstably to one side for a moment before the pilot managed to right it. Behind her, one Raider began spouting black smoke and listing. The warriors on board ceased firing as they struggled to maintain a grip, but mere moments later they were plunging to the ground beneath. The Raider struck with a crash, and was immediately swarmed by bellowing orks brandishing weapons.

'Mistress!' Zesk shouted in alarm, pointing at snub-nosed shapes that were screaming into view around nearby spires. They were orkish creations, so unaerodynamic that Dhaemira could see little explanation for how they were kept aloft other than the stubborn refusal of their pilots to accept the concept of crashing. They were true aircraft, far faster even than her Venom, and bearing down on her at great speed.

'Patience,' she said calmly. 'All is in hand.'

Shards of night streaked into view from behind them: a trio of sharp-edged shapes, even faster and more manoeuvrable than the orkish craft. These were Razorwings, and the orks pulled out of their attack run as they became aware of this new threat – or, possibly, an even more entertaining battle.

That danger was gone, but the damage being done to Dhaemira's escort was continuing. Another Raider came apart in mid-air as some particularly powerful weapon struck it, and one more was limping. Dhaemira could sense that the warriors following her were on the verge of turning tail; few drukhari had any concept of selling their lives dearly if there was any chance of saving them outright, no matter what the subsequent consequences might be. Her pilots were doing their best, jinking and swerving to throw their enemies off, and taking any opportunity to put a turret or walkway between themselves and their attackers, but something needed to change soon.

'There!' she shouted, pointing dead ahead of them as they rounded another spire. It was more hope and distraction than anything else – giving her followers something to focus on, a sense that their goal was within reach and therefore it was worth continuing for the few more seconds it would take to achieve it. However, as they streaked towards this particular concentration of orks, Dhaemira realised that she might actually have been correct.

While nowhere within sight appeared to have been set up as a base of operations as such, she could see more of the orks' strange machinery here than she had elsewhere, and critically it was machinery that did not appear to have any obvious use as an offensive weapon or vehicle. What was more, her keen eyes could make out an exceptionally massive ork clad in immense yellow-and-black armour, who stood a head taller than even the largest other specimens around it. It gestured with a huge weapon that seemed to be part axe and part hammer, the machinery in front of it crackled with power...

...and an entire mob of the creatures flashed out of existence.

'I have found the leader, and the teleportation device!' Dhaemira snapped over carrier wave. 'All forces, to me!'

A barrage of rockets rose up on wobbling smoke-trails from her right, and although most fell wide, three struck a Raider and blew it apart. Another of her vehicles skewed out of control, as something damaged either its steering controls or its thrusters. Some orks actually emerged out of the mass of their fellows on crude jet packs, and while at least two were eviscerated by a Raider's blade vanes and chain snares, the rest either managed their trajectories well enough to land on the deck, or simply got hit by a part of the Raider's exterior but clung on and dragged themselves aboard anyway. Dhaemira did not give the drukhari crew good odds of surviving.

That did not matter. All the lives around her were disposable, and they were closing in on her prey now.

'Focus all fire!' she ordered, pointing her venom blade at the huge ork. The weapons of her remaining craft and their riders opened up, tracking towards it and the other lesser beasts around it. She was almost on top of it now, and she saw it turn, finally alerted to her approach. She leaned forward gleefully, waiting for dull comprehension to dawn in its tiny red eyes as it saw its death approach.

Then something began sparkling, away beyond the ork's leader. Dhaemira just had time to realise that what she had assumed was the ruined back half of an ork vehicle was in fact some sort of wheeled artillery piece, when the bulbous-tipped weapon it bore gave one final bright flash...

...and a wall of translucent energy appeared in front of her, rapidly expanding and pushing everything in front of it, including the startled orks on the ground.

Her pilot began to bank, but even a Venom was not nimble enough to avoid this fate when going at full speed. Dhaemira's reflexes took over, and she leaped clear of her craft just before it, along with most of the remaining Raiders, struck the force-field bubble.

The pinnacle of Commorraghan engineering, compounds stronger than steel yet far lighter, buckled under the impact. As she fell, Dhaemira saw her warriors thrown clear and strike the energy wall themselves, but then she had to put all her concentration into landing. Orks had been shunted forwards and were now crushed together and piled up two- or three-deep below her, with their bellows giving a good indication of what they thought of this state of affairs, so Dhaemira braced herself for an uneven landing on footing that was about to try to kill her. She had little doubt that she could best a great number of these beasts in combat, but their sheer physical strength would be her end if any of them managed to actually lay hands on her...

As suddenly as it had appeared, the orkish energy flickered and dissipated. It was a weapon, then – albeit a very strange one – and not a defensive force field. Dhaemira landed in a perfect crouch on an ork's back, her weapons in each hand, and leaped away again into the empty ground that had just been swept clear of bodies.

The ork chieftain's eyes locked on to hers, and despite herself, Dhaemira shuddered as she attracted the full attention of this monster. It was truly massive: at least half as tall again as she was, and with the bulky muscle common to its species and the thick armour laid over that, it looked more like one of the mon-keigh's Dreadnought war machines than it did a mortal foe. She knew it had realised she was its opposite number – she suppressed another shudder at the thought of this creature considering itself her equal in any way – and that it would now bend all its will towards her destruction, recognising as she did the strategic importance of eliminating the enemy commander.

The ork...

...*laughed* at her.

Sheer fury blazed through Dhaemira's brain, burning away any ghosts of uncertainty. She raised her blast pistol and fired. It was a long shot for her sidearm, but the bolt of darklight struck home.

The ork looked down at one of its armour plates, which, Dhaemira noticed with the faintest scrabblings of trepidation, was now smoking and cratered but had not been pierced. Drukhari armour was far more efficient and advanced than these crude slabs of metal, but if the metal was thick enough and you were strong enough to haul it around like a walking tank, the protection it offered would nonetheless be formidable.

The ork raised its own weapon, and pulled the trigger. Something on it spun around very fast, and Dhaemira leaped aside just in time to avoid the emergence of a crackling black void. It lasted only for a second, but when it cleared it had chewed away a ragged hole in the ground into which she could easily have fitted, leaving behind nothing but the stench of the warp. By Khaine, did even these brutes' *weapons* use teleportation technology?

Dhaemira sprang forward, eager to close the gap between them. A few of her warriors had survived the impact and the fall, and were already raking the mass of orks around them with toxic splinters from their weapons. If she could bring the ork chieftain down then not only could she hold it over her brother, but – as everyone knew – the orks would also devolve into internecine warfare as the beast's lieutenants fought amongst themselves to take its place. That should at least slow them down enough for Dhaemira to solidify her authority, gather a greater force, and return to wipe them out.

The ork gave a massive grunt of effort and hurled its enormous axe-bladed hammer at her. Dhaemira was caught off-guard by the tactic – who threw their melee weapon when they still had a gun? – and the improvised projectile came at her with such force and speed that her evasive roll was almost clumsy. She came back up to her feet with a predatory grin, for although it was still a formidable opponent, the ork had just thrown away its best means of hurting her in close.

The ork did something with its hand, and the weapon *reappeared.* However, it reappeared directly above the ork's head and fell hammer-end first onto the brute's skull, prompting a bellow of rage and anger.

Dhaemira was brought up short in astonishment. The ork had fitted some sort of teleportation device to its hammer, apparently simply so it could *throw it at an enemy and then retrieve it?* That spoke to a far more advanced mastery of warp technology than that with which anyone had credited the arakhia, yet it was being utilised for such a trivial purpose. How could these creatures possess that level of understanding, but be so completely blasé about the dangers associated with it? Did they truly not fear the attentions of daemons? Did they fear *anything?*

The moment of surprised inattention nearly cost her – not at the hands of the ork chieftain, who had kicked its weapon back up into its fist with the sort of glower that dared anyone or anything else to mention what had just happened, but a mob of its underlings which had got just close enough to swarm onto Dhaemira while she was distracted. There were at least a dozen of them, all big brutes covered in scars that looked like the aftermath of ferocious bites, and many with blocky but apparently effective mechanical prosthetics. The first one swung a massive chainblade at her in a flat backhanded blow, and Dhaemira's reflexes kicked back into action.

She swayed backwards like a sapling in a strong wind, letting the chainblade sweep past just above her face, then straightened and thrust with her venom blade in the same motion. The tip went in through the ork's left eye – the right one being another of those prosthetics – and into the brain, but Dhaemira whipped the blade out again immediately rather than risk losing it to the creature's death spasms.

The orks were a tide, but she was the wind; they were a landslide, but she was lightning. Her blast pistol took one full in the face, blowing its skull apart, but even as it fell she was already jerking her head aside to let the solid slug of a different enemy's sidearm flash just past her ear. She pivoted, cutting across the belly of one ork with the tip of her blade as it tried to get behind her, sidestepped the heavy downward swing of another's axe and then, as its blade threw up chips from the ground, swung the elbow of her pistol-arm to open its throat with one of her armour's razor-sharp protuberances. She pivoted again, and the next shot missed her arched back by a hair's breadth to detonate in the stomach of another of her assailants.

She leaped into the air to evade a clumsy swing at her legs, stunned one ork with a kick to the jaw while she was up there and broke its neck with a follow-up roundhouse from the other foot, then turned her blast pistol on the ork that had attempted to cut her down. It was still stooped over, and the darklight bolt struck the crown of its head and bored right through its torso, from top to bottom. She landed on its blade, scooped it up into the air with her foot just as the ork chieftain had done with its hammer, then used another kick to propel the weapon straight into the face of the one which had been shooting at her. The beast went down howling as the powered teeth sawed into its neck.

She took both eyes from one attacker with a single slash of her blade across its ugly, bestial face, and blocked the swing of another's weapon with a thrust kick to the inside of its elbow that snapped its arm, then shot a hole right through the one which looked like it might be their leader, before delivering a jumping knee-strike to the lower jaw of the one whose arm she had just broken, which was the only one still standing. Her patella blade speared through the soft flesh of its throat, up through its mandible and tongue and on into the roof of its mouth, and she savoured a moment of its pain, but she could tell within an instant that the brute's head was too large, its brain was too small, or both. This blow had not killed it, and she hastily disengaged before the one hand that remained fully under its control could seize her. The ork took a lurching step towards her, its arm and fingers outstretched, and Dhaemira readied herself to open its throat and evade its clumsy grasp in the same balletic movement.

The massive shape of the ork chieftain loomed up behind its wounded minion, and clubbed it out of the way with a two-handed swing of its enormous hammer. The force of the blow lifted the smaller ork off its feet and deposited it several yards away, which was no inconsiderable feat given how much it must have weighed, and the chieftain let loose a bellowed challenge so deep and powerful that Dhaemira felt it in her bones. The meaning was clear, even to Dhaemira: no other ork should attack her, lest it suffer the rage of their leader. That was fine by her. There were sufficient orks all around to swamp even a warrior of her skill, but she was confident of her chances in single combat.

That confidence lasted until the ork attacked.

One moment it was stationary, other than its nostrils flaring as it sucked in her scent, and its fingers tightening slightly around the haft of its weapon. Then, without warning, it was in motion. The axe blade flashed towards her head, the ork's stupendous reach combining with the sheer length of the haft to immediately endanger her, but it was the speed of the creature that was the most terrifying. Something that large should not be able to move that fast; it should not be possible! And yet Dhaemira found herself back-pedalling, desperately trying to stay out of reach, with all thoughts of piercing its flesh with her blade abandoned.

This was not a fight, she realised within moments; this was the ork trying to swat an annoyance. She was able to stay ahead of it – just – but the monstrous brute gave no signs of slowing down, and her venom blade could not even reach the hands holding its hammer, let alone any more central part of its anatomy. The hammer itself seemed to tear the air as it was swung, and the gusts of wind it raised buffeted her as she dodged, ducked, and rolled away from it. She fired her blast pistol, but although the bolts struck home, they seemed to do little more than aggravate the beast. She was confident that her venom blade would take its toll, but she couldn't land a blow, and if the ork made the merest contact with its own weapon then it would surely incapacitate her enough for it to finish her off. What was more, all it had to do was get impatient and call on its underlings to join the fray after all, and Dhaemira would be done for.

For perhaps the first time in her life, Dhaemira Thraex found herself utterly at the mercy of another living being, and she *hated* it.

She wondered if the ork could smell her growing fear. Was it relishing her embarrassment? Did it revel in its own ability to have a master archon of the drukhari desperately scrambling to avoid its blows? Or was it utterly oblivious to such things, seeking only the thrill of the fight?

Then, in a desperate snatched glance beyond the ork's left shoulder, Dhaemira saw something that rekindled the faint light of hope within her. She snapped another shot off at the ork's face, which it avoided with a casual-seeming twitch of a neck as thick as her waist, but she had only been trying to distract it for a moment longer.

The rest of her force swept in.

They had attacked on three fronts, each one seeking the orks' leader with the intention of executing it. She had been successful in locating the beast and now, finally, the others were arriving to reinforce her. There were the rest of her vessels, along with those from the Kabal of the Falling Night and Coven of the Red Harvest. A Ravager, flying low, fired all three of its disintegrator cannons into the ork chieftain's back.

For a moment, Dhaemira was outraged. Despite the fact that she had been on the back foot, this was her fight, and her kill. Then her thoughts leapt to the pragmatic: she could execute the captain of the Ravager concerned, and it would still have been her leadership that led to the beast's downfall and struck the first real blow against the invaders.

Then, as the ork failed to keel over in a smoking ruin, but instead bellowed in rage and whirled around, true terror gripped her. What would it take to actually *hurt* this creature?

Nonetheless, it had presented her with its back for the first time in their confrontation – a back with armour that was now scorched, warped and weakened. She leaped forward to bury her venom blade in the monster's flesh, screaming with rage and suppressed fear as she did so.

The... *thing* came at her from her left, a squealing ball of muscle and teeth that clamped its massive jaws down on her sword-arm and wrenched her sideways. Her blow missed its target, and although she clubbed the orkish creature between the eyes with the butt of her blast pistol to make it let go, her chance had gone. The ork chieftain whipped back around with blazing eyes, and swung its hammer again.

This time, the weapon's head made contact with Dhaemira's venom blade, knocking it from her grasp and shattering it in the same instant. Then, as she scrambled back up to her feet, it raised its hammer again with a roar of fury.

'Thraex!'

The shout came a moment before a massive, dark-grey craft hurtled into view, moving fast enough to get to her even before the ork could finish its blow. Dhaemira's hand was seized by fingers of pale ice blue, and she was yanked off her feet and away. The ork's swing buried itself in the ground, causing a small crater of its own, and Dhaemira found herself being hauled over the railings of a Tantalus by none other than Cistrial Virn himself.

Dhaemira took a breath and steadied herself as the Tantalus banked, then realised that her hand and Virn's were still entwined at the same moment as Virn did, judging by how hastily both of them dropped the other's grasp and took a half-step away. Contact poisons to dispose of rivals were far from unheard of.

'I...' Dhaemira began, struggling to find words. She had intervened to kill the ork that had been going to take Virn's life, but drukhari were not bound by debts of honour. Any alliances were made beforehand and usually contracted in exhaustive detail, so that each party knew exactly what would count as a betrayal. By rights, Virn should have let her die and count himself free of a rival.

'We are outmatched,' Virn said stiffly yet hastily, as though seeking to explain his own actions. 'We have killed many, but we cannot strike the telling blow. We need the wych cults, and as many blades for hire as we can muster. Your influence will be needed for that,' he added, with a momentary sideward glance at Dhaemira. 'It would be imprudent to let you perish at this time.'

'I understand,' Dhaemira said, swallowing down a tightness in her throat. After all, she *had* come very close to the sort of death that would be inconvenient for even a haemonculus to retrieve her from, given where her remains would have ended up. 'However, we have not completely failed.' She activated her carrier waves. 'All vessels! The orkish construction with the pylons is their teleportation device. Focus all fire upon it!'

Ravagers and Reapers swept in, concentrating their weapons on the contraption. It looked shoddily built, but like many such things of orkish construction it took a lot more shots than Dhaemira would have expected before it finally exploded. A shockwave of trapped energy ripped outwards, levelling everything around it for several dozen yards including, she noted with fierce satisfaction, the strange artillery piece that had brought her Raiders down.

'There,' she said, in a hollow voice. 'That will contain them for now.' She looked at Virn, but the other archon was staring out over the carnage, apparently ignoring her. No one else was going to take responsibility for giving this order.

'All craft, retreat.'

ELEVEN

Ilyonith Zesk lay still, watched the remaining vessels of the Port Tavarr forces flee back through the webway portal without him, and silently cursed Archon Dhaemira Thraex into the soul-sucking embrace of She Who Thirsts.

Typical archon! He had served her loyally for centuries, not once putting into practice the various schemes he had devised to bring about her downfall and see him ascend to take her place at the head of the kabal. Granted, that was partly because she was extremely paranoid, and Zesk had very few allies he could trust, even amongst his trueborn. However, he had never let his greed overcome his caution, and as a result he had discharged his duty to the highest standards without making even an imperfect grab for power.

And now he was being left behind, abandoned like a promise.

His lack of motion was not completely down to his injuries, although they were severe. He had been thrown from the Venom as it was wrecked against the arakhia's energy field, and landed in a crush of orks. Now his armour was smashed and pierced in a multitude of places, at least one leg was useless, his left hand was missing, and a great rent had been torn in his side by the tip of one of the crude orkish hand weapons. But he was not as dead as the others around him, be they drukhari or arakhia.

Zesk was intelligent enough to realise that what the orks craved most was combat, and that an enemy who was apparently unable to give them this satisfaction was largely beneath their notice. A drukhari force would take their time gathering the wounded to torment them further, and feast their souls upon the wretched unfortunates' agony. The same was true for many of the followers of the gods of Chaos. Orks, though, were more eager to press on to the next fight and find someone new against whom they could test themselves. If Zesk remained still and avoided notice, the odds were good that none of the brutes would come poking around to find out if anyone was still alive. All he had to do was wait for them to leave somehow – their ingenuity on that front might actually serve him well, in this specific scenario – or be exterminated by the larger force that the routed archons would surely even now be trying to assemble. His wounds were severe, but nothing that even a junior haemonculus couldn't deal with, should he merely be able to get to one.

It might take time, and that time would be spent in great pain, but Ilyonith Zesk was no stranger to pain. Granted, he was more usually inflicting it than the other way around, but nothing lasted long in the Dark City without the ability to endure pain to one degree or another. Zesk had survived centuries so far, and he was not going to be cheated out of his rightful place at the head of a kabal just by an invasion of simple-witted brutes who happened to be good at destroying things.

He became aware of a noise approaching, distinct even over the background roar and rumble of the orks doing whatever it was they were doing now their enemies had disappeared again. It was a shuffling, a scuttling, a whispering and a snickering, and even amidst the carnage wrought by an invading force of savages, something about it made Zesk's hackles stand up. He groped around with his right hand, trying to remain unobtrusive. His blast pistol had been crushed – although the ork responsible died when the weapon exploded in its face – and he'd lost his power sword when a chainbladed cleaver made a mockery of his armour and took his left hand off at the wrist. Still, there must be something within reach with which he could arm himself; was that small, thin object under his fingers the hilt of one of his belt knives, with which he had brought down the last of his assailants before collapsing and resigning himself to ingloriously playing dead while his so-called allies fled…?

The noise got closer. It was a high-pitched chittering, like drukhari children who had found a pit of dirgeworms or something equally harmless which could be tormented with no risk to their own safety, but he did not recognise it as coming from any creature native to Commorragh. The hoped-for belt knife turned out to be nothing but a shard of armour – either his own or someone else's, Zesk was unsure – but it was long and sharp, and it would serve adequately to puncture the exposed flesh of a largely unarmoured creature such as an ork. He fumbled it into place between his fingers, ready to slash or stab as appropriate. With any luck, whatever was coming would pass him by, as uninterested in apparently dead and broken bodies as was any other part of the orkish war machine.

The shuffling and chittering was to his left now, and close enough that he thought he might be able to see the source without making any movements that would give him away as still living. He rolled his eyes in that direction, cursing the slightly shifted helm on his head that now marginally impeded his view. Something moved, skittering through the very limits of his vision. It was green, he could tell that much – the bright, vivid green of living orkoid flesh, not the muted colours of the Kabal of the Falling Night. The enemy was close. The enemy was *very* close.

An upside-down face appeared above his, peering down. Ragged bat-wing ears flanked beady red eyes, set on either side of a dagger-like nose so long it was nearly scraping his helmet's faceplate.

The enemy was…

…short?

It wasn't an ork, Zesk realised; it was one of their diminutive slave caste, surprisingly dangerous in large numbers but a negligible threat when alone. He forced himself to remain still in case a sign of life would encourage the slave to call one of its masters. Zesk had no illusions that he would be able to defeat one of *them*, should a hale specimen register that he was still alive.

The slave – the *grot?* Was that the word? – nudged his helmet with its foot. Zesk allowed his head to be rolled to one side despite the utter fury that raged up inside him at such indignity, sufficient to eclipse even the pain of his wounds. He had taken this war plate from the body of his predecessor, and it was one of the finest examples of the drukhari armourer's art, eclipsed within the Kabal of the Hollow Heart only by the suits of Dhaemira Thraex and her junior archons, such as her brother. It galled him to allow it to be sullied by a grot's foot without inflicting punishment on the creature for its transgression, but this was the sensible course of action. Play dead, let its limited intelligence grow bored with prodding an apparent corpse, and let it move on once something else caught its attention–

The grot leaped into the air with a giggle, and came down with its full weight on Zesk's chest.

The breath he'd been holding in his lungs to avoid a tell-tale movement of his breastplate shot out of him in a rushing wheeze, and the wound in his side spat fire through his nervous system. He lashed out with his shiv, his instinctive reaction fully backed up by deliberate anger and spite, and the warp take whatever attention he might attract. The shard of armour went in through one side of the grot's throat and punched out of the other, driven by the power of his hate-fuelled muscles, and the pathetic little creature fell backwards off his makeshift blade with a wet gurgle, clutching at the twin wounds he had opened in its flesh.

Zesk collapsed backwards, most parts of him now in agony and with renewed bleeding from his injuries, but with a grim satisfaction at the life he had just taken. He could hear the grot scrabbling desperately around, even if he couldn't see it, but he had no doubt that it would succumb to its wounds soon. Once it did, there was no chance of any of the orks noticing it: they barely seemed to pay attention to their slaves while they were alive, so another corpse would attract no attention at all.

Still, that dying grot did seem to be making a *lot* of noise. Zesk managed to raise his head slightly, sufficient to get a better view of his surroundings.

The dim light from above was blocked out by multiple small bodies launching themselves at him.

He tried to raise his arms to fend them off, but blood loss-induced weakness and severed muscle fibres foiled him, and the grots landed across him, pinning him down. He tried to thrash and throw them off, but his body refused to obey him. His right arm was trapped, and he felt clawed fingers prising his hand open with surprising strength: the little creatures lacked much in the way of physicality, but they could grip on desperately to fast-moving vehicles or throttle the life out of one of their own kind, and that same wiry tenaciousness allowed them to snatch an improvised weapon away from a wounded drukhari warrior.

He continued to struggle, but to no avail; there were half a dozen of the little wretches, and while he might have made short work of them had he been upright, uninjured and armed, he was in no condition to fight them off as he was. He braced himself for the ultimate indignity of having his throat cut by such a pitiful foe, and being left to bleed out properly beyond the reach of even the most amateurish haemonculus.

However, no blade pierced his flesh, and no long-fingered green hands closed around his throat to finish him off in a more personal fashion. Instead, a new surge of agony washed through him as he was wrenched around on the ground.

Zesk gritted his teeth, determined not to give these miniature monstrosities the satisfaction of hearing him cry out in pain, but the torment did not let up. Now he was actually being moved, dragged and pulled over and past the bodies of those who had fallen in combat around him, while the grots chuckled and gibbered to themselves. Their tongue was garbled and animalistic, of course, but through the haze of suffering washing over him, Zesk was able to discern a repeated phrase, started by one voice and taken up by the others. It had a viciously gleeful sound to it, as though it were a war cry raised up in celebration:

'SPI-KIE!'

'SPI-KIE!'

'SPI-KIE!'

TWELVE

Snaggi Littletoof had to suppress the urge to jump and skip with glee as he led his daring raiding party back through the devastation. They'd found a spikie! What was more, they'd found one that was still alive, but too damaged to do more than wiggle a bit!

Oh, it turned out to have one good stab left in it, as you might expect from a spikie, and Mozz had found out first-hand what happened when you jumped on one of the gits without making sure it was properly dead first. However, Snaggi had managed to heroically subdue the vicious alien warrior – fine, he was prepared to concede that the other ladz might have helped – and now they were transporting their prize back to the rest of his new band of followers with their heads held high.

This was one of the few times when being a grot actually came in handy. Well, Snaggi knew that being a grot was always better than being an ork, or indeed being anything else, because how could it be otherwise? If being a grot wasn't the best thing, then why would *he* be a grot? That sort of logic was inescapable. But Snaggi was also aware – and this was where his towering intellect came in, his ability to see past how he *wanted* things to be and focus on the objective reality of stuff – that being a grot was not always such a good thing *in the galaxy as it was*. Somehow, the orks had turned natural order on its head and put themselves in charge, even though grots were clearly superior, and certainly smarter. That was the sort of injustice that gave him the fiery righteous rage within, which motivated him to fight on against oppression, no matter the odds.

However, the specific circumstances of why being a grot was currently coming in handy was a direct result of this injustice, which only proved to Snaggi how great he was, since he was using the orks' own prejudices against them to ultimately bring about their downfall. Orks only paid attention to grots when they wanted something done for them, or the grots were in the way (in the orks' opinion), or they lacked any better options for a bit of target practice or general kicking. The Waaagh!'s simple presence in this strange place had given the orks plenty of good targets and fun new things to blow up, so the last one wasn't a problem, and orks would rarely go *searching* for a grot even if they did want something done; they were more likely to just give the grot a beating when he eventually showed up, as punishment for not being around when he should have been. That meant so long as Snaggi and his ladz weren't getting underfoot, they probably wouldn't be high on anyone's list to start shouting orders at or demand to know what they were up to.

'Where're we takin' dis git, anyway?' Beez demanded, hauling backwards on the spikie's head to drag it over a bit of rubble.

'Back to da ladz, for starters,' Snaggi said. He had ended up pulling on the arm without a hand, which was entirely coincidental and nothing at all to do with it being probably the least dangerous of the spikie's extremities. The git was still trying to thrash around, but grots were naturally good at holding on to things trying to get away from them, such as squigs, food, or another grot that had just nicked your food. 'Den we'll find da portal an' get out of 'ere!'

'Why?' Swipe demanded. 'We've got 'im. Why not jus' get out ourselves?'

Snaggi smiled sagely. Clearly, the time had come to dispense a pearl of wisdom. 'See, dis is where I can help ya. If yoo're gonna be me underbosses den yoo're gonna need to learn dis next part. Wot we got 'ere?'

'A spikie,' Swipe said, pushing on the leg he was holding. It didn't look to Snaggi as though the spikie's leg was supposed to bend that way, but that was the spikie's problem.

'Right, but it ain't da spikie dat's important, is it?' Snaggi said coaxingly. 'It's what it can do for us. If dis was grub den, yeah, makes sense dat we keep it between us, cos we're da important ones. But we ain't choppin' dis git up an' sharin' it out, are we? Nah, we're usin' it to do a fing, a fing wot's gonna be really impressive to all dose cowards wot didn't come wiv us. An' stuff like dat only gets *better* if dere's more grots around when ya do it, cos den dere's even more of 'em to be impressed by it and say fings like "Wow, dat Snaggi and da underbosses really know what dey're doin', we should stick wiv 'em an' follow dere orders, cos dey'll make fings really good for us!"'

'I dunno,' Nib said dubiously, wrangling the spikie's other leg. 'Dat just sounds like less loot an' grub an' stuff once we get away from da orks.' He clamped one hand over his mouth as soon as he'd spoken, as though a runtherd was going to show up and clobber him for uttering such impudence, and nearly dropped the spikie's leg in the process.

Snaggi sighed and shook his head. 'Ladz. Ladz ladz ladz. How are we gonna *get* da loot an' grub? Sure, we *could* try an' nick it ourselves, but dat ain't da smart fing. Da smart fing is to get da uvvers to do da nickin' for us! Dere's no warboss in da galaxy wot goes around and nicks *everyfing* himself, right? Dey get da best bits from everyone else, so dat's wot we're gonna do, too. Yoo lot are gonna help me prove dat I know dese speshul secrets wot da gods've told me, an' den all da grots wiv any sense will follow us. I'm Da Grotboss cos after all' – he patted himself smugly on the chest – 'I'm da one wot knows fings, an' you lot are me underbosses cos you showed da vision to back me from da start.'

There was a general nodding of heads and chuntering of approval amongst Snaggi's underbosses as they grot-handled the still-bleeding spikie around a corner, although Snaggi noticed there were already a few questions being asked along the lines of why they should be the ones who had to cart the spikie around. He smiled, because that was good, that showed *motivation* – namely, the motivation to make some other git do the work, which in Snaggi's opinion was the only motivation worth having. He'd tried too hard before; he'd assumed that because Gork and Mork spoke to him, he had to do everything himself. That had been a mistake, he recognised that now.

He wouldn't make the same error again. Now he had his underbosses – or 'useful idiots' as he was referring to them in the privacy of his own head – he could get them to do stuff for him, but they would do it because they could then get other grots to do those things for *them* in turn! Say what you liked about orks, and Snaggi would so long as none of the big gits were around, but their hierarchy system worked. He needed *layers* beneath him so he could be at the top without having to concentrate on everything at once, like one of those tinhead buildings with all the steps going up to the top. What were they called? A... ziggurat! That was it. Snaggi's scheme for becoming Da Grotboss was a ziggurat plan.

'Next lesson, ladz,' he said proudly. 'We're gonna start gettin' loot off dis right from da start. Anyone who wants to come wiv us froo da portal's gonna 'ave to pay up! Dat's gonna make 'em even more eager to find some loot once we get out of 'ere, an' we can 'ave some of–'

He broke off, as a small group of figures rose into view out of the ruins around them.

'Well, well, well,' said a voice. 'Wot's goin' on 'ere, den?'

The voice belonged to a beefy grot – or what passed for beefy amongst grots – wearing a bloodstained apron, on the belt of which hung a variety of tools: a small saw, whose rusty teeth had gobbets of flesh stuck between them; a long-bladed, single-edged cutting blade that looked a little keener and narrower than your standard grot stabba; a pair of pliers which made Snaggi's teeth hurt just to look at; and on and on, a veritable arsenal of things that could be used to poke and pry into bits of a body which the Brain Boyz had never intended to see the light of day, and surely too many for a grot with only two hands with which to wield them.

'Oh zog,' Longtoof said in a small voice. 'It's da Disorderlies.'

'Dat's right, squirt,' the newcomer sneered. 'Top grots of da top dok! HOOAH!'

'HOOAH!' the other grots with him chorused, punching the air as one.

Snaggi kept his expression neutral. The Disorderlies were the henchgrots of Dok Drozfang, the painboy who appeared to have had some hand in Ufthak Blackhawk's rise to prominence. Snaggi had gathered that, as a result of this, the dok was regarded as the pre-eminent practitioner of his trade in this part of the Tekwaaagh!, treated with some level of respect by other painboyz and normal orks alike, and the Disorderlies clearly felt that sort of status rubbed off on them. None of them would dream of trying to push an ork around, of course, but other grots…

'Wozzup?' Snaggi said cheerfully, deciding to approach this as though there were nothing at all menacing about the Disorderlies' appearance or general mannerisms.

'Wotcha doin' wiv dat git?' the head Disorderly demanded, pointing at the spikie with one claw.

'Not a lot,' Snaggi said quickly. 'Just havin' a bit of fun, dat's all.'

'A bit of fun?' the Disorderly repeated eagerly. 'So it's still alive?'

Snaggi glanced sideways at Gip, seeking advice from someone who had been around this particular Waaagh! for longer. Gip shook his head almost imperceptibly, confirming Snaggi's suspicions: working for a dok as they did, the Disorderlies were going to be more interested in living bodies than corpses.

'Nah,' he said casually. 'Not any more. It's still leakin' a bit, but it's definitely carked it. Just takin' it back to da boss so he can put da helmet and wotnot on his bosspole an' dat.' He tried an ingratiating grin. 'Y'know how it is.'

The Disorderly focused on Snaggi's teeth in a way that reminded Snaggi very abruptly of the pliers on the other grot's belt, and snorted. 'Dead, ya reckon. We'll see about dat. Sneeza!'

Another grot hurled a chunk of rubble with what Snaggi had to grudgingly admit was an impressive degree of accuracy, in that it landed right on the spikie's chest. The spikie, which had sunk into the sort of torpor common to those who had lost a lot of blood and become largely resigned to their fate, reacted to this by trying to thrash again. It was a fairly pitiful effort, but one that could not be disguised. Still, Snaggi did his best.

'Swipe!' he snapped, redoubling his grip on the arm. 'Stop wiggling da body, dat ain't funny!'

'I didn't do nuff... I mean, yes, Snaggi. Sorry, Snaggi,' Swipe said, picking up on the true meaning of Snaggi's furious glare a second too late. Not that it probably would have made much difference anyway, judging by the gleeful crows that had broken out amongst the Disorderlies.

'You see dat, Sneeza?' the leader asked jovially.

'I did indeed, Squeeza!' the grot known as Sneeza replied, rubbing his hands together before pulling a length of metal fashioned into a crude club from his belt. 'It's alive an' kickin'!'

'Ladz, ya don't understand,' Snaggi began, turning back to the Disorderlies. 'We gotta take dis git to da big boss, even if it *ain't* dead.'

'Gonna be honest, dat sounds like a yoo problem,' Squeeza said, slipping the long-bladed scalpel from his belt. 'Da dok wants a spikie wot's still alive, an' dis one ain't gonna put up much of a fight. Stand aside, an' we'll let ya keep yer hands.'

'Dat's a good deal,' Nib offered tentatively. 'I quite like me hands...'

'Shut it!' Snaggi hissed. He debated the likelihood of impressing the encroaching Disorderlies with his grotboss spiel, but disregarded it. These gits had a taste of power, tarnished and second-hand though it might be, and that would be enough to blind them to the reality of his glory. What was more, they might even take word of his plan to Drozfang, or some other ork who just might pay enough attention to care about it, and that would be disastrous.

'Underbosses!' he announced, dropping the spikie's arm and drawing his weapons. 'Let 'em 'ave it!'

Whether or not his companions would have followed his lead and actually attacked became something of a moot point, because – as Snaggi had planned – the Disorderlies reacted to his defiance by lurching into a screaming charge of their own,

waving their implements of pain and dubious medical proven-
ance as they did so. Grots that might not have taken up arms to
defend a nearly dead spikie for an as yet untested purpose were
far more eager to pull weapons to defend themselves, and the
two somewhat ragged battle lines were drawn.

Snaggi fired his blasta, but Squeeza was very inconsiderately
not exactly where the round went, and it only clipped the other
grot's left shoulder. Squeeza howled in pain but kept coming,
his expression an equal split between bloodlust and fear of the
consequences of his own failure, and Snaggi didn't have time
for a second shot before the larger grot was upon him.

He back-pedalled desperately from Squeeza's first slash, a
diagonal blow that could have caused Snaggi's right hip to
abruptly cease to be on speaking terms with his left shoulder, and
tried to put his stabba through the other grot's chest. Squeeza
managed to knock his thrust away, then grabbed the wrist of
Snaggi's gun-hand as he tried to aim his weapon point-blank
at Squeeza's head. Snaggi dropped his stabba to seize the hand
clutching the scalpel just before the blade got plunged into his
side, and the pair of them staggered around in a half-circle, each
trying to get their weapon into the right position to deliver a
killing blow.

The trouble was that while Squeeza was only beefy by grot
standards, Snaggi was a part of those grot standards, and he
was very definitely physically outmatched by his opponent. The
blasta was gradually forced farther away from Squeeza's head,
and the blade of the scalpel began to prick at Snaggi's ribs. This
was a situation that required all the kunnin' and ingenuity which
had got Snaggi to where he was today.

'Da spikie!' he wailed. 'It's gettin' away!'

The fear of failure exploded in Squeeza's eyes and drowned out
the bloodlust, and he instinctively looked around to check on

the status of his desired prize. The spikie was still where it had been, of course, but the momentary distraction allowed Snaggi to lean forward and clamp his teeth shut on Squeeza's ear.

The larger grot jerked away in panic and pain, and only succeeded in leaving half his ear behind, clamped between Snaggi's teeth. He howled, and his grip on Snaggi's wrist slackened for half a second, allowing Snaggi to twist the weapon around and pull the trigger.

It wasn't a well-aimed shot, but at this range it didn't have to be. A fist-sized section of Squeeza's chest vanished, and this time the other grot's spasm was the result of life rapidly leaving his body. Squeeza slumped backwards, and Snaggi raised his hands in triumph and did a little dance.

'Yeah! How'd ya like dat, ya git? Dat's wot ya get when...'

He tailed off as he looked around him, and saw most of his underbosses fleeing, with Beez lying face down on the ground with a long shiv sticking out of his back. Fury rose in Snaggi. He'd worked so hard, he'd found them the spikie, he'd killed a grot much bigger than him to keep it, and now the gits were *running away?*

'Cowards!' he bellowed at their rapidly retreating backs. 'Come back! Come back an' fight! Grots ain't dangerous!'

Something hit him in the back of the head, and then the ground loomed up and headbutted him in the face.

THIRTEEN

Ufthak stared at the ruins of the tellyport platform, and fumed.

It hadn't been a perfect solution to the problem, but it had been *something*. Sure, they'd been firing mobs off into who knows where, even more disorganised than a Waaagh! usually was, but it had been progress of a sort. Ufthak had hoped that one of them might have had the brains to secure the portal and open it from the other side, but maybe he'd been expecting too much; after all, he suspected that it wasn't as though the spikiez had just thrown a bolt or something. Maybe what they needed was a spikie. But did they just need to be near the portal, or did they have to do a special thing?

'Nizkwik!' he bellowed, and waited.

He didn't have to wait long. The little git clambered out from where it had been taking shelter behind the still-smoking body of a meganob who'd taken a direct hit from a big spikie gun, and hurried up to where Ufthak was standing.

'Yes, boss?'

'Where's dat mate of yers?' Ufthak asked. 'Da one wot's been froo dese fings before. Snaggi?'

Nizkwik's face fell. 'Snaggi?'

'You lookin' to make me repeat meself?' Ufthak asked, hefting the Snazzhammer meaningfully. 'Cos dat flippy spikie git wot shanked Uzgit's mob ran away before I could give it a good pastin', so dere's a pastin' goin' spare, if ya get me drift.' That had been infuriating: Ufthak was quite impressed with how the spikie warboss – if that was what it was – had sliced its way through an entire mob of beast snaggas in a matter of seconds; however, it hadn't wanted any part of him once he'd tried to close with it, almost as though it was scared of getting hit. Typical spikiez, only wanting to fight when they thought they could win. Their gods were probably wimps.

'No, boss!' Nizkwik said hurriedly, waving its hands. 'No need for dat! Just a bit confused, cos Snaggi said he was doin' a secret fing for ya, an' dat's why he ain't here.'

Ufthak wrinkled his brow. 'Secret fing? Why da zoggin' heck would I get a *grot* to do a secret fing? Dere ain't nuffin' secret goin' on.'

'Ya mean,' Nizkwik said, its expression sliding into delighted malevolence with the inexorable slowness of hot squig grease flowing across a tilted cooking pan, 'dat he was *lyin'*?'

'Zogged if I care,' Ufthak huffed. 'So yoo're sayin' ya don't know where Snaggi is?'

'No, boss!' Nizkwik said eagerly, then bit its own knuckles as it realised what it'd just admitted to. Ufthak booted him; the little grot went sailing through the air and collided with a Deff Dread, then fell to the ground with a muffled, 'Sorry, boss.'

'Zoggin' grots,' Ufthak muttered, spinning the Snazzhammer absent-mindedly. Well, there was nothing for it. He wasn't going to go looking for Snaggi, or send anyone else to do it; it was utterly beneath him. The grot should be *here*, just in case it was needed. Now Ufthak just had to remember to give it a clobbering next time he saw it, to teach it a lesson. Or for something to do.

Well, if he didn't have the grot around to prod for more information on exactly how these things worked, they'd simply have to do the best they could. Probably just as well. What were the odds of a grot actually knowing anything *useful*? Besides, even if Snaggi were here *and* Ufthak could find a spikie, the chances of the git making the portal do what he wanted were slim.

'Wot dis needs,' Ufthak said firmly, 'is some good old-fashioned orky know-wots.' He looked around. 'Boffin!'

'He's not 'ere, boss,' someone piped up. It was one of the mekboy's spannerz, a singed-looking Bad Moon with a skull that was rather more pointy than most, and the expression of an ork who had come to accept that the world in which he was so interested was always going to explode at him, and not in a fun way. Nazlug, Ufthak remembered, that was his name.

'Mork's teef,' Ufthak grumbled. Was no one where he wanted them to be? 'Well? Whereizzee?'

'Went to get some more tools to repair da tellyporta, boss,' the other ork said somewhat sheepishly, gesturing at the ruined structure next to him, then edging surreptitiously away from Princess, which was sniffing him with interest.

Ufthak raised his eyebrows. 'He's got tools wot can repair *dat*?'

Nazlug gave the shrug of an ork who felt unqualified to comment on the exact nature of his mekboy's abilities, and Ufthak sighed. He could already feel the momentum of the Waaagh! stalling. They'd found and killed most of the spikiez in this bit of their home, but he was sure there was a lot more of it somewhere. The raiding force that had come through and blown the tellyport pad up had to have come from *somewhere*, after all.

However, knowing it was there was no use if he couldn't get to it, and although his ladz had just had an invigorating scrap against the spikiez, the gits had disappeared once it became obvious they weren't doing very well.

The trouble was, orks didn't just stop fighting because the enemy had disappeared. If you'd stomped them all then that was one thing; then you could have a fungus beer, laugh about the best bits with the ladz, and call it a job well done. Sure, you'd need to find some more gits before long, but that was what the Waaagh! was for, wasn't it? See the galaxy, and kill anything you found that fancied a scrap. That was the orkish way. When the enemy disappeared halfway through a fight, though, that was a different matter entirely. That wasn't *satisfying*. Your blood was up, you wanted something to hit – or something to hit you, even – and there was nothing around that fit the bill.

Except, of course, other orks.

And there was nothing wrong with orks fighting other orks, of course there wasn't. It was the way of things: across the galaxy, orks fought with other orks more often than they fought anyone or anything else, mainly because another ork was always willing to have a scrap and there was usually one within arm's reach. Gork and Mork wouldn't have it any other way.

But the truth was that Ufthak felt it was simply a *waste* for the ladz to start fighting each other now. The point of a Waaagh! was that it was orks under one boss, all gunning for the same enemy, whoever that might be. That was why a warboss was a warboss; he was the boss all other bosses followed, rather than just being one of many all fighting each other. If the Tekwaaagh! started scrapping amongst itself now, with the spikiez so close at hand – okay, so Ufthak didn't know exactly where they were, other than 'on the uvver side of da gate', but they were definitely close in a *feeoretical* sense – then it would be a disaster.

It would be proof that Ufthak wasn't ready to be a big boss, and while he wasn't that bothered whether or not he lived up to Da Meklord's assessment of him, Ufthak himself very much liked being big boss.

They needed some more spikiez to stomp, and sharpish, or things were going to get fractious. In fact, things already were. Away past a blazing Stompa that had been set on fire by a lucky shot to the fuel tanks, a big mob of Bad Moons shoota boyz were squaring up to a dozen Deathskull tank-bustas, who were outnumbered but considerably more heavily armed. Mork only knew how the spat had started – it could have been anything from who got a choice bit of loot to someone treading on someone else's toe – but it was about to spill over from strong words into violence, if the gathering crowd of grinning onlookers and the grots hastily taking bets were anything to go by.

Part of Ufthak wanted to just let it happen, and have a good old laugh while bits of ork flew everywhere. However, that wasn't going to help him find and stomp the spikiez who needed stomping, so he shouldered the Snazzhammer, whistled for Princess – which came trotting after him, hoping for treats like a severed limb – and strode towards his ladz to get them to think again. Or just think once, even; that might be enough.

Ufthak was passing through the shadows beneath the Stompa when he recognised the ork at the head of the shoota boyz: Deffrow, formerly one of Ufthak's own mob, who'd gone and got himself a mob of his own now his former nob was the big boss. He was sneering and waving the power klaw he'd had fitted to replace the hand that got mangled when he hit a humie mekboy with a stikkbomb, and it looked like the tank-bustas' nob wasn't too impressed with the gestures Deffrow was making, judging by the way he was fingering the butts of his rokkit pistols. Ufthak drew in a breath to begin a bellow that would put both of them in their place…

…and the darkness attacked him.

One moment he was walking through the shadows, deeper patches of blackness in an already dim world cast by the fires above, and the next *something* was clawing its way out of a patch of darkness at head height and reaching for him with a claw on which strange glyphs glowed with a cold fire. A humie would have frozen in fear and shock, and had its throat clawed out. It would take more than a suddenly sharp shadow to trouble Ufthak Blackhawk, however, and he responded to the threat as soon as it revealed itself by whipping the Snazzhammer up and delivering a blow that snapped the limb in question and drew a squealing snarl of pain from whatever it belonged to.

A dozen more suddenly sharp shadows, though? That might cause a problem, and that was what was coming for him now.

They dropped from above, pulled themselves from the ground, and squeezed out from the shadowed metal pillars of the Stompa's legs. They were bipedal, with hides of midnight hue, clad in ragged dark leathers and clutching curved blades that reflected only the faintest glimmers of light. Apart from that, they were in no way uniform: some were covered in glyphs lit from within by cold fire like the arm he'd swatted, and some had skins that were unmarked; some leered with mouths full of sharp fangs beneath blazing eyes, and the faces of others were featureless pools. All they had in common was their obvious murderous intent.

Princess leaped at one with a bloodthirsty battle squeal, and everyone started fighting at once.

One of the shadow-gits thrust its hand at Ufthak and pale fire billowed from it, as though it were a Deffkilla wartrike's exhaust rocket. Ufthak managed to jerk his head aside from the blast, which whipped past his left ear like a cloud of aggressive ice – *cold* fire? This place just got weirder and weirder – but the slight shift in his momentum brought him directly into the path of one of those glimmering blades. The curved tip arced downwards into his chest, but stopped with a *ping* as it struck an armour plate. Weird or not, these gits' actual weapons seemed solid enough.

Ufthak lashed out with a punch that struck an inky-black face with a satisfying crunch of breaking bones and splintering teeth, even though the mouth wasn't visible at the moment his fist made contact. The shadow-git dropped like a poleaxed grot, and fell straight through the shadows on the floor and out of sight. Ufthak would have paused to gape at that, but he had no time to do so: the rest of the shadow-git's mates were on him.

They were scrawniez of some sort; he could tell by the infuriating way they moved, all flowing grace and supple evasion, with a speed of reaction that would have left even a beakie swinging clumsily at blurred after-images, and a regular humie crawling on the floor looking for its guts within a second. They had a savage edge though, these shadow-gits, and they leant into their blows more. Scrawniez and spikiez alike usually poked and probed, hesitant to commit to an actual fight unless they were sure they weren't going to get hurt back; these ones swung as though they held a grudge against the air between them and him, and were trying to carve straight through Ufthak to get to something on the other side.

It was quite bracing, really.

He roared, and swung the Snazzhammer, pulverising one of the shadow-gits with a single blow, but another one blasted him with cold flame from his left, sending spikes of icy pain down his flank. He blocked a blade with the Snazzhammer's haft, only to find a second worming its way between armour plates, through his hide, and between his ribs. He grabbed that git with his free hand and hurled it into one of its mates, but then something stabbed him in the back of his right leg, which buckled beneath him and brought him down to one knee. He punched backwards with the Snazzhammer, not even bothering to turn the weapon around, and the butt of its haft caught the culprit in whatever served as its throat.

And still they fought. Ufthak caught a glimpse of Princess dragging one away by its leg, the shadow-git's utterly alien face still somehow conveying the startled expression of something which was far more used to being the one doing the unwanted dragging, but the others were pressing in on him in a welter of throaty snarls and glinting blades. He grabbed one by the throat, but the weapon of its neighbour hacked into his bicep. He tried to sweep them away with the Snazzhammer, but one of his enemies had grabbed on to the weapon's haft and weighted it down, then sank suddenly appearing teeth into the flesh of his hand. Ufthak yelled in pain and outrage, and let go of the Snazzhammer; the shadow-git staggered back with it, barely able to take the weight of the massive weapon.

Ufthak drew a slugga from his belt – a faithful old weapon that had been with him since his time as a regular boy in Badgit Snazzhammer's mob – and pumped shots into the bellies of two of the shadow-gits right in front of him. They also staggered backwards, but only due to the impact of the slugs, which had torn right through them and left wet holes behind. Ufthak emptied the weapon into a third body, roared in fury as something sharp pierced his shoulder, dropped the slugga, and lashed out with an open-handed slap that not only mashed a shadow-git right in the face, but had the added bonus of triggering his palm button.

The shadow-git that had stolen the Snazzhammer was trying

to manoeuvre the hefty weapon around into a position to take a swing at Ufthak when the weapon disappeared, taking the git's hands with it. The strange creature screamed – a high keening noise that set Ufthak's teef on edge – and the Snazzhammer reappeared square in Ufthak's grasp, just like it was supposed to do every time.

Well, so long as the zoggin' thing did it when it really counted.

He energised the head and punched it forwards, obliterating the midsection of one of his attackers, then surged upright. The sharp pain in his leg was still there, but it was no longer a surprise, and he'd become accustomed to it. Besides, he had a whole bunch of different new pains now, courtesy of his assailants, so all in all it was more of a baseline, as it were. However, he'd been whittling the shadow-gits' numbers down, and none of the wounds they had dealt him were sufficient to stop him. He was Ufthak Blackhawk, Ufthak Gargantsmasha, and he hadn't been stopped when his head came off his body that time; he wasn't going to get dragged down like some weedy grot by this bunch of gits.

He spun the Snazzhammer, and the butt of the haft cracked one shadow-git under the chin, flooring it. He whirled around with the weapon's momentum and carved clean through another with the axe blade, and lashed out with his left leg to kick a third so hard in the chest that it sailed clean out from under the Stompa and into what passed for daylight beyond. Princess sprang and bore the handless one to the ground, the squig's happily ravenous squeals hitting nearly the same pitch as the ragged, tearing screams of the luckless alien being torn apart by its fangs – and that left two.

One leaped at him, reaching out to engulf him in ice fire again, but Ufthak was too quick this time: he grabbed the thing's arm and directed the blast up and away from him, then leaned forward and simply bit the shadow-git's head off. His jaws enveloped its skull without difficulty, and his teef crunched a slender spine and crushed and sheared their way through the narrow column of flesh. He chewed once – it tasted cold and dark, like licking the space between stars – and spat the mangled mouthful out.

The last shadow-git, the one he'd cracked on the chin and knocked down, didn't wait to meet its end. It dived for the blackest patch of shadow left and vanished, just before Princess pounced. The squig hit the Stompa's leg face first and rebounded with a confused whine.

Ufthak looked out into the light, just in time to see the shadow-git he'd kicked out there get engulfed in flame, explosions and shoota fire. Deffrow's mob and the tankbustas they'd been arguing with had taken their sweet time to notice that their boss was being attacked by weird alien things, but they were at least emphatic in dealing with it once they had.

'Yoo good, boss?' Deffrow called once the smoke had cleared, and a few dark, wet gobbets were all that was visible of the last attacker.

'Nah,' Ufthak said.

'Nah?' Deffrow looked sideway at the tankbusta nob, then sidled a little closer. 'Did da gits getcha?'

It wasn't concern on Deffrow's face; orks were rarely concerned by their own injuries, let alone those of others. It was simple interest, because if Ufthak had been badly hurt and was about to keel over then the entire leadership of this part of the Tekwaaagh! might be up for grabs, and Deffrow would want a running start at it.

'Dat ain't it,' Ufthak said, striding out from beneath the Stompa. He threw the Snazzhammer up into the air and caught it again with a meaty *thwack*, but he wasn't really interested in showing off right now.

He was *furious*.

'Sendin' shadows at me!' he bellowed, causing every single ork looking at him to take a step back in alarm. 'Zoggin' *shadows*? Not comin' to face me one-on-one like a proppa warrior, not comin' at us wiv guns an' blades and dose zippy flyin' wotsits? Dis ain't a *fight*! Dis is a zoggin' *insult*! I ain't standin' for it! Zog Da Meklord, an' zog da Tekwaaagh! Dese gits've made it *pers'nal*, an' I'm gonna wring dere scrawny little *necks* for it!'

He stopped, panting slightly with how hard he'd been screaming. His boyz were staring at him uncertainly now, clearly wondering exactly what was going to happen next, and how many of them were likely to end up as squig food as a result. Orks didn't often lose their temper, because most things that might cause them to do so were just an excuse to have a fight, which was a good thing, and so nothing to get angry about. When a large ork actually flipped, things got unpredictable.

Ufthak could actually feel himself vibrating, he was so angry. The zoggin' *cheek* of it! To send their shadowy little kommandos – or whatever the spikie equivalent was – to try to take him out! And the worst thing was, there was very little he could do about it. He could smash *this* place up fine, oh yes, he could blast it and bomb it and wallop it with the Snazzhammer until every remaining spikie skulking somewhere in the ruins was a fine paste, and the buildings themselves were just monochrome dust, but that wouldn't help him get at the ones that had caused this.

He whirled around and stared at the portal: the thing separating him from his enemies, yet also the only way to them. The infuriatingly alien, incomprehensible…

Wait.

Absolute fury was surging through him in the aftermath of the fight – not just the usual exhilaration and aggression that was a part of such activity, but a burning anger unlike anything he'd felt before, and it was unlocking things as it went. The sheer desire to get at his enemies, to get his hands on them and make them pay for their arrogance and hubris, made him think about things in ways he never had.

'Someone get me Da Boffin!' he bellowed. 'An' also one of his spannerz wot no one likes, an' a shokk attack gun, an' a weird-boy wot ain't exploded anyone's head recently. I am gettin' *froo* dat git!'

'Now, I ain't usually da one askin' dis,' Da Boffin said, 'but… are you sure dis is gonna work?'

'Yes,' Ufthak replied, and to his astonishment, he was. The trick was holding on to his anger enough to retain his concentration, without letting it take hold of him so much that he clobbered his best mekboy. 'Simple, innit? Shokk attack guns make a sort of weird tunnel, right? Just like shokkjump dragstas do, like wot me an' Mogrot used to get froo dat humie Gargant's shields dat time. Only da gun makes a tunnel ya shoot snotlings down.'

'Gotcha,' Da Boffin said, nodding.

'So if we link da gun up to da portal,' Ufthak said, nodding towards the cables that had been shoved into the scrawniez' archway in places Da Boffin had felt were most suitable, 'we can make our *own* tunnel to da uvver side!'

'Well, I ain't sayin' dat's a bad idea,' Da Boffin said, 'particularly since it ain't gonna be me holdin' da gun.' They both glanced over at Nazlug, who looked about as dejected as it was possible to be if you were an ork with a massive gun bolted to his shoulder plate ('in case it all goes a bit weird, we don't wantcha lettin' go of it accidentally, do we?'). Then their collective gazes travelled down the other cable now attached to the shokk attack gun, which terminated in a metal spike driven into the skull of a weirdboy known as Uzkop.

'Dat part, though,' Da Boffin said thoughtfully. 'Dat's wot's stumpin' me.' Uzkop himself was whimpering, although that possibly had less to do with the spike in his head and more to do with the natural state of a weirdboy when surrounded by other orks. Even Ufthak could feel the energy of the ladz he'd gathered together: aggression and frustration in equal measure, just the sort of thing that could charge up a weirdboy's brain and bring forth his devastating powers. If you were lucky, you could aim the git at the enemy and have him melt their faces off. If you were unlucky, on the other hand, he'd explode a bunch of your boyz' heads, possibly including yours and quite possibly including his own. Uzkop was clinging desperately to his copper staff, which helped earth the power, while his two burly minders hovered nearby in case they were needed.

'Makin' da tunnel's just da first part,' Ufthak said. 'We still gotta make da tunnel go where we want it to, an' since da git wiv da gun can't see wot he's shootin' at, we need somefing else to do da targetin'. Dat's wot da weirdboy's for.' It all seemed so *simple* somehow, as though the knowledge had always been there within him, just waiting to be discovered. The spikiez had given him a problem, and he'd come up with a solution.

This was when all the finkin' finally paid off.

He turned around. The Waaagh! – or a large part of it, anyway, those the nobs had been able to round up – were assembled in as close to good order as orks were ever likely to manage. There wasn't a great deal of jostling or shoving, the speed freeks were managing to keep their engine revving under control, the beast snaggas were preventing their squighogs and smasha squigs from rampaging off and eating anyone. Even the Stompas weren't sounding their war-horns. Every one of them seemed to sense

MIKE BROOKS

that something big was about to go down, and they were willing to hold their natural exuberance in check for the moment, just to see what was going on and whether they could get a good fight out of it.

Ufthak reached out his hand. Nizkwik shoved the shouty cone into it, and Ufthak raised it to his mouth.

'ALRIGHT, LISSEN UP!' his enhanced voice bellowed with a crackle and squeal of feedback, focusing every ork's attention on him. 'DA SPIKIEZ FORT DEY COULD HIT US AN' LEG IT, BUT WE AIN'T GONNA STAND FOR IT, ARE WE?'

'NO!' the Tekwaaagh! thundered as one, raising various weapons into the air and shaking them vigorously.

'SO WOT WE'RE GONNA DO IS, WE'RE GONNA GO FROO DIS FING AND GIVE 'EM A GOOD OLD KICKIN'!' Ufthak continued, to roars of approval. 'WE'RE GONNA FIND 'EM, AN' WE'RE GONNA STOMP 'EM INTO DA DIRT! AIN'T DAT RIGHT?'

'YES!' the Tekwaaagh! hollered joyfully. Ufthak grinned, turned around, and pointed at Nazlug.

'Fire it up!'

The spanner obediently clenched the shooty-lever, and the three-pronged shokka on the front of the huge gun began to spin. The charged orbs at the end of each arm sparked with energy, dragging blazing trails through the air as they moved faster and faster, until Nazlug was half-obscured behind a whirring circle of blue lightning. The first telltale signs of inter-dimensional disturbance began to flicker in front of him, the beginnings of the shokka portal that could move things from one place to another without bothering about the space between.

'Now!' Ufthak shouted, and Da Boffin threw his switch. The power that was starting to build up in the shokk attack gun was abruptly rerouted, flowing into the scrawniez' portal, and the air

158

within the archway, which had been empty and unremarkable, crackled and came to life. It became opaque, shimmering with a cold light, like an aurora reflected on the waves of an arctic sea.

'Staff!' Ufthak bellowed, and Uzkop's minders ripped the staff from his grasp. The weirdboy's eyes went wide, then were eclipsed by a bright green glow from within. He began to twitch uncontrollably, and the minders grabbed him to keep him in place.

All that Waaagh! energy, flowing into Uzkop from the assembled orks, began to build up. Every part of it was focused on one thing: finding the spikiez that had attacked them, and making them pay for it. No matter where they were, no matter where they'd hidden, the thing at the forefront of every ork's mind was getting to them. Ufthak had made sure they were concentrating on it.

Energy crackled out of the spike in Uzkop's head and skittered along the cable that linked him to the shokk attack gun, and the gun's whirring took on a new tone, like the distant rumble of thousands of angry voices. The portal flickered, wavered, then stabilised again with a slightly different pattern of shifting light within it.

It had worked. Ufthak knew it had, although he couldn't verbalise how. However, he didn't need to. He clapped Da Boffin on the shoulder, ran to his trukk, and vaulted up into the back. Nizkwik scrabbled on after him, and Princess bounded up behind.

'Mogrot!' he roared, as his sidekick threw the trukk into gear. 'Step on it!'

The vehicle lurched forward, and behind him Ufthak heard the almighty roar of his ladz, united again in a single purpose, surging after him with their war cry on their lips.

''ERE WE GO, 'ERE WE GO, 'ERE WE GO!'

FOURTEEN

The throne room of the Kabal of the Hollow Heart was the centre of Dhaemira's power. It was the grandest hall in her entire spire, a massive space that occupied the entire width of Heart-point, albeit the narrower portion near the apex of it. Above it were her decoy chambers – too easily accessible from the outside to be considered safe, in a city in which gravity was a mere annoyance to most, and inconsequential to many – and the roof on which she had met Zothar Oridraed and sent him to his death. Beneath her were her real chambers, buried in the midst of the tower but equipped with sympathy windows, so she could look out over her domain from the structure's actual exterior without presenting herself as a target for assassins. Below that were the torture chambers and dungeons, and farther down still were the barracks, mess halls, training rooms and armouries for her warriors, who stood ready to repel any assault coming in from ground level.

Which was not, of course, to say that there were not other

guard stations throughout the spire, since Dhaemira's ancestors had not been so foolish as to leave no protection between themselves and the wretched creatures they captured and tormented. Dhaemira herself had her own private staircases and anti-grav shafts by which she traversed her home, each one coded solely to her palm-print, eye-scan, blood chemistry or breath, and with the method of security used to access each switching on a pattern that only she knew. The tower had several virtually impregnable chambers in which Dhaemira could take shelter in the case of an emergency, as well as a variety of exits, many of which were known only to her, and all of which had a variety of lethal countermeasures to ensure no one came up them the wrong way.

With all of those thoroughly prudent precautions against attack in mind, it might have seemed strange that Dhaemira sat openly on her throne in the middle of a huge space in which there were a multitude of shadows and places to hide. The throne room was, after all, filled with statues of her forebears, mighty edifices honouring the Dark Muses, and grand depictions of the general superiority of the drukhari over all other species of the galaxy, leaving plenty of places in which assassins could conceal themselves. Dhaemira let herself be seen within it for two reasons.

Firstly, while paranoia was prudent, being seen to be paranoid was not. Dhaemira's authority as master archon rested on others perceiving her as strong, and an archon who cowered behind closed doors and bodyguards practically invited open plotting against themselves. Her presence and visibility was just another trap, designed to encourage the overconfident to spring their schemes only to see them shatter against her defences, like cheap blades on good armour.

Secondly, there *were* plenty of assassins hiding in the shadows and alcoves of the throne room, because Dhaemira had stationed them there herself.

However, perhaps the most dangerous – or at the least, most unnerving – of them all was currently on one knee on the floor in front of the steps that descended from Dhaemira's throne. His skin drank in light rather than reflected it, apart from the cold glow emanating from the sigils of destruction etched into his flesh. His fingers ended in savage talons, and the darkness of his face did not hide the glint of his fangs.

Dhaemira leaned forwards in her seat. 'Define "failed".'

Kherazul of Aelindrach did not raise his head to look at her. Curtains of lank, colourless hair fell on either side and in front of his face, obscuring much of it from view. It was a strange sight to see a mandrake so cowed; Dhaemira would have enjoyed the novelty of the experience, had the reason for it not been so infuriating.

'The arakhia was too strong, and too ferocious,' Kherazul intoned, in a voice that sounded like claws scraping across lead. Although Dhaemira could not be sure, she did not think that the creature's mouth moved when it spoke. 'We wounded it, but could not kill it. Only I escaped, in order to bring you word of its continued existence.'

'Did you not set on it when it was alone?' Dhaemira asked. That was the point of mandrakes, surely – to attack enemies when they thought they were safe? Or were orks just so gregarious that it was impossible to get one by itself?

'It was alone,' Kherazul replied. 'Save for its… pet.' Now he raised his head, and fixed his cold eyes on her. 'This arakhia is a fell creature. Not just brutal, but swift and cunning. It slew my kin without needing any aid from its own.'

Dhaemira ground her teeth in irritation. The mandrakes had been Maculatix's idea, although the slaves to pay them had come from Dhaemira's dungeons. It should have been enough. The fact that the ork chieftain had not only survived the attack, but also butchered its assailants by itself, spoke strongly of just what a formidable creature it was.

On the other hand, if an entire pack of mandrakes could not bring the ork down with a surprise attack, Dhaemira's own inability to land a blow on it did not seem quite so humiliating. Maculatix had not openly laughed at her in the wake of their retreat from Sabregate, but Dhaemira could tell that he wanted to. Seeing his expression when he heard how abysmally his plan had failed would be the very small, faint silver lining of this thoroughly unwelcome cloud.

'And your payment?' she asked, biting off her words slowly and deliberately.

'Will be returned,' Kherazul replied tonelessly. The fees mandrakes demanded for their services from the drukhari nobility who hired them could vary wildly, but the investment was almost always a secure one. Dhaemira was now glad that Kherazul had only asked for captives to take back to the shadow realm of Aelindrach, rather than something more esoteric. At the very least, they were easier to demand be returned than one's own true name, or a heartbeat, or any other such strange request.

'See that it is,' Dhaemira said. She wasn't quite sure what she would do if it was not – she hardly wished to launch an assault on Aelindrach in search of retribution, even if the orks weren't a more pressing concern – but there were appearances to be maintained. Besides, killing Kherazul for his failure would guarantee that she would not see her investment back, so this promise was probably a cunning move on the mandrake's part.

'You may leave,' she said, and the mandrake rose to his feet. He did not head for the door, simply for the nearest patch of true shadow, into which he vanished without trace. It was an uncomfortable reminder of how deadly he and his kind were.

Except to this ork chieftain, apparently.

She stood and held out her arms. Servants rushed forward with her cloak and fastened it about her shoulders quickly and efficiently, then backed away with their faces lowered as she began to descend the steps to the throne room floor. Everyone could tell that the master archon was in a foul mood, and no one wished to be on the wrong side of her temper.

No one apart from family.

'Dear sister,' Dhalgar said, emerging from behind a massive plinth carved into the shape of bodies contorted in pain. 'How it grieves me to see your failure laid bare.'

Dhalgar Thraex, when not a pile of bloody meat in the aftermath of having a vehicle land on him, was tall enough to look Dhaemira in the eyes, not to mention confident enough. He was currently arrayed in his second-favourite armour – his actual favourite not having survived his first encounter with the orks – and was resting the wrist of his left hand lightly on the pommel of his sheathed blade. Dhaemira did not trust that sword at all; she did not know from where Dhalgar had got it, and even in a city of cursed weapons and foul creations, it had an unpleasant, twisted aura all of its own.

'You will note that I am still hale and whole,' Dhaemira pointed out, 'rather than just returned from the Red Harvest's ministrations. You may wish to consider that when you next open your mouth.'

Dhalgar smirked. 'Why, because I was the victim of an accident caused by my pilot's poor decision-making, whereas you ran from a fight?'

'Because I might just send you back there,' Dhaemira snapped, taking a step to stand toe-to-toe with him. Dhalgar did not flinch or step backwards, but his lips pursed thoughtfully, and his next words were, if not respectful, at least delivered in a neutral tone rather than a barely disguised sneer.

'The mandrakes were your idea?'

'Maculatix's,' Dhaemira replied.

'And now?'

'Now I speak to my allies, and we consider our next move,' Dhaemira said. 'The immediate threat of the arakhia's teleporting was ended. Now we need to prepare a more concerted attack to wipe them out once and for all. There are still alliances to forge, primarily with the wych cults.' She eyed him. 'Are you capable of resuming command of your shard?'

'Of course,' Dhalgar said with a snort. The Shard of the Cruellest Light was the largest faction within the kabal aside from Dhaemira's own court, as befitted the master archon's only living blood relative. The other three shards – the Void Ascendant, the False Hope, and the Eyeless Gaze – had their own archons, each of whom Dhaemira actually trusted more than she did her brother, although that statement still stretched the definition of 'trust' to breaking point. However, Dhalgar was a fearsome warrior and a talented strategist when he wasn't trying to show off, and so he was – for now, at least – worth keeping around.

'Then do so,' Dhaemira instructed him. She pushed past him, forcing him to step aside. 'Come. I have a war to plan.'

'You have made an alliance with the Falling Night?' Dhalgar hissed into her ear, as their Raider pulled alongside the dark green Tantalus that bore Cistrial Virn and his bodyguard.

'The other kabals have acknowledged my authority and look to me for direction,' Dhaemira replied quietly. 'Virn and Maculatix stand with us. Port Tavarr is as close to united as it has been since Fahrrul died. What about this arrangement do you find disagreeable, brother?'

'Virn cannot be trusted,' Dhalgar said firmly, looking straight ahead as though refusing to sully his eyes with a glance at the archon in question. 'You are a fool if you do so.'

'Who says I trust him?' Dhaemira replied with a snort. 'His interests and ours align for now, and he is intelligent enough to realise that.'

All the same, her mind went back to that moment when she had been plucked out of peril by Cistrial Virn, and those moments she spent dangling above the roaring mass of the ork horde before being hauled aboard the Tantalus that now ran alongside them. Would Dhalgar have come to her rescue? If he had, would he have let her fall into a roiling mass of alien savages, blame a faulty grip, and then seek to take command of her kabal? Dhaemira was fairly sure she knew the answer to that question. Ambition drove Dhalgar just as surely as it drove her, but her brother lacked patience and long-term thinking. If he gained command then the kabal would undoubtedly fall to ruin – not immediately, perhaps, but certainly after a few decades.

More importantly, if he gained command then it would be because Dhaemira was dead, which was a far greater incentive to keep Dhalgar in his place.

'Do you at least approve of our choice of allies within the wych cults?' she asked, as their small group of craft banked around a ruined spur of what had once been a building, but which now resembled nothing more than an angular headland of pitted, dark stone. Indistinct, shuffling shapes fluttered uneasily as the flyers passed close by: a colony of gloomwings, roosting in the shadows and waiting for the diseased light of the captured sun to wane a little before embarking on a hunt through Port Tavarr's streets and skies. An outsider might question why the drukhari still needed enclosed homes, since there was no weather to speak of in Commorragh, but only if they had not seen the predators that stalked the Dark City's shadowed streets.

'The Cult of the Deathly Sorrow?' Dhalgar nodded. 'Numerous, fierce and, unlike the Silver Shards, not hungry for your blood. There are certainly worse choices that you could have made.'

His tone made it sound as if it were sheer luck that had guided her to this choice, rather than a careful analysis of fighting strength and allegiances. Dhaemira snorted again, and forced herself not to rise to her brother's baiting.

Still, her position as master archon could survive no more mistakes. The orks had demonstrated themselves to be unpredictable enemies who appeared able to frustrate even the best-laid plans. Even more infuriating was the fact that this seemed to happen through sheer chance or blind luck on the creatures' part, as though the universe bent itself to accommodate whatever was most convenient for them with little regard for the rules that governed the lives of other species. Being outwitted by an adversarial mastermind such as a scheming fellow drukhari, or an Asuryani farseer capable of surveying the skeins of fate and guiding their milk-blooded followers down the most beneficial paths, or even the daemonic intelligence of one of the servant-beasts of Chaos – these were outcomes for which the wise archon prepared themselves. The crude hammer of the orkish war machine, and their bestial resilience and savage ferocity were dangerous, but being outflanked by them? Being forced to react to unexpected stratagems, and their bizarre technologies? It was humiliating.

Her flotilla passed through a massive arch that was carved into the shape of two daemonic-looking entities bound together and facing away from each other, their horns interlocked and their clawed arms twisted back to be wrapped around the other's neck, and their expressions contorted into ones of horrified pain. Perhaps it had been intended as a monument to Commorragh's triumph even over the denizens of the warp, or perhaps the artist had simply had a particularly active imagination. Either way, it was an isolated structure now, damaged and corroded by time, and surrounded by the dead and broken shells of abandoned buildings in which nothing lived save for the most desperate of Commorragh's residents, and the beasts that hunted them.

Up ahead, however, was something far more vibrant.

The arena of the Cult of the Deathly Sorrow was the size of a city of a lesser species: a gigantic circular amphitheatre sunken partially into the ground, the walls of which were set with hundreds of thousands of seats, varying from narrow, uncomfortable perches for the poor to luxurious private boxes for the wealthy and influential that were practically second homes. A sizeable chunk of Port Tavarr's population could and did come here on a regular basis to watch hekatarii of the cult engaging in gladiatorial combat – either with each other, with captured beasts, or with alien fighters – and skyboard and jetbike riders racing through specially constructed courses, with each new turn providing the potential for a gruesome, high-speed death (and that was leaving aside the fact that the rival contestants would be trying to kill each other even as they raced).

This was just one of several such arenas within Port Tavarr, and Port Tavarr was merely one of the innumerable sub-realms that made up Commorragh, greatest of all cities and surely the largest contiguous inhabited area within the galaxy – if indeed it was 'within' the galaxy at all, thanks to the strange nature of the webway. Regardless, it gave Dhaemira a certain chill to look at the Arena of Deathly Sorrow and consider not just how mighty the forces were that dwelled within it, but how even that strength paled in comparison to the drukhari race in total. Truly, her kind were still the unquestioned rulers of the galaxy, no matter how many pathetic planets the orks or the mon-keigh laid claim to.

She had often come here to sample the delights of the gory, pain-wracked spectacles it offered, because while there was a delicious intimacy – and far greater individual gain – to be had from torturing a victim yourself, the sheer unpredictability of the games offered its own thrilling reward. The sudden reversal of fortunes on the arena floor that saw a bleeding warrior cut down their now-overconfident opponent, or a proud reaver losing control of their jetbike or careering into an unseen razor-net and briefly becoming an agonised smear on the wall – these moments imbued the spectator with a rush that could never be achieved when one was in full control of events. Sometimes it was not so much about the quantity or even quality of the soul nourishment extracted from another being's suffering, but the overall experience of it.

Now, however, they were not approaching for the purposes of leisure. Their craft descended towards the wide roof, which had space for hundreds of Raiders, but were greeted by the rising shapes of skyboards and reavers coming up to meet them. It was not just drukhari, either: Dhaemira saw the dark shapes of razorwings keeping pace with a couple of the skyboards, the massive carnivorous avians flanking the beastmasters that had broken them in.

'It appears that Xurzuli is not welcoming visitors at present,' Maculatix shouted across from his Raider. The master haemonculus' tone was light, but Dhaemira could sense the tension that lay beneath. Were they too late? Had some hitherto-unconsidered rival made an approach to the Cult of the Deathly Sorrow, seeking to usurp power within Port Tavarr? She loosened her blast pistol in its holster.

'What business do you have here?' the lead reaver demanded. His blank-featured mask contained a voice amplifier, which sent his words booming and crackling around them. 'The next games are not until darktime.'

'We come to speak with Succubus Xurzuli Mindrex,' Dhaemira called back. 'I sent a scourge ahead.'

The reaver laughed. 'Your little bird must have fallen prey to something on its way here. My mistress has not mentioned that she is expecting guests.'

'Then you can tell her that some have arrived,' Cistrial Virn said. He was standing at the very prow of his Tantalus, his hair whipped by the winds that trawled through Commorragh despite the apparent lack of atmospheric processes to create them. 'Master Archons Cistrial Virn of the Kabal of the Falling Night and Dhaemira Thraex of the Kabal of the Hollow Heart, and Master Haemonculus Maculatix of the Coven of the Red Harvest. As well as our underlings,' he added, with a sideways glance that was not directly aimed at Dhalgar, but was also not directly *not* aimed at him. Dhaemira felt her lips quirk in a smirk as her brother let out a hiss of anger.

'Yes, yes,' the reaver said. 'I know your colours, and can read your iconography.'

'Then perhaps you should see whether your mistress wishes to reconsider her position,' Dhaemira called to him. 'We are on a matter of some urgency, and we would rather seek what we need elsewhere than bandy words with a gatekeeper!'

She was too far away to read what could be seen of the reaver's expression, but the way he pulled his jetbike back and down made it clear enough that he was passing on their words. For her part, Dhaemira was thinking furiously. What had happened to her messenger? Scourges were practically untouchable in Commorragh, since the sensitive messages they carried were too important to the functioning of society for it to be any other way. A natural fate was not out of the question – there were plenty of aerial predators in the Dark City, after all, some of them large and savage enough to trouble even one of the drukhari who had mastered the skies on their own grafted wings – but it was unlikely. Could a particularly desperate enemy have attempted to sabotage this meeting?

Her eyes slid sideways to Dhalgar of their own accord, but Dhaemira got her paranoia back under control with some effort. Dhalgar wished for the orks to be destroyed just as much as she did – more so, perhaps, since he must yearn to atone for his indignity – and an alliance with the Cult of the Deathly Sorrow was a great step towards achieving that. It would not serve his purposes to undermine her – not yet, at any rate.

'Well, well,' Virn said, just loud enough for Dhaemira to hear him. 'It looks as though our host may have discovered her manners after all.'

A Venom was rising up from the arena's rooftop, and in the passenger compartment Dhaemira could see the distinctive shock of night-black hair that marked Xurzuli Mindrex out from a distance. Her mane was nearly as long as she was tall, and only a high clasp atop her head kept it bound up and under some form of control. She was surrounded by five other warriors: five of her bloodbrides, the finest wyches under her command. Not all of them were female, of course, since 'bloodbride' was a title rather than a description; indeed, Xurzuli herself had only taken on a female form in the last few decades since ascending to the rank of succubus, in the same way as every Asuryani warrior who explored the warrior aspect of the Howling Banshees was female, and most incubi were male. Some roles within aeldari society overrode the tenuous grip of biology: it was one of the few constants across all the varied strands of the species' existence.

'Grand Succubus,' Dhaemira greeted her as the Venom rose into hailing range. 'I understand that my message did not arrive?'

'No, I received it,' Xurzuli replied. Her voice and posture were lazy, but it was the laziness of a reclining predator which was nevertheless ready to pounce should prey present itself. Succubi were the pinnacle of death-dealing within the drukhari, and Xurzuli was one of the best among them. Dhaemira was a fine warrior, but she had few illusions about who would win in single combat between her and Xurzuli Mindrex.

That was one reason why it was so important to recruit the succubus to their cause. The wych cults lacked the massed fire-power of the kabals, or the sheer resilience and immunity to pain of the haemonculus covens, but they were unmatched for quicksilver lethality.

'I found it somewhat amusing,' Xurzuli continued, fixing each of them with a stare, one after another. Her eyes had been altered or replaced, and no longer had any whites, merely dark pools. 'These arakhia must be formidable indeed, for you to come begging my aid.'

Dhaemira bristled, as she could feel the others doing as well. To accuse another drukhari of *begging* was a calculated insult. Virn opened his mouth – to list, Dhaemira was certain, the iden-tified assets of the ork force in order to drive home exactly how serious a threat they were. Virn had that kind of mind, neat and ordered. Dhaemira found her fellow archon's mastery of details quite impressive – not that she would ever admit that out loud – but something told her that it was not what was required here.

'Their leader slew an entire pack of mandrakes by itself,' she said, before Virn could frame his first syllable.

Xurzuli straightened: the predator had detected a rustling in the long grass. 'By *itself*?'

'So I was informed by the lone survivor,' Dhaemira confirmed.

She let that statement hang in the air for a moment, accompanied by its unspoken connotations: a mandrake, one of the terrors of the shadows, admitting how it and its kin had been bested by a single alien warlord.

'Intriguing,' Xurzuli said. 'This sounds like a creature whom it might be most invigorating to face in combat.'

Dhaemira shot a look at Virn, who gave the briefest of nods in return. Jumping in when your ally was about to speak might put fractures in an alliance, but the archon of the Falling Night could recognise when another had seen a quicker route to victory.

'Very well, my friends,' Xurzuli said, and now she no longer lounged against the rail of her craft but was upright and alert, every muscle of her lean body prepared to spring. 'The Cult of the Deathly Sorrow will assist you in bringing death and suffering to these invaders. I have but one price.'

Dhaemira schooled her expression. 'And that is?'

'This chieftain must be taken alive,' Xurzuli purred. 'I will have it in the arena, and will make great sport of it there.'

Dhaemira gritted her teeth. 'That would be unwise.'

'You think to tell me what I can achieve in my own arena?' Xurzuli snapped.

'Not at all,' Maculatix cut in, 'but plucking the cursed thing away from its followers and getting it here may well prove impossible. We know the arakhia, and we know how they work – if their leader is slain, their internal coherence will fall apart and they will tear themselves to shreds as the remaining lieutenants fight to establish dominance.'

Out of the corner of her eye, Dhaemira saw Cistrial Virn shooting another glance at her. She ignored her fellow archon and former rival for primacy after the death of Lord Fahrrul, and kept her attention on Xurzuli instead.

'A swift strike to annihilate this monster and its coterie, a swift strike of the sort the wych cults excel at, is our surest strategy,' Maculatix continued. 'That is why we have approached you.'

'I agree with everything you have said,' Xurzuli replied. 'However, my price remains the same.'

Dhaemira closed her eyes in frustration for a moment.

'Think about it, my friends,' Xurzuli said, slipping back into her lazy tones. '*Removing* the arakhia from its followers is functionally the same as killing it, is it not? It will still leave them leaderless, and prone to fighting amongst themselves. Once that occurs, we can pick them off at our leisure.' Her expression hardened. 'You let me worry about how I will achieve this, but if that creature is damaged in any way by any of your warriors, this alliance is concluded. Do we have an accord?'

Dhaemira looked at Virn, and then at Maculatix, but there was little she could do. They needed a wych cult, and a powerful one at that – but also one that was not going to react to seeing them by drawing its blades and going for their throat. The Cult of the Deathly Sorrow was the only one within Port Tavarr to fit that bill.

'Very well,' she said. 'The warlord is yours, but it *must* be neutralised.'

'Consider it done,' Xurzuli said with a smile, which faltered as a noise reached their ears. It was far off and faint, but distinct nonetheless.

Something had exploded. And as the noise came again, and again, it became apparent that this was not going to be an isolated incident.

'What is that?' Xurzuli asked, her expression no longer so supercilious.

'It is the arakhia,' Dhaemira said. Somehow, she knew what had happened without seeing it, even before carrier waves began to broadcast the latest development to the assembled nobility.

'They've breached the portal,' she said, with grim certainty. 'They're in Port Tavarr.'

FIFTEEN

When Snaggi woke up, he was already on his feet. Or more accurately, he was being dragged along while upright and his feet were acquiring friction burns from the ground.

'Wossit? Woz goin' on?' he slurred, trying to force his legs into some semblance of movement.

'Da portal, boss,' said a voice from his left, and Snaggi looked around to see Gip there, supporting him with one shoulder under his arm.

'It's opened, innit?' said a voice from his other side, which proved to be Swipe. Snaggi looked ahead of him, and blinked furiously to get his eyes to cooperate.

One of the massive, pale arches through which the spikiez had swept on their ill-fated counter-attack had activated again, and was filled with the shimmering light that Snaggi remembered so well. However, rather than disgorging slender, bloodthirsty warriors attired in razor-edged armour, the portal was currently swallowing the massive, blocky, and fume-belching shape of a

Stompa. The light closed behind the enormous walker's back, and a massive cheer went up from all around.

'Wot da blazes are ya doin'?' Snaggi hissed, disentangling himself from his supporters. 'We don't wanna go froo dere! Dat's where all da orks are goin'! We wanna find da portal we came in froo, an' leg it dat way!'

'Yeah, well, don't fink we've got a choice in it,' Gip muttered. 'Runtherds, innit.'

Snaggi chanced a look over his shoulder, and grimaced. His burgeoning mob of followers were trotting along at a fair clip, each one wearing the grim, slightly constipated expression of grots heading towards a fight not because they wanted to – since the only fight a grot wanted to take part in was one where the enemy didn't know they were fighting, and also were facing the other way and had their backs exposed for a bit of enthusiastic stabbing – but because the possibility of what lay ahead was less alarming than the certainty of what followed behind. In this case, what followed behind was a pair of runtherds: surly orks whose calling in the great, chaotic melting pot of orkish society was to beat on grots, snotlings, and squigs until they did what they were told. Each one had a fearsome-looking grot lash in one hand, while the other held the leash of a squig-hound, a ferocious beast more than capable of tracking down runaways and biting them in half.

'Ah, zog it,' Snaggi muttered. 'Wot happened to da spikie? After yoo lot *left me* to get clobbered by da Disorderlies,' he added, nastily.

'Dey carted it off, boss,' Nib said, from behind him. 'Next fing we know, word's gone out dat da big boss has got da portal open an' we're all goin' froo to give da spikiez a taste of boot levver. Apparently dey tried to kill da big boss wiv shadows or somefing, an' he weren't pleased.'

Snaggi tried to imagine that. Ufthak Blackhawk was…
unyielding was perhaps the best term, in that the git just wouldn't
let go of something once he'd set his mind to it. Snaggi was used
to orks being either obsessive and narrow-sighted on a particular
area of focus, like some of the painboyz and meks he'd encountered, or easily distracted by something flashy. Blackhawk gave
off the disconcerting impression of actual long-term thinking,
and definitely the notion that he might hold a grudge. If the spikiez had gone and properly riled him up, rather than just being
the obvious target for the orks' incessant need to fight something, this was not going to end quickly.

'So anyway, since da portal opened right after da Disorderlies nicked dat spikie we found, we figured dat wot yoo said
was right,' Swipe said quietly. 'Dat's how to open da portal! So
we're wiv ya, boss. Yoo obviously know wot's wot!'

'Yeah,' Gip said, with the slightly uncertain expression of a
grot who'd cynically thrown his lot in expecting a bit of rank,
and found to his surprise that there might be something underneath to believe in after all. 'I guess da gods *do* speak to ya.'

'Well, yeah,' Snaggi muttered, through his throbbing head.
'Course dey do. I ain't gonna lie to ya.'

'So wot now?' Nib asked, his voice betraying his nervousness.
'Are we gonna make a break for it? A darin' escape?'

'Nah,' Snaggi said quietly, eyeing up their surroundings. 'We're
smack in da middle of da Waaagh!, wiv a couple of runtherds
behind us – we ain't goin' anywhere except froo dat portal.
We gotta take dese fings slow,' he added, to their disappointed
expressions. 'Orks are about as bright as a dead glow squig, but
dey're gonna realise somefing's up if we try to leg it here'n now,
and dey'll just clobber us. Since we *lost da spikie*,' he added with
deliberate emphasis, 'we're gonna 'ave to go along wiv 'em for
now, den get away when dey're concentratin' on duffin' up da

spikie's mates. Find anuvver one wot's nearly dead, an' try da same fing again. Dis time wivout leggin' it an' leavin' me to get clocked in da zoggin' head, maybe?' he finished, with more than a little venom.

He looked around him again. All of his original audience were here, each one of them hurrying along in a desperate bid to avoid the attentions of the runtherds, but they were swallowed up in a much larger mass of grots. Runtherds tended to herd all their charges together, regardless of origin: orks were part of distinct mobs, and took their orders from a particular nob, but grots were just grots, and no one cared. As a result, it took Snaggi a few more seconds of furtive searching before his eyes lighted on the distinctive truncated nose he was looking for.

'Back in a minute, ladz,' he announced to his immediate followers, and dropped back into the crowd. He was jostled and shoved, but he jostled and shoved back, until he managed to position himself just behind and to the side of his target.

'Gekki Shortnose,' he announced, in the same tone of voice that one might use to pronounce the doom of an entire dynasty. Gekki jumped, and nearly fell over his own feet as they continued hurrying forwards.

'Wot do *yoo* want?' the other grot demanded, once he'd gathered himself. Snaggi could tell that Gekki wanted to square up to him, but he was too scared of the runtherds, so he kept trotting forwards, and Snaggi kept trotting just behind him. 'I fort yoo was gonna find a spikie an' use it to get us all out of here!' Gekki continued accusingly, looking back over his shoulder.

'I was,' Snaggi agreed. 'Ran into a bit of trouble. Dok Drozfang's Disorderlies showed up an' nicked da git from us, an' I can't help but wonder how dey knew where to find us.'

'Well?' Gekki said, after Snaggi had left a meaningful pause. '*I* don't know!'

'No?' Snaggi said. 'Ya didn't like me, Gekki Shortnose. Ya didn't *believe* me. Ya didn't *trust* me. I reckon yoo were scared dat I might be right,' he added, deliberately raising the volume of his voice: not enough for the runtherds behind to hear him, but definitely so that other nearby grots could. 'I reckon ya went and found da Disorderlies, an' told 'em wot we were up to, an' which way we'd gone, in order to mess me plans up!'

'Dat's ridiculous!' Gekki protested. 'I wasn't even watchin'!'

'Dere's one fing yoo're forgettin',' Snaggi told him. 'Da gods speak to me, Gekki Shortnose, an' dey told me wot ya did!'

He had his stabba out before the other grot realised what was about to happen, and sliced it across Gekki's scrawny neck. Gekki coughed and bubbled as blood began to flow, stumbled, fell, and was immediately tramped on by the grots following behind.

'*Oi!*' a runtherd bellowed, angered more by the disruption than the death, because who cared if a grot died? Who cared if twenty, fifty, a hundred grots died? Not the runtherds. Snaggi scuttled away through the mass of grots around him as one of the big gits came lumbering forward, then settled down into the same half-panicked rhythm as his fellows. The runtherd, failing to find an obvious culprit for the commotion, contented himself with laying about with his grot lash a couple of times on general principle, then fell back to survey the group from the rear again.

'Wot did ya do?' Swipe hissed in horror, from Snaggi's left.

'Da git betrayed us,' Snaggi said, shoving his still-bloody stabba back into its sheath. 'He got wot was comin' to him.'

'Are ya sure it was him?' Nib asked.

'Course I'm sure!' Snaggi snapped. 'Da gods told me!' And if that wasn't completely true – if he hadn't had the same green-tinged visions he'd had in the past, if he hadn't heard the same booming voices that were part explosion, part dakka, and part engine roar, with their words that were individually unintelligible but still capable of a generalised *sense* of what the deities were getting at – well, so what? Snaggi was a prophet of Gork and Mork, and it was surely just downright lazy to expect the gods to do all the hard work on that front. They couldn't be expected to make every little decision for him, so he would do what he knew was best, safe in the knowledge that he had their favour.

After all, if he was doing something really wrong, they could always tell him so, couldn't they?

'Just remember, ladz,' he said, as the shimmering portal loomed up in front of them. 'Dere's only one fing worse'n an ork, an' dat's a *traitor.*'

The expressions of the other grots around him were a mixture of awe, belief and fear. Snaggi grinned. He might currently be being herded along by orks with whips and beasts, who would happily feed him into the teeth of the enemy without a second thought, but right at this moment he also had *power*.

And that was a start.

SIXTEEN

Ufthak had to admit, he was impressed.

The spikiez' strange bubble city was still too dark, too weird, and extremely pointy, but it was also *big,* and an ork could respect size. With very few exceptions, the biggest ork would be in charge; bigger guns were shootier; the reasons Gargants were so big was because it was the closest an ork could come to a visualisation of their gods, and their gods were, essentially, *really* big orks.

The spikiez' bubble city wasn't as big as a planet – at least, this part wasn't – but it somehow felt bigger because it was obviously not a natural thing. Planets were planets; Ufthak didn't really think about them, other than watching and cheering from orbit when a fleet's big guns started giving whoever was down there a proper headache prior to the ladz dropping in and letting 'em have it up close (which did not mean that the big guns would stop shooting; many an ork's fun had been ended by an over-enthusiastic and under-aimed barrage from their own ships). Planets were supposed to be big; they wouldn't work otherwise.

Someone or something had built this place, and it was bigger than any other made thing Ufthak had ever seen. There was no ork war machine that would look impressive in these surroundings, not even a ship. Ufthak knew that because far, far above, the tiny shapes of spikie ships were just visible.

'We ain't in space,' Ufthak said to Da Boffin, peering through the make-bigger lenses the mekboy had given him. They brought the sharp, angular vessels into larger and clearer focus, and he could somehow tell, despite the distance and lack of obvious scale, that these were full-sized voidships rather than more of the little skimmers they'd seen so far. 'How are dey stayin' up dere?'

'Probably some sort of gravity-gubbinz,' Da Boffin opined, taking the make-biggers back and looking again. 'Da gits seem to like dat sort of fing, floatin' about everywhere like da ground's too good for 'em.'

'Sez yoo,' Ufthak said, looking meaningfully down at Da Boffin's current method of propulsion.

'Yeah, but dis just makes stairs easier,' Da Boffin said, slightly defensively. 'Da wheel was zoggin' annoying for dat. Ain't like da battlewagons've gotta worry about stairs, so I ain't lookin' to make any of 'em float just to show off.' He sucked his teef thoughtfully, and looked through the lenses again. 'So, boss. Wot's da plan?'

'Stomp da gits,' Ufthak said. As if to put the emphasis on his words, something else exploded as a Stompa's supa-rokkit detonated like a tiny sun. A chain reaction of secondary explosions followed, each one a ball of crackling dark energy shot through with veins of white lightning, and a spire some distance from the original explosion began to crack and fall.

'Sort of got dat,' Da Boffin said. 'I meant after. Let's say ya stomp all da gits in 'ere, teach 'em a lesson for sendin' hungry shadows after ya an' everyfing... What 'appens next? Are we stayin' here an' fightin' whoever shows up after dat?'

'S'pose we'd probably better get back to da rest of da Waaagh!,' Ufthak admitted. 'Da Meklord wouldn't be callin' us all togevva unless he'd got a big old fight planned, an' we don't wanna miss out on it.'

In truth, he was chafing at the idea of being summoned like a grot that hadn't done a task, and he still hadn't found anything particularly fancy he could show off like Da Meklord would be expecting. On the other hand, he was already tiring of this place. Not the fighting – that was good fun, and he had a grudge to settle – but the actual *place*. Impressively large though it was, it was dingy and dull, and Ufthak's orkish mind was rebelling against it. The whole *point* of orks was to be loud and colourful and extremely violent, and these surroundings were the anathema of that. They were old and dark and monochrome, and sound didn't quite carry properly. They were already partially ruined, so even the most enjoyable bit of destruction still felt a little as though you were just hastening a process that was going to occur anyway.

'So we're gonna need to get out of 'ere at some point?' Da Boffin said.

'Yeah, reckon so,' Ufthak said. 'Guess we can just go back da way we came, get back to dat planet I was on. Don't feel quite right, tho.'

'I know wot ya mean,' Da Boffin said, nodding. 'Orks ain't meant for goin' backwards.'

'Trouble is, we dunno wot uvver gates are gonna get us anywhere,' Ufthak continued. 'Could grab a spikie an' twist bits off it until it told us, I guess, but I ain't sure da gits wouldn't enjoy it.'

He frowned as a thought occurred to him. 'On da uvver hand… Gimme dose back a minute.'

Da Boffin handed the make-biggers over, and Ufthak put them to his eyes again. He scanned quickly across the shadowy vista laid out in front of him, but there was as yet no sign of any massive counter-offensive from the spikiez as the first wave of the Waaagh! pushed deeper and deeper into this new battle-ground, so he turned his gaze upwards again.

'Dose are definitely spikie spaceships, ain't dey?' he said.

'Yup,' Da Boffin confirmed. 'I seen da like before, several times. Nippy, blurry little gits, but dey come apart as soon as ya land a proppa shot on 'em.'

'So dey're gonna need to be able to get into space,' Ufthak reasoned. He searched around for a few seconds, then let out a triumphant grunt. 'Got it! Dere's a massive portal up dere in da ceiling-fing, big enuff for a ship to get froo. Dat's gotta lead outta dis place an' into space, and once we're in space we can go anywhere we want, jus' like before.'

'Maybe,' Da Boffin said, 'but we ain't got a ship.'

'We ain't got a ship *yet*,' Ufthak corrected him with a grin, and pointed upwards. 'Reckon ya can make one of 'em go?'

'Well, it's a bit more complicated, innit?' Da Boffin said. 'I mean dere's "go", yeah, but dere's also "stop". An' "left", an' "right", an' "up", an' "down", and den dere's da really teknical stuff like "up-left", an' "down-right", and–'

'Dis is a yes-or-no question,' Ufthak cut him off. 'Can ya fly da zoggin' fing?'

'Yeah, shouldn't be too hard if spikiez can do it,' Da Boffin said with a sniff. 'Dey might be all fancy and flip around unneces-sarily an' dat, but dere machines have got to be pretty simple to control, given how much time dey spend runnin' away.' He sucked his teef again. 'Any one of 'em take yer fancy?'

'Dey're all a bit weedy,' Ufthak muttered, which was the honest truth. Ork ships were blocky and solid, even if they were actually the halves of two different ships welded together. If there was an enemy in sight then you shot them, and if that didn't work then you rammed them: simple tactics, but effective ones, and ones which required a robust vessel to carry them out. Spikie ships were as spindly as the beings that made them, and just as prone to snapping in half if you hit them in the spine.

On the other hand, a lot of them could still deliver a decent punch. A silhouette caught Ufthak's eye and he refocused the make-biggers, kicking the magnification up as far as it could go. There was something very familiar about that…

'Zoggin' 'eck,' he muttered. He had been shot at enough by the spikiez' darklight guns to recognise their shape and profile by now, and the one he was looking at right at this moment was underslung along the belly of a spikie void-craft, and that made it *massive*. Ufthak tried to imagine the level of damage that thing could kick out, and found that he couldn't smile wide enough to envisage it. Now *that* was something not only worth having just for the destruction it could cause, but also as a prime candidate for taking back to Da Meklord and showing him that Ufthak Blackhawk *could* come up with the goods.

'Alright, I know which one I want,' he said, handing back the make-biggers. 'Da biggest one, wiv dat zoggin' great gun on da underside. Ya see it? Yoo gonna be able to get it for me?'

'Don't worry about it, boss,' Da Boffin said, beaming. 'I'll get a bunch of da ladz togevva, an' we'll get right on it. Nazlug! Yoo're in charge while I'm gone!'

Nazlug looked up in surprise, and the other spannerz around him backed away from his fire-singed shape uncertainly.

'Dere's gotta be a quick way up,' Da Boffin added, looking

around them. 'I can't see da spikiez climbin' stairs all da way to da top, don't fink dey've got da patience for it.'

'Dat's yoor problem now,' Ufthak told him. He felt a lot more at ease now he had a plan in place for getting back out into the galaxy and receiving the acclaim he was due, once he was done here. He unslung the Snazzhammer from the sticky-metal on his back and twirled it, then hopped back up onto the rear of his trukk. 'Mogrot! Get us to da fightin'!'

'Yoo got it, boss!' Mogrot replied happily, and mashed the go-pedal to the floor. The trukk accelerated away, but Ufthak's attention was caught by the smallest of details. Just for a second, before a Deff Dread got in the way and blocked his view, he was sure he saw a grot staring at him from out of a crowd of other grots that had just come through the portal. The strange thing was that the grot did not seem to be staring at him in awe, or fear, or the slack-jawed incomprehension so common to its kind; instead its expression was one of undisguised malice. What was even weirder was that although one grot looked a lot like another, Ufthak could have sworn that it was that runty git Snaggi Littletoof.

He shrugged, and turned away to let the headwind pull his lips back from his teef. So what? It wasn't as though a grot was important.

If you could say one thing for Mogrot Redtoof, it was that he generally used relentless enthusiasm to overcome whatever obstacles he found himself facing as a result of his lack of actual brainpower. If you could say a second thing about him, it was that ever since an escapade involving a shokkjump dragsta, a broken bridge, and a humie Gargant, he'd got it into his head that any vehicle could fly without issue if you drove it fast enough.

'WAAAGH!' Mogrot bellowed, and hauled on the wheel to

send the trukk careering off the side of the raised roadway on which they'd been driving, directly onto the mass of spikiez below them.

'Zoggin' idiot!' Ufthak yelled, but there was nothing for it now: the trukk was dropping like a yellow-and-black stone, with only seconds before it hit the ground. He leaped over the side, followed by a happily squealing Princess (which appeared to be assuming that this was a game) and Nizkwik, who was little more intelligent than Mogrot under most circumstances, but had a far better-developed sense of self-preservation.

Ufthak only had a moment to size up what was underneath him before he landed on it. He got a brief impression of a bipedal mass of misshapen pallid flesh, bulging with artificial muscle and studded with vials, devices and implants. It looked up at him, its attention caught by the rapidly descending shadow overhead, and he saw a bronzed mask, lined with dark slits which gave no clue as to the appearance of the face beneath, on a head that was disproportionately far too small for the body on which it perched.

Then the energised blade of the Snazzhammer's axe head smashed into that mask and carved it in two, followed in rapid succession by the thing's head, neck and torso. The monster fell apart in a welter of blood and guts, not even its formidable physique capable of standing up to the Snazzhammer when driven down by the twin forces of gravity and Ufthak's powerful arms. Ufthak had the very briefest sliver of satisfaction, just as his boots touched the ground, and then the trukk exploded behind him.

The powerful jet engines which gave a vehicle that size such immense speed needed a lot of fuel to power them, and it all went up at once. The fireball licked out, carried on the wings of a wave of concussive force so powerful that it smacked Ufthak in the back and knocked him onto his face in the messy remains of the thing he'd just killed, while Princess and Nizkwik sailed past at what had been his head height. He'd have been in trouble, had the force of the blast not flattened all the spikiez around him as well, and left everyone in the same buffeted and slightly deafened state.

All the same, this was no time to be lying around. Ufthak pushed himself back up, wiped his hands clean of bloody gunk to grip the Snazzhammer properly, and began to swing.

The spikiez here were strange ones, not like most he'd seen. Your regular spikie was just a pointier scrawnie, with more hooks and sharp edges, and generally either hidden behind their surprisingly tough armour, or moving so fast that the gits barely needed it. These ones actually had some heft to them, looked as though they got more than one meal a week, and appeared to have largely disregarded war plate in favour of a few bits of flappy cloth here and there and some surprisingly form-fitting leg coverings. The sculpted flesh of their torsos was bare – exceptionally bare in some cases, apparently lacking skin altogether and with the wet grain of muscle exposed to the air – and they pressed forward without bothering to try and dodge or block his blows, as though pain held no fear for them.

To be fair, that suited Ufthak fine, because he wasn't inflicting pain so much as catastrophic injury. He simply swatted aside the first two that came at him, knocking the first one to the right and the second one to the left with massive impact wounds in their chests, then brought the Snazzhammer straight down on the next, crushing it to a pulp. He lashed out again and knocked the head clean off another, reached out and grabbed the neck of a fifth with his free hand, broke it with a twist, and hurled the rapidly dying thing into two more of its fellows.

That broke the initial rush. The few remaining creatures fell back into the shadows, gibbering and hooting wetly from behind their featureless metal masks in voices that sounded more animalistic than anything else. Ufthak paused for a moment, and took a breath.

'Mogrot!' he bellowed, without turning around. 'Yoo dead?'

For a moment, there was no reply. Then: 'Nah, boss. Landed on me 'ead! Hey look, dere's a bunch of da ladz! Over 'ere, boyz!'

'Yoo wrecked me trukk. I *liked* dat trukk,' Ufthak said. He frowned, as a new shape appeared in the shadows in front of him. It seemed to have more arms than was usual. Had the spikiez teamed up with the bugeyes? Ufthak had heard of some unlikely alliances being forged in the crucible of necessity, but he didn't think the bugeyes teamed up with *anyone*.

'Sorry, boss! Won't 'appen again!'

The many-armed shape scuttled forward, but it didn't move like a bugeye. They were all ferocious fluidity, whereas this thing had an insectoid jerkiness to it. It was a spikie, Ufthak could see that now. It had too many arms, and a long coat, but it was definitely a spikie. He wondered why it was moving so strangely.

It was a distraction.

The big gits came at him from either side: two more like the one he'd killed when he landed, bigger even than him, and far larger than the little ones he'd just slaughtered. Each one lashed out with a massive cleaver as long as many an ork was tall, their breath hissing through the slits in their masks as they put all the power of their grotesquely over-muscled bodies into the coordinated blows.

They were coordinated too well, each one striking for his neck. Ufthak managed to catch both strikes on the Snazzhammer's haft, which through some miracle of Gork and/or Mork didn't break, then went on the offensive. These things were swift for their size, but were they the equal of Ufthak Blackhawk, big boss of the Tekwaaagh!?

He swayed away from one blade while punching the head of the Snazzhammer into the knee of the other git, caught the wrist of that one as it staggered and yanked it across to block its mate's next strike with its back. The massive cleaver hewed into pale flesh and deformed, protruding bone, and Ufthak shoved as hard as he could. Both his enemies went staggering, and as the injured one collapsed, it wrenched the blade out of the other one's hand.

The one still standing came for him, but it had to step over its mate to do so, which gave Ufthak an extra moment to set himself. The big git lashed out at him with the strange device that encased its left hand, but Ufthak met the blow coming the other way with the head of the Snazzhammer and shattered both device and the hand within, then used the axe head of his weapon to carve his enemy open diagonally. It flopped backwards, flesh and bone separating to expose glistening innards, and Ufthak brought the Snazzhammer down on the head of its prone companion just in case it got any ideas about getting up again.

A sharp sensation in his ribs alerted him to the fact that the four-armed spikie had scuttled forward and stabbed him with some very sharp fingers. Ufthak didn't even bother with the Snazzhammer; he just grabbed it by the head and hoisted it up to eye height while it wailed in pain and thrashed in a futile attempt to escape his grip.

'Wot's da big idea?' Ufthak demanded angrily. 'Woz dat meant to 'urt? Who d'ya fink yoo're dealin' wiv, my lad?' He simply squeezed: the spikie's skull cracked within a second, and it went limp. Ufthak threw it away, then shook his hand a few times to get the brains off, and looked around to see what else was going on.

What remained of his trukk was on fire. Nizkwik and Princess had re-emerged from where they'd been thrown by the blast, both moving a bit gingerly. Mogrot, blackened with soot, had clearly found a few enemies of his own to scrag, and was cheerfully approaching with a knot of boyz that included the familiar shape of Dok Drozfang.

'Boss!' the painboy said cheerfully as he stomped up. Ufthak could remember when Drozfang had been an imposing figure of saws and pinchers and syringes; these days he was just another ork, the top of his head barely reaching Ufthak's chin. 'I got me grots to get a spikie wot woz nearly dead, just in case it would come in handy, but I gave it a shot to perk it up a bit an' da git carked it, ungrateful little toe-rag dat it woz. Want us to grab anuvver one, if we can?' He looked around, and his brow furrowed. 'Of course, ya don't tend to leave nuffin' alive when ya fight, so we'd 'ave to go lookin' somewhere else.'

'Nah, don't bovver,' Ufthak said. 'We can grab one if we need it.' He scratched at his ribs where he'd been stuck. 'Dese are some right weird gits, bodies lookin' all strange an' dat – reckon yoo could learn somefing from 'em?'

He'd intended it as a joke, since Drozfang had always enjoyed mucking about with body parts – which Ufthak wasn't going to complain about, since transplants were a standard procedure for orks, and had saved his own life – but he wasn't prepared for the grimace that crossed the painboy's face.

'Urgh, no fanks, boss. I 'ad a quick look in some of da underground bits we just came past once da spikiez fightin' us were dead, and by da Great Green, dese ladz need dere heads lookin' at. Dere was one fing I saw wot had four faces, an' if any of 'em was da original den I'm a six-legged squighog.' He shuddered. 'Not sure even Grotsnik would like wot dese gits are up to, an' dat's an ork who don't take no for an answer when he asks if ya want some new legs.'

'I know wot ya mean,' Ufthak said, surprised to find that he actually did. 'Seems like anyfing wot should be fun, da spikiez find a way to make it weird.'

'Say, boss,' Drozfang said, 'yoo're scratchin' a lot.'

'Hmm.' Ufthak realised that he was indeed scratching at his ribs yet again. 'Yeah, one of da gits got me wiv 'is fingers. Didn't 'urt, but it's...' He broke off, as a sharp pain lanced through his side. 'Wot da zoggin' 'eck...?'

'Oh dear.' To Ufthak's shock, the dok actually looked worried. 'Dat ain't good. I've seen dis before when da spikiez've been about. Dey like poisons, dese ladz.'

'Poisons?!' Ufthak thundered, then leaned on the Snazz-hammer as it felt as though someone had dug a choppa into his side. 'Da bloody cheek of it!' Poison wasn't just cowardly, it was *pointless*. The whole purpose of a fight was to see how good you were and have a laugh in the process, not to stick someone once and then run off laughing behind your hand until they fell over. How could that count as winning?

'Yeah, an' da itchy sort is especially nasty,' Drozfang said, rooting through his kitbag. 'Makes ya start growin'.'

Ufthak looked at him. 'Don't sound so bad.'

'Makes ya start growin' *faster'n yer skin can keep up*,' Drozfang elaborated. 'Saw it happen to a couple of ladz a while back, dey ended up just burstin'.'

Ufthak screwed his face up. 'Dat sounds... I mean, sorta hilarious, but it ain't exactly da way I wanna go out.' He winced again. 'Okay, yeah, definitely somefing wrong in dere. Fairly sure fings shouldn't be pulsin' like dat.'

'Got it!' Drozfang exclaimed triumphantly, pulling a syringe out of his bag. 'Dis should do da trick! Hold still, boss!'

Ufthak eyed him uncertainly. Normally, letting a painboy inject you with anything was very low down on the list of things a sensible ork was prepared to tolerate, but Ufthak was pretty confident that Drozfang was invested in his survival. After all, Drozfang had mainly risen to prominence within the Waaagh! due to his association with Ufthak's rising star. As a result, he reluctantly let the painboy stick him with the needle and depress the plunger, although not without a shudder of misgiving.

'Right, now ya might feel a bit off for a while,' Drozfang said in a low voice, 'but dat's only normal wot wiv da mixture goin' on inside ya. Main fing is, ya shouldn't burst out of ya skin now.'

'Dat's good,' Ufthak nodded, blinking heavily. 'Dat's good.' He frowned and squinted upwards, as something caught his attention. 'Wossat?'

'Dat's *not* good!' Drozfang bellowed. 'Shootas out, boyz! Da sky-gits are comin'!'

Ufthak had wondered when they were going to show up. Apart from the few who had attacked when the Waaagh! first arrived in Spikie City, there had been precious few of the small, zippy gits of which you normally got so many in a spikie warband. Now they all seemed to be coming out of the sky at once, blocking out what passed for light in this place: the gits on their flying planks, the gits on the flying, single-seater warbikes that went nearly as fast as a fighta-bommer, and even the gits that had their own wings. They were banking between the spires, strafing the land-bound orks beneath them with their weapons. There weren't enough of them to turn the tide of the battle on their own, but they were going to be a zoggin' nuisance until the boyz could muster enough massed firepower to knock them down.

'Is it just me,' Mogrot began slowly, 'or are a *lot* of 'em headin' dis way?'

Ufthak squinted again, trying to focus both his eyes and his brain through what increasingly felt like thick fuzz.

'Like, a *lot*,' Mogrot added. He didn't sound worried – that would involve being able to comprehend cause and effect, which was usually beyond him – but he was definitely turning the concept over in his head. In fairness, Ufthak thought muzzily, there was a lot of space in which he could do so.

'We can't take 'em all at once!' Drozfang yelled, as the first ragged volleys of shoota fire failed to deal much damage to the incoming horde. 'Scatter!'

Ufthak watched the orks around him diving for cover behind wreckage, corpses, and corners of buildings, and wondered what the fuss was about. Even the first spattering hiss of needle fire from the sky-gits striking stone and thudding into the flesh of the spikiez he'd killed didn't really register as a problem.

'Boss!' he heard Drozfang yelling desperately. 'Get over 'ere!'

Ufthak frowned. Why was the painboy giving *him* orders? He began to turn to give Drozfang a piece of his mind, and a series of whickering thumps heralded the arrival of a line of darts in his arm. Ufthak looked down at them, wondering how they'd got there. The pain hit a moment later, but only for a moment, because then a new fuzziness – sharper and darker, somehow – began to spread through him. He was dimly aware of steely coils lashing around his wrists and ankles, and then the ground began to drop away from him. His last sight was of Princess leaping upwards and latching on to a floaty-plank with its teeth, only to be kicked in the snout until it let go and dropped back to the ground with an outraged squeal, and then blackness flooded over him completely and erased all sensation and awareness.

SEVENTEEN

'We have their chieftain,' Maculatix said, the words slipping between his sharp teeth like envenomed blades. The leaders of Port Tavarr were in a luxurious suite within the massive edifice that was the arena of the Cult of the Deathly Sorrow, and surrounded by delicacies and delights of all kinds. From the agonised crystalline statues of enemies who had fallen prey to the Glass Plague, to the artwork depicting various debauched acts, and even the mon-keigh strapped to a rack and subjected to nerve stimuli simulating the sensation of being slowly roasted alive over an open flame, Xurzuli had spared no expense on the decor. Maculatix's glass was filled with twice-tested pleasurewine, and he was reclining on an artificed couch that moulded itself to his form, but the master haemonculus was still far from relaxed.

'The initial strike was a success,' he said impatiently. 'Why are we not cutting the arakhia to shreds while they are leaderless?'

'You are free to take your forces and do so, of course,' Xurzuli Mindrex said lazily, nipping a sliver of cured volanti liver off the spike-blade of a long rondel. Dhaemira presumed the weapon was not coated with toxins, but she would not put it past the succubus to have ingested an appropriate antidote as a matter of course. Wyches might delight in the thrill of combat and the spray of arterial blood, but that did not mean they did not find satisfaction in the bloated, discoloured flesh of a poisoning victim.

'You may have forgotten,' Maculatix said crisply, 'but the purpose of this alliance was to destroy these vermin! Instead, you have your prize and have retreated again, as though you fear them.'

Xurzuli raised one perfectly sculpted eyebrow. Her blood-brides did not stiffen in response to the insinuation about their mistress' courage, since a wych was always ready to flow into deadly motion, but they definitely bristled. Still, no weapons were drawn, since Xurzuli's followers would not commence violence without her permission. If they had, then Maculatix's haemoxytes would have undoubtedly responded: the master haemonculus' prized wracks would be slower than their opposite numbers, but Dhaemira could not even begin to guess what obscene flesh-grafting and hidden biological enhancements lurked beneath their scarred skins.

'Master haemonculus,' Dhaemira said smoothly, rising to the role of peacemaker since no one else seemed to want to. 'The crux of the plan was to let the arakhia tear *themselves* apart. Our host managed to spirit her prize away, as agreed. The arakhia advance has stalled, and they are inevitably inflicting casualties upon themselves as the new hopefuls try to secure their status. Should we intervene too soon, we risk them uniting against us once more as the obvious threat. We can use this time to prepare new defences, ready our own troops and make the smaller kabals, covens, and cults fall into line, and be ready to greet the filth with murder as soon as they show any sign of regaining cohesion.'

'And you seized your own captives to have your fun with, did you not?' Xurzuli said to Maculatix.

'That is hardly the point,' Maculatix said loftily. 'Besides,' he added, 'your facilities here are rudimentary at best.'

'Our dear master haemonculus is probably just edgy since the foe was taking bites out of his domains before they were halted,' Xurzuli said lazily. She walked languidly to a table to which a naked Asuryani was strapped, and began to carve herself a piece of meat from his thigh. The trapped aeldari was so tightly secured that his attempts to thrash in pain produced almost unnoticeable results, and the puncture marks on his throat showed where his vocal cords had been severed, meaning a breathy hiss was the only disruption to Xurzuli's snacking. 'Mmm,' she added. 'Will you not try some? We have administered no sedatives, so his flesh is free of those bitter aftertastes.'

'My *domains* contain devices and locations of critical importance to all those with whom I am allied,' Maculatix snapped, waving away the succubus' offer of freshly carved flesh. 'It is in no one's interests for them to be overrun by vermin!'

'Are you saying that you are unable to defend your own halls?' Dhalgar asked, with what Dhaemira considered to be a singular lack of diplomacy.

'I would have thought you would be particularly keen to see my facilities preserved, given how recently you required them,' Maculatix responded acidly. His scissorhand snicked open and shut twice, as though he was subconsciously considering removing one of Dhalgar's limbs. Dhaemira hoped he would not, mainly because her kabal's honour would force her to respond in some manner, despite the fact that she would be secretly delighted.

Maculatix and Dhalgar continued quarrelling, in the low-key, barbed-tongued way of drukhari who had no imminent intention of drawing blood. Dhaemira sighed, and crossed to where Xurzuli stood.

'I would like to see the captive,' she said.

Xurzuli looked at her in what appeared to be genuine surprise, and swallowed the bloody morsel on which she had been chewing. 'Whatever for? You will see it tonight, when the games begin.'

That was another reason why Xurzuli was not keen to move immediately against the orks: the Arena of Deathly Sorrow hosted nightly games that the population of Port Tavarr paid great sums to attend, and the cult was not going to miss a show simply because of an invading army. The death and destruction occurring in a different part of the sub-realm would be ignored, since to do otherwise would be to admit that there was actually a threat.

'Call it simple curiosity,' Dhaemira said. In truth, she was not sure why she desired to see the ork, but it was an impulse and she was drukhari, so she indulged it.

'By all means,' Xurzuli said. 'It is being held in one of the dungeons.' She snapped her fingers, and a mon-keigh slave in the colours of the Cult of Deathly Sorrow stepped forwards, hands folded at the waist and head bowed. 'Take the master archon to see the new alien gladiator.'

The slave merely bobbed her head – she made no verbal acknowledgement of the order, because to utter 'yes, mistress' would be to suggest that there was a possibility of 'no, mistress' – and turned to lead the way. Dhaemira caught Cistrial Virn's eye as she made to follow; the archon of the Falling Night looked over at her enquiringly, and for a moment Dhaemira had a strange urge to invite her rival to accompany her.

'Can you make sure they don't do anything foolish?' she said instead, flicking her eyes towards the ongoing squabble.

Cistrial's eyes widened slightly in surprise at this demonstration of trust, but then he gave the faintest of wintry smiles, and inclined his head briefly in agreement. Still, Dhaemira felt the other archon's eyes on her as she exited the chamber, and had to fight against the expectation of a knife between the shoulder blades. Cistrial's words and actions appeared to suggest that their unexpected alliance remained firm for so long as the orkish menace persisted, but Dhaemira had picked up on oddities – lingering glances, and Cistrial positioning himself to always be near Dhaemira, yet slightly behind her or to the side, so he could observe her without her observing him in turn – that suggested there was something else going on.

She pushed her doubts to the back of her mind. Whatever her rival's motivations, Dhaemira was convinced that self-interest would see their alliance hold for now. The last thing either kabal could afford was for hostilities to erupt between them when their forces were already in such close proximity. Such a conflict would be brutal, devastating, and lead not only to Port Tavarr being weakened, but also to the bloodied remnants of each kabal surely being swallowed up by untouched rivals.

The slave led her down, away from the sweeping vistas of views enjoyed by the suite, and into the arena's windowless bowels. Passing groups of wyches gave Dhaemira hard stares, but nothing more; no matter the temptation of setting them-selves against such a lauded noble, Xurzuli's underlings knew better than to give insult to their mistress' guest and ally, lest they be the one strapped to a table with their flesh on offer for the enjoyment of all.

Had the slave guiding her been one of Dhaemira's own then she would have engaged herself in idle amusement with it, such as tripping it, pulling its hair, or otherwise accosting it. Good manners prevented her from doing so to someone else's property, but she did not bother to hide her aggravation at their pace, despite the slave's apparent attempts to hurry. The mon-keigh were just so slow and cumbersome, unless artificially enhanced in some manner. The warriors known as Space Marines were the most obvious example, greatly swollen in size and strength – and indeed speed – and encased in their primitive yet durable armour until they posed a credible threat even to aeldari fighters. Thankfully, such specimens were very few in number; the mon-keigh were a frail race by nature, and most haemonculi agreed that they had such specific requirements for genecrafting and fleshsmithing that such amusements were best carried out on other species. It was only humanity's dogged perseverance, their half-remembered yet broadly functional technology, their indifference to their own casualties, and their cloying faith in their dead god that made them such a galactic nuisance.

And then at the other extreme, Dhaemira reflected, there were the arakhia. Immensely durable, alarmingly and unpredictably innovative, and with an approach to technology which appeared to consist largely of deciding that they were going to achieve the desired result and daring the universe to prove them wrong. Unlike the mon-keigh, who could be pain-trained with relative ease into complete obedience and to perform moderately complicated tasks, an ork with any semblance of freedom would try to kill its master without hesitation. Should any drukhari find a way to control the beasts, or bring them into service, their power might even threaten the dominance of Asdrubael Vect himself.

They had reached the dungeon levels now. Wailing and gibbering reached Dhaemira's ears as they walked down row after row of cells and cages, and she could smell the sweat and fear coming off the slave in front of her. The mon-keigh's fear of drukhari was ever-present but repressed, lest it overwhelm and paralyse her, and so cause her to be executed as uselessly disobedient. The creatures around them were a new and different source of terror, however, and the slave had insufficient mental barriers in place to prevent herself from being compromised. Something slammed wetly and heavily against the door of a cell to their right, the slave jumped and gave a small squeak of fear, and Dhaemira couldn't help herself.

'Fear not, child,' she said softly, sliding her fingers through the slave's hair and clenching them into a fist at the back of the mon-keigh's scalp. 'I will protect you.'

The slave went stock-still, frozen in place by Dhaemira's touch, and the words that she understood despite the language not being her own. Her eyes, wide and terrified, flicked towards Dhaemira's face, and the archon saw two emotions writ large in the dark pupils: yearning for the protection Dhaemira's words had offered, and fear at the knowledge that she was being toyed with. There was no protection here, and the slave knew it, but that did not stop her from wishing for it with all that remained of her soul.

Dhaemira leaned close and breathed deeply, taking the scent of the slave's terror down into her lungs. Her own soul, ancient and wizened though it was, rejoiced in the suffering of another, and Dhaemira withdrew with a sigh of contentment. The refreshment was mild and brief, but enjoyable nonetheless.

'How much farther?' she demanded, and the slave jumped, then scurried off to lead the way again like a prey animal realising that the predator had withdrawn without striking. Dhaemira followed her, smiling.

The slave stopped, with another squeak of fear, when they rounded a corner and were confronted by a hideous masked form. Dhaemira did not pause, for she knew the raiment of a beastmaster when she saw it.

'You,' she snapped. 'Where is the new arakhia?'

The beastmaster regarded her silently for a moment, his mask unreadable. Then he nodded. 'You must be the archon I've been hearing about, the new ally. I'm Karfynd, the mistress' chief beastmaster. Come, it's right here.'

He gestured with his whip to the cage in front of him. Dhaemira drew level with him and looked inside, through massive bars nearly as thick as her own waist, and the shimmer of some manner of force field.

She drew her breath in sharply, and had to force herself not to take a step backwards. 'What in the name of all the Muses...?'

The cell was dimly lit, so much so that the slave was unlikely to be able to see anything within, but Dhaemira's eyes could penetrate the gloom well enough. However, she was struggling to believe them.

'The force field does not confer any sort of magnifying effect?' she asked, already sure that she knew the answer.

'No,' the beastmaster said. It was hard to tell with his mask on, but Dhaemira thought she could sense a sort of stoic amazement emanating from the other drukhari. The beastmaster knew exactly what he was looking at, but he had no idea how it had come to be.

'Then what has happened?' Dhaemira demanded. 'I fought this beast, not a day ago!'

'We believe it was injected with electrosteroids by a flesh gauntlet,' Karfynd said. 'Normally that would cause massive, uncontrolled muscle growth that would rip its skin open, but it seems to have been given some sort of counter-injection by one of its own kind. Then the sedatives used to put it under in order to bring it here slowed its metabolism, giving the counter-agent time to work, and now...' He gestured. 'Well, some of the growth has occurred, but as you can see, not how we would have expected.'

The dark mass within the cell sat up from where it had been lying on the floor, and Dhaemira met the gaze of two red eyes in a head the size of her torso. Then the ork heaved itself to its feet, its head going up, and up, and up...

The slave began to whimper, and Dhaemira caught the acrid scent of urine: the mon-keigh had lost control of its bladder in its terror. It was an understandable reaction for the weak-minded when faced with this monstrous creature, but it hardened Dhaemira's will. She had placed her hands on this slave without exacting such a level of terror. How dare this crude beast outdo her?

'Thank you for the information, beastmaster,' she said coldly. 'I wish to be alone with the creature.'

Had he been her underling, Dhaemira could have dismissed him without question. Here, in Xurzuli's realm and speaking to Xurzuli's servant, her authority was less complete. However, Karfynd apparently decided that he had no intention of arguing with an archon, so he slapped his coiled whip across the legs of the slave to make her walk, and moved off down the corridor to leave Dhaemira facing the ork chieftain on her own.

It had been big before, but it was massive now. Its clothing had ripped and torn, and there were gaping spaces between the remaining plates of its armour. It was somewhere between two and three times her height, easily larger than the biggest grotesque. She looked at its enormous fingers, as thick as her arms, and suppressed a shudder at the thought of them wrapping around her body. The creature could likely crush her to death with one hand, should it be able to catch her.

'Are you capable of speech, beast?' she asked softly. The ork's ears twitched, its eyes narrowed, and it took a single seismic step towards the bars of its cage.

'Can you speak?' Dhaemira said again, but this time she spoke

in the mon-keigh tongue they called Low Gothic. It was a bar-
baric, blocky language that stuck between the teeth, but it was
widely used and understood by many species across the galaxy,
since humanity's xenocidal manifesto did not preclude some
of its individual members from trading and negotiating if they
thought there was a benefit to be had.

The ork took another step. It was now standing right up
against the bars. It did not grab them, like a prisoner might; it
simply ignored them and stared straight at her, as though its
incarceration was of no concern.

'*Yeah,*' it said in Low Gothic, its voice a rumble as deep as
an earthquake.

EIGHTEEN

Something had happened involving the Waaagh!, the ladz, and some sort of spikie counter-attack involving sky-gits, but Da Boffin was no longer paying attention. Like many oddboyz, he was broadly capable of functioning within orkish society – indeed, his special interests were critical to it – but only for so long as those special interests were not massively overstimulated by a specific discovery or problem. He'd been given a task by Ufthak, which was to capture the biggest spikie ship with the massive gun on it, and so that was what he was going to do.

This wasn't just a question of loyalty to the big boss: Da Boffin hadn't heard of *any* mekboy capturing and flying a scrawnie ship before, of any sort, so this had become a matter of personal pride. He couldn't wait to see what sort of weird gubbinz they had on their craft, let alone how he might be able to integrate and override them with his orky know-wots.

Of course, he still had to figure out how to get to the zoggin' thing.

'Dat fing's gotta be *miles* high,' said Dreggit, one of his spannerz, looking at the spire to which the target ship was attached far, far above. 'I mean, we could fight our way up it, sure.' He nodded vigorously, as though to convince himself of the truth of what he'd just said. 'But it's gonna take a zoggin' long time. Also, da spikiez will probably realise wot we're up to, an' try to make it difficult for us.'

'Might even move da ship before we get dere,' Da Boffin said, scratching his chin.

'Whoa.' Dreggit's jaw dropped open. 'Dat's *proper kunnin'*. Good job we got yoo around to fink of stuff like dat before da spikiez do.'

'Yeah,' Da Boffin said absently. He'd amassed a sizeable chunk of ladz – not much compared to the full strength of the Waaagh!, but certainly enough to kick a bunch of spikiez off their own ship – but he'd only done so with the promise of a good scrap, so they weren't going to stick around indefinitely. That was the problem with being a mek instead of a big boss: even in the Tekwaaagh!, Da Meklord was the only mekboy with any real authority.

So, they needed to get up very high, and they needed to do it fast enough that the spikiez didn't realise what was happening before it, you know, happened. Aircraft? No, that was no good. The Waaagh! didn't have anything which could fly that could transport more than a few ladz at a time. What about putting the ladz into trukks and having the aircraft fly them up? Da Boffin dismissed that idea as soon as it occurred to him, since quite apart from the varying performance of different craft, flyboyz were notoriously capricious. They'd be more likely to forget they had something attached to them and try to zip off in different directions to blow things up.

What about fixing up some of the spikiez' wrecked vehicles?

They could float. Da Boffin toyed with the idea for a few seconds, then discarded it. Nicking one of the gits' thrusters and making himself hover with it was one thing, but trying to get a whole bunch of their sky-trukks back into working order – let alone getting orks of lesser intelligence than himself to pilot them – was something else entirely. They were zippy, wobbly things, and likely to be unforgiving of inexpert handling. He had no idea how many orks they would carry, either, given the weight discrepancy compared to their usual cargo. After all, the things had barely put up any resistance when the Waaagh!'s traktor kannons had wrenched them down into the ground…

'Dat's it!' Da Boffin exclaimed, snapping his fingers. 'Dreggit, yoo're finkin' about dis all wrong!'

Dreggit blinked. 'I am?'

'We don't gotta get up to da ship,' Da Boffin said, warming to his moment of inspiration. 'We just gotta get da ship down to *us!* Bring all da traktor kannons up! We'll pull dat fing right off da tower it's stuck to an' get it down to where we can reach it!'

'Brilliant, boss!' Dreggit said happily. 'But do ya reckon we've got enough kannons? We ain't got any of da real big space hulk-catchin' ones, an' dat fing might not be a space hulk, but it's still a fair old size.'

Da Boffin sucked his breath in between his teef, in the time-honoured manner of an expert considering his opinion. Then he reached out and clipped Dreggit round the back of the skull.

'Ow! Wossat for?'

'Yoo're finkin' about dis all wrong, Dreggit!' Da Boffin barked. 'We can't just pull da ship down! It's too big! Dis ain't like a space hulk, wiv proper planetary gravity wells an' atmosphere an' dat! Da spikiez are messin' around wiv gravity up dere, an' as soon as we tug da ship outside of it, it's gonna fall right on us an' squash us flat!'

'If yoo say so, boss,' Dreggit muttered, rubbing his head.

'I *do* say so,' Da Boffin said. 'Now, go an' get da zoggin' kannons!'

To Dreggit's credit, he took a precautionary step away before speaking. 'But boss, ya said we *couldn't* traktor da ship down to us. Ya literally said dat just now.'

'Don't tell me wot I said like dat somehow makes you da smart one!' Da Boffin roared, rounding on his spanner. 'Keep up, Dreggit. Of course we can't traktor da ship down 'ere, any grot could see dat! But who says a traktor beam can only work one way?'

Dreggit frowned. 'Uh… Dunno, who?'

'Well, whoever does, dey're wrong!' Da Boffin said irritably. 'We ain't gonna traktor da ship down. We're gonna reverse-traktor ourselves *up!*'

NINETEEN

A thrill ran through Dhaemira as the monster spoke. It was a jolt of excitement prompted by the rare sensation of a new experience, since she had never before in her centuries of life conversed with an ork. However, it was also a chill of fear – deliciously uncommon in itself – at the notion of an ork that could comprehend and respond using language. It barely mattered that the language in question was a primitive one; the sheer possibility of communication with this species felt like a gulf had opened up beneath her. The galaxy – or her understanding of it – had changed, and change sat ill with a culture that had existed in the same way for tens of millennia.

'Do you have a name, creature?' she asked, fascinated and appalled at the same time. In response, the ork coughed out a collection of aggressive-sounding syllables. Then it grinned at her, showing a mouth full of massive ivory fangs, and spoke again.

'In da humie language, yoo'd call me Ufthak Blackhawk.'

The name was barely any smoother when rendered into mon-keigh sounds, but it was at least vaguely intelligible. Dhaemira stored it away for reference. Anything she could learn about this brute and its kin might be of use in ensuring her victory.

'I know yoo,' the ork said, unprompted. Its brow was furrowed in concentration. 'Yoo're da spikie boss wot made like ya wanted to fight, but just danced around a lot.'

Dhaemira bristled, but she had little comeback. She'd not even managed to land a blow on the monster, and it was only thanks to her own immense skill and agility that it had failed in its own attempts.

'Ya took out Uzgit an' his ladz well enuff,' the ork said. 'Dat woz some good scraggin'.'

Dhaemira blinked. Had the thing just… *complimented* her?

'So,' the ork said, looking around its cell as though seeing it for the first time, 'I ain't dead. Guess yoo gits've got a plan.'

'You will be placed into the arena this evening,' Dhaemira said. 'There you will be matched against the deadliest oppo-nents and the most dangerous beasts that Commorragh has to offer, until you die.' She smiled at the thought, until she realised that the ork was smiling back at her.

'Sounds good to me.'

'"Good"?' Dhaemira folded her arms. 'Did you not under-stand me, you witless brute? This is a death sentence for you!'

'Gonna die at some point,' the ork replied with a shrug. 'Might be today, might be tomorrow, might be when da sun blows up an' fries everyfing. So long as it's violent or funny, I ain't bovvered.'

Dhaemira was rendered speechless for a few moments. It was one thing to scoff at the orks' disdain for casualties, to assume that they were mindless beasts that had no concept of mor-tality. It was quite another to be smacked in the face with the realisation that they understood it and simply *didn't care.* Every aspect, every single facet of drukhari society was concentrated on extending one's lifespan for as long as possible. They sheltered in the webway to avoid the attention of She Who Thirsts, they nourished their souls with the suffering of others in order to stave off their own deaths. Nobles such as herself devoted great swathes of their wealth to their own protection, in the certain knowledge that others of her own kind desperately wanted her dead simply so they could seize the resources she controlled and use them to lengthen their own lives that bit further.

The notion that orks didn't fear death, that there was no lurking, malicious entity – that they knew of – waiting to torture them for all eternity in the darkness that lay beyond their final breath... Why should this species of barbarians enjoy such luxury? Why should they be so carefree? How could they have such life, such *vitality,* and still seek to squander it amidst the thunder of guns? For the briefest of moments, Dhaemira had a vision of something else: a life in which the shadow of She Who Thirsts did not cast a subtle blight on every waking moment and trail its fingers through her dreams; a life in which she did not have to cling desperately to her own existence by torturing other beings, lest she suffer far more hideous torments when the spark of her own soul sputtered out. A life in which she could just... live.

It made her *furious.*

'You are savages!' she hissed. 'Do you even know *why* you fight?'

'Yeah,' Ufthak said. 'Do ya know why yoo do?'

Dhaemira frowned. 'What?'

'Orks always fight,' the massive creature rumbled. 'Always 'ave. It's wot we woz made for, but it ain't just dat. It's wot da gods want, but it ain't just *dat.* See, da more we fight, da bigger we get.' It tapped itself on the chest with one massive finger. 'Da bigger we get, da smarter we get.' It tapped itself on the side of the head. 'An' da smarter we get, da better we get at fightin'. If we don't fight, we get slow an' stoopid, an' den we might forget about da gods. We might forget about tellyportas, an' Gargants, an' boomdakka snazzwagons–'

'You're just making words up now!' Dhaemira broke in angrily, then took a step back as the ork lashed out with a punch. It passed between the bars and struck the force field, which held with a crackling boom of energy, but the thing's arms were long enough that it would have reached her had that protection not been there.

'I woz *talkin'*,' the ork growled, and the hairs on the back of Dhaemira's neck stood up as the subsonic harmonics of the creature's voice shivered through her bones.

'I've seen yoo lot fight,' Ufthak continued. 'Dunno why ya do it. Ya don't enjoy it.'

'We do!' Dhaemira snapped, but the ork waved her words away.

'Nah. Yoo enjoy *killin'*. Yoo enjoy showin' off, provin' dat yoo're better'n da uvver gits an' makin' sure dey realise it, but ya don't enjoy *fightin'*. How're ya gonna enjoy fightin' when ya can't take a punch?' It held up one arm. 'One of yer mates cut dis hand off once – I had to get a new one off some git wot probably didn't deserve to 'ave two of his own. An' dere was one time before dat when me whole body got blown out from under me head, dat woz a good laugh. Dat's how ya can tell it's a good fight, but yoo spikiez would just sneak up behind gits an' stab 'em in da back like a buncha Blood Axes.'

'You seem particularly sure of your own delusions,' Dhaemira scoffed. 'And I do not, incidentally, know what a "Blood Axe" is, nor do I wish to learn. But tell me something, creature – if you are so intelligent, and you know us so well, why was it so easy for Xurzuli's underlings to capture you?'

'Weren't dis smart before,' Ufthak said. 'I woz gettin' dere, but I weren't dis smart. Den dat git stabbed me wiv da grow-juice, an' when I woke up everyfing was smaller'n wot it woz, an' me brain woz bigger.'

'And much good may it do you!' Dhaemira said, affecting a gaiety that she did not entirely feel. This ork, this serious, calculating ork that accepted its imprisonment but which she could tell was ever alert for any sign of weakness or opportunity, had rattled her. 'I trust you realise that your army is even now going to be tearing itself apart as your subordinates try to elevate themselves to your former position.'

'Da strongest'll win,' Ufthak said with another shrug. 'Dat's da way of it. Da Waaagh! will get started again, an' dey'll come for yoo like we woz doin' anyway. 'Specially since I'm da only one wot knows how to get 'em out of 'ere,' it added slyly.

Dhaemira regarded it carefully. 'You're what?'

'I know how da portals work,' Ufthak said carelessly, leaning on the bars of its cell with one hand and inspecting the fingers of the other. 'Gotta 'ave one of yoo gits around, usually. Mind yoo, I managed to force dat one wot got us froo into dis bit of wherever da zog we actually are. Just needed a bit of finkin' from me, an' a powerful urge from da ladz to kick all of yer teef in.'

Dhaemira bit her lip. The ork's ploy was blatant, especially to one such as she, who had been steeped in the byzantine power plays of Commorragh's high societies since before she could walk. It was angling for her to release it, and dangling the prospect of it leading its army away as the reward for her cooperation.

Fine. She could play along, if only to demonstrate to it how superior her intellect was, no matter how large a brain it had now.

'But why would you "get them out of here"?' she asked innocently. 'After all, all you wish to do is fight, and you still have plenty of enemies here.'

Ufthak didn't reply for a few seconds. It just looked at her, its head tilted slightly to one side. Then it grunted, and spoke.

'Are you da boss?'

'What?'

'Da boss. In charge,' Ufthak elaborated, as though she had somehow not comprehended the meaning of the words, as opposed to why it was asking. 'Do da uvver spikiez do wot ya say?'

'Yes,' Dhaemira said firmly.

Ufthak leaned closer to the bars. '*All* of 'em? Dere's not a single spikie wot tells ya wot to do?'

An image of Asdrubael Vect flashed unbidden into Dhaemira's mind – only an image, for she had never been privileged enough to lay eyes on the Living Muse, but his cold, cruel visage was burned into her memory from hologlyphs and statuary. She wanted to lie, because it burned her to admit weakness in front of this *brute*, but the tiny tendrils of worry that the Overlord of the Dark City would hear of even this tiny disobedience had already taken root in her brain, and brought forth their fruit in the form of all the painful, terrible ways his displeasure would make itself known.

'Yeah, fort not,' Ufthak said with a deep chuckle when she didn't answer immediately. 'Yoo're *a* boss, but yoo're not da *real* boss.' It stood back again. 'An' dat's da same as me.'

Dhaemira raised her eyebrows. 'You are *not* in charge of this rabble?'

'Dis lot? Oh yeah,' the ork said. 'But dat's just a part of da Tekwaaagh!, see? Da rest of 'em are out dere somewhere, led by Da Meklord, Da Biggest Big Mek. He's been givin' da orders for as long as I've been in da Waaagh!, an' to be honest,' it continued conspiratorially, 'I'm gettin' a bit sick of it. I could stay 'ere an' keep stompin' yoo gits, make a little empire of me own in yer back yard, but dat ain't really satisfyin'. We've 'ad a good scrap, now I wanna get back out dere an' have a word wiv Da Meklord about who should *really* be in charge.'

It grinned again, and Dhaemira realised it was waiting for her response. The void-cursed thing actually thought it had appealed to her through some sense of kinship, of shared struggle, and was waiting for her to release it!

It would be disappointed.

'The more you fight, the bigger you get, and the smarter you get,' she said, as if musing. 'And you have no fear of the arena since you are unconcerned by a violent death, nor indeed when your life ends so long as you consider that end to be a worthwhile one. So what would happen,' she added, approaching right up to the force field that separated her from the monstrous beast, 'if you were to just… stay there?'

Ufthak blinked. 'Wot?'

'No arena. No death. No mobs of your own kind, and certainly no *fighting*,' Dhaemira said. 'Just those four walls, with everything else out of reach. I wonder how long it would take you to degenerate, if your body does not get whatever hormonal stimulus violence evidently releases within its cells. Will you shrink? Will you lose the intelligence that allows you to converse with me? Will you eventually lose even the memory of your own gods? Not that you would be of much interest to them, by the sounds if it, if you remained cooped up in a cell without the ability to engage in combat of any sort.'

Very slowly, with an audible creaking of flesh and popping of joints, Ufthak's massive hands clenched into fists.

'It will be fascinating to observe,' Dhaemira said lightly. 'And observe it I shall, because no matter how long you continue to draw breath, I will be here. The army that was once yours might make us bleed before they die, but they will die, and they will never reach here, or find you. No one will rescue you. No one will even *kill* you. I will take great pleasure in watching you wither, in the process losing every semblance of self that a beast like you can claim to have. You see, while you need to fight, all *my* people require to survive is the suffering of others. Normally we inflict that through physical pain, but with such a naturally resilient wretch as yourself,' she said with a smile, 'I am intrigued to see whether your growing despair will suffice.'

'See, I fort we might've had some sort of agreement comin' along,' Ufthak growled. 'I fort you might be *smart*. Turns out yoo're just as stoopid as every uvver weedy little scrawnie wot finks dey know how fings are gonna go. How's dat been workin' out for ya so far? Have da orks been doin' everyfing ya fort we would, an' nuffin' else?'

Dhaemira refused to be browbeaten by this towering wretch. She kept her superior smile on her face and stepped backwards from the cage, then turned and began to walk away.

'Fightin' should be *fun*,' Ufthak continued to rumble from behind her. 'Yoo lot can't even get dat right, wiv yer knives an' yer "look at me, I'm da best" nonsense. If yoo were a proppa fighter, yoo an' me would be scrappin' right now!'

Dhaemira continued to walk away, and the monstrous ork began shouting louder and louder behind her, until its voice filled the entire dungeon like thunder.

'Alright den, spikie! Yoo gotta know I'm gonna get out of 'ere, an' one way or anuvver I'm gonna find ya, an' I won't be fightin' for fun. I'm gonna make ya suffer! Ya hear me, spikie? *I'm gonna make ya SUFFER!*'

TWENTY

Da boss is gone.

The words ran through the Waaagh! faster than buggy fuel through a grot's digestive system.

Da boss is gone.

It wasn't always even actual words, or at least not *those* actual words. It was a sense, a feeling, some form of innate knowledge that spread from one ork to another without the individual vectors being conscious of it. One moment the ork knew what they were doing and why, and the next there was a splinter of uncertainty worming its way inwards. Without a big boss, who was in charge? If two nobs were arguing over something, who was going to set them straight and tell them what the truth was? Something didn't have to be factual to be the truth, not yet; truth was whatever orks told the galaxy it was. Whatever the ork in charge said the truth was then *became* the truth, and then the Waaagh! would set itself towards making sure the galaxy reflected the truth.

Now the truth was *da boss is gone,* and that meant that all other truth was briefly suspended until a new boss was found. Of course, various orks had their own ideas about the truth of who the new boss was going to be.

Various orks, and one grot.

Snaggi was aware of the change before any of his followers were. He'd experienced it before, although he'd had the advantage at that point of being the one who'd caused a Gargant head to fall on top of the warboss in question, so the state of affairs had been pretty obvious. However, he recognised the way the air prickled as new tensions began to flow out through the assembled orks around them.

He adopted a suitably heroic stance – feet apart, fists on his hips, and head tilted back slightly – then closed his eyes ostentatiously. When he was sure that enough of his followers would have noticed, and just before any runtherds nearby started to twig that something odd was going on, he opened his eyes again and gasped theatrically.

'Da big boss has gone!'

The heads of the grots around him whipped around, until he was the centre of a crowd of wide eyes and attentive ears.

'Da gods told me!' Snaggi announced. It wasn't difficult to sound both shocked and excited, given that was exactly how he felt. What in the name of the Great Green had the spikiez pulled out that had allowed them to off Ufthak Blackhawk? More importantly, how could Snaggi Littletoof, Prophet of Gork an' Mork and the first-ever grotboss, turn this situation to his advantage?

One thing was for sure, dallying wasn't going to achieve anything.

'Dis is our chance, ladz!' he announced. 'Who's da obvious choice to replace Ufthak?'

The assembled grots looked at each other, and came up with a variation of mumbles on a general theme of uncertainty.

'Exactly!' Snaggi said with glee. 'Dere ain't one! Dat means confusion, an' confusion is something we can use! Da ork war machine can't function wivout us, so dis is our chance! Nick stuff, hide stuff, an' break stuff. By da time da orks've worked out who dey *fink* is in charge, da Waaagh! ain't gonna be goin' anywhere! If dey want da vehicles to go, or da guns to shoot,' he continued proudly, 'dey're gonna 'ave to come beggin' to us. *Beggin'!*'

'Uh, boss?' Nib asked, tentatively raising a hand. Snaggi hated it when grots did that, since it usually meant they were either slowing his momentum with a ridiculous question or, more rarely but more frustratingly, had come up with what they thought was a logical hole in his argument that he would momentarily and inexplicably be unable to answer, despite the obvious difference in intelligence between them and him.

'Yes, Nib?' he said, warily.

'Why wouldn't da orks just stomp us for wreckin' everyfing?' Nib asked. 'I mean, dey're gonna be pretty mad.'

'Maybe, maybe,' Snaggi said. '*But,* ya gotta remember dat dere's gonna be a zoggin' big scrap while dey work out who's in charge, an' dat ain't a fight for grots. Wot ork's gonna say he should be in charge because *grots* won da fight for 'im? None of 'em! So wot I'm sayin' is,' he continued, 'dere's gonna be a lot less orks in a while, but da same amount of us as dere is now, so maybe dey're gonna have to listen to *us* for a change!'

'If dere's gonna be a lot less orks, wot's gonna stop da spikiez from scraggin' us?' another grot asked, in the nervous tones of one who had seen a bit of scraggin' as performed by spikiez and had already decided that he wanted no part of any such thing.

'Yoo gotta stop finkin' dat da orks are gonna protect ya!'

Snaggi barked, stepping forward and slapping the other grot around the face. 'Da shame of it! Ain't ya worked it out yet? Da only fing we're good for, so far as an ork finks, is dyin' in wotever way dey choose! Yoo can bet yer last toof dat'll mean gettin' shot by da spikiez' poison needles, or somefing just as bad! Wotcha got to lose?'

'Well, all me innards, for starters–'

'Look, if freedom an' glory was gonna be won froo cowardice an' petty feevin' den grots would already have it!' Snaggi said, turning in a circle to address his audience. 'We gotta fink bigger! We gotta take *risks*! *We* need to be da ones in charge of all da best stuff. So get out dere, an' seize da means of destruction!'

'Yoo heard da boss!' Gip shouted, leaning into his role as Snaggi's right-hand grot and general heavy. 'Get to it!'

'An' sharpish!' Snaggi added, as movement caught his eye. 'Dere's a runtherd comin'!'

The crowd of grots scattered like a gathering of corpse squigs exposed to the light by a body being turned over – a sight many of them were familiar with, since the dead often had things worth nicking but rarely fought back, unless it was a very bad day – and Snaggi went with them, for there was no sense blowing his cover by being found making inflammatory speeches. He hastened along through the gradually increasing chaos of the ork army, cursing his natural aura of greatness, which drew distrustful orks towards him. He didn't want to *be* average, but it would be useful for others to sometimes *perceive* him as average, rather than the smart, charismatic leader of exceptional grace–

'Oof!'

'Oof!'

Snaggi fell in a tangle of limbs, not all of them his own. He feared for a moment that he'd collided with an ork, but he knew that was wrong even before he'd managed to thrash himself free. The force of the impact and the pitch of the clumsy git's grunt led to one conclusion: another grot.

In fact, it led to one *specific* conclusion.

'Nizkwik?' he said, picking himself up.

'Snaggi!' Nizkwik yelled, lurching back to his own feet. 'Yoo gotta come quick! Dey've taken da boss!'

'Dey've *taken* da boss?' Snaggi said, frowning. 'Who's taken 'im?'

'Da spikiez!' Nizkwik wailed, as though that should be obvious. 'Dey came wiv dere sky-gits an' shot 'im full of darts, but den dey grabbed 'im an' flew off! He dropped da Snazzhammer an' everyfing! Da boss has been *captured*, an' no one knows wot to do!'

Snaggi hesitated. On the one hand, Ufthak out of the way was still Ufthak out of the way; it would likely lead to strife within the Waaagh!, and exactly the sort of confusion he was banking on to make his grab for power.

On the other hand, Ufthak out of the way was a very different proposition to Ufthak being dead. The big old git was likely to take some killing anyway, and Dok Drozfang had by all accounts saved him when he should have been a goner once before, but Snaggi would have been prepared to take his chances on even an eighty per cent or so likelihood of Ufthak actually having carked it. An Ufthak who'd only been captured, though? That was a problem. There was a very low chance of him actually being dead, since the spikiez probably thought they could have some fun with him, and given his stubbornness and general ingenuity, quite a high chance of him somehow finding his way back to the Waaagh!.

Snaggi was a visionary, but he was a realistic one. Seizing control from Ufthak Blackhawk, an established and massive big boss, was going to be a long shot; that was why he hadn't tried it yet. Seizing control from a newly minted successor was far more achievable, albeit still risky. Going to all the trouble to seize control from said newly minted successor, but with the very real chance of Ufthak returning and being very displeased with what he found? That, to Snaggi, seemed like a poor use of his time and energy.

'So why'd ya come lookin' for *me*?' he asked, which seemed to be the logical next question, at least while he figured out how to ditch Nizkwik.

'Yoo're da smartest grot I know!' Nizkwik wailed. 'None of da orks've got any ideas about how to find da boss! Dey're all just standin' around arguin'!'

'Course dey are,' Snaggi chuckled, thoroughly tickled by the mental image conjured by Nizkwik's words. 'Course dey are! Bet none of 'em even fort about trackin' da signal from da hammer, eh?'

Nizkwik's eyebrows squeezed up close together, in an external representation of his two brain cells trying to fire a few neurones and work out what Snaggi meant. 'Da signal from da hammer?'

'Yeah,' Snaggi said, still laughing at the thought of how much smarter he was than all the other orks. 'I used to work for a mekboy, y'know! Da Boffin modified da Snazzhammer so da boss can tellyport it back to 'im, but in order for dat to work, da hammer an' da boss' wrist armour have gotta know where da uvver one is, right? So dere's gotta be a signal between 'em. If ya hooked up a gizmo to da hammer, den yoo could work out wot direction da boss is in, an' follow it right to 'im!' He laughed, and slapped Nizkwik on the back. 'Dat's da problem wiv orks, dey ain't got da brains!'

'Snaggi,' Nizkwik breathed. 'Yoo're a genius!'

'Yeah, I know,' Snaggi said modestly, then frowned as Nizkwik turned and began to sprint away. 'Oi! Where're ya goin'?'

Realisation struck with the speed and force of a squiggoth's kick, and left Snaggi breathless. He'd been *tricked!* He'd been *betrayed!* Not only had Nizkwik shamelessly unearthed the crucial information that only Snaggi's wisdom could have known, the little git was now going to claim it as his own too!

Well, the buzzer squigs were out of the jar now, and no mistake. One way or another, the orks of the Tekwaaagh! were going to find out how to track down their missing big boss, and so scupper Snaggi's best chance of overthrowing the unjust power structures and becoming Da Grotboss in truth. Only one question remained: was he going to let Nizkwik take the credit, and complete Snaggi's humiliation? Or was he going to salvage what he could from his fellow grot's treachery, and at least trick Ufthak into thinking that he was loyal when the big boss was retrieved, in order to get the brute to lower his guard for some as-yet-unformulated scheme in the future?

There was only one answer to that question.

'Get back 'ere, ya little toe-rag!' Snaggi bellowed, and set off in pursuit of Nizkwik's rapidly receding form.

TWENTY-ONE

Ufthak was angry.

He was angry because the spikie had sassed him, and he was angry because despite being angry, he hadn't been able to grab it and rip it apart. He was angry because he knew that the spikie knew that, and had sassed him not just to make him angry, but to make him angry *because* he couldn't get to it. It had knowingly made him angry with his own anger, and that just made him even angrier.

However, as the immediate anger began to cool slightly, Ufthak noticed a different feeling. It was an unfamiliar one – a sort of hollow in the middle of him, a bit like being hungry, but without any notion that eating something would make it go away. He'd never really experienced anything like it before, although on the other hand, he'd also never experienced anything like being trapped in a small metal cage with no prospect of anything to fight, or any way to get out. He'd hammered on the walls, and the force field beyond the bars, but even his impressively large new frame had been unable to make much more than a dent.

He considered the possibility that this was a specific emotion relating solely to being trapped in a small metal cage with no prospect of anything to fight or any way to get out, but he had a nasty feeling that it was the 'despair' the spikie had talked about.

It was not a concept with which Ufthak was familiar, because there were very few situations in a normal ork's life where it would apply. You were either fighting, or you were doing the things that you did between fights, like eating, or sleeping, or repairing the weapons you used to fight, or travelling to find a fight, or so on. If you didn't find a fight, you could always punch the ork next to you and start one; your nob didn't always like that, but then you might end up fighting the nob, which was still a fight, so the basic goal had been achieved.

The point was that orks lived in the moment, and those moments were often violent, which suited them fine. You found fights, you had fights, and then you were either looking for the next fight, or you were dead – which wasn't ideal, since it meant no more fights, but at least showed that you'd really put your all into the last one. The notion of no fights, and not being able to find a fight, not even having another ork next to you to punch...

Ufthak didn't understand spikiez, and was fairly sure he didn't want to either, since he'd probably have to tie his brain into knots to do it, but the spikie boss had seemed to be telling the truth when she said that they needed others to suffer. It certainly explained a lot about why they did some of the weird things they did (although it opened up a bunch of other questions that he was equally fairly sure he didn't want to dwell on – finkin' had its limits, after all). An ork would never consider having a giant enemy on hand and *not* fighting them, but if a spikie thought that the captive would enjoy the fight, might they not keep them caged up instead? It was vicious, and weird, and therefore fitted in with everything Ufthak knew about the gits.

Still, scrawniez of all flavours had a tendency to think they were smarter than they actually were, which left them open to making mistakes. He thumped the wall once more, to no obvious effect, then glared across the dark corridor at the cell facing him on the other side. There was something in there, although he couldn't make out exactly what.

'Oi!' he shouted, using the humie language. 'Yoo! Got any ideas fer how to get outta dis place?'

There was a dry slithering sound, as of scaled coils shifting against each other, and then dark, viscous liquid splattered against the opposite cell's corresponding force field. It began to drip downwards, smoking as it did so.

'Guess dat's a "no",' Ufthak muttered, and sat down to wait for whatever opportunity might present itself.

The passage of time was hard to mark in the spikie city anyway, let alone in the windowless depths of wherever Ufthak was. However, he had been waiting long enough to grow actually, properly hungry when the next development occurred.

That development being that the floor gave way beneath him and dropped him into a shaft.

'*Wot da zog?*' he bellowed in surprise as he fell, bouncing off the walls as he did so with clatters and bangs when his armour plates made contact. He reached out, spreading his arms and legs, and managed to brace himself. The palms of his hands grew unpleasantly warm in the process, but he'd experienced far worse, and he came to a halt spreadeagled above an ongoing drop that the dim light from his cell above failed to penetrate.

Ufthak considered for a moment. He might, with an enormous amount of effort, be able to climb back up to his cell. But what would be the point of that? He didn't *want* to be in his cell;

that was quite possibly the worst place for him to be. Unless the spikiez had some equivalent of a rogue mekboy pulling levers for the fun of it – which, granted, wasn't out of the question – being dropped down a chute was actually an improvement. It suggested that someone wanted him somewhere for something, and there was a good chance that would either be a fight, or he could make it into one.

'Here goes nuffin',' Ufthak muttered, and let go.

Whatever other fancy tricks the spikiez might be able to play with gravity, they weren't doing it here. He plummeted downwards, and was just starting to consider the likely consequence of his new and greater weight impacting on a flat surface after a fall from this height – a consequence for which words like 'splatter' might be appropriate – when the shaft began to curve and his fall turned into a fast and somewhat uncomfortable slide. He had time enough to see slits of light ahead of him – a grate of some sort – before his feet hit it, it gave way, and he was through.

And falling again.

The drop was only about that of his own height this time, and he landed in dust and a cacophony of noise with nothing bruised other than his pride. He sprang back up to his feet – his new bulk didn't seem to have slowed him down, at any rate – and took stock of his surroundings.

First of all, the exit through which he had just slid was already sealing itself shut again. It was set in a wall that rose considerably higher than his head, and ran off as far as his eye could see on either side of him. And above it…

Spikiez. Lots and lots and *lots* of spikiez.

There were far more of the gits than he could count, and Ufthak found that he could count quite high now. They were mainly seated, although here and there was one jumping up or moving about, or two – or more – pressed up against each other in a manner that suggested they were completely oblivious to their surroundings. A lot of them were looking at him, and a lot of them were shouting. It didn't sound like a war cry. It sounded... Well, it sounded like a thin, weedy version of the roar that orks might make when watching a race between the speed freeks.

Somewhat distrustfully, Ufthak turned away from the wall of shouting spikiez and looked behind him.

It was... war.

Only different.

Far above him, spikiez tore through the sky on their flying warbikes, engaged in combat with other spikiez on floaty-planks as each group slalomed through poles and narrow towers that rose up from the arena floor. Ufthak saw a hail of glittering shards pierce the body of one of the plank-riders, which lost control of its ride and began to fall the long distance to the ground as a limp shape trailing blood. The biker that had made the kill pumped the air with its fist in celebration as the noise of the crowd swelled, but clearly forgot to keep paying attention: it flew into *something* that Ufthak could barely make out as more than a few faint, shimmering lines strung between towers, and then both it and the bike it was riding on came apart into several pieces as neatly as if they'd been chopped by a giant, invisible cleaver.

Off to Ufthak's right, a massive two-legged reptilian roared. It was larger than many a squiggoth, with an enormous, sharp-toothed head balanced out by a long tail, and powerful hind legs on which it moved with surprising speed and surety as it ran down the tiny figures around it. Ufthak grunted as he recognised them as scrawniez – even thinner than usual, clad in rags, and with only rough stubble where many of their kind boasted long, flowing hair. Prisoners or slaves, then, or some other group that had fallen foul of whichever boss was running this. They had very un-spikie weapons, little more than sharpened poles. There was no evidence of poisoned darts or the sort of bitterly sharp blades that were the spikiez' usual hallmark, and also no evidence that the crude tools they did have were serving as any sort of deterrent to the predator.

Far to Ufthak's left, a more even sort of battle was taking place. The ground looked to have been laid out especially for the purpose, with pools of glistening blue water, bulbous-trunked trees, and strangely smooth white walls. A ragged group of humies were exchanging weapons fire – mainly their light-zappa guns and their tiny, chattering shootas – with a group of blue-skinned fishboyz. There were fewer of the fishboyz, but Ufthak reckoned they had a good chance: everyone knew they couldn't fight worth a damn once you got up close, but their guns were the business. The humies were hanging back, unwilling to risk the small area of open ground between them and their enemies, but Ufthak could instantly tell that was a mistake. His analysis was borne out when a brilliant bolt of energy seared from one of the fishboyz' guns and stabbed straight through a wall to incinerate a humie crouching behind it.

Ufthak chortled. You couldn't win a dakka war with fishboyz; you had to take the hits to get in close, then let 'em have it. 'They don't like it when you hit 'em inna face,' as Badgit Snazzhammer had said once, and Ufthak had seen the truth of that several times.

Thinking of Badgit reminded him that he didn't have a weapon. He closed his hand experimentally and felt the button depress, but the Snazzhammer failed to materialise anywhere remotely near him. Da Boffin had said there was a range limit on the tellyporta, but that it should work within any distance

Ufthak was capable of throwing it. The spikiez had obviously taken him rather further than a hammer throw away from his ladz.

Two objects blurred down at him from the sky, and he threw one arm up to shield his face and drew the other back ready to lash out, but the flying things stopped just short of punching range. When they didn't start shooting, Ufthak lowered his arm a bit and studied them.

They were strange, except they were spikie things, so 'strange' was sort of expected. They appeared to be giant, independent lenses, kept aloft by one or more of the myriad blinking lights and protrusions on the frames that surrounded them. They bobbed loosely in the air, buffeted by air currents from distant explosions or swirled up by the overhead races, but the lenses themselves remained steadily fixed on him.

'Dis place,' Ufthak said firmly, 'just gets weirder an' weirder.'

The air flickered somewhere in what was presumably the arena's middle – not that Ufthak could really see the other side, given the variations of terrain and ongoing battles that were in the way – and a truly massive spikie appeared. It was taller than a Gargant, but Ufthak could see the haziness and rough edges that made it clear it was a projection rather than the real thing. Just as well: even he would have struggled to fight a spikie that big.

The spikie began to speak in their silly, fluid language. Ufthak waited a couple of seconds to make sure he hadn't suddenly learned how to understand it, then was going to go back to looking for a weapon, when two things happened in quick succession. Firstly, he recognised another spikie, just in shot behind the one that was on its feet and speaking: it was the boss from the dungeon, the boss he'd fought before! It was looking very displeased, and Ufthak grinned as he realised what must have happened. That boss had wanted him to stay trapped, but *this* boss had decided it wanted him to fight in the arena after all! Well, that was entertaining.

Secondly, two images of himself appeared in front of the speaking spikie. He was rather smaller, and being looked down on; the spikiez were seeing him as the flying lenses were seeing him. The speaking spikie gestured to him with a sneer, and the crowd erupted into raucous jeers and bellows.

Ufthak shrugged. He couldn't care less what spikiez thought about him. It looked like he was being given the opportunity to fight, which suited him, and he didn't care if it also suited them. Perhaps he'd find a way to turn the tables on an entire arena full of spikiez; if not, he'd have a good scrap on the way. What more could he ask for?

The ground a little way in front of him started to shake, and then a cage erupted from the arena's dirt floor. There was a moment's dramatic pause, and then the front dropped open. A large shape emerged, twisting itself to get its overlarge shoulders through the doorway. The multiple dim lights from above glinted off familiar armour, made from the same substance that still decorated much of Ufthak's torso.

Ufthak's face broke into a broad grin. They'd given him his very own beakie to play with!

TWENTY-TWO

The beakie, Ufthak noted, didn't seem particularly pleased to be there. That was a bit odd, since beakies were the most ork-like of all humies: they didn't tend to run away from a good scrap, and kept fighting even after they'd taken a proper kicking, so you'd have thought that this sort of place would be great for one of them. However, beakies also hated anything that wasn't a humie, and rather than enjoying a fight because it meant they could kill some non-humies, they sometimes appeared to resent the fact there were even non-humies for them to fight in the first place. There was an underlying current of bitterness that seemed to suck out a lot of the joy that should have been there.

It was all rather confusing. Ufthak didn't actually *hate* anyone or anything, not really. There were plenty of things he didn't like that much in the galaxy, and which he thought were weird or odd or annoying, but he could fight most of them, so they weren't that bad. Beakies, though, they had a hatred that *burned*.

Still, Ufthak wasn't the one who'd put the beakie here, whereas presumably the spikiez had, much like they had with Ufthak. Beakies were capable fighters; perhaps this one would be willing to listen to reason.

'Oi, beakie!' Ufthak yelled in the humie tongue, pointing at the crowd behind him. 'Wanna scrag dese gits?'

The beakie – armoured in dark blue apart from its gauntlets, which were a vivid crimson – didn't answer. It just reached into the cage from which it had just emerged, pulled out a chain-choppa, ignited the motor with a flick of a switch, and charged at Ufthak with a bellow.

Oh well.

Ufthak hadn't faced a beakie since he'd become a nob, let alone since the growth spurt he'd experienced after becoming big boss. He remembered them as ork-sized or larger, swift and deadly and encased in armour that was nigh-impossible to crack. You needed a rokkit launcha or a power klaw to really get at them, or to hold one down and a bunch of the ladz to give it a going over with their choppas until someone found a gap or a weakness.

That was then, however, and 'ork-sized' was a poor descriptor given the size of orks was far more variable than that of humies. Ufthak waited until the beakie came into range, then lashed out with a punch.

Humies had short arms anyway compared to orks, although their legs were somewhat longer. Ufthak's fist thudded into the beakie's chest before its chain-choppa could even reach his torso, and although his knuckles smarted a bit immediately afterwards, beakies were nowhere near as solid as he remembered. The overgrown humie staggered back and sat down in the dirt of the arena floor with a startled expression on its face, and pieces of splintered decoration dropping off its breastplate.

'Yoo got any mates wiv ya?' Ufthak asked, shaking his hand out. 'Somefing to make dis a bit more interestin'?'

This was apparently the wrong thing to say, judging by the way the beakie leapt back to its feet and flew at him again. Rage made for an excellent motivator, it seemed, and Ufthak had to step back and swat the chain-choppa away a couple of times as the beakie tried its best to bury the whirring teeth of its weapon into his flesh. Within a few seconds, however, it became clear that no matter how angry the beakie was, it wasn't going to be able to be more than an irritant to him. Somewhat disappointingly, Ufthak found that he was simply too big and too quick for a regular beakie to give him any trouble.

He could have killed it easily enough, taken the choppa off it and pulled its limbs off one by one, maybe even beaten it to death with its own leg. But while the beakie hadn't seemed interested in helping him spoil their captors' party, what if he didn't give it a choice in the matter?

Ufthak caught the beakie's choppa arm in his hand, and began to spin. He whirled around three times on the spot, dragging the beakie around with him, then let out a massive grunt of effort and heaved the beakie high into the air.

His aim was true. To be honest, Ufthak had been considering the whole thing a win-win scenario: if he hadn't made the throw, then the beakie would have flown head first into the wall that formed the arena's edge, which would have just been funny, but it sailed upwards, thrashing as it went, and easily cleared it.

Then it came down amidst the crowd of startled spikiez.

One thing you could say about beakies was that they were always ready for a fight. Now denied the opportunity of carving chunks out of Ufthak, the beakie clearly decided that it was going to make the best of a bad job, and began laying about it with its weapon. Spikiez scrambled to get away from the raging, armoured killer newly arrived in their midst, but even their lightning-fast reflexes and general agility were of limited use when they were hemmed in on all sides by others of their kind, many of whom had been seated and some of whom were too caught up in the secondary entertainments offered by chemical stimulants – or each other – to immediately realise what was going on.

Spikie warriors, when appropriately armed and armoured, could certainly give a beakie a good fight. These weren't warriors, however, but indolent spectators with only a knife or three about their persons, and no great desire to buy time for their fellows by sacrificing their own lives. Ufthak watched the bloodshed for a few moments, then turned away with a laugh.

Spikiez. They started an awful lot of fights with an awful lot of enemies for a species that feared their own deaths so much.

The flying lenses closed in on him again, although they remained out of his reach. That was the cue for the giant projection of the spikie boss to reappear, towering above the arena. It wasn't smiling any longer, which amused Ufthak no end. He made the rudest hand signal he could in its general direction, and although he suspected that the watching crowd didn't know the gesture's exact meaning, the general intake of breath and change in tone of the noise around him suggested they had at least gleaned an idea of it.

The spikie spoke once more, its voice amplified until it rolled around like thunder, or distant explosions. Then it made a chopping gesture with its hand, and its image blinked out again. Ufthak looked around expectantly. He doubted he was going to get rewarded for his creative disposal of the beakie, so presumably another and more dangerous opponent was on the way, which to be fair was not that far off from a reward anyway. He'd be satisfied so long as he wasn't about to get vaporised by one of their darklight guns, although if that was the only way the spikiez thought they could kill him, then he'd still consider it as kind of a compliment.

Sure enough, the familiar whine of spikie lifter-engines swelled overhead. There were four of the small bike-types, but they weren't moving to attack; instead, they had a large crate slung beneath them, suspended on tethers. Ufthak eyed them, wondering if he could get aboard one when they landed – and if so, whether it would have enough power to lift him, since he probably weighed ten times as much as your average spikie now. But it seemed that the gits were ahead of him on that one. They came to a simultaneous halt with the crate still some way off the ground and disengaged the tethers at the same time, sending the crate plummeting, then sped away before it even hit the ground.

The crate looked sturdy enough, but was presumably rigged to come apart on landing, since that was what happened as soon as it hit the ground. Ufthak squinted through the dust raised by the impact, trying to work out what was inside. There was a huge, dark shape in there, but…

Something bellowed, and Ufthak stiffened in surprise. He knew that voice. But that wasn't possible.

The crate's occupant lumbered out of the dust-cloud and beat its chest, roaring with primal ferocity. Ufthak's blood, which had been fired up at the prospect of another fight, chilled in his veins. It felt as if the bottom had fallen out of his stomach.

The creature he faced was his size, possibly even larger, but whereas Ufthak still had typically orky proportions, the same could not be said of this monstrosity. It was grotesquely swollen, with ampoules dug into its flesh and glistening auto-injectors visible all over its frame. Its right arm was disproportionately long; its left shoulder was higher than the right and had a third arm attached beneath it, growing out of its ribcage and surrounded by slabs of grafted muscle. The skin of its back was stretched tight by the lumpy protrusions of a malformed spine, but it still moved with a fearsome, simian speed and strength.

It was typical of the work of the spikie painboyz, from what Ufthak had seen: brute-forcing a body to go far beyond what natural biology had ever intended, and including their own deranged alterations into the mix.

However, that was not what was horrific about it. The thing that truly set Ufthak's teef on edge was the fact that the thing's skin was the same deep green as his own, and the tiny face almost buried between the massively enlarged shoulders was one he knew.

'Deffrow?' Ufthak breathed. 'Wot da zoggin' 'eck?'

It was Deffrow, there was no doubt about it. His right arm no longer terminated in a power klaw, but in a forearm and hand that had presumably been taken from another ork and grafted on before he had been subjected to whatever had caused this massive, unnatural growth, but those were definitely his features. Ufthak searched his former underling's face, looking for a sign of recognition, but he found none: Deffrow's pupils were pinpoints that moved wildly, as though he was massively overstimulated.

Then they fixed on Ufthak, and he charged.

There was no warning, no swearing or accusation of poor leadership, or even a simple 'Waaagh!'. The roar that emanated from Deffrow's mouth lacked even that level of sophistication. It was an animalistic scream, and nothing more. Ufthak had the barest second to set himself, and then Deffrow was on him.

Many of the galaxy's species might have been taken aback by the assault of one of their own, especially one so horrifically altered. Ufthak was disgusted by what had been done to his fellow ork, but fighting other orks was something he had done many times before, so that in itself was no problem for him to get his head around. The problem came more from the fact that Deffrow now had three hands, whereas he had only two.

'Get a zoggin' grip!' Ufthak roared, blocking two punches but taking the third in the ribs. *'Oof!* Wot's da big idea? Spikiez got into yer 'ead?' He landed a solid left hand on Deffrow's jaw, to little effect, and then Deffrow grabbed Ufthak's wrists with two of his hands and drew the third one back, before landing his fist squarely between Ufthak's eyes.

'Ow!' Ufthak bellowed, as stars erupted in his vision. He spat out a toof, but his eyes refocused on Deffrow's upper left fist drawing back for a second go, and he knew he didn't want to taste another. This time when Deffrow punched, Ufthak managed to sway his head to one side, then twisted it around and clamped his jaws shut on the other ork's forearm.

Deffrow roared in pain, and pulled his arm back. At least he could still feel pain; for a moment Ufthak had been worried that the spikiez would have pumped him full of some sort of drug to prevent it, but of course the gits wanted the maximum amount of suffering on both sides. Ufthak had no intention of giving up his brief advantage, so he threw his entire body forward into an enormous headbutt that saw his forehead hit dead centre on Deffrow's face.

The lack of appreciable neck also meant Deffrow's body no longer had any way to cushion such a blow, and even his newly massive frame was going to struggle to operate when what was left of the brain controlling it had taken such a hit. Ufthak was a bit wobbly himself, but he had enough wherewithal to wrench his arms free of Deffrow's loosening grip, and to bury one foot in the other ork's gut. It felt like kicking a Gargant's side, but it caused Deffrow to stagger a step sideways. Ufthak moved with him, staying closer to the one arm than the two, and lashed out with another punch that sent Deffrow reeling again. He looked around hastily, searching for a weapon, but to no avail; the spikiez had obviously intended for them to beat each other to death with their bare hands.

Deffrow certainly appeared willing to oblige. He lunged for Ufthak with his right hand outstretched, looking to hold him in place while his two left fists got busy on the pummelling. Ufthak twisted, grabbing the grasping hand by the wrist and shoving his hip into Deffrow's oncoming body, then wrenching forwards and downwards. Deffrow's feet left the ground, and his massive body described an ungainly arc through the air before landing in the dirt with an impact that felt like a bomb had gone off.

Ufthak didn't waste any time. There was no sign of the ork he knew any longer, in terms of what might charitably have been referred to as intellect. Whatever the spikiez had done to Deffrow after they'd snagged him, presumably at the same time as they'd grabbed Ufthak, it hadn't been limited to bulking him up. He was properly gone now, as mindlessly killy as any bugeye, and there was only one way to deal with that.

Whatever dubious benefits the spikiez' interventions had granted Deffrow, his malformed frame did not lend itself to getting back up off the ground very easily once it was down there. Deffrow had one moment to thrash, to little success, before Ufthak began pounding away on the other ork's face, his left hand on Deffrow's right shoulder and one knee on his gut. Ork skulls were notoriously thick and resilient, capable of withstanding an astonishing amount of blunt force without sustaining damage that a painboy couldn't fix given a few metal plates and a bit of glue, but Ufthak was a lot bigger than he used to be, and he hit a lot harder.

Also, he was angry.

The first punch landed flush. Deffrow half-blocked the second with his upper left arm, but his lower one had already gone limp. If Ufthak had been thinking about it, he might have surmised that the newly grafted limb was not as easy to control if there was any disruption to the nervous system, but he was more concerned with finishing the job. The third punch slipped past Deffrow's defences and struck home again. The other ork's eyes rolled back in his head for a moment, and now none of his body seemed to respond to him any longer. He flailed, but it was as though all of his new muscle had turned to water.

Ufthak kept punching. He kept punching until Deffrow had gone still and there was nothing left of his face except a green-and-red ruin, because Ufthak had no intentions of letting the git get back up again behind him. Deffrow had been a decent nob, but he'd got himself snatched by the spikiez and turned into their weapon, and that was no way for an ork to live. Ufthak knew that he'd prefer death to that, so it stood to reason that Deffrow would have as well, had there been enough of him left to verbalise it.

He wasn't going to be verbalising anything any more. Ufthak drew back his fist and landed one more punch, just to show the spikiez that he wasn't bothered about beating one of his own nobs to death.

When his fist made contact with what remained of Deffrow's face, the ground shook.

It shook hard enough, in fact, to send Ufthak sprawling sideways off Deffrow's corpse. As the green killin' rage began to subside and the roaring in his ears quietened, Ufthak realised that the noise of the arena around him had changed – and not just because of whatever the beakie had been up to in the stands behind him. An explosion was an explosion, pretty much, but that noise above him was the full-throated thunder of proper engines, not whiny spikie lifter-jets, and the sound rolling out across the arena was not the sizzling of humie light-zappas or fishboy megablastas.

'I know dose guns,' Ufthak said.

TWENTY-THREE

The games in the Arena of Deathly Sorrow were widely regarded as the best in all of Port Tavarr, and indeed farther afield still. The Cult of the Silver Shards might best them in terms of the sheer barbarity of the environments in which their gladiators competed, but the Deathly Sorrow's entertainments were superior in size, spectacle, and variety. Dhaemira had attended before, but never at the request of the cult's grand succubus, and never in such luxury. From her seat in the Grand Box, she could follow any flens as it flew around the arena tracking the individual contests and combats, and have its signal sent to her personal screen. She could even, if she so wished, view particularly entertaining deaths or displays of martial prowess again, or slowed down, or from different angles. Meanwhile, slaves were on hand to offer her the very finest victuals and drinks taken directly from Xurzuli's personal kitchens.

It was a vulgar display of wealth and power, but impressive nonetheless. The mistress of the Cult of the Deathly Sorrow wanted there to be no doubt about how little she needed her current partners. Once the orkish threat was dealt with, Dhaemira would not be surprised if Xurzuli Mindrex intended to become the dominant force in Port Tavarr herself. It would be unusual – wych cults usually steered clear of such overt political manoeuvring, instead preferring to ally themselves with kabals for mutual benefit, and cut ties if it seemed they'd miscalculated – but not exactly unheard of.

Beside Dhaemira, Dhalgar chuckled with delight as he watched a flock of razorwings bring down a bulbous, warty biped of a species Dhaemira did not recognise, and tear it apart. Her brother was lapping up the spectacles on offer and savouring the wisps of psychic torment they produced, and appeared to have quite forgotten his earlier spat with Maculatix, who was himself observing the rampages of an enslaved grotesque – captured from the Coven of the Twisted Blade, if Dhaemira was any judge – with macabre relish. Xurzuli was in a fine humour, announcing the various contests and combatants to the crowd, and projecting herself into a towering image in the arena's centre that went, in Dhaemira's opinion, some way towards representing the sheer size of the succubus' ego.

Dhaemira looked to her other side, towards Cistrial Virn. She was simply checking what her fellow archon was doing, which was always wise when in close proximity to someone of whose motivations one could not be entirely sure. She was startled to meet Cistrial's eyes, since the other archon was already looking at *her.*

'Ah,' Dhaemira said, and swallowed with a throat that had inexplicably become treacherously dry. For his part, Cistrial's eyes twitched: a virtually invisible movement, but as obvious as a guilty flinch for someone as experienced at reading the micro-languages of drukhari interactions as Dhaemira. Cistrial had clearly not intended to be seen looking at her; had the archon of the Kabal of the Falling Night been harbouring treacherous intent?

'Are you enjoying the games?' Cistrial said lightly, but his tone was too deliberately casual. Now he looked away, as though returning his own attention to the spectacle, but his screen was flicking through the feeds one flens after another. It was a cover, and a poor one.

'Indeed,' Dhaemira said. Their alliance was still important, and she was unwilling to risk it by confronting her rival over such a small thing. 'This is as grand a show as any I can remember seeing.' Her words sounded stilted and lifeless in her mouth, but what was said was said.

'Ah, but my friends, the best is yet to come,' Xurzuli said from in front, leaning backwards until her blade-laced hair drooped down between them. 'I have high hopes for the next addition!'

She straightened in her seat and manipulated a small control. Nothing happened for a few seconds, but then the feeds switched to focus on a specific grille gate set into the arena wall.

'What are we supposed to be looking at?' Cistrial said, the tone of his voice very different to the artificial lightness it had contained a few moments before. Now it was strong and sure, and the question clearly contained the implication that he felt the lack of an obvious subject to observe was not down to his own lack of perceptiveness, but rather a failing on the part of their host.

'One moment,' Xurzuli said, although she was clearly annoyed at the apparent delay. However, a few moments later the grille gate clattered open, and deposited a massive figure at high speed into the dirt of the arena floor.

Dhaemira had been half-expecting this, but even so she found herself leaning forward and her hands clenching the armrests of her luxurious seat. 'Xurzuli! You released the arakhia?'

'Of course,' Xurzuli said, her expression half-contemptuous, half-puzzled. 'Why would I not?'

'Did I not tell you of my conversation with the creature?' Dhaemira bit out. 'It admitted that its kind thrives on combat.'

'Which is just as well, since *I* intend to thrive on *its* combat,' Xurzuli said with a malicious laugh. 'My price for joining your alliance was that we take the beast alive – did you honestly think I would let it rot uselessly in my dungeons?'

She engaged her projection once again, and stood up to let the arena drink in her grandeur. Her image towered above them all as she began to speak.

'Honoured guests and snivelling wretches! The Cult of the Deathly Sorrow is proud to introduce our latest showpiece, the massive and deadly leader of the arakhia warband that has been making such trouble in Sabregate and Port Tavarr!'

A pair of flenses flickered down and focused on Ufthak Black-hawk, who glowered up at them. Even at this distance removed from the creature, even knowing that it could not see her, Dhaemira felt the power and intensity of its stare.

'The first challenge for our newest guest is an old favourite, with many arena kills to his name,' Xurzuli announced, sadistic glee dripping from her voice. 'What is more, I am informed that the specific caste of mon-keigh warriors to which this Marqus Dias belongs harbours a particular hatred of the arakhia! Let us see how they fare against each other!'

A cage rose up from the arena floor, and disgorged a bulky, armoured shape familiar to anyone who had waged war against the mon-keigh for any length of time.

'A Space Marine?' Maculatix said, steepling the fingers of his natural hands. 'However did you procure one alive?'

'I cannot go sharing the secrets of my beastmasters, now can I, master haemonculus?' Xurzuli chuckled. 'Come now, this should be a good show!'

'The Space Marine does not stand a chance,' Dhaemira said bluntly. Xurzuli glared at her, and Dhaemira went back to watching her feed in silence.

She was proven correct in short order. Ufthak knocked the mon-keigh warrior over, fended off a furious rush that would have butchered many an opponent, then simply whirled the Space Marine around and hurled it into the crowd with a truly shocking display of strength. Dhaemira could not have even lifted the mon-keigh giant encased in its armour, although in fairness, nor would she have tried to. Ufthak's method of disposing of its opponent was far cruder than she would have employed, but still brutally efficient.

'Dhaemira's assessment was accurate,' Cistrial commented. He glanced slyly at Dhaemira before adding, 'Perhaps it would have been beneficial to consult someone who had actually fought the creature before you assigned it a somewhat underwhelming opponent.'

Xurzuli did not acknowledge that with a response. A flens had followed Marqus Dias into the crowd, and was detailing the slaughter that followed as the enraged killer took its frustrations out on the paupers who packed the seats closest to the action. There were no fancy flens arrays for them to sample the myriad delights as they wished; they simply took in what was in front of them, and lived with the risk of occasional peril from unexpected escapees. The cult could have erected a barrier, of course, but where would the fun be in that?

'Someone subdue the mon-keigh before it reaches anyone important,' Xurzuli commanded in clipped tones. Then she turned to Maculatix. 'Master haemonculus, shall we see how the arakhia responds to a familiar face?'

'It is hardly my finest work, given the limited time and tools with which I had to work,' Maculatix said with false modesty. 'However, I am intrigued to see how the contest goes.'

Xurzuli nodded – as though there was any chance of the succubus being gainsaid in her own arena – and got to her feet once more. Her gigantic simulacrum filled the sky again, along with smaller images of Ufthak, although even these were still large enough to be seen by all.

'The beast wishes to play, it seems,' Xurzuli declared. 'Very well. We shall see how it fares against its own kind!' She made a chopping gesture with her hand, and her image winked out again. However, as the succubus' voice finished thundering around the arena, Dhaemira cocked her head and listened intently.

Cistrial leaned in close to her, until their foreheads were nearly touching, and Dhaemira's hands clenched again. It was an entirely natural reaction to a potential enemy being so close, but she had no intention of flinching backwards.

'Do you hear that too?' Cistrial asked in a low voice, and Dhaemira forced herself to concentrate on what she had been listening to in the first place, rather than her rival's face mere inches from her own.

'Yes,' she said quietly, after another couple of seconds. Now she did sit back, unease stirring in her stomach. The sounds of combat in the arena were loud and pervasive, but there was a new noise that Dhaemira was certain she had not heard before. Or rather, she had heard it before, but not here.

She had heard it elsewhere in Port Tavarr, and in Sabregate, because it was the distant sound of massed ork weapons fire.

'I said we were not to be disturbed!' Xurzuli snapped, which took Dhaemira by surprise for a moment until she realised the succubus must be speaking to an underling who was addressing her by carrier wave. Dhaemira could see Xurzuli's eyes glistening as she watched the cage being brought in by four reaver jetbikes, and recognised the signs of hyper-focus. The ability to turn all of one's concentration onto a foe was a potent tool in the combat arsenal of a wych, but it had the disadvantage of blinkering them to more general threats. Many were the bands of wyches who had plunged deep into the ranks of an enemy but, once caught up in their desire to spill blood, failed to notice that they were being encircled by the wings of the enemy's force.

That, Dhaemira thought somewhat smugly, was why you needed an archon. The kabals indulged themselves in the hedonistic bloodshed of battle, but never to the exclusion of their own self-preservation. However, it seemed that Xurzuli was going to need some prompting.

'The arakhia are coming!' Dhaemira said urgently. 'Listen, Xurzuli – can you not hear them?'

The face that the succubus of the Deathly Sorrow turned towards Dhaemira was a furious one, but it seemed that she could no longer block out the truth. Nonetheless, she laughed.

'So what if they are? This arena is a fortress as much as it is a stadium! Do you honestly think they can penetrate it?'

'Yes,' Cistrial said, before Dhaemira could reply. 'You have only encountered the arakhia when you have been raiding, Xurzuli – when they are hard to hurt, but slow to react. They have a fearsome blend of cunning and brutality when they are the ones attacking. We still do not even understand how they managed to turn a deactivated webway portal to their own will to get here in the first place!'

Xurzuli's expression shifted into one almost of petulance, but she listened to the carrier waves for a moment, then hissed in frustration. 'They are attacking the far end of the arena, trying to force entry. The wall is holding so far, but they are bringing up those crude Titan-equivalents.' She smiled, showing her teeth. 'Of course, there is nothing to say that the brutes can even hit a target the size of a wall with their guns.'

Dhaemira cast a glance at the flens feed. Ufthak had been grappling with Maculatix's creation – a massively enlarged ork with a third arm grafted on – but had now gained the upper hand and was methodically staving its former comrade's skull in with its fist. Ufthak reached back for one final punch.

When it landed, the ground shook.

'I think they hit the wall!' Dhaemira said urgently. A pall of smoke and dust was already rising from the far end of the arena, visible despite the miles between them and it.

'Then they have come to their own deaths!' Xurzuli spat. The succubus rose to her full height, and the circular roof of the arena began to disgorge vehicle after vehicle as her warriors left their seats and piled into them, ready to take the fight to the brutish invaders. Xurzuli gestured, and suddenly Dhaemira's ear was buzzing with carrier-wave signals from her own underlings desperately trying to get her attention.

'You blocked our transmissions?' she demanded angrily. 'Why?'

'You would have insulted me by giving the glories of the greatest show you have ever seen less than your full attention?' Xurzuli scoffed.

'Had we done so, we might all have learned of the arrival of the arakhia's army before *they blew a hole in your wall*,' Maculatix said, his voice dripping with scorn.

'Your creation was a substandard disappointment,' Xurzuli said, as though the haemonculus had not voiced anything of relevance. 'I shall not be seeking out your services for the creation of arena combatants again. Now, come. We have business to attend to.'

Two craft descended into view. One was a Raider, packed with Xurzuli's bloodbrides. The other was the grand succubus' personal Venom, with a completely empty passenger bay.

'And what business is that?' Dhalgar asked, not without a little trepidation. For once, Dhaemira's thoughts aligned with those of her brother, since Xurzuli rapidly appeared to have moved beyond the strength of will and self-belief one would expect of a succubus in control of a powerful wych cult, and into the realms of delusion.

'The arakhia chieftain, of course,' Xurzuli said. She vaulted aboard her craft, and seized up the agoniser and glaive that awaited her. 'Since my captive mon-keigh and Maculatix's creation could not end its existence, perhaps the combined forces of the brave leaders of Port Tavarr will be enough? Unless you would prefer to stay here,' she added, 'and let me claim its head all for myself.'

Dhaemira glanced at the others, but found unanimity looking back at her. Despite the treacherousness of her brother, the tenuousness of her alliance with Maculatix, and the ongoing confusion of Cistrial Virn's motivations, none of them wanted to let Xurzuli Mindrex take on Ufthak Blackhawk alone. Should she do so, and win, then she would surely eclipse them.

None of them intended to let anyone else seize enough power to be the uncontested ruler of Port Tavarr, and that meant working together – for now – to prevent any one of their number becoming pre-eminent.

'Of course not, Grand Succubus,' Dhaemira said on behalf of them all as they boarded Xurzuli's craft. 'Let us slay the beast together.'

TWENTY-FOUR

Ufthak grinned with delight as the thunder of orkish guns reverberated through the arena. The spikiez he could see in the crowd – those that hadn't been killed by, or run away from, the beakie – were clearly unsettled by what was going on, and Ufthak was enjoying every moment of it. Sneering, superior gits that they were, acting as though being tall and spindly and living for a long time made them better than everyone else! It was about time someone drove into their home and taught them a thing or two.

The spikiez weren't the only ones who'd realised what the enormous explosion and new timbre of gunfire meant. The remaining humies and fishboyz had stopped shooting at each other and were hunkered down, their guns turned towards the direction of the new sounds. Their huddled shapes had the air of captives who had been killing each other on the basis that their captors would kill them anyway if they didn't, but now realised their captors might not be in charge any longer, and weren't entirely sure if this was an improvement from their perspective. Ufthak was tempted to walk up to them and give them a kicking on general principle, but there seemed little point to it; it would be far more amusing to wait for them to decide to get some revenge on spikiez.

Speaking of which...

The sound of screaming jets announced the arrival of more spikie vehicles, coming in fast and high at first, then killing their forward momentum and dropping directly down towards him. One was a flying trukk, packed with the really flippy spikiez that didn't wear many clothes, presumably in case they got in the way of the flipping. The other was one of the small, zippy flyers, and Ufthak's eyes narrowed as he saw who was riding in it.

There were a couple he didn't know – a cadaverous, multi-armed spikie that looked a bit like the one that had stabbed him with its fingers, and which floated like Da Boffin now did, and a pale-haired, pale-skinned one in dull green armour – but he recognised the other three. One had been projecting itself above the arena, and seemed to be in charge of this place. The second was the one Ufthak had been talking to from his cell, the spikie boss that had carved up Uzgit and his ladz. The third took a moment, but there was something very familiar about its armour and its stance. He'd never seen its face before, but the expression of fear-wracked hatred was exactly what he would have expected, bearing in mind their previous meeting.

'I know yoo!' he bellowed, pointing at the spikie, who actually flinched a little. 'Yoo chopped me hand off, an' I dropped a trukk on ya!'

The spikie hid its face by donning a cruel-looking helmet – which added the question of how it had grown back the arm that Princess had bitten off to the first question of why it wasn't still a very flat smear somewhere – and it and its companions readied their weapons. There were a lot of whips, swords, and general pointy implements in evidence, and here was Ufthak without a weapon of any sort.

It wasn't right. If the spikiez had to send a whole bunch of their bosses to kill him then fair enough, he'd take that as as good a way as any to get sent to meet Gork and Mork, but it seemed a bit anticlimactic to be fighting them with his bare hands. If only he had the Snazzhammer with him, to give them a proper fight...

But hang on a second.

He must have dropped the Snazzhammer when the sky-gits had drugged him. Surely one of the ladz would have picked it up? It was a zoggin' fine weapon; the whole point of getting Da Boffin to stick the tellyport homer on it was to make sure that no one pinched it once Ufthak had thrown it at something, so no self-respecting ork would have just left it on the ground. And if the ladz were *here*, then that presumably meant the hammer was too, which meant it should be back in range.

This was no time for half-measures. Ufthak faced the spik-iez and slammed the palm of his hand into his chest, button and all.

TWENTY-FIVE

Dhaemira seized the Venom's rail, ready to vault out of it, just as the ork chieftain beat its chest once in a typically bestial manner...

...and disappeared.

There was a long moment of silence.

'What,' Xurzuli Mindrex said, her tone of voice one that threatened immediate and profligate violence if occurrences did not stop disappointing her, 'just happened?'

TWENTY-SIX

Ufthak quite enjoyed the sensation of tellyporting. The world went really colourful and loud for a moment, everything screamed at you and sometimes tried to eat you, and then you arrived where you were going all pumped up and ready to fight whatever you found. However, he was normally expecting it, so this one took him off-guard a bit. He staggered a step to his left, and collided with something solid.

'Wot?' he said, and realised that his right hand was holding something. He looked at it.

It was the Snazzhammer.

'Boss!' a voice shouted gleefully. Ufthak blinked away the last vestiges of disorientation, and realised that instead of standing on the arena floor and waiting for the spikie bosses to come and try to kill him, he was in the back of a trukk and Mogrot Redtoof was right in front of him. Behind Mogrot, Princess bounced up and down and squealed in excitement.

'Zoggin' 'eck!' Ufthak bellowed, causing the orks around him to cower away for a moment. 'Dis fing was s'posed to come to *me*, not me go to *it*! I woz about to 'ave a really good scrap!'

He looked around. The trukk was at the head of a wide front of ork vehicles powering forward into the spikie arena, firing their weapons for all they were worth. Fighta-bommers roared overhead, guns blazing as they engaged spikie flyboyz and sky-gits. Behind him, the earth-shaking footfalls of Stompas were only drowned out by the explosions kicked up as their massive munitions thundered away to detonate in the stands, blowing great chunks out of the enormous structure.

'On da uvver hand, dis is alright, I guess,' Ufthak conceded with bad grace. He looked down. 'Why's da floor sticky?'

'Well, boss, yoo're standin' where Skarbad woz,' said Wazzock, another of Ufthak's former mob who had since gone on to take charge of a mob of his own. These were the slugga boyz currently crammed into the back of the trukk, all pressed up against the sides since Ufthak took up a great deal of space these days. 'We gave 'im yer hammer to hang on to in case we found ya,' Wazzock continued, 'but I guess ya found us instead. He sort of exploded when ya turned up.'

Ufthak grunted. 'How'd ya know where to look for me?'

'It woz da grot!' Mogrot said excitedly. 'Yoo know, boss, *your* grot.'

Ufthak wrinkled his brow. 'Wot, Nizkwik?' He couldn't imagine Nizkwik knowing where to look for his own hands.

'Nah, yer uvver grot,' Mogrot said. 'Not da stoopid one, da stabby one.'

Ufthak was going to say something scathing about Mogrot referring to any other multi-celled organism as 'stoopid', but the git had at least managed to latch on to an appropriate frame of reference. If you had to assign roles to the two grots who followed Ufthak around, then Nizkwik was definitely the stupid one, and Snaggi was undeniably the stabby one. Ufthak decided to have a quiet word with both Da Boffin and Dok Drozfang, once this mess was sorted out, to make sure that Snaggi never ended up in a Killa Kan no matter how eagerly he volunteered.

'Alright, Snaggi,' he said. 'Wot happened?'

'He woz babblin' somefing about da signal wot links yer hammer an' yer armour,' Wazzock said. 'Nazlug bodged up somefing wot pointed us in da right direction for a bit, but–'

'Don't tell me,' Ufthak said, putting his hand over his eyes. 'It blew up.'

'Yeah,' Wazzock said. 'But den we saw dis place, wiv a giant spikie standin' in da middle of it, so tall we could even see it over da walls! It kept appearin' an' disappearin', but we fort it looked like somefing worf fightin', so we all headed over to see wot woz wot.'

'Good ladz,' Ufthak said, 'good ladz.' He hefted the Snazz-hammer. It was more or less the size of a regular choppa to a regular ork, at least in his hand as it was now, but it would still kill spikiez just fine.

'So *is* dere a giant spikie here?' Mogrot asked eagerly.

'Nah,' Ufthak said, and Mogrot's face fell. 'But don't worry,' Ufthak added, pointing. 'Dere's still plenty of da gits to scrag!'

They were coming in fast: a veritable horde of them, now the spikiez had got themselves sorted and worked out that they were actually under attack. Sky-trukk after sky-trukk was dropping down, filled with warriors and spitting fire into the thundering orkish convoy. The ladz were answering in kind, naturally, with trukk-mounted big shootas coughing streams of rounds into the air, and the passengers firing off their own weaponry with great abandon, albeit not great accuracy. Still, the sheer volume of fire and the density of the attacking spikiez meant that many of the incoming vehicles were clipped and began to spin, veer, or simply drop like stones depending on how they had been damaged. Ufthak heard a new scream of engines behind him, and a mob of stormboyz powered up into the air, aiming to take the fight to the enemy in their own element. However, they weren't the only ones with that idea.

'Spikiez comin' in!' Wazzock yelled, and discharged the skorcha part of his combi-shoota into the air. The gits were swinging down on lines from one of their vehicles, closing in on Ufthak's trukk with an almost sickening agility, grace and accuracy. Wazzock's tongue of dirty yellow flame engulfed one spikie and sent it tumbling with an ear-rending screech, but its mates were unscathed, and they landed on the trukk with knives drawn.

Of course, there wasn't a great deal of trukk to land *on* that wasn't already occupied by ork, so combat was instantaneous. This wasn't the hack and slash of a ruck on solid ground, where orks would pile forward trusting to momentum and brute force, while spikiez danced out of the way and tried to stick them with knives while staying out of reach. This was close and desperate and bloody, with no room for finesse, feints or mistakes. One spikie landed knees first on an ork and plunged twin daggers into his neck with a shrill yell; another was broken clean in half as the momentum of its swing met an ork choppa coming the other way at waist height. Spikie pistols shot splinters of solid poison into ork eyes and roaring ork mouths, and sluggas blew holes in spikie chests large enough for the spikies in question to fit their own heads into, had they been particularly limber.

One spikie actually backflipped off the line on which it had been swinging, and lashed out with a whip that coiled around Ufthak's hammer arm. Pain flared through the limb where the whip's serrated edges sawed through his sleeve and touched his skin, but he ignored it and yanked his arm backwards. The spikie was too startled to let go of its weapon, and found itself tugged straight into Ufthak's fist with an impact similar to if it had landed in front of a trukk going at full speed. Ufthak stamped on it for good measure, grabbed another one and hurled it bodily off the trukk – it landed on its feet, but immediately got run over by a battlewagon – then finally got enough room to clobber a third with the Snazzhammer, right on top of its head. The sheer force of the blow immediately reduced the spikie in question to a height more akin to that of a grot, somewhat bursting it in the process.

'Heads up!' Ufthak roared. The convoy had been approaching a large area of the arena floor that was taken up by tall, woody plants, presumably so the spikiez could watch their captives engage in jungle warfare or have them hunted by forest predators. Huge shapes were now emerging from between the trunks, and thundering towards the Tekwaaagh!'s trukks with obvious malice. Ufthak saw the enormous forms of the strange, swollen spikiez he'd fought back before he got drugged and grabbed, but there were other creatures there as well that he'd never seen before. It looked like the spikiez of the arena had emptied their dungeons of every big and nasty monster they could find, and pointed them all at the orks.

The collision of the two battle lines was cataclysmic, a tremendous smacking of metal into flesh where, for a wonder, flesh did not always come off worst. For every beast that got mashed by a ram bar and ground under huge, knobbly wheels or rusted metal tracks, another one used a combination of massive size and unnatural nimbleness to hit a trukk at an angle and topple it. The ork advance began to slow, as overturned vehicles blocked the progress of those behind, and unharmed vehicles braked to let their passengers out so they could get stuck into the fighting.

Mogrot, Wazzock, and those of Wazzock's ladz that hadn't

already been knifed to death piled gleefully over the sides and started laying about themselves as their trukk slewed to a halt, but Ufthak paused for a moment to look up at the spikiez still circling above them. The scraggin' spikiez were down here, slitting throats and getting bludgeoned into oblivion in turn, but the shootin' spikiez were still up there, taking potshots from over the side of their flying trukks and picking off the boyz one by one. What was more, most of the ladz weren't paying attention to them any longer; they had plenty to keep them occupied at ground level, what with the scraggin' spikiez and the dungeon creatures. Who cared about the gits above you when you had a roaring monstrosity in front of you with tentacles for a tongue or knives for hands, right there in reach of your choppa?

Ufthak, that was who. Finkin' could be a pain in the head sometimes, but Mork damn it, Ufthak wasn't going to let the spikiez get one over on him just because they could fink too. They'd found a way to slow his ladz down and hold them still to shoot them more easily? Well, then he needed to solve this problem.

He hurled the Snazzhammer. It flew upwards, tumbling end over end, until the axe blade side of it *thunked* into the hull of a spikie vehicle. One of the crew looked over the side, a tiny helmet peering down at the vessel's new adornment.

'Princess!' Ufthak said, whistling. 'Who'za good squig?'

Princess apparently came to the conclusion that it was indeed the good squig in question, and leaped joyously at Ufthak. He caught it under his left arm, raised his right hand, and triggered the button.

At the absolute worst, nothing would happen and he'd have to find a new weapon. More likely, the Snazzhammer would come back to him and he'd be back where he'd been a few seconds ago. There was, he realised in the middle of closing his fist, the faintest possibility that the Snazzhammer would come back to him *with the spikie flyer still attached*, which would be... interesting.

Instead, the world screamed at him for a second, and then he was hanging off the Snazzhammer's handle a Stompa's height or more above the ground.

The spikie vessel tilted at the sudden extra weight, and Ufthak propelled his left arm upwards. Princess squealed with delight as it flew up, the sound only becoming muffled when its fanged maw engulfed the helmet of the spikie that had looked down. The spikie staggered backwards with a scream that ended abruptly as Princess bit its head off, and Ufthak clamped his fingers over the flyer's edge.

Back in the days when he'd been a regular ork boy, he'd never have reached it. He was far bigger now, however, and his arms were far longer. He heaved himself up and onto the vehicle, his swaying weight causing it to yaw unevenly, but the spikiez on board were too busy concentrating on Princess to notice him at first. The squig was bounding around with great enthusiasm, looking to bite as many different things as possible, and the spikiez were reacting as ranged troops often did when faced with a fast-moving, immediate threat in their midst: they were attempting to shoot it, usually missing, and sometimes hitting each other.

Ufthak wrenched the Snazzhammer out of the flyer's hull behind him, and set to work.

It didn't take long. The spikiez might have been nimble, but their silly skinny vehicle gave them very little room in which to take best advantage of that agility. One sweep of the Snazzhammer carried three over the edge in various states of injury, and then it was already all over bar the shouting. One of the gits managed to land a sputter of poisoned splinters into Ufthak's

chest, but the brief wave of dizziness that followed was not sufficient to prevent him from swatting it over the side with his free
hand just before he clobbered another with the Snazzhammer,
while Princess tore the leg off a third. That one overbalanced
over the side; the one doing the steering, which had seen Ufthak
marching down the flyer towards it, clearly decided that its mate
had the right idea and leaped off of its own accord before he
could reach it, leaving the vessel empty apart from Ufthak, Princess and some corpses.

'Right,' Ufthak said with some satisfaction. 'Dat's dat.'

Or it would have been, were it not for the fact that there were
many other spikie flyers around them, none of which he was
able to get to, and many of which had noticed the scrap that had
been taking place. Ufthak became aware of a growing encircle-
ment of other flying trukks surrounding the one on which he
stood, becalmed and still and a very easy target.

'Oh zog,' Ufthak said, just as the spikiez opened fire.

There was a big difference between shaking off the effects of a
few splinters – probably helped by his recently increased mass,
meaning the poison was stretched further, like how three orks
would get through a box of shoota shells faster than one – and
ignoring the concentrated fire of whole trukkloads of spikiez.
Ufthak hunkered down as well as he could behind the steering controls, but the sheer size that had so benefited him a few
moments ago meant that there was nowhere he could fully take
cover, even had the gits not been all around him in any case.
He could throw himself over the side to escape the barrage and
hope he landed on something soft, but that seemed an outside
chance: the arena was not exactly a welcoming environment,
and orks didn't call spikiez 'spikiez' for no reason. Even if he
landed on the gits he'd just pitched overboard, he'd still be pulling helmets and pauldrons out of his flesh for a week.

Ufthak put his fist through the control panel, on the basis that it was unlikely to make things actively worse.

The flyer lurched forward with a strained whine, and a lot of the spikiez' shooting was abruptly passing through the empty air behind it. The vehicle directly in front of them tried to twitch to one side, but the sheer speed of the spikiez' own vessels worked against it, and Ufthak's craft rammed into it before it could complete its evasive action.

The wickedly sharp ramming spike at the front of Ufthak's flyer scraped down the side of its sister, and then the inevitable happened: spiky protuberances entangled and interlocked, and the two craft began to spin around each other, whirling through the air.

The spikiez aboard the other craft had to hang on desperately as their vessel's momentum threatened to spin them clean off it. Princess clamped its teeth around the central mast, the centrifugal force lifting its entire body off the deck. Ufthak took a few seconds to pick some of the larger, more obvious splinters out of himself and waited for at least one sort of spinning in his head to stop, then mashed the control panel again.

This time the engines cut out completely, and the flyer began to drop. The other one was still locked up with it, but its straining engines could not keep the weight of both vehicles aloft, and they began to spiral down towards the ground. Ufthak peered over the side, waited until he saw a battlewagon underneath him, and jumped.

It wasn't a soft landing, but it was at least a close one. He didn't fall far, and the wagon's roof held rather than collapsing beneath him, although it did bend a little under his suddenly arriving weight. The battlewagon itself wasn't moving, given it was now mired in a mess of the other vehicles that had come to a halt when orks and spikie monsters started laying into each other.

'Boss?' someone behind him shouted, and Ufthak turned around to see the gunner of the battlewagon's killkannon staring at him from behind the sights of his gun.

'Ya see dose fings?' Ufthak bellowed, pointing at the still-descending spikie vehicles directly in front of the battlewagon. 'Krump 'em!' He held up one hand. 'Actually, wait a sec.'

A round, red, squealing shape bounded into view and landed next to him. Princess squealed happily, an arm sticking out of its mouth.

'*Now* krump 'em,' Ufthak said. He leaped off the side of the vehicle, with Princess beside him, and the killkannon opened fire.

Ufthak would never have claimed that orks were the best shots in the galaxy. Even his own Bad Moons clan were no more accurate than the rest of their kin; they just made up for it by owning guns that fired more shots in the first place, since if you had enough dakka then every enemy's survival rate dropped to zero. The battlewagon's gunner was a Bad Moon, and probably average in every respect, but even he was going to struggle to miss a target of that size directly in front of him.

The killkannon went off with a sound like a god clearing its throat, and the spikie flyers came apart like a grot in a pen of gnasher squigs. Ufthak ducked as a piece of one sailed past his head, followed by a piece of spikie a moment later, and banged on the side of the battlewagon.

'Good shootin'!' he yelled. 'Now get blastin' da ones still up dere!'

'I'd love to, boss!' the gunner called back. 'But we ain't got no more dakka!'

Ufthak wrinkled his nose at him. 'Ya wot?'

'Yeah, beats me,' the ork said, opening the door and clambering out with a slugga and a choppa in his hands. 'Fort we 'ad loads, but it's all gone. Da engine's run dry as well, so we can't even run da ones on da ground over. Just gonna 'ave to give da gits a kickin' da old-fashioned way. *Waaagh!*'

He leaped off the wagon and went piling into the ruck, leaving a nonplussed Ufthak behind him. What was more, the other nearby guns, which had been taking shots at the circling spikie flyers, were falling silent as well. What was going on? How were they running out of ammo and fuel? This was a Waaagh!, for Mork's sake!

Well, there was nothing for it. Ufthak couldn't come up with fuel and ammo on the spot; and even if he could, that was grot work. He'd just have to do what he did best.

'Ready for anuvver scrap?' he asked Princess, who bounced up and down and squealed in what Ufthak was prepared to take as an affirmative. 'Alright, let's go!'

He'd got three strides deep into the melee, and had just lopped the head off something with too many eyes and too little skin, when the sky began spitting death.

Orks and spikiez fell around him, cut down by indiscriminate fire. Ufthak just had time to wonder what was going on when a zippy flyer shot in and disgorged five shapes that tumbled elegantly to the ground.

'Oh, it's *yoo*,' Ufthak said in humie, as the five spikie bosses drew their weapons.

'Are you going to run away again?' called the one who had spoken to him in his cell, whipping her blade back and forth.

'Don't need to,' Ufthak said with a shrug. 'Got me hammer now.' He picked up half a dead ork, and hurled it as far as he could in the other direction. 'Princess, fetch!'

The squig bounded joyously away, and Ufthak set his feet. He wasn't having anyone say he needed a squig to help him fight his battles.

'Right den, spikiez, let's make dis clear.' He took a firm grip on the Snazzhammer, and grinned at them.

'Come and 'ave a go, ya zoggin' gits!'

TWENTY-SEVEN

'Now, I'll grant ya, dis ain't da best situation,' Snaggi said, ducking as half a spikie flew past his head.

'Ain't da best?!' Swipe wailed. 'Da orks kicked in da spikiez' front door an' started trashin' dere house! Dere's spikiez all around us, an' dey've all got knives!'

'Also, da orks ain't got much fuel or ammo left!' Nib yelled. He pulled the trigger of his blasta, then ducked down in panic behind the trukk where they were sheltering. 'Oh, Mork help me, I hit somefing!'

'Dat's a good fing, ain't it?' Longtoof said, puzzled.

'Not when it means it's noticed me!'

The spikie came over the trukk like a migraine through a fungus beer hangover, sharp-edged and merciless. Longtoof was impaled by its serrated blade before he'd even worked out what was going on, and the spikie laughed behind its helm, but it had misjudged the fury of Snaggi Littletoof, Grotboss and Prophet

273

of Gork an' Mork. More specifically, it had misjudged the mentality of grots in general.

If a grot was faced with danger, its usual instinct was to run. However, if a grot was *surrounded* by danger, with nowhere safe to run to, the deeply buried fight instinct would come to the fore. Snaggi, thanks to his enormous intelligence, had already worked out that there were two ways to get grots to fight: convince them that they were going to easily win, or convince them that everywhere else was just as bad and so they might as well try to kill the thing in front of them.

'Scrag it, ladz!' Snaggi yelled, and stuck his stabba into the joint of the armour behind the spikie's knee.

The spikie wobbled, and a dozen grots converged upon it with the killer instinct of small and vicious beings that had suddenly seen a chance to knife something without getting gutted in return. Nib grabbed on to the spikie's choppa-arm to prevent it from pulling the blade back out of Longtoof's chest – Longtoof himself was already drooping, so didn't get much of a say in the matter – and the rest piled onto the lanky git, bowling it backwards to the ground and setting to work. Spikie armour was tough, but it still had gaps, and grots were experts at finding their way around obstacles. Within seconds the spikie's throat had been opened, and also someone had hacked off one of its hands for reasons of which Snaggi was not quite certain, but wasn't going to question right now when there were more important things to worry about.

'Nib!' he snapped. 'Wot woz dat about da orks being low on fuel an' ammo?'

'Well, yeah,' Nib said, pulling the spikie's blade free and waving it experimentally while Longtoof fell over with a groan that everyone ignored. 'Da ladz got to work, just like yoo said to. Hide stuff, nick stuff, an' break stuff, right?'

'Dat woz when we fort Ufthak was gone!' Snaggi said, exasperated. 'We woz tryin' to seed maximum confushun while da orks were fightin' each uvver to take over! Dere's no point doin' it when dey were just comin' to find 'im again!'

'Right, boss, I can see dat,' Nib said, nodding. 'Fing is, after ya told us to do it, ya never told us to *not* do it.'

'So yoo're tellin' me,' Snaggi said slowly, in a voice that he hoped conveyed his displeasure, 'dat da Waaagh! just drove into da middle of a nest of spikiez, but ya *ditched all da ammo?*'

'But ya said not to fink dat da orks would protect us from da spikiez!' Swipe said. 'Ya said–'

'I know wot I said!' Snaggi thundered, rounding on him. 'But Mork alive, ladz, context! *Context!* I can't do all da finkin' for ya!'

'Why not?' someone else piped up. 'Ain't dat da point of bosses?'

'Yeah,' another grot added. 'No one said I 'ad to fink for meself in dis revolushun! Dat's a swindle!'

Snaggi growled in frustration. Was it too much to ask to have underlings who knew exactly what they should be doing and had the intelligence to predict your wishes at any given moment, but still looked up to you and treated you as a divine oracle? *He* didn't think so.

'Alright, ladz,' he said with resignation, 'I'd hoped to avoid dis, but I ain't sure we got much of an option no more. I fink we're gonna 'ave to fight.'

'We just did fight,' Nib said, pointing at the dead spikie.

'Nah, I mean proper fightin',' Snaggi said. 'Not scraggin' one git wot walked into da middle of us. Da spikiez'll kill us if dey get da chance, probably proppa slow an' uncomfortable like. Da orks ain't gonna stop da spikiez from killin' us *as such*, but so long as dey're around, dey're gonna be tryin' to kill da spikiez, which means da spikiez ain't gonna be concentratin' on us.

So wot we needs to do is use dat distraction an' stab a whole bunch of da gits while dere's still enuff orks around to keep 'em busy. Den we can get out of 'ere, one way or anuvver, an' start da plan again once we're somewhere a bit less deadly.'

'Explain to me again how it is we're gonna kill da spikiez,' Gip said. 'Dey're all fast an' flippy, and we ain't gonna outnumber 'em like we did dat one.'

'Simple,' Snaggi said. 'We need more ladz! Everyone go an' find every grot ya can! Yoo all know where dey're gonna be hidin' out! Bully 'em, bribe 'em, or if dat don't work, tell 'em da troof. Remember, da more ladz yoo can get wiv us, da more of 'em dere is to hide behind!'

It didn't take long. The grots had stuck with the orks, because what else were they going to do when the Waaagh! got moving? Grots liked going fast just as much as orks did, and they liked watching the big guns blow stuff up just as much as orks did. Also, although none of them had verbalised it in the same way Snaggi had, all of them knew that if the orks zogged off, then the spikiez lurking in the shadows that wouldn't have chanced their arm with the main body of the Waaagh! would certainly creep out to have their way with a bunch of grots.

Now, however, the spikiez were everywhere and everyone was trying to kill everyone else, and there wasn't even anywhere to run away to. As a result, a quick conversation along the lines of 'come over 'ere, we're gettin' some ladz togevver' was an automatic winner, since every grot felt safer with a couple of other grots around, whom he could shove in front of himself if something dangerous showed up.

It wasn't exactly more grots than Snaggi had ever seen before, since he'd been around a Waaagh! or two, but it was certainly more than he'd ever seen in one place and listening to him. They were huddled together in what passed for the middle of the ork lines, although with the way the battle was flowing backwards and forwards – not to mention side to side – that definition was about as solid as a Blood Axe's promise, so he didn't have the time for lengthy speeches.

'Fellow grots!' he bellowed. 'It's da day of rekke... rekkin... It's da day of findin' out wot's wot! Dere's a whole bunch of spikie gits around us wot want to scrag us. Are we just gonna quake an' cower in our boots?'

That didn't get the reaction Snaggi was hoping for. There was a general uncertain mumbling, following by one grot in the front row sticking his hand up hopefully.

'Just to check... Is dis somefing we're votin' on?'

'No!' Snaggi yelled. 'We ain't votin' on nuffin'!'

'Well, it's just dat it sounded like a question, ya see, so we fort–'

'We ain't votin'!' Snaggi shouted. 'I ain't askin' yer opinions! I'm tellin' ya dat we *ain't* just gonna quake an' cower in our boots! We're gonna get out dere, an' show dese spikie gits wot fink dey're *better*'n us why dey're wrong about dat! Yoo all know how it's done! Trip 'em up, bring 'em down, slit dere froats!'

Another grot stuck his hand up.

'Wot about dose of us wot ain't got no boots?'

Snaggi considered drawing his blasta and just shooting the git, but managed to restrain this very understandable impulse through an almighty effort of will that only went to demonstrate his truly astonishing levels of empathy and understanding towards his fellow grots, even those who were marginally less intelligent than squig dribble.

'No boots?' he said. 'Simple. Nick 'em off da spikiez! Slit dere froats, nick dere boots!'

'Slit dere froats, nick dere boots?' the grot repeated, and those immediately around him nodded excitedly.

'Slit dere froats, nick dere boots!'

'Slit dere froats, nick dere boots!'

'Boss,' Gip muttered, leaning close to Snaggi. 'Are spikie boots even gonna *fit*–'

'Sssh!' Snaggi hissed. 'Not now, Gip! Somefing speshul's goin' on.'

The phrase was spreading outwards through the grot crowd, jumping from one bald green head to another like squig lice in a market pen. Grots that a moment ago were looking more than a little dubious about the merits of engaging in combat against well-armoured, highly agile, and thoroughly sadistic killers were now pumping their little fists in time, drawn in by the chant's seductive wiles. Weapons were raised into the air, fear disappeared from faces, and all of a sudden what had been a cowering mass of terrified individuals was united in purpose: a burgeoning Grotwaaagh!, just waiting to be unleashed.

'Slit dere froats, nick dere boots!'

'Slit dere froats, nick dere boots!'

'See, Gip?' Snaggi said with satisfaction. 'Three syllables – works every time.'

'If ya say so, boss, but wot's a silly-bull?' Gip asked.

Snaggi ignored him. Instead, judging that what passed for Waaagh! energy amongst grots was reaching its peak, he risked making himself into a more obvious target for any watching spikiez and hopped up onto the highest thing nearby: the bucket of a squig catapult that had been abandoned after the loaders had run out of pots of buzzer squigs to hurl at the enemy.

'Forward, fellow grots!' he declared, waving his stabba in the general direction of the spikiez – which, to be fair, could have been pretty much any direction, including upwards. 'For survival, da glory of da Grotwaaagh!, an' better footwear for all!'

'WAAAAGH!' the assembled horde bellowed, a few octaves

higher than the cry was normally delivered at, and surged forwards. Snaggi wouldn't like to count them, mainly because counting was something he felt that someone else should do for him, but there were a *lot* of grots. Most of them were from mobs that had slipped away from the runtherds, but there were also oilers and orderlies of meks and doks whose bosses weren't important enough for the grots concerned to have derived any clout from their role; muckers-out of squig pens; fetchers, carriers, and message-runners; even the crews of those mek gunz that had run out of ammo. All of them had come together for one purpose, under one leader: him, Snaggi Littletoof!

'Oi, Snaggi!'

Snaggi looked down, and saw to his general contempt the familiar face of Nizkwik looking up at him.

'Wot do *yoo* want?' he asked, then froze in horror. Had Nizkwik been in the crowd just now? Had he heard Snaggi speak? Had Snaggi said anything about overthrowing Ufthak, or just about scragging spikiez? He was *fairly* sure it had just been about scragging spikiez, but–

'Good speech!' Nizkwik said encouragingly. 'Yoo really got 'em fired up, da boss'll be dead pleased!'

Da boss'll just be plain dead, when I get my way, Snaggi thought with the glee of one who knew that the grot to whom he was speaking was barely capable of forming his own thoughts, let alone perceiving those of a genius and master of deception.

'Yeah,' he said out loud, 'I was proud of– *Don't lean on dat!*'

'Wot?' Nizkwik asked, looking at his right elbow, but it was too late. The squig catapult's mechanism, designed – if the word could be applied to something put together by a mekaniak working more on instinct and intuition than actual measurements – to be operable by a grot's comparatively weedy arms, was not robust enough to withstand Nizkwik's weight.

Clunk!

'Arrrrgggghhh!' Snaggi yelled, as the counterweight dropped and the bucket went up, with entirely predictable consequences. A good-sized pot of buzzer squigs was not much smaller than a grot, and while it was also a bit lighter, the contraptions that launched them were built for range (since any good mek knew that no grot was going to be reliable once the enemy got too close). Snaggi hurtled through the air, getting a brief, jumbled, and not-entirely-useful overview of the battle from above as he went. He managed to twist around, desperate to see where he was going.

A nightmarish visage loomed up in front of him, floating on a skyboard.

'Arrgh!' Snaggi yelled again, and stabbed reflexively.

Momentum could achieve a lot, including surprise and penetration. Snaggi's stabba struck home and punched deep into the chest of the thing a moment before he collided with it, and the force of the impact knocked both of them clear off the board. The spikie – if that was what it was, for its face was like no spikie Snaggi had ever seen before – was attached to its ride by a chain, which arrested their joint fall a few feet down. The board began to veer, the spikie burbled as blood gouted from its body, and Snaggi desperately clawed at it to try to get some sort of grip with which to hold on. His knife was already slipping free...

His groping fingers caught on the edge of something, and he tightened his grasp, but it came away just as his stabba succumbed to his weight and came loose with a sucking sound. He fell, landed with a thump, looked at what was clenched between his fingers, and shrieked.

The spikie's face had come off in his hand.

Snaggi was not a squeamish sort, but pulling people's faces off was the sort of thing that spikiez did. There wasn't any *point* to it other than causing pain and suffering beyond what any ork, or grot, would be interested in inflicting. If someone needed killing, then you shanked them – if you were a grot, preferably when they were looking the other way. You might make an example of some git what had got too big for his boots, but that was generally by duffing him up a bit more than was needed for him to learn his place, just to make sure everyone else got the message. Pulling faces off? Where was the mileage in that?

Then Snaggi realised two things.

Firstly, the badly bleeding spikie was being borne away by its skyboard, and it was still in possession of its face: in fact, its face looked a lot more face-like than it had a moment ago. The ugly, bulbous, near-shapeless and deeply pitted thing in Snaggi's hand – which also stank, for some reason – was a *mask*.

Secondly, there were several huge, multi-eyed monsters with entirely unreasonably large claws closing in on him with demeanours that were rapidly shifting from curious to predatory.

If there was one thing that Snaggi had learned to do in this cruellest of galaxies, it was to survive. There was no way he could fight these things, and no way he could run from them. The spikie had been hanging around directly above them and wearing this mask, and also wielding a whip that was lying next to where he had fallen, having dropped from the spikie's hand after he'd stabbed it. Presumably, therefore...

Snaggi pulled the mask over his head, cursing the spikie's strange head shape and unnatural eye positioning as he did so. Then he grabbed the whip, and screamed as loud and as feral as he could manage.

It was simple small-creature tactics: make a loud noise, and do whatever you could to convince the bigger things that you weren't an easy meal. What Snaggi would have given for that skyboard, so he could get properly out of their reach! That was long gone now, though, so he had to make the best of what he had.

The creatures started backwards, clearly taken aback by what their senses were telling them. The thing in front of them was certainly food-sized, but it didn't *sound* like food, and what was more, it didn't *smell* like food. The largest ventured forwards again, still uncertain of how to react.

Snaggi took a deep breath, and cracked the whip.

It wasn't an ideal weapon for him: he lacked the height to get the proper action. However, long experience of being under the command of runtherds had given him at least a theoretical understanding of how whips worked, or he'd never have learned when and how fast to duck. The length of it snaked out, and caught the largest beast across the nose.

The monster reared back, snarling in pain and confusion. Snaggi panicked for a moment, certain that he was about to be torn limb from quivering limb, but some instinct pushed him forward – the same instinct that had driven him to dream of becoming Da Grotboss in the first place; the one that said that once you started moving, it was better to keep moving in the same direction than to stop and wait for all your bad choices to catch up with you…

He ran forward, ducked under a swipe of the monster's claws that was more reflexive than aggressive, and launched himself at its back. He grabbed hunks of purplish fur and hauled himself up while it lumbered around in a circle, trying to work out what was going on, until he was sitting between its massive shoulder blades. The others in the pack were watching perplexedly, clearly not quite sure what had happened and not yet making any move to reach out and either swat him off, or cram him into their own mouth and start chewing.

Which left Snaggi Littletoof riding considerably higher than was normal, with a good view of the fight going off around him, and astride a towering monster over which he appeared to have at least nominal control.

'Alright den,' he said, a grin spreading over his face as the adrenaline coursed through his veins and his thumping heartbeat served to remind him that somehow or other, he wasn't dead yet. He yanked on the monster's ear with one hand and showed it the whip in its peripheral vision with the other, and it turned in the direction he was pulling. 'Yes! Oh, yes! Dey larfed at Snaggi Littletoof, but who's larfin' now, eh? *Who's larfin' now?'*

The next quarter-revolution of the monster brought an interesting tableau into view: the massive – somehow even more massive than before? – shape of Ufthak Blackhawk, wielding the Snazzhammer as he fought not one, not two, but *five* spikie bosses coming at him from all angles. This was *destiny*. This was *fate*. This was Gork and Mork presenting Snaggi with a gift and daring him to take it.

'Ladz!' Snaggi said, drunk on power. He raised his whip, and pointed it at the brawl.

'Lunchtime.'

TWENTY-EIGHT

Ufthak Blackhawk was fighting all five of them, and while it wasn't necessarily *winning*, it certainly wasn't losing as quickly or as emphatically as Dhaemira Thraex would have liked.

Five of the most dangerous combatants in the galaxy – three archons, a master haemonculus, and a grand succubus, a rank only achieved through being one of the greatest gladiatorial fighters ever to set foot in Commorragh – should have over-whelmed any enemy in short order, even one as physically imposing as this massive brute. That hadn't happened, and what was even more frustrating was that Dhaemira was pretty sure she knew *why* it hadn't happened, but could do little to fix it.

The simple fact was that she and her nominal allies were not used to working as a team. Xurzuli had long ago left behind the sort of arena combat in which the rank-and-file wyches engaged, where one group would fight against another, or against a squad of captured mon-keigh, or a ferocious beast. If the succubus took to the arena now it was to fight by herself – perhaps against a plethora of foes, or against one exceptionally deadly opponent in a display bout, or an underling challenging for her status. In open battle, she went and killed where she would, and the rest of her cult did their best to keep up. Combat was now the ultimate expression of Xurzuli Mindrex's ego, and there was no room for compromise; she expected others to either be doing as she wished, or to get out of her way.

The rest of them were no better. Maculatix was as jerkily unpredictable in a fight as he was in matters of politics or strategy, and Dhaemira had to pull a cut more than once because the master of the Coven of the Red Harvest suddenly appeared in front of her making an attack of his own. Dhalgar was a vainglorious fool, overeager for revenge for his previous humiliation by the monster, yet clearly – to Dhaemira's eyes, at least – scared of the consequences if he actually got too close. As a result, his contributions mainly consisted of a relentless slew of vituperous curses, some half-hearted blows with his blade that never came close to reaching the ork's flesh, and a great deal of posturing and getting in the way.

Of all the other four, and rather surprisingly, Cistrial Virn was the one with which Dhaemira was able to work the most effectively. However, even that was far from perfect; they were almost awkward around each other, often having the same idea at the same moment and nearly colliding, or otherwise inconveniencing themselves.

'I had an angle!' Cistrial raged, as Dhaemira dragged him backwards.

'And the ork would have had your head in return!' Dhaemira snapped, as the massive hammer whistled through the spot where Cistrial had been standing a moment before.

'And why would you care about that?' Cistrial demanded, shaking his arm free from Dhaemira's grasp. He seemed unreasonably angry for someone who had just been saved from decapitation, but Dhaemira understood; she would also be galled to feel she owed something to a rival.

'Your assistance is still required to defeat this menace,' she said crisply.

'Besides,' a voice added, in a similarly factual tone, 'your face is aesthetically pleasing, and it would be inconsiderate of you to get it destroyed.'

It took half a moment for Dhaemira to realise that it was in fact *her* who had said that as well, and that her mouth had run on far in advance of her brain. A flurry of unfamiliar emotions ran through her in the time it took for startled comprehension to spread across Cistrial's face, and then she dived back into the fray with the determination of one for whom immediate obliteration was no longer the worst possible option.

The trouble was, Ufthak Blackhawk moved faster and with more precision than should be possible for anything that size, which is not to say that it was faster than the drukhari with which it was battling, but combined with its great size, strength, and reach, it was fast *enough*. A mere scratch from Dhaemira's venom blade – a replacement from her armoury for the one the ork had previously shattered – would be enough to incapacitate most foes, although the deeper the wound, the faster the poison would spread. However, Ufthak was so big she was not sure that she could rely on even the virulent toxins that coated her weapon to perform as she would normally expect. A glancing blow from the ork's energised hammer, on the other hand, could be quite enough to debilitate her given the force with which it was being wielded.

Xurzuli attacked with a scream, lashing out with her agoniser. The whip's micro-serrated coils wrapped around the ork's forearm, which should have been enough to connect to its nervous system and overload it with pain stimuli, but Ufthak merely grunted and used its other arm to swing its hammer in a wide circle, over which Xurzuli vaulted as effortlessly and gracefully as if she were performing an acrobatic routine. Dhaemira lunged in, seeking to bury her venom blade between the monster's ribs while it was distracted–

–and her legs were taken out from under her. She landed on her side, just as one of Ufthak's enormous feet swept past above her in an unsighted kick that could have shattered most of the bones in her sternum. She rolled aside desperately as the ork brought its hammer down at her, then was tugged clear by her ankles.

'What–' she began, then stopped as she realised she had been pulled almost into the arms of the crouching Cistrial Virn. The other archon's long-hafted spear was immediately obvious as the reason why Dhaemira's legs had disappeared from under her.

'Turnabout is fair play,' Cistrial said with a wicked grin. 'I too cannot allow my ally to die yet. And in addition,' he added, leaning close, 'I have tasted pain and despair many times from another drukhari, and while mortification is not as nourishing, it has the benefit of novelty. Perhaps I shall have to trick you into accidentally complimenting me again.'

The accusation of imperfection stung Dhaemira into action, and she rolled away and up to her feet. '*Accidentally?* I can assure you, I do not make mistakes!'

'Then your words were honestly meant?' Cistrial said, and there was the briefest flicker in the icy wall of his composure.

'Of course!' Dhaemira said. She saw an opening, and long experience at politicking and preying on the insecurities of others made her strike for it instinctively before she had even considered her words. 'Why? Do you doubt yourself?'

'Do not be ridiculous!' Cistrial snapped. 'I... am beautiful, and clearly you would be attracted to me!'

'Then we are in agreement!' Dhaemira said, even as a small part of her brain wondered what in the name of the Living Muse was going on.

Cistrial readied his spear again, and nodded towards where Ufthak Blackhawk had just taken one of Maculatix's arms off with his axe blade, leaving the haemonculus scuttling backwards and cursing. 'We should probably–'

'Yes,' Dhaemira said, with considerable certainty and no little relief.

They attacked together, Cistrial probing high with his spear while Dhaemira went in low. Ufthak had been battering Maculatix backwards while fending off jabs from Xurzuli's glaive and largely ignoring the ineffective Dhalgar, but the huge ork broke off its pursuit of the haemonculus as the two archons began to press it from behind. It whirled around with a stentorian bellow, and slammed its hammer down; Dhaemira and Cistrial dodged to either side, and although the ork swatted Cistrial's answering spear-thrust away, this time Dhaemira's blade penetrated its defences and the point parted cloth to dig into the creature's right thigh. Ufthak made its counterstroke, but Dhaemira was already rolling away, although the energy field that crackled around the head of the hammer passed so close to her head that her hair began to smoulder in the moment before she got clear.

'Grand work!' Maculatix cackled, lunging for the ork's back with his flesh gauntlet poised.

However, the master haemonculus had miscalculated. A normal enemy would be incapacitated within seconds, but an ork of this size was no normal enemy. Ufthak didn't even look; it just rammed the haft of its hammer backwards, so hard and so fast that the blunt tip of it slammed straight into Maculatix's chest, punched through his ribcage, and emerged through his spine.

Even a haemonculus' resilience and immunity to pain had its limits. Maculatix sagged like a marionette with its strings severed, his expression more one of shock than anything else. Ufthak shook his body back off the hammer's haft, then used the weapon's head to flatten Maculatix's skull against the ground.

'One down,' the huge ork grunted in the mon-keigh tongue.

Then it staggered, and dropped to one knee.

'Now you die, beast!' Xurzuli snarled, charging forwards. Dhaemira went with her, venom blade held ready, with Cistrial Virn at her side–

Until Cistrial cried out, and staggered, and dropped with Dhalgar's blade between his ribs.

'*No!*' Dhaemira shouted, aghast. Cistrial was too powerful, too *perfect* to be brought low by Dhaemira's wretch of a brother... And yet there Dhalgar was, twisting his foul sword in the wound and relishing in the agony he was bringing forth. The blade gave off a tangible aura of spite now it had tasted flesh, and Dhaemira could hear its soundless laughter. There was a drukhari soul bound into the weapon, lending its viciousness to Dhalgar's own.

'Come, sister!' Dhalgar shouted gleefully. 'Let the succubus have her kill! We can take control of the Kabal of the Falling Night, and power will be ours in any case!'

'No,' Dhaemira repeated, more quietly, and attacked.

She knew the look in her brother's eyes. His ambition would not be slaked even by subsuming the Falling Night into their ranks – which would be no easy feat in any case, since Cistrial had various subordinate archons of his own who would want to stake their claim to the kabal rather than see it taken over by outsiders – but Dhaemira's decision was not predicated solely on the knowledge that it would only be a matter of time before Dhalgar turned his blade on her. Cistrial Virn was not just aesthetically pleasing; there was something about him that Dhaemira *admired*, and she wanted time to study that feeling, to examine it and pull it apart, so that she knew exactly how another might take advantage of her. She could not do that if the object of her attentions was dead.

It took Dhalgar a moment to understand her intent, so caught up was he in his premature triumph. He only withdrew his blade from Cistrial's side to parry Dhaemira's first strike at the last moment, and then he was back-pedalling before her attacks, Cistrial's blood flicking around as his blade darted from side to side.

'This is folly!' Dhalgar spat. 'You would slay your own blood over this *rival*?'

'Do not pretend that the bonds of blood would hold you!' Dhaemira snarled. 'And yes, Dhalgar, because rival or not, he is worth ten of you!'

'What are you idiots *doing?!*' Xurzuli screamed from somewhere behind Dhaemira. 'The beast is regaining its strength!'

Dhalgar screamed. For a moment Dhaemira thought it was in horror at Ufthak's recovery, but that seemed unlikely: the huge ork would have to get through Xurzuli and Dhaemira before it could reach him. Then she heard the rapid, heavy tread of feet behind her, and threw herself to one side on instinct.

The clawed fiend tore through the air where she had just been standing. Dhalgar fled before another, trying to ward it off with sweeps of his blade. The presence of the fiends was not a complete surprise – they were huge and vicious arena creatures often goaded into battle by beastmasters, although they had a tendency to fly into berserk rages that could endanger allies and foes alike – but what was definitely unusual was that the one which had just tried to attack Dhaemira had one of the orks' small slave caste riding it, wearing a stolen beastmaster's mask and wielding a whip. Not just any beastmaster's mask, in fact: Dhaemira recognised it from when she had spoken to Ufthak in the dungeons.

'Karfynd was slain by one of *you?*' she scoffed, as the slave – grot? – hauled on the side of the fiend's head and managed to bring it around to face her. The beast roared, but Dhaemira was quicker. Her blade slashed out twice, carving an 'x' shape into the hard muscle of its chest. There was no delay in the toxins taking effect here, and the fiend staggered while the grot on its back clung on desperately.

Dhaemira risked a look behind her. Ufthak Blackhawk, bleeding from various gashes inflicted by Xurzuli, clubbed down another clawed fiend with its hammer. Xurzuli herself fended off a second, expertly severing its spine with her glaive, but the moment of inattention cost her. Even her preternatural agility and reflexes were insufficient to avoid the next blow Ufthak launched, aimed directly at her.

It was very hard to land a blow on a succubus, but when you were as strong as an ork the size of Ufthak Blackhawk, you only needed to land one.

The hammer's axe head carved Xurzuli Mindrex, grand succubus of the Cult of the Deathly Sorrow, into two separate pieces. She hit the ground at the same time as the clawed fiend Dhaemira had just cut with her blade; the grot that had been riding on its back scurried past Dhaemira, running for the massive shape of Ufthak Blackhawk. The huge ork was clearly not quite fully recovered from the toxins Dhaemira had introduced into its system, but its red eyes latched on to her with recognition and malice.

A scream made her look back around again, only to see Dhalgar transfixed by the blade of Cistrial's spear. Her brother had brought down the fiend that had attacked him and had been coming for Dhaemira while her attention was on the ork, but Virn had stabbed him from where he lay on the ground, and his spear's head had found the gap between Dhalgar's armour plates to lodge just above his hip.

Dhaemira batted Dhalgar's half-hearted parry away, disarming him in the process, and plunged her blade into the corresponding gap on the other side. Dhalgar spluttered and collapsed to his knees as the venom began to take hold. He was no longer a threat; he would be paralysed in moments, and dead within a minute. Dhaemira harboured no regrets. Her brother had been a rival from the moment he was born, he had also been useful enough – just – to outweigh it. Now he had outlived his usefulness, although, it had to be said, not by very long.

Which was no guarantee that Dhaemira would survive much longer. With her brother dealt with, she turned her attention back to Ufthak Blackhawk. Cistrial Virn had wrenched his spear back out of Dhalgar with a cry of pain at the effort it took him, and was trying to lever himself up to his feet, but he would be of little use in a fight save as a brief and barely mobile distraction. Ufthak was bleeding and slightly poisoned, but merely looked all the more invulnerable for it as the creature took its first step towards her. It had taken the best that five drukhari lords had to offer and had, for various reasons, outlasted them. It was an arakhia, a Child of Destruction, and at this moment it looked as inevitable as a drukhari's final death.

Something that, of course, any drukhari would try to ward off for as long as possible.

'You said you wanted to get back out into the galaxy!' Dhaemira shouted in Low Gothic, readying her blade. 'To fight your... your *Meklord* and take command! Why not do that? Why not just leave?'

Ufthak paused in its stride, worked its mouth, and spat out a tooth. 'Workin' on it.'

Dhaemira's brow creased in confusion, but at least while she was conversing with the beast, it wasn't attacking. Perhaps it lacked the brain power for both. '"Working on it"? What in the name of all the stars and souls does that mean?'

'Dhaemira,' Cistrial said weakly. 'Look up.'

Dhaemira had no intention of taking her eyes off Ufthak, but then something began to press in on her eardrums. It was noise, gradually starting to make itself heard over the din of battle, but it was something else as well: a change of pressure, a massive displacement of air.

And with it came a shadow.

Certain that she was making a mistake, but unable to ignore what was happening, Dhaemira looked around and up. What she saw took a moment to process, but when her brain had caught up with her eyes it sent a cleansing wave of pure fury coursing through her.

'That is *Heart's End*,' she breathed, looking up at the distinctive, wasp-waisted shape of her flagship descending towards them. The vessel's thrusters were firing, and it was somehow navigating the gravity well of Port Tavarr, although not with any degree of grace. Its engines were overcharged, and what should have been minor corrections were being accomplished with clumsy bursts that sent it rocking drunkenly back and forth. It almost looked as if it was being flown by...

Being flown by...

'Da Boffin needed a bit of time to get 'imself sorted, I guess,' Ufthak rumbled, 'but da lad's come up wiv da goods.'

'You've taken my *ship*?' Dhaemira yelled, rounding on the ork that was grinning at her infuriatingly.

'Ain't *yoor* ship no more,' Ufthak said. 'But yeah, dat's our way outta here. All we need now is to get on it, an' find a way to get it froo dat gate fingy right up dere.'

Dhaemira looked up again. Far above, where her ship *should* have been at anchor, she could just make out the burning wrecks of other drukhari vessels, and beyond them was the Portgate, which led out of Port Tavarr and into the wider webway. The *Heart's End* had been taken, and it had wrought havoc on the other ships berthed around it before it had come careering down here in search of its new masters. She would undoubtedly have been informed of this, or even noticed it for herself, had the orks not been creating so much chaos across the entire area.

'Of course,' Ufthak continued, his voice somehow roughening even further, 'last time we spoke, I woz talkin' about makin' yoo suffer. I ain't as fancy as yoo spikie gits wiv yer skinny little knives an' yer pain-jabbers, but if yoo wanna keep us here den I guess I ain't gonna have anyfing better to do.'

'If you stay here then you will be worn down and slaughtered, piece by piece!' Dhaemira spat. 'You and all your followers will die!'

'So will yoo an' a lot of yoors, an' we ain't da ones scared of dyin',' Ufthak replied, spinning its hammer. 'Make yer choice, spikie. Cos dat's a big old gun on dat ship wot used to be yoors, an' I reckon Da Boffin can have a *lot* of fun wiv it before he crashes.'

Voidbreaker. The largest dark lance ever crafted, and surely the cause of death for many of the ships now burning in the zero-gravity anchorage far above. Dhaemira thought about what that weapon might do, were it to be discharged here. It could annihilate the arena and everything in it in short order, for starters.

Losing her flagship would be like losing a limb, but limbs could be regrown for the drukhari nobility. The most powerful succubus and haemonculus in the realm were dead, and the archon she had considered her closest rival appeared to be an ally beyond all drukhari norms, ready to stand and die with her.

All she needed to do was to get the orks out of Port Tavarr, and the authority she'd craved could still be hers.

'You need a way through the gate,' she said, her voice hoarse in her throat. 'You need one of us.'

'If dat's wot it takes,' Ufthak said. 'It'd be easier'n da uvver way I came up wiv before.'

Dhaemira reached a decision.

She reached into a belt pouch and pulled out a tiny vial of sleek black glass, then knelt beside Dhalgar's spasming form. His helmet was the work of a moment to remove. The face beneath was deathly pale, and he was foaming at the mouth as his internal organs failed. Death was imminent – or would have been, had Dhaemira not had the antidote to her blade's venom to hand.

She broke the top off the vial, and emptied the contents into her brother's mouth. It dripped between his teeth and flowed over his swelling tongue, and he had just enough consciousness left to recognise what was going on, and swallow. The antidote took effect nearly as quickly as the venom had, and his shaking began to subside almost instantly.

Dhaemira didn't wait for him to recover fully, even though he would be weak for some time to come from the poison ravaging his body. She picked him up and threw him towards Ufthak, and he stumbled and collapsed into a pile at the massive ork's feet.

'Take him,' she said. 'He'll need to feed on something's pain if you want him to survive for long. But I couldn't care less if he does or not,' she added.

'Somefing's pain?' Ufthak repeated. He grabbed the grot that had been cowering behind his leg, which tried to make a break for freedom far too late and was snared by a hand as big as it was. 'Reckon we can manage dat. In fact,' Ufthak added with a grin, looking to its left, 'dat gives me an idea...'

Dhaemira was not about to ask the ork what its idea was, but nor was she certain what was going to happen now. Were the beasts actually going to try to land the *Heart's End*? The ship had never been intended to manoeuvre in gravity, let alone make planetfall, even in an artificial environment like Port Tavarr. Besides which, it was immense; Dhaemira was not sure that it could fit inside the arena, and ork piloting had always seemed to be more a matter of luck than of judgement.

Then Ufthak, the grot in its hand, and her brother flared brightly. Dhalgar's expression drew into a rictus of horror for a moment as he realised what was about to happen, and then they disappeared.

'They're teleporting *again*?' Cistrial rasped, leaning on his spear.

'How did they build one so quickly?' Dhaemira demanded of the empty air, turning to look up at the *Heart's End*. 'And out of what? Did they just haul a load of their junk aboard my–'

She broke off as light flared around them, again and again and again. Entire groups of orks disappeared in the middle of a fight. Vehicles that had been there one moment were gone the next. Drukhari, recognising the deadly occurrences for what they were, scrambled desperately away from any nearby orks in an effort to avoid being dragged through the warp with them. Most were successful. Some were not, and their despairing screams, cut off almost as soon as they began, were nearly enough to make Dhaemira feel sorry for them. Still, Ufthak might have a few other candidates to use to get through the webway gate if Dhalgar's soul had been torn from his body by daemons during his unexpected trip, which at least reduced the likelihood of the ork returning and looking for a new victim.

In under a minute, the vast majority of the orks were gone. Some of the larger walkers had been left, presumably because it would have taken too much power to move them rather than because the orks had carefully measured the space available in any individual cargo bay aboard the *Heart's End* and found it lacking. Dead orks had been left as well, but they were not the only green-skinned shapes still on the surface of the Arena of Deathly Sorrow.

A very large group of grots gradually realised that not only were they now alone in the midst of the enemy, but that they weren't going anywhere either. Above them all, the *Heart's End* began a rather shaky turn, pointing its nose back up towards the Portgate. The grots, it seemed, were staying behind.

Orks might not feel much pain or much fear, but their diminutive slaves were a very different matter. For drukhari who had been fighting for their lives a moment before, many of whom had taken grievous wounds in the process, the grots were like a cup of water placed before someone dying of thirst. Here, at last, were victims that were unlikely to offer much resistance. Deadly weapons were discarded, and knives were drawn that were nearly as sharp as the smiles on the faces of those wielding them.

Dhaemira inspected Cistrial's wound. It was deep, and Dhalgar's cursed blade had caused it to fester already, but it was not fatal. 'A brace of those wretches should meet your needs, I believe,' she said, addressing the other archon. 'And I am sure we can find a lesser haemonculus to assist. Indeed, given Maculatix's fate, I suspect there will be many who would wish to ally themselves with the power that we could become together.'

'You would help me?' Cistrial asked, wincing in pain.

'Of course,' Dhaemira said. 'Lord Virn, Port Tavarr is ours for the taking, battered though it might be. After that, who is to say that our talents combined could not take us considerably further? Assuming, that is,' she said, looking Cistrial in the eye with rather more effort than should have been required for an archon to whom projecting confidence was second nature, 'you wish to enter into such a... partnership.'

Cistrial's eyes searched Dhaemira's face. In search of deception? Or in search of something else?

'Yes,' the archon of the Falling Night said after a long moment. 'Yes, I would– I believe that would be... very beneficial. To us both.'

Something skittered inside Dhaemira's chest. Her ambition, recognising another opportunity to increase her power.

Certainly that, and nothing else.

TWENTY-NINE

'Ya don't want me to bring dat big bunch of grots up, boss?' Da Boffin asked, as he swung the spikie ship around.

'Nah, leave 'em,' Ufthak said. 'Dey'll keep da spikiez busy for a bit, an' make sure dey don't try anyfing fancy like shootin' us down. Course,' he added, 'it's a bit weird how so many of 'em were all in da same place wivout any runtherds around.' He looked at Snaggi Littletoof, who was staring back out of the window with an expression that hovered halfway between horror and relief. 'Yoo know anyfing about dat, runt?'

Snaggi jumped, and backed away from the window. 'Me, boss? No, boss.'

'Don't listen to 'im, boss!' a new voice piped up, and Nizkwik hurried into the bridge area. 'I was *dere*. Snaggi got a whole bunch of 'em fired up, an' ready to fight for da Waaagh! It was amazin'!'

'Is dat so?' Ufthak said, narrowing his eyes. On the one hand, grots who were actually prepared to fight were a sight more useful than grots usually were. On the other hand, it sounded suspicious.

'Ah, Nizkwik,' Snaggi said, in a voice that could have stripped paint. 'Fank da gods yoo made it out, I fort yoo woz dead.'

'Not me!' Nizkwik said, happily oblivious to Snaggi's tone. 'An' guess wot else got tellyported up!'

The little grot turned and whistled, then shrieked in alarm as Princess bounded in with jaws slavering.

'Ya zoggin' idiot!' Snaggi yelled, as the squig chased the two grots around and out into the corridor beyond. 'Why'd ya *call* it?'

'I fort da boss would want to know 'is squig was okay!'

Ufthak grunted, and turned away. Everything was back to normal there, at any rate, although he had a nagging feeling he should be keeping a close eye on Snaggi Littletoof. He immediately dismissed the thought as nonsense. He was an ork, and a massive one at that. Snaggi was only a grot. What harm could it possibly do, except to itself?

The spikie that the other spikie had thrown at him was curled up in a ball, panting and whimpering. Ufthak prodded it with his boot, waiting to see if it pulled knives out of anywhere and lunged for him.

'Oi.'

This garnered no response, which irked Ufthak. What was the git so scared of? Had it never been tellyported before?

He reached down, grabbed it by its head, and hoisted it bodily into the air. The spikie wailed and flailed, then froze as he tightened his grip warningly.

'Lissen carefully,' Ufthak said in Humie. 'Last time ya tangled wiv me I left ya wivout an arm, an' squashed flat. Obviously dat ain't enuff to off one of yoo lot, so I'm guessin' dere's quite a bit I could do to ya before ya die from it, an' as I understand it, yoo lot *really* don't want to die, so you ain't gonna be lookin' for a quick way out. Wot's more,' he added, 'if it looks like yoo're gonna die, I could let da painboyz have a go at ya, see if dey can keep ya around. Not even orks trust da painboyz, so I fink somefing like yoo might wanna avoid dat, am I right?'

The spikie didn't speak, but something about its expression suggested to Ufthak that whatever spirit it had was breaking, if not already shattered. He'd thought as much; it had yelled a lot when they'd been fighting, but didn't seem to dare go near him. It was basically a grot, just taller and a lot less green.

'Or,' he continued, 'if ya piss me off, I could just tellyport ya somewhere. Don't fink yoo'd like dat. Maybe I could just telly-port ya *nowhere*.'

The spikie's eyes widened in horror.

'See, now we're gettin' somewhere,' Ufthak told it, grinning. 'So here's da deal, spikie. We're takin' dis ship out of dat gate fing up in da sky, an' we're leavin'. Den I'm off to have a con-versation wiv me boss about who's really in charge now, but dat ain't none of yer business. All *yoo* gots to do is make sure dat gate opens for us. If ya can do dat, we're good. Can ya do it?'

The spikie tried to nod. However, given it was being held up by its head, it didn't have a great deal of success.

'Yes,' it said, sullenly.

'Say, "Yes, *boss*",' Ufthak told it.

The spikie glared at him, but only for a moment. Once he began tightening his grip a little, it hissed at him, but then bared its teeth and spoke through them.

'Yes, boss.'

'Dere's a good spikie,' Ufthak said. 'Now, I'm gonna let go of ya. Get us froo da gate, an' we're larfin'. Try anyfing kunnin' an' I'll rip *both* yer arms off dis time, an' put ya in a cage for da grots to poke.'

He opened his hand. The spikie dropped and landed with the

grace inherent to its kind, but backed off and put its back against the wall rather than stab anyone. Even though this ship belonged to its kind, it already looked out of place: Da Boffin had rigged up his own control systems to make the alien machine do what he wanted, and crude levers, large buttons, and trailing wires abounded.

'So yoo made it go, den,' Ufthak said, switching back into Orkish. 'Good job.'

'We got all manners of go,' Da Boffin replied, beaming. Then his smile faded. 'Except one. I've figured out wot most of dere stuff does, but da spikiez ain't got nuffin' wot looks even a little bit like a warp drive. Dey must use dere tunnel fings to fly any-where dey wanna go.'

Ufthak grunted. 'Ugh. I just wanna get out of dis place, can't be bovvered wiv tunnels an' dat. Okay, so we get a new ship as soon as possible, one dat can go into da warp so we can find Da Meklord.' He paused, as another thought struck him. 'Did ya get Mogrot up?'

'Pretty sure, yeah,' Da Boffin said. 'He was wiv Wazzock's lot.'

'Good,' Ufthak said, nodding with satisfaction. 'Da git owes me a new trukk.' He pointed at a light that had just started flashing urgently on one of the control panels. 'Wot's dat mean?'

'Dat is…' Da Boffin checked a gizmo that was plugged into about three different things. 'Temp'ral instability. Means dere's some weird warpy stuff goin' on. Somewhere behind us, by da looks of it.'

'Wot, like Chaos gribblies an' dat?' Ufthak asked, wondering if they'd left the spikiez' arena too soon.

'Yeah, might be,' Da Boffin said. 'Reality might be comin' apart just a little bit, dat sort of fing. We did a lot of tellyportin', and I don't fink dis place is exactly *real*, if ya get me drift. Not like planets.' He flicked the instrument. 'Might come to nuffin'. Wanna check it out, just in case?'

Ufthak thought about it for a few seconds, then shook his head. 'Nah. Chaos gribblies is fun, but killin' 'em ain't exactly *satisfyin'*, wot wiv how dey just dissolve. Let's find a proper ship wiv an engine wot'll get us froo da warp.'

'Wotever yoo say, boss,' Da Boffin said, feeding more power to the engines and accelerating their climb. 'Seems a shame to let da spikiez have all da fun, tho.'

Ufthak grinned. Chaos gribblies tended to be fairly single-minded, were often quite hard to hurt, and rarely seemed to pay much attention to thoughts of their own mortality.

'Oh, don't worry,' he told Da Boffin. 'I don't fink dey're gonna be havin' much *fun*...'

THIRTY

The star was all big and red, and near it – as stars went, which meant it was still a long way away by any other standards – was another that was smaller, and more yellowy. Three planets orbited the big red star, and it was around the central one of these, a green-and-blue rocky world, that the ships of the Tekwaaagh! were clustered. There didn't seem to be much in the way of void combat going on; if whomever the Waaagh! was fighting had possessed ships at any point, they'd either been destroyed or had fled. The surface of the planet was a different matter, though. Even from a distance, Ufthak could see the grey pall that obscured great swathes of the world. A lot of stuff was burning, which was a pretty reliable sign of a good fight.

It had been a bit of a trek to get here. They'd found an exit large enough for the spikie ship that had brought them out not far from a humie shipyard. The humies, it seemed, were not expecting a spikie ship either piloted or crewed by orks, and the shipyard's defenders had been overwhelmed in short order.

However, it had taken Da Boffin and his undermeks a while to hack together enough different bits to make a ship that an ork wouldn't be embarrassed to fly in, so they hadn't been as swift in answering Da Meklord's call as Ufthak would have liked. Then they'd had to follow the signal from the shouty box back to where it came from, which involved flying through the warp, and the warp could be zoggin' difficult when it wanted to be. Orks were mostly happy to go wherever it took them, safe in the knowledge that they'd probably find a fight wherever they emerged, but Ufthak had a specific destination in mind, and that always took a bit longer.

Thankfully, it seemed that the Waaagh! hadn't moved on anywhere, and now here he was in his own ship. It was a kroozer, since they'd not had the time or the resources to make anything truly massive and impressive, but it was big enough. Ufthak had called it *Starsmasha*, because that sounded quite killy.

'How's it goin' in dere, spikie?' Ufthak asked, rattling the cage that hung on one wall. The spikie inside – Dhalgar, apparently – whimpered. It had thought it was cunning by waiting until they were involved in the battle at the humie shipyard before trying to stab Ufthak, but it hadn't stabbed hard enough. It still had both of its arms, but it also had a nasty-looking series of gashes across its face, as though inflicted by a clawed hand.

'Please...' the spikie burbled, still curled up in a ball. 'Please don't go through the warp again.' It had not been Ufthak, or indeed any other ork, that had inflicted its injuries.

'Ain't a promise I can make ya,' Ufthak said cheerily, and the spikie whined. Ufthak moved away from it, and began studying the read-outs in front of him.

'Where's da *Mork's Hammer*?' he asked. The bridge of the *Starsmasha* was a heavily adapted humie one, but Da Boffin had left a lot of their instruments in place. Say what you want about humies, at least they weren't spikiez; they made devices you could understand without being a mekboy and running it through a bunch of wires first.

'Dat one,' Da Boffin said, pointing.

'Alright den, just like we planned,' Ufthak said, and cracked his knuckles. Most warbosses would be down on the planet at the heart of the scrap, but Da Meklord was a bit weird. He liked to tellyport down in his Mega-Gargant, or just stay in orbit and blow stuff up with his ship's guns. That was what happened when you had a mekboy in charge, Ufthak supposed – particularly a Bad Moons mekboy. Ufthak was a Bad Moon, and appreciated a good bit of dakka as much as the next ork, but there was a time and a place for it. You had to get your hands dirty, or how did anyone know you were really the boss?

He leaned over and pressed the 'on' switch on the shouta. 'Dis is Ufthak Blackhawk on da *Starsmasha*. Any of yoo gits listenin'?'

The speakers erupted in noise. Some of it was ork kaptins who recognised Ufthak's name or his voice and greeted him enthusiastically, or told him to zog off again just as enthusiastically, or often both one after another. A lot of it was just noise; orks didn't hold with the notion of staying quiet – unless they were Blood Axes – so if an ork had a way of making noise he would usually be using it. If he had a way of broadcasting that noise far and wide to anyone listening, or unable to *not* listen, so much the better.

Then a new voice cut through, deeper and more powerful, and not sounding best pleased.

'Dat yoo, Ufthak? Yoo decided to join us, den?'

Back in the day, Ufthak might not have recognised sarcasm when it was directed at him. Now, however, his brain was easily developed enough to know what it was, and he didn't much appreciate it.

'Well, yoo asked so nice,' he said. It might have just been his imagination, but he didn't think that the voice coming out of his own mouth was any lighter in pitch or timbre that Da Meklord's, which suggested that he was easily the same size as Da Biggest Big Mek now. The slight pause before Da Meklord answered suggested that he'd noticed it, too.

'An' wot loot have ya got for me? Took ya long enuff to get 'ere, so I'm hopin' it's gonna be worth da wait.'

'Me too,' Ufthak said, with complete honesty. He'd picked the *Mork's Hammer* out by eye now, a particular shape and set of lights in orbit over the planet beneath that was starting to turn casually towards the *Starsmasha*, as though welcoming it to the group. There was nothing between the two ships, and Ufthak had a feeling that Da Meklord was ordering his 'eavy guns to be ready to open fire, just in case.

'So, boss,' he said casually, 'yoo wanna come over an' check on wot I got for ya? Dis ship's got somefing well speshul on it, an' you're gonna want to see it up close.'

There was a pause. Then: *'Alright, I'll come an' look at me new ship. Stay where yoo are.'*

Ufthak bristled at that – *his* new ship? – but he held his peace. Finkin', that was the key. It had got him this far, in one form or another, and it could take him a bit further. He looked out of the viewport, wondering how long it would be before the *Mork's Hammer* came alongside them. Or would Da Meklord just leave his ship where it was, get into a boarding craft and come over like that?

'Boss,' Da Boffin said, wrinkling his brow at a whirring dial, 'we're gettin' a massive power spike from da *Mork's Hammer*.'

Ufthak grunted. That could mean anything, when Da Meklord and his ship was concerned. 'Are dey chargin' up dere guns?'

'Don't fink so,' Da Boffin said, scratching his head. 'Looks more like–'

The air pressure suddenly increased dramatically, and Ufthak's ears popped. He whirled around as the air on the bridge began to shimmer, and Da Boffin's various spannerz scrambled out of the way. They knew what was coming.

The distortion resolved into half a dozen blocky shapes, which snapped into an almost too-sharp reality. Then, with a stink of ozone, Da Biggest Big Mek himself stood on the bridge of the *Starsmasha*, along with a group of orks Ufthak loosely recognised as Da Meklord's most trusted underlings.

He was immense, decked out in proper Bad Moons black and yellow. One arm of his mighty mega-armour terminated in a kustom kombi-weapon with multiple barrels and various bizarre-looking ammunition feeds, and the other hand clutched the Shokkhammer, his tri-headed weapon that could literally knock chunks of his enemies into the warp. He dripped with trophies and gadgetry, for Da Meklord had an intense and unending fascination with anything teknologickal, and his back banners proclaimed his many triumphs in artwork rendered by press-ganged grots.

Ufthak whistled. 'Nice tellyportin'. Yoo get da idea from Badrukk?'

'Dat git?' Da Meklord growled. 'I'd like to see 'im tellyport a Mega-Gargant into a fight. Zoggin' amateur.' He straightened, raising his chin in what Ufthak realised was an attempt to look down his nose, which was more difficult than it had been, because the two of them were now of a similar size. 'So, Ufthak Blackhawk. Wot's da loot?' He looked around, and sniffed. 'Dis don't look nuffin' speshul.'

'It's not da ship as such, it's wot's on it,' Ufthak said. 'Or rather, wot's underneaf it. An' I could show ya, but dere's a problem.'

'A problem?' Da Meklord said, tilting his head to one side. 'Wot sort of problem?'

Ufthak took a deep breath. This was it. Even for an ork, even for an ork as big and strong and smart as he was, this was not something to do lightly. However, since he was by now quite heavy, it was probably all good.

'Da problem where you're da warboss,' he said, flexing his shoulders, 'an' I don't fink ya should be.'

In other species, there might have been more circling and snapping, more jibes and insults. It didn't work that way for orks. Ufthak had laid down a challenge, and Da Meklord wasn't going to let it sit there doing nothing. Da Biggest Big Mek raised his kombi-weapon, the ammunition feeds clicking and humming as the auto-loaders crammed rounds into breeches, but Ufthak was already moving.

He sprang forward and swung the Snazzhammer at the weapon, and the energised head smashed the worky bitz into a splintering shower of debris that rained across Da Meklord's nobs, who hurried back out of the way. This wasn't a fight they could get involved in; one way or the other, Ufthak or Da Meklord needed to put their opponent down themselves.

Ufthak adjusted his grip and swung the Snazzhammer back the other way, trying to take Da Meklord's head off as he had so many others, but the sheer size of his adversary defeated him; the bulky shoulder plate of Da Meklord's mega-armour got in the way, and although the blow sent the warboss staggering sideways, it did little more than crumple and scar the metal. Then Da Meklord snarled, and went on the attack.

Ufthak blocked three blows from the Shokkhammer, because he had no desire to have parts of his body disappearing – that was the sort of thing that could really ruin your day. He dropped the shokk rifle; it was too cumbersome for use at this sort of close range, and he needed a free hand. He made a grab for the Shokkhammer's haft and managed to catch it, then swung the Snazzhammer at Da Meklord with a toothy grin. Much to his surprise, Da Meklord's free hand emerged from the wreckage of his kombi-weapon and, with shameless imitation, caught the Snazzhammer just below the head.

'Yoo're gonna have to do better'n dat!' Da Meklord spat, fury written all over his face. He heaved, seeking to force Ufthak backwards through sheer mass and strength, but to his visible astonishment, Ufthak held his ground.

'So're yoo,' Ufthak grunted. Mork's teef, but the git was strong! Ufthak was holding Da Meklord in place for the moment, but it was taking everything he had. How long could he keep it up? The servos in Da Meklord's armour were whining and complaining, but they weren't giving up; machines generally didn't get tired, they just worked until they broke.

'Dere's no way yoo can win dis,' Da Meklord said with an ugly laugh. 'You ain't strong enuff!'

Mork curse him, but the git might be right. Ufthak strained again, but he couldn't twist either weapon out of Da Meklord's grip, and it was all he could do to prevent the warboss from managing the same thing. He needed another plan. He needed to do something unexpected. What was the most unexpected thing he could do that might also work?

He let go.

Da Meklord took a stumbling half-step forward, taken unawares by the sudden lack of resistance. Ufthak ducked under the big mek's left arm to come up behind him, clasped both arms around the other ork's waist, and put everything he had into one gigantic heave.

Not that long ago, this would have been a futile attempt; hilariously so, in fact. But Ufthak had been fighting, and he'd been winning, and he'd also been pumped full of a very potent mix of drugs that had accelerated an ork's natural propensity to increase in size and strength. He was much stronger now.

Strong enough to bodily lift another ork in mega-armour,

hoist him over his head, and dump him onto the top of his skull on the floor.

The noise was cataclysmic. It sounded as if someone had thrown a very large spaceship into a planet made of metal. Ufthak fought his way back to his feet, conscious that the left side of his chest was telling him in no uncertain terms that he was a zoggin' idiot and it would be having no part of him trying something like that again, but it had been worth it. The entire top of Da Meklord's armour was crumpled, the servos and gears were spitting and stuttering, and the big mek's head was somewhat flatter than it had been merely seconds before.

And still the git was getting up. You didn't become a warboss if you could be stopped by even a moderate dent in your head.

Ufthak drew his shoota with his left hand and pointed it at Da Meklord's face, but Da Biggest Big Mek snarled and lashed out with the Shokkhammer, and suddenly not only was Ufthak's shoota gone, but his hand was as well. He stared at the stump for a moment, until his brain caught up with events and told him that the Shokkhammer had knocked it clean into the warp, *and was coming for his head next.*

'Time ta go!' Da Meklord cackled, drawing the Shokkhammer back for another attack. His armour was busted, and his head was busted even more, but the git still had enough about him to keep on swinging. Ufthak didn't even have the Snazzhammer; it was well out of his reach, abandoned on the deck where it had slid out of Da Meklord's grasp.

Ufthak closed his fist.

The Snazzhammer appeared in his hand instantly, and Ufthak swung it with a speed and strength born of desperation. The energised hammer surface connected with the haft of the Shokkhammer and snapped it, sending the whirling triple head into one of the watching nobs and obliterating him.

Then, on the backswing, the Snazzhammer's choppa side split Da Meklord's skull in two. Not even Da Biggest Big Mek could withstand that: he fell backwards, stone dead.

Ufthak leaned on the haft of the Snazzhammer for a moment, then eyed the remaining nobs. 'Any of yoo lot got somefing you wanna say?'

They looked at each other. No one could have accused them of being geniuses, but they were smart enough to see which way the wind was blowing. 'No, boss.'

'Good.' Ufthak raised his voice. 'Someone get Dok Drozfang! I'm gonna need a new hand! Again,' he added bitterly, staring at the stump. This would be the third.

'Can I do da fing, boss?' Da Boffin said eagerly. 'Can I do it?'

Ufthak nodded. Some occasions were momentous enough to be marked by a statement of intent, just so no other gits got ideas. He drew himself up to his full height.

'Fire da Black Kannon!'

Da Boffin pushed a lever up as far as it could go, twiddled three dials to maximum, and slammed his hand down on the biggest, reddest button on the ship's entire control panel.

Ufthak became aware of a thrumming noise building beneath him. Most of the *Starsmasha* was built from humie vessels, of course, because their hulls and their technology were far easier to work with than spikie stuff, not to mention considerably more durable. However, there was one very important bit of Ufthak's new ship that retained its spikie origins.

The massive darklight gun mounted under the nose of the *Starsmasha* discharged a moment later, sending a titanic bolt of sputtering black nothing arcing towards the *Mork's Hammer*. Da Meklord's ship was equipped with a force field, as you'd expect from something designed by Da Biggest Big Mek himself, but there was only momentary resistance from it before it was burned out and the bolt of negative energy slammed into the superstructure of the Tekwaaagh!'s flagship. It burned a hole right through the other kroozer – at least, until it hit the fuel stores. Then the *Mork's Hammer* came apart in an explosion like a little sun of its own, just as electricity sparked all across the *Starsmasha*'s bridge and everything went dark.

'We got it!' Ufthak bellowed with glee. 'Who's da warboss now, eh?' He groped for the switch of the shouta and flicked it. '*Who's da warboss now?*'

There was no reply.

'Boffin?' Ufthak said. He hoped the tone of his voice adequately communicated his displeasure at not being able to gloat over this display of utmost shootiness.

'Da Kannon knocked out a bunch of systems, boss,' Da Boffin's voice replied. 'Fried 'em good an' proper.'

Ufthak digested this. 'Wurf it,' he grunted.

'Wurf it!' Da Boffin agreed. 'Anyway, let's 'ave a look...' There was clanking, and the sound of a spanner at work. 'Alright, should be able to talk to da rest of da fleet now.'

'Can we shoot da Black Kannon again?' Ufthak asked hopefully.

'No idea,' Da Boffin admitted. 'It weren't meant to be hooked up to a ship like dis. We can't shoot it right now, anyway. Maybe in da future, when I get a bit more stuff back online. We might just have to hope da gits remember wot it does.'

Ufthak shrugged. 'One shot was good enuff. Anyone else can step up to me da old-fashioned way if dey want to, an' I'll put 'em on dere arse.'

He flicked the shouta activation switch again.

'Now, listen very carefully, ya gits,' he began, ''cos I'm only gonna say dis once. Da Meklord was interested in fancy gubbinz, an' don't get me wrong, yoo can have a lot of fun wiv fancy gubbinz. But it ain't right to be goin' around da galaxy wiv dat as yer focus. We're *orks,* not humie cogboys. So now we're doin' fings my way. Da Boffin's yer new head mekboy, Dok Drozfang's yer new head painboy, an' dis ain't da Tekwaaagh! no more.'

He grinned in the darkness, and the red light of the distant star reflected off his teef.

'Dis is Waaagh! Ufthak, an' it's time to set da galaxy to burnin'.'

ABOUT THE AUTHOR

Mike Brooks is a science fiction and fantasy author who lives in Nottingham, UK. His work for Black Library includes the Horus Heresy Primarchs novel *Alpharius: Head of the Hydra*, the Warhammer 40,000 novels *Warboss, Brutal Kunnin, Da Big Dakka, Renegades: Harrowmaster, Huron Blackheart: Master of the Maelstrom,* and *The Lion: Son of the Forest,* the Necromunda novel *Road to Redemption* and the novellas *Wanted: Dead* and *Da Gobbo's Revenge.* When not writing, he plays guitar and sings in a punk band, and DJs wherever anyone will tolerate him.

Bleeding Hearts

Anyone who has ever suffered from a broken heart knows that love has its dark side. But just how deep that darkness can be may surprise you. *The Scary Book of Valentine's Day Love* bravely ventures into this bottomless abyss, collecting tales of deadly and dastardly loves from all over the globe, including:

The Boy Killed by Kisses: A dream scenario quickly turns nightmarish

The Hook: The legend of the crazed killer who stalks Lover's Lanes everywhere

La Sayona: Be careful with your wandering eye—Venezuela's "Sackcloth Woman" is ready to pounce

The Chocolate Cream Killer: There's nothing sweet about a treat from Christiana Edmunds

Whether you love a good scare or just can't stand the sickeningly sweet side of Valentine's Day, *The Scary Book of Valentine's Day Love* is all the company you'll need this holiday.

cidermillpress.com

RELIGION / Holidays / Other
USD $16.99 / CAD $21.00
ISBN 978-1-40034-889-3

51699

9 781400 348893

About Cider Mill Press Book Publishers

Good ideas ripen with time. From seed to harvest, Cider Mill Press brings fine reading, information, and entertainment together between the covers of its creatively crafted books. Our Cider Mill bears fruit twice a year, publishing a new crop of titles each spring and fall.

CIDER MILL
PRESS

BOOK
PUBLISHERS

"Where Good Books Are Ready for Press"

501 Nelson Place
Nashville, Tennessee 37214

cidermillpress.com

THE SCARY BOOK OF
Valentine's Day Lore

BOOK PUBLISHERS

CIDER MILL PRESS

Illustrations by Neil Evans
Tim Rayborn

So Terrifying Tales of Romance from Around the World

Valentine's Day Lore
THE SCARY BOOK OF

Table of Contents

Troubled and Tragic Love Stories .. 72

Ghosts and Urban Legends 94

Murders Most Foul 122

Unusual Customs around the World 142

Introduction

What would the world be like without romance? Pretty dull, actually. All over the world, poets, artists, writers, musicians, and many more have spent centuries praising love, bringing us to a point where much of the culture we now know is built around it. Take a quick look around (or through your social media feed) and you'll see it: love is everywhere. As such, romance often takes center stage in our thoughts, even (especially?) when we would prefer it didn't. We're in love with love, so much so that we have a holiday focused on it. Of course, not everyone is in love with that development—while some people adore Valentine's Day, as many, if not more, people despise it.

Yes, love is grand, but it can also be painful, either leading to heartbreak or darker consequences like anger, jealousy, revenge, and murder. This little book takes a look at some of the darker alleys on the map of the heart, from historical mishaps to weird myths, from strange urban legends and ghosts, to tragedy, murder, and odd customs, all in the name of love, romance, and desire. Just where did the idea of Valentine's Day come from, anyway? And who was Valentine, if he even existed?

We'll examine those questions first, before trotting off through the thorny rosebushes in search of the weird, the unsettling, and the horrifying. While Valentine's Day itself has spawned a few good tales, the lore of love cannot be limited to a single day—just as romance is not limited to a single day, nor are the jealousies, errors, and tragedies that can attend it.

Love comprehends all things, and as you'll soon see, it makes folks do some pretty strange things. Such as sending a valentine to someone you hate. Stalk others who are in throes of passion and exact your murderous intentions upon them. Reassemble your one true love's body after it was brutally dismembered.

All of these situations and many others will be discussed in this book, and they just might leave you feeling very differently about the affairs of the (sometimes bloody) heart. Love and desire will always be with us, but so will the darker parts of human nature, and when the two collide the results can be downright deadly. So, grab some chocolates and—if you're so inclined—someone you love and explore the legends and tragedies of our romantic obsessions.

History

People have been in love for as long as there have been people. History is filled with romances gone wrong, lusts unsatisfied that led to tragedy, and various other horrors. This section looks at some of these twisted tales, as well as the possible origins of Valentine's Day itself. Have you ever wondered what running through the streets of ancient Rome naked and whipping people has to do with our modern day of love? Probably nothing at all, but it's fascinating to think about...

More Than One
St. Valentine

If there is a Valentine's Day, there must be a Valentine. So, who was this person, and why do they have a day named after them? Well, that's the big question, and it's not so easy to answer. There were probably two, and possibly three, men living in the third century who might be the one the day honors, and all of them met a bloody death. The Catholic Church honored all three and listed February 14 as the day they were martyred. Safe to say that Valentine's Day does indeed have a bloody origin!

Valentine might have been Valentinus, a priest who lived in Rome. At some point, he was arrested and held captive by a wealthy Roman named Asterius. While imprisoned, Valentinus would talk with Asterius about his religion. According to the legend, Asterius told Valentinus that if he could cure Asterius's daughter of her blindness, he and his family would leave behind the Roman gods and embrace Christianity. Valentinus went to the girl, prayed, and, so the story goes, restored her sight. Asterius was so impressed that he and his whole family converted. The Roman emperor Claudius II heard about this healing and conversion, and was furious. He ordered that Valentinus and Asterius, as well as his whole family, be executed. Their heads were cut off, but some devotees of Valentinus snuck his body away and had it buried elsewhere.

A similar story comes from Umbria in central Italy, where a bishop (not a priest) named Valentinus convinced a high-ranking Roman to convert to Christianity and was executed.

Another legend states that a certain Valentinus secretly performed marriages for Roman soldiers. Emperor Claudius II was convinced that unmarried men made better soldiers, so he outlawed marriages for his troops, but Valentinus went ahead and performed weddings for them anyway. And so, off with his head. Yet another legend says that Valentinus helped Christians escape from Roman prisons, seeing how terribly they were treated there. Once again, he was found out and got the chop. There is even a legend that Valentinus himself sent a message of love to a young lady (which probably meant he wasn't a priest in this version), signing it, "From your Valentine."

Now, you might be wondering what a guy getting his head whacked off with an axe has to do with a day for romantic love, and that's a good question. February 14 was set aside to honor Valentine throughout the Middle Ages and beyond, but it seems that the fourteenth-century English writer Geoffrey Chaucer (of *The Canterbury Tales* fame) might have been the first person to specifically associate the day with romantic love. There was something of a folk tradition that February 14 was the day when birds began to mate again (this is backed up by some ornithologists, by the way). In Chaucer's poem of 1375, "The Parliament of Fowls," he wrote:

> For this was on Seynt Valentynes day, whan every foul
> cometh ther to chese his make [i.e., "choose his mate"]

For various reasons, this idea of mating on the day seemed to catch on with other writers, and over the next few decades, Valentine's Day started to be associated with romantic love in quite a few literary works. So, is it Chaucer's fault that people have to buy chocolate, cards, and gifts for February 14 rather than commemorate a guy who got brutally decapitated by an axe? It may well be!

Lupercalia, the Wild Roman Celebration

Lupercalia was an annual festival in ancient Rome, celebrated on February 15. In fact, the word "February" comes from the day's other name, dies Februatus, or "day of purification." The Romans and earlier Etruscans also honored a god named Februus, a god of purification, though Lupercalia itself is probably related to a Greek festival called Lykaia, which honored wolves, and possibly the god Pan, who some Romans might have called Lupercus. Yes, it's all pretty confusing!

What isn't confusing is that the day was one for some crazy goings-on. The importance of wolves to Rome is obvious, since its founders, Romulus and Remus, were said to have been suckled by a female wolf when they were infants. Celebrations for the day first appeared in the city of Rome, at the site where the two infants were believed to have been raised by the wolf. A ritual took place on the day, which involved an animal sacrifice, usually a goat. Men between the ages of 20 and 40 were devoted to this rite, and would come forward to have their heads anointed with the animal's blood and then washed with milk. They were supposed to laugh as this was done.

Afterward, there was a meal, and straps were cut from the flesh of the sacrificed animal and given to the young men. They would then go out into the streets, naked or barely dressed, and try to swat anyone they met with these straps. Women would willingly let themselves be hit, because they thought it would bring fertility, good luck in pregnancy, and good health.

It was said that some women were so taken by the men who swatted them that they sought the men out and even married them, thus making the ritual something of a self-fulfilling prophecy!

In any case, after running naked through the streets for some time, the men would return to the cave and the festival would come to an end. While the celebration started in the city of Rome itself, it eventually spread to other parts of Italy and the greater Roman Empire, and the ritual came to be regarded as a kind of general fertility rite that was practiced at the end of winter. Roman emperors, such as Caesar Augustus, encouraged the festival, though later Christians were appalled. Lupercalia continued to be celebrated after the adoption of Christianity for a period, past 391 BCE. Pope Gelasius I (reigned from 494–96 BCE) complained that people were still indulging in Lupercalia during his time, calling them a "vile rabble," but it seems that even he wasn't able to ban the celebrations completely.

So, what does this festival have to do with Valentine's Day? Well, given the Christian dislike of it, and its date (February 15), some people have thought that the Catholic Church abolished it and replaced it with a day honoring Valentine, though there isn't much evidence for this. Gelasius did endorse February 14 as a day to honor the martyred Valentinus, but it wouldn't become a day associated with romantic love for about 1,000 years. Blending a fertility ritual and a holiday for love doesn't seem too far-fetched, to be sure, but as we've seen, Lupercalia was its own thing, and it's more of a coincidence that two different holidays, one for love and one for fertility, happened to fall one day after another on the February calendar.

The Châtelain de Coucy and His Heart

uy de Coucy, also known as the Châtelain de Coucy (active from 1186–1203) was a French nobleman and trouvère, a kind of poet and composer. He wrote a number of songs that have survived, and a few are appealing even to modern listeners. Not much is known about his life, but it's what allegedly happened after he died that makes him worthy of being included in a book about horrifying love stories.

According to legend, he fell in love with a noblewoman, known as the Lady of Fayel. Unfortunately, she was already married. This wasn't too much of a problem for Guy, since many of these medieval poets and musicians liked to write about their powerful loves for ladies who were not available. This pitiful emotional state was, in fact, one of the main features of medieval love poetry, long before country music and angsty teenaged diaries.

When the lady's husband, Lord Fayel, found out, he was not pleased. So he came up with a plan to get Guy to leave, permanently. Pretending to be Guy's friend, Lord Fayel suggested that he and Guy go on a pilgrimage to the Holy Land together. Guy agreed, but Lord Fayel backed out at the last minute, forcing Guy to go it alone. Lord Fayel was delighted with his cunning plan, for he'd gotten rid of his rival and set him up to face many dangers on his journey. Sure enough, while on the pilgrimage, Guy was mortally wounded. Knowing he would never see Lady Fayel again, he told his servant to remove his heart after he died, embalm it, and send it to her, to prove that he loved her even after death.

The servant carried out his romantic, if gruesome, wish, and sent back the heart. But Lord Fayel discovered this plan. He managed to have someone intercept the package with the heart inside and bring it to him instead. He told his cook to prepare it as part of the meal and to serve it to his wife.

After she'd finished, Lord Fayel then smugly informed her that she'd eaten Guy's heart, and now he was gone forever. The lady replied that if true, she had eaten the most perfect food, and would never eat again. She died, of starvation or grief, soon after, and Lord Fayel was left alone with his remorse and guilt.

So, did this tragedy actually happen? Probably not. The story went around in the thirteenth century, but in some versions, there are different characters. One told of a troubadour from southern France and another of a singer from Germany. Since it's unlikely that there was a big trade in removed hearts across Europe, the whole story is probably just a farfetched tale. The real-life Châtelain de Coucy did go on a crusade in the 1190s, and died in eastern lands in 1203, so those facts were probably one source for the legend, romantic and icky as it was.

Henry VIII Makes Valentine's Day an Official Holiday in 1537

A king proclaiming a holiday for love! What could be more of a classic ending to a fairy tale? Everyone falls in love, and everyone lives happily ever after! Except it didn't happen like that at all. Henry VIII gets some credit for proclaiming February 14 as the "official" holiday of Valentine's Day (even though it was already in the Catholic church's calendar), and that's the day that would stick all the way into modern times.

But it wasn't meant for secular love; it was a continuation of the idea of the religious holiday for the saint. Indeed, the day would continue to be a feast for St. Valentine's martyrdom in the Catholic church up until 1969, when Pope Paul VI removed that element, but that's a story that need not concern us.

In any case, Henry wasn't keen on Catholic holidays. As you might know, he married the Spanish princess Catherine of Aragon back in 1509. But over the course of the next twenty years, she had no sons (at least none who survived), and Henry grew ever more frustrated and paranoid that he wouldn't have a prince to take the throne when he died. Henry was also a notorious philanderer, and by 1531, he had his eyes set on the noblewoman Anne Boleyn. But he couldn't just be with her; he had to get rid of Catherine, and the only way to do that was to have his first marriage declared invalid. Of course, the pope refused, and Henry got angry. As a result he broke with Rome and the Catholic church, created his own Church

of England, and used his power as the head of it to annul his marriage with Catherine.

Once he'd sent her away, he was free to marry Anne, which he did in 1532. The first child she had was a girl, Princess Elizabeth, who would grow up to be Queen Elizabeth I. It wasn't long before Henry's eyes were wandering again, and he became drawn to Jane Seymour. He seemed to genuinely fall in love with her, but now he had to get rid of Anne. He couldn't just annul their marriage, as he had with Catherine, so he devised a much more sinister plan: he looked for evidence that she'd committed adultery, found it, and had her head chopped off. Whether she was actually unfaithful or not is still debated.

With Anne dead, Henry married Jane and together they produced Edward, the son Henry so badly wanted. Only Edward died due to childbirth-related complications. Henry would marry three more women over the next few years: Anne of Cleves (whom he divorced), Catherine Howard (whom he also accused of adultery—probably with reason—and beheaded), and Katherine Parr, who outlived him (whew!).

While all this was going on, Henry was tearing apart the country by replacing the older religion of Roman Catholicism with his new English variety. This involved closing all of the monasteries and taking all their wealth for himself, and executing various advisors as traitors. It's probably just as well that Valentine's Day wasn't especially well known as a day for earthly love yet; with Henry's track record, who would have wanted to take part in it?

Hector Berlioz's Romantic Obsession

Hector Berlioz (1803–1869) was a brilliant and innovative French composer, perhaps best known for his *Symphonie Fantastique*, which he admitted was inspired by his experiences under the influence of opium. It tells the not-so-charming story of a young artist who is obsessed with a woman he cannot have. He finally gives into madness and murders her, and his own funeral distorts into a black mass. As you can imagine, this musical work was pretty controversial when it premiered in Paris in 1830. Fellow composer Franz Liszt declared it was a work of genius, while Felix Mendelssohn described it as "utterly loathsome."

The most disturbing thing about the work was that it was, in part, autobiographical. Earlier that year, Berlioz had met an Irish Shakespearian actress named Heather Smithson, and fell head over heels for her, but she refused to have anything to do with him. His frustration over her refusal might well have influenced his bizarre musical work, but that wasn't the end of the story.

In 1830, he also met a woman name Camille Mokke, who wanted to win his heart, just to show she could do it. Soon, they were engaged, but Berlioz had to go to Rome to accept a prestigious prize he'd won, the Prix de Rome. While there, Camille's mother wrote him a rather nasty letter, telling him that she was ending their engagement, and that she was going to marry her daughter to another man, Camille Playel, a wealthy owner of a piano factory.

Furious, Berlioz began to plot the murders of both Camilles and the mother, too. He bought women's clothing and obtained guns. His plan was to wear a disguise, gain access to their homes in Paris, and then shoot all three people. He set off from Rome, ready to go down in infamy. Except Berlioz made a misstep almost immediately: in Genoa, he realized he'd left behind his disguise on another train! At his wit's end, he decided to end it all by jumping off a cliff into the sea, but he landed near a fisherman, who pulled him to safety.

Berlioz finally reached Nice, and decided to give up his plan altogether, telling himself that Camille and her mother were a waste of his time. Then, he went back to Italy and wrote a sequel to the *Symphonie Fantastique*, in which he used his rage to less dangerous purpose. Back in Paris, he met up again with Smithson, and this time, they hit it off, getting married in 1833. But this story has no happy ending. Within eight years, he'd gone off Smithson and taken a new mistress. Berlioz and Smithson separated in 1844, and even though Berlioz still provided for her, he ended up marrying his mistress. But after she died in 1862 (Smithson, in case you were wondering, died in 1854), he fell in love again ... it just never ends! But this new woman died in 1864, and Berlioz eventually died himself in 1869, lonely and broken.

His bizarre story is one of those "truth is stranger than fiction" tales, and how the volatile romantic obsessions in Berlioz's music were uncannily realized in his own life.

Victorian "Vinegar Valentines"

We often like to think that the Victorians (at least the upper-class ones) were prim and proper, and enjoyed an artistic culture that was obsessed with cuteness and sweetness. The Victorians, with the help of Charles Dickens, essentially invented the Christmas card, after all. And they went all in on Valentine's Day as a celebration of romance, including all of the usual expressions, especially flowers and cards.

And while it's true that there could be a lot of sentimental feelings expressed in those cards and in the art on them, there was also a dark side to their holidays. Christmas ghost stories were quite popular, for example (Dickens' *A Christmas Carol* was not the only example), and when it came to Valentine's Day, the Victorians had a very unique take on the day, especially for people that they didn't like: "vinegar valentines."

These delightfully subversive and sometimes awful creations were basically anti-Valentine's Day cards. You didn't send one of these to someone you loved, but to someone you disliked. Beginning in England in the 1830s or 1840s and continuing for the next several decades, it's thought that at their most popular, vinegar valentines made up almost half of all Valentine's Day cards sent!

The cards could have messages that mildly poked fun at the recipient, or they could be vicious, depending on the feelings of the person sending the card. Illustrated with often-grotesque drawings, they might mock a particular person, or even their whole profession. You could send such a card to anyone you

disliked, and have it tailored to them: it could be a horrible boss, a greedy landlord, a corrupt politician, an ex, or a terrible family member. Even worse, these cards were often sent COD, meaning the recipient had to pay the postage due on them.

Since many of them were destroyed, we have only a few surviving cards, but let's look at a few of the messages from those:

> 'Tis a lemon that I hand you, and bid you "skidoo,"
> Because I love another, there is no chance for you!

> Pray, do you ever mend your clothes, or comb your hair?
> Well, I suppose, you've got no time, for people say, you're
> reading novels all the day. Don't imagine anyone will
> take you for a gentleman.

As you can imagine, such cards often didn't go over well, and even if we see them as funny now, there are reports of fights, lawsuits, and suicides coming about because of these biting communications. There was one case of an angry husband who shot his estranged wife after receiving one. But often, such cards were sent anonymously, to protect the senders from such a retaliation.

As the trend went on, more and more people began to push back against it in letters to newspapers, calling them vulgar and cruel, which they certainly could be. Eventually, their popularity died down. But for several decades in the 1800s, vinegar valentines ruled the day, and the sensitive souls out there might have needed to approach February 14 with a little bit more apprehension than many folks do today.

The Boy Killed by Kisses

Is it possible to be loved to death? Apparently so! While this tragic tale is about birthday wishes, rather than Valentine's Day follies, it merits a place in this collection of love gone awry. Plus, the boy in question had his birthday on February 15th, so it's basically a Valentine's Day tragedy, anyway. After reading this, you might think that this story must be an urban legend. It certainly has a lot of the characteristics of a popular tall tale, but it was faithfully reported in a New York newspaper, which detailed the autopsy and printed a photo of the boy, dressed in choir robes.

It seems that the poor victim in question, George Spencer Millet, turned 15 the day after Valentine's Day in 1909. George was well-liked at the insurance company where he'd worked for the past eight months (apparently, he was doing that rather than going to school, a not uncommon occurrence for kids at the time).

According to the article, he "met death while fleeing from the kisses of frollicking [sic] stenographers in the office of the Metropolitan Insurance Company." They just don't write newspaper articles like they used to! Also, "The Frolicking Stenographers" really needs to be a band name.

In any case, the report went on to say that George, "was killed by a penetrating wound to the heart." Further, "the wound penetrated ... beneath the eighth rib. The wound took an upward course."

Apparently, the ladies wanted to give him kisses for his birthday, and perhaps for Valentine's Day as well, and began chasing him around the office, maybe playfully, but at some point, it seems that they got a bit too aggressive. In trying to get away from them, George tripped and fell. He had an ink eraser in his shirt pocket, a small blade meant for scraping ink off of a page and this tool became a deadly weapon, as he fell on it, and accidentally stabbed himself through the heart. He knew what happened right away and even cried, "I am stabbed!" as he bled out everywhere. He died in the ambulance.

One can imagine how horrified those poor women must have felt. The coroner conducted a serious investigation, issuing subpoenas to several people, including, according to the newspaper report, "several of the young women who were chasing him at the time in order that they might kiss him." Presumably, the investigators concluded that it was all a tragic accident, but the poor boy's death must have cast a pall over the office for a long time afterwards.

Millet's gravestone in a Bronx cemetery reads: "Lost life by stab in falling on ink eraser, evading six young women trying to give him birthday kisses in office Metropolitan Life Building."

Special thanks to J. W. Ocker for uncovering this weird and grim story.

The St. Valentine's Day Massacre

The infamous St. Valentine's Day Massacre had absolutely nothing to do with love or celebrating the holiday; quite the opposite, in fact. It was an act of brutality showing the high levels of mob activity in Chicago during the 1920s, crimes that the city government and police couldn't (or wouldn't) stop. Various gangs slugged it out on Chicago's streets, each trying to gain the upper hand and establish their empires, but no one was more ruthless than Al Capone, who wanted to be top dog for every illegal enterprise, from bootlegging to gambling, and he had no problem taking out his rivals.

When Prohibition became American law in 1920, those involved in the organized crime world saw a perfect chance to make huge amounts of money by producing and selling alcohol illegally, and make huge amounts of money they did. Gambling and prostitution dens also brought in a hefty amount of cash. Capone was probably worth $100 million by the end of the 1920s, an absolutely stunning sum for the time ($100 million in 1925 would be worth more than $1.8 billion today) and he lavished some of that wealth on charities, like soup kitchens and other community institutions, which made him very popular with the locals. A shrewd man, to be sure.

In his quest to become rich and powerful, Capone ordered hundreds of hits and murders during his reign over the underworld, but he was always careful not to be directly linked to them, which was why the police and even the early FBI had such trouble catching him. As you might know, he was eventually arrested for tax evasion. Hey, whatever works.

In any case, one especially brutal slaying took place on February 14, 1929. At the time, Capone's main rival was an Irish gangster named George "Bugs" Moran. Capone was determined to strike hard at his enemy, and sent some of his own goons, dressed as policemen, to a garage on the north side of the city. There, they found seven of Moran's men working on a bootlegging operation. The fake police officers gunned them down, firing off approximately seventy rounds of ammunition. When the real police arrived, they found just one man, Frank Gusenberg, still alive, but he refused to talk and died shortly afterward. Bugs was actually on his way to the garage, but arrived after the shooting and was thus unharmed.

The murders, soon branded the St. Valentine's Day Massacre, shocked even those used to the city's gang violence. Capone, who was at his home in Florida, denied having anything to do with it, though most investigators believed him to be responsible. Bugs blamed Capone, while Capone said that Bugs had done it, presumably to frame Capone. Once again, Capone escaped justice, and since no one was ever charged with the murders, it's still one of the more shocking unsolved crimes in American history.

Myth

The world's mythologies are filled with love stories of all kinds, from the sweetest to the worst. On the awful side, there are plenty of romantic tragedies and bloodbaths: gods and goddesses behaving badly, heroes who are not so heroic, loves won and lost, jealousies and reconciliations, horrible discoveries, and bizarre fates. The Greeks in particular seemed to have a tale for just about every romantic entanglement you can think of, with every orientation and point of view on display. Ancient Egypt, Africa, and the Viking world also have their own disturbing and violent contributions. The obsessions of love were a preoccupation of the immortals, and often they handled it about as well as the rest of us.

Isis and Osiris

The classic myth of Isis and Osiris has several versions, as you might expect from an extremely old tale; there is evidence of the Egyptians worshipping Osiris from as far back as 4,500 years ago. He was an early form of the god that dies and is resurrected, and he was crucially important for Egyptian culture. According to the myths, Osiris, along with his queen Isis, and his brother Set, were the offspring of the sky goddess Nut and the earth god Geb, and he ruled Egypt fairly and with justice. There is less written about his reign than his grizzly end and return.

Set was jealous of his brother and felt that he should be the one to rule. Why did he hate Osiris? There are different versions of where the grudge came from, with some stories claiming it was because Osiris was carrying on with Set's consort, Nephthys, and another version that says Osiris kicked Set at some point, and he never got over it.

In any case, Set began to plot his brother's downfall, and came up with a creative way to do it. He threw a lavish party and invited Osiris to attend. There, he presented a wooden box to all of the guests, which he had instructed be made to fit Osiris perfectly. Set then proclaimed that whoever could fit perfectly in the box would win it. Various guests tried, but none could do it. Then Osiris gave it a go and settled inside with ease. Set, along with his accomplices, slammed a lid on the box, trapping Osiris. They took the chest to the Nile River and threw it in, believing themselves to be done with him.

Upon hearing the news, Isis, consumed by rage and grief, went in search of Osiris's body, and found it in the river. She wanted

to make sure that he received the proper funeral rites (funerals were a big deal to the Egyptians). But, hearing of her efforts, Set managed to get to the body and cut it into fourteen pieces (some versions say forty-two), which he then scattered across Egypt. Set then took the throne for himself, as he'd always wanted.

Not to be denied, Isis went in search of her husband's body and was able to reassemble Osiris's corpse, with the help of the gods of the dead, Anubis and Thoth. She found all the parts except for his male member, so a new one had to be made. Anyway, they put him back together and mummified him, and with the artificial member, she was able to conceive a son with his restored body, whom she then hid from Set. That son, the hawk-headed Horus, grew up to avenge his father's murder. He defeated Set in combat, banished his uncle, and ruled in place of Osiris, who had now become lord of the Underworld.

Isis's love for Osiris saved Egypt, and for this she was worshipped for centuries, an esteem that sustained itself all the way through the fourteenth century, when it is claimed that some Egyptian women still went to Isis statues for healing and help with pregnancy.

The Many Affairs of Zeus

L et's be honest, the words "faithful husband" and "Zeus" don't really go together. In spite of being king of the Greek gods, being married to Hera, goddess of marriage, and accomplishing lots of great feats, Zeus had the libido of a 15-year-old boy and was constantly causing problems and fathering children who then created further trouble. Unfortunately, women had little to say in such matters, especially where gods were concerned, so Zeus could go about doing what he wished, up to and including rape. The Greek myths are filled with examples of his adultery gone wrong. Here are just a few:

Alcmene: Zeus wanted the lovely daughter of the king of Mycenae for himself, so he took on the form of her husband, going so far as to tell her all about "his" recent military exploits. When her real husband returned, he realized that she'd been tricked and forgave her. Eventually, Alcmene gave birth to two children, one by Zeus, and the other by her husband. Zeus's son would grow up to be none other than Hercules, though Hera, furious with her husband, tried to make his son's life miserable as often as she could, and eventually saddled Hercules with his legendary twelve labors.

Danae: She was the daughter of the king of Argos. This king had heard a prophecy that his grandson would kill him, and, since Danae was his only child, he locked her away in a tower (or a tomb in some versions of the story), where she could never meet a man. But Zeus came to her as a cloud, and, after changing into a shower of gold, impregnated her. The king knew that only Zeus could have done this, and so, unwilling to risk the god's wrath, he sent both mother and infant away, putting them in a chest and casting them out to sea. Zeus and

Poseidon saved them and brought them to the island of Serifos. Danae's son, Perseus, would grow up to become one of Greek mythology's greatest heroes.

Europa: She was a princess of Tyre, a city in Phoenicia. Zeus desired her and one day appeared to her and her friends as a white bull. After they had pet him, Europa climbed onto his back, and he took off toward the ocean. She had no choice but to hold on. He swam with her to the island of Crete, lay with her, and once again, fathered a child. She had three children by him; each of them became a king, and the whole continent of Europe was named after her.

Lamia: A queen of Libya, Lamia was seduced by Zeus, and had several children by him. In this case, Hera was enraged and killed each child; some versions say that she even forced Lamia to eat them. This cursed fate drove Lamia mad, and eventually she retreated to a cave, coming out at night to look for children to consume. Oh, and since she couldn't close her eyes to sleep, Zeus gave her a new pair that she could remove from her head!

Leda: She was the wife of Tyndareus, king of Sparta, and, of course, Zeus wanted her. He came to her in the guise of a swan that was trying to escape a bird of prey. In this form, he seduced her, and eventually she gave birth to two children, one from Zeus and one from her husband. By all reports, Zeus's child didn't have feathers, at least.

Hermaphroditus

As we've seen, the ancient Greeks had no shortage of fascinating myths that still tell us much about them, their beliefs, and ourselves. The story of Hermaphroditus is definitely one of the stranger ones, and seems entirely appropriate in a book about the horrors of love.

Ovid, the Roman writer who died in 17 or 18 CE, tells us that Hermaphroditus was the son of Hermes and Aphrodite (hence his name), and that he was cared for by naiads (water spirits) at Mount Ida in modern-day Turkey. He was very beautiful, as was his due, given who his parents were. By the time he was 15, he was bored with his idyllic home and wanted to see more of the world. So, he visited nearby cities, hoping to satisfy his craving for new sights.

It was in a forest near one of these cities, Caria, that he would meet his bizarre fate. Hermaphroditus came to a pool, in which a nymph named Salmacis lived. She took one look at the young man and was immediately overcome with desire for him. She tried to seduce him, but he was not interested in her advances and pushed her away. She left in a bit of a huff.

She was not to be denied, however, and when he slipped into the pool (thinking she had gone), she returned, basically assaulted him, and refused to let go. Hermaphroditus struggled to get free of her, but his situation became even worse. She prayed to the gods that the two of them could be joined together forever as one being.

Of course, the gods, being mischievous and unpredictable, granted her request. She and Hermaphroditus melded together

and became one being, forever joined as a creature of two sexes. Also, the pool was now enchanted and anyone else who bathed in it would be subject to the same fate. And from the name Hermaphroditus, of course, we get the term "hermaphrodite," for any living thing that has female and male sex characteristics in one body.

Hermaphroditus was well known in the Greek world, and even worshipped as a god in Cyprus and elsewhere. They came to be regarded as something of a protector of marriage, since they signified man and woman fused together. Others thought that the idea was horrifying, and that such a conjoined being could only be a monster. In any case, Hermaphroditus was most often shown in art as a human with a woman's breasts and a man's genitals, a symbol that emphasizes the unusual nature of Salmacis's desire.

Oedipus

Ah, the infamous Oedipus! The tragic king who's so well known that he even has a whole psychological condition named after him. Most people probably have some vague notion of who Oedipus was, and what happened to him, but this entry is a perfect chance to dive a little deeper into the character's tragic tale.

He certainly had what can only be called a horrific love life. As a mythical king of the city of Thebes, he is a main character in two plays by the ancient Greek playwright Sophocles: *Oedipus the King* (also known as Oedipus Rex) and *Oedipus at Colonus*. A third play, *Antigone*, is an equally depressing sequel set after Oedipus's death.

The basic story is filled with all sorts of unsavory details. Not long after Oedipus was born, a seer uttered a prophecy that he would kill his father, King Laius, and marry his mother, Queen Jocasta. Needless to say, neither of them was particularly happy about this prediction, so they decided to murder the baby and thus escape their horrible fate. Of course, they couldn't bring themselves to commit that terrible act, so they asked a servant to do it for them.

But the servant likewise couldn't harm the child, and instead gave baby Oedipus to a childless couple, who took him in and raised him. He grew up with no knowledge of his parents or his royal heritage. Eventually, though, he heard about the prophecy and, wanting to spare them, ran away from his adoptive parents, thinking that they were his real parents. This move set the prophecy in motion.

Some time later, Oedipus met Laius on the road and they got into an argument, not knowing who the other was. Oedipus killed him (part one fulfilled). He then saved Thebes by solving the famed riddle of the Sphinx: "What goes on four legs in the morning, two in the afternoon, and three in the evening?" The answer is a human being, who crawls as an infant, walks upright through life, and then needs a cane, a "third leg," in old age.

Quite pleased with himself, he became the new ruler of Thebes, and married the widowed queen who was—you guessed it—his own mother, without knowing her true identity (part two fulfilled). When they both eventually found out, Jocasta killed herself, and Oedipus blinded himself and went into exile, eventually dying in the town of Colonus.

But they'd already had children together, and the curse was far from through with the family. Their sons, Polyneices and Eteocles, fought, and Polyneices died. Their sister, Antigone, wanted to bury him in Thebes, but King Creon (brother of Jocasta) refused to let her, and sentenced her to die when she went against his command. She killed herself before she could be executed. Creon's son, Antigone's son, Haemon, and Creon's wife, Eurydice, killed themselves in quick succession, leaving Creon alone to regret his cruelty.

All because a young man accidentally romanced his own mother.

Orpheus and Eurydice

The tragedy of Orpheus and Eurydice is one of the greatest tragic love stories in all of mythology, inspiring countless retellings in plays, operas, and more.

Orpheus, as the son of Apollo, was blessed by the gods with a stunningly beautiful voice that would attract listeners far and wide. During one of his performances, a young lady in his audience, Eurydice, caught his attention. Soon, they fell in love, and couldn't bear to be apart—naturally, they decided to get married. The wedding day was one of great celebration, but when the day ended, disaster struck.

In some versions of the myth, a shepherd named Aristaeus hated Orpheus and desired Eurydice for himself. In others, a lecherous satyr saw the young bride and wanted her. Either way, the assailant attacked, and Orpheus led Eurydice away, fleeing together to protect her. In her attempt to escape, she stepped into a vipers' nest and was bitten by a venomous snake, dying soon after.

Devastated, Orpheus was determined not to let her go, and devised a plan for reviving her. Taking up his lyre, he journeyed to the realm of the dead, and pleaded for the release of his new bride. His words and music were so moving that Hades and his queen, Persephone, were deeply moved. Hades agreed to let Eurydice return to the mortal world, following Orpheus back, but he warned Orpheus that this gift came with one condition: on their journey back to the realm of the living, he must not look behind him, and he must not look upon her until she had fully emerged into the light of the living world. If he did, she would be drawn back to the underworld again, and would never escape.

Orpheus agreed, and eagerly began his journey home. He pushed on, never once looking behind him, even though he wanted to. Finally, he made it to the surface; he'd done it! Hearing Eurydice behind him, he turned in joy to embrace and kiss her. However, she had not yet crossed over into the living world, and Orpheus watched in horror as she faded in front of him, drawn back to dwell in the land of the dead forever. If only he'd waited another ten seconds!

Afterward, Orpheus was inconsolable, and never the same again. He was destined to die a tragic death of his own, being torn apart by Maenads, female devotees of the wine god, Dionysus. Some versions of the myth say this was because he gave up his devotions to the gods, while others say that he swore off any women at all (favoring only men from then on), and that these crazed women killed him as a result. But after the attack, his disembodied head fell into a river, and floated down toward the Mediterranean Sea; it sang the whole way. His head drifted across the sea to the island of Lesbos, where the people placed it in a shrine, along with his lyre.

The Darker Side of Eros/Cupid

When we think of Cupid, most often we imagine the chubby, happy, flying cherub who flits about with his tiny bow and arrow, shooting "love darts" into unsuspecting folks to make them fall in love. From Disney films to Valentine's Day cards, Cupid seems to be the ultimate in cute, cuddly, and sweet. This image (combined with the biblical cherubs), however, only goes back to the Renaissance, and was definitely not always the image of Cupid.

Indeed, in the thirteenth-century French poem "The Romance of the Rose, "the "God of Love" is a major player in the story. He shoots an arrow into the Lover, who falls in love with a rose held in a castle. The Lover then besieges the castle to take the rose by force. The story is weird, surreal, and filled with allegory and politics.

Going back even farther, Cupid is the Roman version of the Greek god Eros, who was said to be the son of Ares and Aphrodite, though early myths identify him as one of the original gods. In 414 BCE, the playwright Aristophanes wrote his comedy, *The Birds* (no, horror fans, this work has nothing to do with the Alfred Hitchcock film). In it, he wrote that Eros sprang forth from a primordial egg and then mated with Chaos itself to produce the human race, which isn't what we would consider a romantic origin story.

Like Aphrodite, Eros is a god of love and sex, and as such, he represented both delight and danger, because, as we're finding out in this book, love and death really do go together!

Eros was said to be beautiful, and his power was considerable. He could make anyone, god or mortal, bow to obsessive love and lust, and that made him a force to be reckoned with. Through his works, Eros could control minds and wills, and madness, violence, and war resulted from those put in the throes of obsession.

Eros's reputation was well established in ancient Greece, when he was said to have caused some gods to burn with love and desire, and eventually lose their minds. Later on, the early Christians took Eros to be a real threat, with writers such as Isidore of Seville believing that he was a demon sent to tempt minds into lust and bring ruin. Whether as a primordial god or the son of Aphrodite, his behaviors were pretty much the same, and his mother did nothing but encourage him. While she was worshipped by far more people over time, Eros definitely had his own followers, possibly those who hoped that they could appease him and somehow master their own hearts, misled by wishful thinking.

Callisto and Artemis

T here are multiple versions of this strange and tragic myth, but they follow the same basic plot. Callisto was a nymph and a devotee of the Greek goddess Artemis, the virgin goddess of hunting and the forest. Artemis required her companions to remain virgins as a sign of loyalty.

But Zeus, who, as we've seen, couldn't control himself, lusted for Callisto and wanted to have her as another of his conquests. Instead of appearing to her as a swan, he decided to come to her disguised as Artemis. With that deceitful plan, he went to her and proceeded to seduce her in his female form. Despite this same-sex union, Callisto became pregnant. Afterward, she returned to the real Artemis and her other companions, but said nothing, perhaps wondering how her lady had been able to make her pregnant.

Callisto was able to hide the pregnancy for a while, but eventually Artemis saw her when she was bathing, and the truth came out. The real Artemis, who of course knew nothing about this fling, was enraged that Callisto had broken her vow, even though she had been deceived. What happened next depends on the version you read. In some versions, Artemis transformed Callisto into a bear as punishment, in others, Zeus's wife, Hera, enraged by his many infidelities, was the one who turned poor Callisto into a bear. In still others, Zeus turned her into the animal to hide her from Hera's wrath. No matter what happened, she was banished to the wilderness, where she gave birth to a son, Arcas.

Here, the myth takes on various twists and turns. In some, Callisto went off and wandered in the wilderness for sixteen years. When her son, now grown, was out hunting one day, he found her and was about to spear her with his weapon. Zeus saw this and intervened, saving her. He then placed her in the sky as the constellation Ursa Major; some versions say that Arcas was placed there as well, as Ursa Minor.

In another version, Hera ordered Artemis to shoot the bear just after giving birth, and Artemis obeyed, but Zeus intervened and saved Callisto, placing her in the night sky and shepherding their infant son away. In yet another version, Artemis accidentally killed Callisto while hunting, not realizing that the bear was the nymph in a new shape.

No matter which version you read, things turned out badly for poor Callisto, the victim of a god's lust.

Pyramus and Thisbe

The tale of Pyramus and Thisbe is a classic of star-crossed lovers whose story ends in grief. First appearing in the ancient world, it was adapted many times over the centuries, perhaps most successfully when William Shakespeare inserted a version of it into his romantic comedy *A Midsummer Night's Dream*. Unfortunately for the lovers themselves, in their original tale, all was not well and didn't end well.

The most famous version outside of Shakespeare's was written by Ovid. It's the earliest surviving version of the story, dating from the year 8 BCE, but it was certainly based on older myths.

Pyramus and Thisbe were a young couple who lived in neighboring houses in ancient Babylon. Unfortunately for them, their parents hated each other, and they forbade their children from seeing each other. Rather than discouraging the young couple, the two found a way to communicate by speaking through a crack in the wall between their homes, and declared their love for one another.

But this wasn't enough for them, and they eventually concocted a plan to meet secretly, by a tomb near a mulberry tree, and then flee from their families and enjoy their lives together. It might have worked, except that Thisbe arrived first. There, she saw a lioness who had just killed its prey, and its mouth was still bloody. Fearing for her own life, Thisbe ran away, but her cloak fell to the ground. The lioness gnawed and chewed on the cloak, leaving blood from her jaws all over it.

Pyramus arrived soon after, but saw Thisbe's torn and bloody cloak on the ground, and the tracks the lion had left. Pyramus assumed the worst, and, overcome with grief and despair, he drew his sword and stabbed himself, his blood splashing on the white flowers of the mulberry tree.

Thisbe returned to tell him what happened and that she was all right, but she saw him lying dead at the base of the tree. Crying out in anguish, she prayed to the gods that the two of them might be buried together, to be joined in death as they couldn't be in life. She then took up Pyramus's sword and stabbed herself with it, lying down beside him to die.

The gods heard her prayer and, as part of granting her wish, they turned the flowers of the mulberry tree red, to signify the blood these two faithful lovers shed for each other.

Of course, the story has obvious connections to Romeo and Juliet, which it influenced. That tragic tale of young love originated in fifteenth-century Italy, and had already been retold several times before Shakespeare adapted it. So, he managed to work both Pyramus and Thisbe and Romeo and Juliet into his own plays, and audiences across the globe have been the beneficiaries ever since.

Apollo and Hyacinthus

Hyacinthus was an extremely good-looking prince in Sparta who attracted the attention of quite a few notable people. He was admired by men and women, but was only interested in men. The most important of his suitors was the sun god, Apollo, but Hyacinthus also had the attention of the god of the north wind, Boreas, the god of the west wind, Zephyrus, and a man named Thamyris. Poor Thamyris probably never had a chance, and the winds didn't fare so well either, because Hyacinthus chose Apollo to be his lover, and how could he not? Would anyone really turn down a god so great?

Apollo was said to be madly in love with Hyacinthus, and showed the young man all of his lands, while traveling in a chariot drawn by swans. Apollo even gave up spending time at some of his other beloved places (such as Delphi) in order to be with Hyacinthus. Apollo taught his young lover many skills, such how to play the lyre, how to properly use a bow and arrow, and how to become a better athlete.

But, as you might imagine, their romance doesn't have the happiest of endings. Once, Apollo showed Hyacinthus how to play a game called quoits, where the players try to toss rings or a discus. Apollo went first, but being a god, he was far stronger than the other players, and threw the discus far into the sky. Hyacinthus ran after the discus to retrieve it, but as it hit the ground, it bounced back up and struck him in the head, causing a fatal wound. Another version of the myth says that Zephyrus, jealous that Hyacinthus had spurned him for Apollo, deliberately blew the discus so that it struck the young man dead.

Either way, poor young Hyacinthus died in Apollo's arms, despite his efforts to save the young man's life. Even a god could not change a mortal's fate. Apollo was so distraught that he actually wanted to become mortal, so that he could join Hyacinthus in death, and he begged his uncle Hades, lord of the underworld, to kill him. But Hades could not, since death was not the fate of the gods. Apollo vowed to remember the young man in song and to create a flower, the hyacinth, from his blood.

In another myth, Apollo was able to bring back Hyacinthus and give him divinity; he was honored in Sparta and elsewhere. In a three-day festival, people mourned his death on day one, and then probably celebrated his divinity on the third. This event not only honored the return of spring and the growth of flowers and other vegetation, but was another of the many death-and-resurrection myths that were so common in the ancient Mediterranean world.

The Loves of Narcissus

We all know the term "narcissistic," and most people probably know that it comes from a Greek myth about a young man named Narcissus, a handsome teenager who was enamored with the love of his life … himself. But the story is a little deeper than that, and like the other entries here, is beset with tragedy, broken hearts, and death. We'll look at two other people who dared to adore Narcissus and then the grim fates of all three.

Ovid tells the story of a nymph named Echo, gifted with a beautiful singing voice and the ability to talk easily. Unfortunately, she angered the goddess Juno (Hera), possibly because she had run interference for Jupiter (Zeus) while he was out cheating on Juno. As punishment, Juno cursed Echo with no longer being able to initiate conversations on her own; she could only repeat what others had said.

Meanwhile, Narcissus, a beautiful young man whose parents were a nymph and a river god, had become rather full of himself and disinterested in the affections of others. Once, while out hunting with friends, he became lost in the woods, and he attracted the attention of Echo. She was immediately smitten with him, but because of her curse, had no way to tell him. Narcissus called out, asking if anyone was there, and she repeated his words. He said, "come here," but all she could do was say the same to him. He then invited his mystery caller to come with him, and she thought this meant he was interested in her, so she ran to him. He rejected her advances and commanded her not to touch him. Humiliated, she ran away. In time, her form dissolved, leaving behind only her voice, which can still sometimes be heard when one speaks in certain open areas.

A young man, Ameinias, also fell in love with Narcissus, who rejected him with the same harshness as he rejected Echo. Ameinias was so upset that he killed himself with a sword that Narcissus had given him as a gift.

Seeing Narcissus's cruel behavior, the goddess Nemesis decided to punish him. One myth says it was Echo's fellow nymphs who asked Nemesis to take revenge, while another tells us that Ameinias called upon the gods and asked for justice with his dying breath.

In any case, Narcissus was fated to finally fall in love ... with himself. He came to a pool of water to drink and saw his reflection. At once, he was struck by his own image and fell in love. Since his reflection could not return his love, all Narcissus could do was stare longingly at the water. Before too long, he also wasted away. When he bid his own image farewell with his dying breath, Echo answered, "farewell."

Heracles and Deianira

The story of Heracles (more commonly known by his Roman name, Hercules) and Deianira was yet another tale of love and loss. But Heracles, despite being a "hero," was, like many of his colleagues, more than a little disloyal, and rather like his father, Zeus. He was hardly a model husband to Deianira. Still, his strange death hardly seems one worthy of a demigod who had accomplished so much.

Deianira was the daughter of Althaea and Oeneus, the king and queen of Calydon, though some versions say that Dionysus, the god of wine, was her father. In any case, Achelous, the river god, wanted to marry her, but Heracles saved her by wrestling with the god and winning. In another, far less pleasant version of the story, Heracles took her by force and then promised to marry her, as if that was some consolation.

While he was away doing heroic deeds, the centaur Eurytion wanted to marry her, and her father agreed, but Heracles returned and killed the centaur.

Another account says that the centaur was named Nessus, and that he tried to kidnap her. As they were crossing the river Euenos, Heracles arrived in time and rescued her. He shot the centaur with an arrow, mortally wounding him. As Nessus lay before Deianira, dying, he convinced her to take a vial of his blood, telling her that if she mixed it with some olive oil, it would create a powerful potion that would prevent Heracles from ever being unfaithful to her.

Knowing that Heracles had quite the reputation for his wandering eyes, Deianira readily agreed. Of course, it was a lie.

Meanwhile, Heracles was off carrying on with others and fathering illegitimate children. Deianira even heard rumors that he'd fallen in love with another woman, Iole. Angry at his behavior, she mixed some of the blood with oil and smeared it on his lionskin shirt (some versions say it was a cloak she'd woven for him), thinking that it would do the trick, and make him return to her as a faithful husband.

When the time came for Heracles to put on the garment, he was in for a nasty surprise. The centaur had deceived her. The blood was a deadly poison and burned Heracles's skin, but he couldn't remove the garment . Seeing death as the only option, he asked his friends to build a funeral pyre, and they reluctantly agreed. They lit it and he threw himself in the fire, burning himself alive.

Seeing this, Zeus took pity on his son and asked that Athena bring him to the heavens, so that his suffering would end. Meanwhile, Deianira, overcome with guilt at the centaur's trick, stabbed herself, or hanged herself, depending on the version in question. And thus ended the unhappy marriage.

Siya and Maadi

The Soninke people of West Africa tell of how their ancient empire came to an end through a rebellious love. It's quite a love story, and also features a multiheaded snake that demands sacrifices.

Long ago, the empire of Wagadu thrived, but it only did so because of the generosity of Bida, a giant, seven-headed snake. Bida would bring rain and gold to the kingdom, but in exchange, it wanted the sacrifice of one young woman each year. Reluctantly, the people agreed, and so every year, they would set out to find someone that they knew would please the snake. The unfortunate victim would be brought to Bida's well and thrown in.

One year, they chose a woman named Siya Yatabéré, who was engaged to a man named Maadi. They told her to resign herself to her fate, and informed Maadi that his wedding was cancelled. But Maadi, who dearly loved Siya, wasn't about to accept this decision, and promised her she would not die in Bida's jaws. He prepared himself, and on the appointed day, he came to the well, where Siya waited, dressed in ceremonial garb for her sacrifice. She tried to send him away, saying that she was willing to sacrifice herself to save the empire, but Maadi refused, hiding nearby and waiting for Bida to emerge.

Finally, the snake raised one of its heads from the well. Maadi struck it with his sword, chopping it clean off. He did the same with five more heads, and finally the seventh and final of Bida's heads popped up. This head spoke, declaring that because of this betrayal, Wagadu would see no rain for seven years, nor would it have gold, and the kingdom would fall into ruin.

Maadi ignored the warning and sliced off the final head. He gave his sword, shoes, ring, and cap to Siya, and then he went and told his mother what he'd done. Surprisingly, she stood by him, understanding that he had killed the creature for love, and swore to protect him from the anger of the nobles.

Indeed, when they discovered that Siya was alive and how she'd managed to survive, the rulers were furious. They demanded that everyone try on the shoes, ring, and cap to see who they fit. They fit Maadi, of course, and he confessed. His mother intervened and protected him, saying that she would take charge of the country in exchange for her son's life and the freedom to marry Siya. The nobles agreed, and the couple were able to wed and live happily.

But the snake had spoken the truth. The rains didn't come, and Wagadu grew drier and drier, until it could no longer survive, and its people had to disperse. Maadi had won his love, but doomed the empire.

Loki, Angrboda, and Sigyn

Loki, the great trickster of Norse mythology, was always up to something, and this behavior most definitely extended to his private life. Loki was able to change his physical form and gender, apparently depending on his mood. He once changed into a mare and, after getting together with a stallion, gave birth to the eight-legged horse Sleipnir, who would become the god Odin's trusty steed.

Among his other exploits, he wooed and won the sorceress Angrboda, whose exact identity is not known. Their offspring were three of the most intriguing and frightening beings in all of Norse mythology: the goddess Hel, the guardian of the underworld and the land of the dead; the giant wolf Fenrir, who eventually fights and devours Odin at Ragnarok (the end of the world); and the even bigger Midgard Serpent, who will fight Odin's son Thor at Ragnarok. Thor will kill the beast, but the serpent will also kill Thor with its poisonous breath.

Knowing that the other gods would disapprove of their three unusual children, Loki and Angrboda tried to keep them secret, but eventually the gods found out and took them away. Hel was given her own realm, Fenrir was bound, and the serpent was thrown into the ocean. Loki remained pretty resentful about these actions, and would eventually exact his revenge.

Loki also didn't limit himself to only one romantic partner. He was later accused of transforming into a female again and giving birth to other monsters, whose identities are unknown. Further, he married a goddess named Sigyn, and together they had two sons of their own, Narfi (or Nari) and Váli, also known as Nari and Narfi.

At some point, Loki went too far when he crashed a banquet of the gods and proceeded to attack everyone there with insults and slander. He was thrown out of the hall, and sent away, but the gods remembered and decided to teach him a lesson once and for all.

After a long search, they found Loki and captured him. They changed Váli into a wolf, who then attacked his brother, Narfi, killing him. The gods took Narfi's intestines and made them into bonds, which they used to bind Loki to large rocks in a cave. The winter goddess, Skadhi, making good on a promise to get revenge after Loki insulted her at the banquet, then hung a serpent over him, whose venom dripped onto his face and burned like acid. Sigyn came and held a bowl over his face to catch the dripping poison and spare him the pain, but she occasionally had to dump the excess venom out of it. When she was gone, the snake's venom returned to burning his face.

Sigyn remained devoted to him in this way until the end of the world, though many might wonder what she saw in him, and why she was so loyal to her husband, when he wasn't loyal to her.

Troubled
and Tragic
Love Stories

Beyond the realms of myth and legend, there are countless examples of romance gone wrong—stories that would give Romeo and Juliet a run for their money. Sometimes, all people want to do is be in love and be happy, only to have insurmountable obstacles put in their path, or face a world that simply won't let them be. These true stories of love and loss, triumph and tragedy might bring a tear to your eye if you're a hopeless romantic, or they might just prove your point, if you're a cynic.

Harmodius and Aristogeiton

Harmodius and Aristogeiton were citizens of classical-era Athens, lovers who both died in 514 BCE. These two men found themselves swept up in the political events of the time, and would later be remembered as heroes. At the time, Athens had been experimenting with democracy (though only a privileged few, all of them men, were allowed to vote). Not everyone loved the idea of voting, however, and sometimes, men would take power without going through the usual procedures, becoming tyrants. The word "tyrant" wasn't necessarily considered negative, though; it just meant someone who held power outside of the usual way. Of course, power corrupts, and, all too often, those who became tyrants for the good of the city eventually got greedy and became, well, tyrannical.

And so it was that a man named Pisistratus became Athens' tyrant in the mid-sixth century BCE. He seems to have done a lot to help the poor, reduced corruption among the wealthy, and funded the arts and sports, and was, therefore, pretty popular. Unfortunately, when he died in 527 BCE, his son, Hippias took over along with his brother, Hipparchus, who began to enjoy his power a little too much, leading to a decline in popularity for both.

It so happened that Hipparchus's eye was drawn by a handsome young man named Harmodius, but Harmodius was already very much attached to Aristogeiton, and refused. It might have ended there, had not Hipparchus turned it up a notch. He invited Harmodius's younger sister to carry a

ceremonial offering in an important Athenian festival, and she agreed. On the day, however, he publicly humiliated her, accusing her of not being a virgin, and chasing her away.

This was a humiliation for Harmodius's whole family, and, given that Hipparchus was already known to be abusing his power, this act was the last straw for Harmodius. He went to Aristogeiton, and together, the two plotted with a few others to assassinate both Hippias and Hipparchus, using their corruption as an excuse to enact revenge. On the day, at the Panathenaic Games, a sporting event held once every four years, they put their plan into action. Finding Hipparchus, they stabbed him to death, but unfortunately, Harmodius was killed by guards. Aristogeiton was arrested, and Hippias saw to it that he was tortured until he revealed the other conspirators. Aristogeiton resisted and even mocked Hippias after pretending to cooperate, and tradition says that Hippias killed Aristogeiton himself.

Afterward, Hippias became more and more of a true tyrant, executing citizens based on little more than his cruelty and paranoia. This turned many people against him, and he even allied himself with the hated Persians to try to stay in power. He was exiled eventually, and though he tried to return later on, he failed, and died without returning to Athens. Later on, writers would praise Harmodius and Aristogeiton, the tragic lovers, for their role in preserving Athens and its institutions.

Abelard and Héloïse

Peter Abelard (1079–1142 CE) was a French scholar and philosopher. He was also a gifted speaker and a lecturer at the University of Paris in its early days, and his teaching attracted students from all over Europe. One story says that he was once forbidden from teaching at the university for a time, so he simply set up class outside. When the authorities objected, he moved his classes across the Seine and carried on, and the students kept coming. With such a devoted following, Abelard became rather full of himself.

As his star continued to rise, he had the chance to become the tutor to Héloïse d'Argenteuil, who was the niece of a man named Fulbert, a canon (clerk) at Notre-Dame Cathedral. The two fell madly in love and used their "teaching sessions" to engage in a passionate affair. News of this tryst spread fast, and soon everyone whispered about how the great Abelard was carrying on with his student. Everyone, it seems, except Fulbert.

When he found out, of course, he forbade them from seeing each other. The two continued to have an affair in secret, and, unfortunately, Héloïse became pregnant. So, Abelard did what most arrogant, career-minded men would do: he sent her off to Brittany to cover it up and, allegedly, to protect her reputation. She gave birth to their son and named him Astrolabe, an instrument used to calculate latitude that had recently been imported into Europe from the Islamic world. Poor kid must have been teased mercilessly at school.

Abelard did offer to marry her, and amazingly, he even got Fulbert's blessing for it, but Abelard also wanted the marriage

kept secret so that the scandal wouldn't hinder his career at the university. Héloïse didn't like this, but eventually agreed. Fulbert decided to tell everyone, embarrassing them both, and Héloïse then denied they were even married. She decided she'd had enough of scandal and gossip and, with Abelard in agreement, she went to live in the convent of Argenteuil outside of Paris.

Fulbert was enraged when he found out about this, thinking Abelard had forced her to go away to protect his reputation. So, he sent some men to attack Abelard one night in his home. They took hold of him and, with a large knife, castrated him. Abelard was left a eunuch, but the criminals were later caught and had their eyes gouged out and their own genitals cut off, so, hooray?

Abelard himself decided to retire to a monastery, but he and Héloïse often wrote letters to each other, letters of love, philosophy, and discussions of many other topics. At one point, Abelard decided to declare that he'd never loved her at all, but maybe he was still angry about all he'd lost ...

Infante Peter and Inês de Castro

"**I**nfante" in this case doesn't mean a baby; it was simply a title given to the male children of Spanish and Portuguese kings. Peter (1320–67 CE) was heir to the throne of Portugal. Like so many royal children, he had to make do with all of the politics, scheming, and back-stabbing that went on around him. People at this level of society most often didn't marry for love, but to do their duty, make political alliances, and/or bring wealth to the family.

Peter was engaged to Constanza Manuel, granddaughter of King James II of Aragon, as that union made for a strong political alliance. Except when Constanza arrived in Portugal in 1340, something unfortunate happened: Peter met her lady-in-waiting, a beautiful young woman named Inês de Castro. It wasn't long before Peter had fallen head over heels in love with Inês, and she with him. The two began an affair in secret.

This wasn't all that unusual. During the Middle Ages (and later), male monarchs were pretty much expected to have mistresses, and their advisors and even the church looked the other way, as long as they fathered legitimate children with their wives. In Peter's case, he really was in love with Inês, which made things a bit more complicated for his marriage. Still, Constanza did become pregnant, but she died in child-birth in 1349 CE.

Peter could now marry Inês, or so he thought. His father, King Afonso IV, knew what had been going on and refused to let him marry her. Peter refused to marry any of the other women

his father proposed, and the two clashed over it. Peter started living with Inês in secret, and promised her brothers important appointments at his court when he became king. Afonso worried that Peter's promises would give Portuguese power to Aragon. Even worse, Peter claimed he had married Inês against his father's wishes and that they now had children of their own.

So, Afonso decided to take matters into his own hands. He sent three of his soldiers to find Inês at a monastery. They took hold of her and cut her head off in front of one of her children. Peter, mad with grief and rage, raised a rebellion against his father. King Afonso won that battle, but he died soon after, and Peter became king in 1357. With all the power at his disposal, he had Inês's murderers arrested, and, according to legend, he executed them by ripping their hearts out with his own hands.

He then proclaimed that he and Inês had been lawfully married and named her queen of Portugal. In 1360 CE, he had her body exhumed and moved to a royal monastery, where his own tomb would be, so that they could lie together for eternity. Denied lasting happiness in life, he saw to it that they could be together in death.

Shah Jahan and Mumtaz Mahal

Shah Jahan (1592–1666 CE) was the fifth emperor of the Mughal Empire. As ruler of a vast number of territories in Central Asia (large parts of India, modern Pakistan and Bangladesh, and Afghanistan), he was no doubt used to a lavish lifestyle that set him above all others. He had the best food, enormous palaces, the finest clothing, even multiple wives—and it was with one of these wives that a timeless love story was born.

Shah Jahan was engaged to Mumtaz Mahal (1593–1631 CE) when they were both teenagers. At that level of society, marriages were pretty much exclusively political. Indeed, by the time the two married, Jahan already had one wife, and would later take a third, but it was Mumtaz who captured his heart. He wanted little to do with his other wives, and was fully devoted to Mumtaz. Their marriage was a happy one, and she had several children with him. Pre-modern medicine, childbirth could be far more dangerous to the mother and child if anything went wrong, and Mumtaz died in 1631 from childbirth complications. A grief-stricken Jahan commissioned a grand building that would be her mausoleum, the world-famous Taj Mahal in northern India.

This stunning masterpiece of architecture is one of the most famous buildings in the world, attracting millions of tourists every year. It took over thirty years to complete, and stands as a monument to Jahan's true love. Later in life, Jahan was

deposed by his own son, Aurangzeb, during a struggle for power among his successors. Jahan was held prisoner, though he continued to live in luxury. When Jahan finally died, Aurangzeb had him buried in the Taj Mahal next to Mumtaz, as he'd wished.

It would be a classic, tragic love story, but more sinister rumors have also plagued the figure of Jahan over the years. Legends say that after the Taj Mahal was finished, he ordered the architect, Ustad Ahmad Lahori, to be blinded, so that he could never again design something so wonderful. Then, in an act of horror and brutality, Jahan ordered that the artisans who had created exquisite works of art in the shrine have one or both hands chopped off, for a similar reason. This cruelty might have extended to the laborers as well, all in some bizarre attempt to keep anyone from outdoing this monument to his beloved wife.

While a gruesome story, there is actually no evidence that Jahan ever ordered these horrible acts to be done to anyone. In fact, a king who executes or maims some of his workers, once an amazing project is completed, is a common rumor through-out history. A similar tale was told about Ivan the Terrible in Russia, for example, when he had the Cathedral of St. Basil the Blessed in Russia built. This slander shows up usually when politicians or historians are trying to push a particular agenda, but Jahan doesn't seem to be the monster that some obviously want him to be.

King James I and George Villiers

King James I of England (and VI of Scotland) ascended to the English throne in 1603, following the death of Queen Elizabeth I, who had reigned for almost forty-five years. During his reign, the English (for better and worse) established their first permanent settlement in America, and two of the English language's great masterpieces appeared: the King James Bible and the First Folio of Shakespeare's plays.

In his personal life, James endured a lot of turmoil. His beloved older son, Prince Henry, died in 1612, leaving the much less competent Charles (later Charles I) as the heir, whose reign would lead to the English Civil War. When it came to romance, James was a bit of a disaster. While married with children, James also took a liking to various young men in his court. This was pretty well known among the nobility, and everyone tended to look the other way.

In the course of these dalliances, James met a young man named George Villiers. Whether it was love at first sight or not, George quickly became a royal favorite, and James would neglect his wife and family to spend time with him. In one palace, there was even a secret hallway connecting their bedrooms. The king was so enamored of George that he began to heap gifts, titles, and responsibilities on him. George was knighted, became a Gentleman of the Bedchamber, was made a baron, an earl, and finally Duke of Buckingham, which is a lot of gifts for someone who was just James's "friend." This made other courtiers envious and resentful, but they couldn't

really do anything, as long as George had the king's protection. It didn't help that George could be arrogant, and a bit of a screwup when he was entrusted with various diplomatic and military assignments.

George publicly stated that he "admired" Anne of Austria, who was the queen consort of King Louis XIII of France, which was more than a bit scandalous if true. However, he might have just said this to take the heat off of himself and the king. Indeed, in private letters, James referred to George as his "wife" and himself as George's "husband."

After James died in 1625, George played the game well enough to stay in favor with the new King Charles I, at least for a while. It's possible that he had been conning James all along to secure wealth and power for himself, and never returned the king's affections. In any case, his luck ran out in 1628, when a soldier named John Felton stabbed him, allegedly because George had denied him a promotion. The wound was fatal, and so unpopular was George by that time that many hailed Felton as a hero.

James How, aka Mary East

In the mid-eighteenth century, in Poplar, a small village outside of London, Mr. James How and his wife owned a public house, the White Horse Tavern. Despite being friendly and respected in the neighborhood, they were very secretive. They never had guests over, didn't hire their own maid, and never had any children. They didn't even have any employees at the tavern; they did all the work themselves. This behavior was odd, but no one really gave it much thought; eccentricity among the well-off is a long-established British trait, after all.

But after some thirty years together, Mrs. How became ill. James took her to stay with some relatives, but her condition worsened, and she died soon after. James was heartbroken, but the situation would only get worse. Two men soon showed up at the tavern, illegally impersonating constables. In private, they demanded £100, or they would arrest him for a crime he hadn't committed. They took James to see a certain Mrs. Bentley, who had actually been blackmailing Mr. and Mrs. How for years, and was not interested in losing her cash cow.

James agreed to pay the £100, and wrote them out a draft from the bank, but the blackmailers were in for a surprise when they went to cash it. They were arrested, and charged. At the trial, the whole town found out the Hows' secret when James arrived, but not as James. Dressed as a woman, "James" confessed to really being Mary East. She and her female partner had lived as a married couple for decades, and Mrs. Bentley, who'd found out, had been blackmailing them for years.

It turned out that when Mary and her companion were young, they had been engaged to men who were arrested for being highwaymen. Realizing that they had feelings for each other, they decided that their best course of action was for one to assume the role of a man, and to live as husband and wife in a new town.

The *London Chronicle* reported: "Being intimate, they communicated their minds to each other and determined to live together ever after. After consulting on the best method of proceeding, they agreed that one should put on man's apparel and that they would live as man and wife in some part where they were not known ... The difficulty now was who was to be the man, which was soon decided by the toss-up of a halfpenny, and the lot fell on Mary East ... Mary, after purchasing a man's habit, assumed the name of James How."

Mrs. Bentley was charged and punished with jail time, and Mary saw justice done. Remarkably, she then resumed her life in Poplar, but as Mary, not James, and was still well-liked by the locals. When she retired, another paper declared that she and her wife had lived in "good credit and esteem," and had acquired their wealth honestly and with "unblemished character." In spite of the tragic death and difficulty that followed, this love story shines as a rare example of acceptance in that time.

The tragic story of Doña Carmen and Don Luis still casts a shadow over the Callejon del Beso ("Alley of the Kiss"), in Guanajuato, a city in central Mexico. On one very narrow section of that street, anger, jealousy, and possessiveness famously brought two young lovers to their doom.

The tale goes that the lovely Doña Carmen was the daughter of a wealthy but cruel man, who hid her away from friends and potential suitors. Due to this isolated life, she became lonely and increasingly miserable. Her father's intention was to marry her off to the wealthiest man he could find, thus enriching himself, and he wouldn't tolerate anyone else getting near his daughter.

Fate has a way of undoing the plans of tyrants, and it happened that Doña Carmen met a young laborer (some versions say a miner), named Don Luis. He was poor, but kind, and she was quickly drawn to him. They often would meet and talk at a nearby church, away from her unsuspecting father. But word got back to Carmen's father, and in his fury, he locked her away in their home and threatened to send her off to a convent.

Hearing this, Don Luis came up with a way that he could still see his beloved: he managed to take up residence in the house directly opposite hers. The two houses were only separated by a very narrow street. Indeed, the upstairs bedrooms were so close that their balconies almost touched, and so Doña and Don were able to meet in secret and hold hands across the *callejon*.

For a little while, this plan worked, and they fell more and more in love, but fate, while bringing them together, also had a cruel plan in store. Hearing voices one night, her father rushed to the door of Doña Carmen's bedroom. Shoving aside Doña Brigida, her lady-in-waiting, he entered his daughter's room and found her on the balcony, holding hands with her beloved Don Luis.

Enraged, he drew a dagger and stabbed her in the chest. Don Luis, in shock and heartbroken, managed to plant a final kiss on her hand as she died. It was said that he stayed with her for a long time afterward, though why the father didn't try to kill him as well, or take her body away, is not mentioned. In any case, Don Luis knew that he couldn't live without Doña Carmen, so he jumped down a mine shaft to his death. The father's fate is not recorded, but one can only hope that he faced some kind of severe justice.

The place where the lovers met is still a site for couples to visit. Indeed, at its narrowest, the alley is only a little over two feet wide, and the balconies above do almost touch. It's become a tradition for couples to go there and kiss on the third step of a stairway that leads upward to the rest of the alley, just below the balconies.

Anne Lister and Ann Walker

Anne Lister (1791–1840) was a wealthy landowner in West Yorkshire who wrote extensively about country life in the early nineteenth century. She was a successful businesswoman and dedicated diarist who provides us insights into the time period and herself. Anne also had a hidden side, which she wrote about in a secret code. In all, she wrote about five million words in a collection of books, some of which were later hidden in the walls of her family home, Shibden Hall. When one of the family descendants, John Lister, found her more-clandestine diaries in the 1890s and deciphered them, he was shocked by what he read. A friend told him to burn them, but he decided to wall them up again, and there they stayed until the 1980s, when they were rediscovered and saved.

The diaries revealed that Anne was quite the womanizer, and had succeeded in seducing a number of respectable ladies throughout England. At some point, she met a wealthy young heiress named Ann Walker, and was smitten with her. Some have suggested that Lister romanced Walker because she needed her money, but based on Lister's writings, it seems that she was genuinely drawn to "the other" Ann. Happily for Lister, Walker felt the same, and the two began an affair in secret, while posing as "companions" for the public.

Some people might have suspected that they were up to something, simply because Lister didn't dress in a "ladylike" manner, wearing all-black clothing (more common for men at the time) with more masculine cuts. Some people even called her "Gentleman Jack," a sobriquet meant to insult her lack of femininity.

Lister didn't care. She won Walker's heart and they even took communion together at a church in York in 1834, exchanged wedding rings, and then lived together as "companions" at Shibden Hall. Their marriage was not "official," of course, but a plaque outside of the church now commemorates it as the first gay marriage in England.

They might have lived happily for many years, but Lister had an insatiable desire to see the world, and traveled with Walker. On one of their trips, they visited the area that is now the Republic of Georgia near modern Turkey, having come south from Russia. Lister caught a fever of some kind, became very sick, and died on September 22, 1840. Heartbroken, Ann Walker nevertheless saw to it that Lister's remains were brought back to England (quite a challenge in the 1840s), and buried in the main church in Halifax, near Shibden Hall. Walker inherited an interest in the hall, but it seems that some others tried to edge her out of it. She went to London, but was able to come back to the hall in 1845 for a few years.

She died in 1854, having never married a man, and, as far as we know, never having had another relationship with a woman. Whether loyal to Lister's memory or unable to form a bond with someone else, hers was a tragic ending to a daring love story in a time when society definitely would not have approved.

Ghosts and Urban Legends

Though they've passed on, ghosts are not immune from the problems of love. In fact, love lost or gone wrong is often what causes these restless spirits to haunt the living or a given area. Hand in hand with ghosts come urban legends, those famous stories that a "friend of a friend" told you, and that you both swore must be true. But most often, these stories have many versions , and are told in many different countries. Maybe there's some hint of truth in them, but we can never know for sure. Romance gone wrong is also a classic feature of many of the best urban legends. So here is a sample of both ghosts and legends for you to enjoy, and maybe to tell others by flashlight ...

A Man Thinks He's Buying Gloves for His Sweetheart, but Oh No!

Urban legends are great fun, no matter what the topic, and part of the entertainment is that there will always be people who insist they are true. The following story, dating back to the 1920s, probably isn't true at all, but it deserves to be. It's not so much scary as hilarious and somewhat embarrassing.

A certain fellow wanted to buy a present for his new girlfriend for Valentine's Day. They hadn't been together for too long, so he needed to make sure that he got her something that was thoughtful, but not too extravagant. He decided that a nice pair of gloves would be perfect, so he and the girlfriend's younger sister went shopping. Finding what he wanted at a certain boutique, he bought them and had them wrapped. At the same time, the younger sister bought some fancy new underwear.

The shop mixed up the two boxes and sent the panties to the man's girlfriend, but with his note. In that missive, he explained that he was buying this gift because she had the habit of not wearing any when it was cold outside. Further, based on her sister's advice, he had gotten her a shorter pair that were easier to take off. They were a good color, and the woman who sold them had a similar pair that she had worn for three weeks, which were hardly dirty at all. Just to be sure, the man had asked the saleswoman to try on this pair, and they looked really nice. He told her that he wanted to be there to help put them on her the first time, since others would likely

touch them before he would be able to. He also advised her that after taking them off, she should blow into them a little, because they might be a bit damp.

In any case, he was looking forward to kissing them often over the next year, and he hoped that she would wear them the next time he saw her.

Signing the card with "all his love," he had one last piece of advice: that according to the latest fashion trend, she should wear them folded down a bit, so that a little fur might show.

And that was the end of that budding relationship!

A Man's Horrifying Blind Date

This urban legend is part of the mistaken identity genre of urban legends, where everything seems to be going great until some awful revelation ruins everything.

There are many versions of this legend, but this one is appropriately updated for the modern world. (Though it's set at a time before exchanging pictures online was the norm and people were more likely to remain anonymous.)

A young man is lonely and goes looking for love on the internet; that's his first mistake. He ends up meeting someone in a chat room. He and this other person hit it off right away and start writing each other privately. This back-and-forth goes on

for some time, and it all seems to be going well. They keep the conversations light and don't tell each other much about themselves—always a sensible safety precaution online.

Finally, they arrange to meet in person, in a public place. In some versions, it's a café, in others, a beach. They set a time and a date, both excited for the big day.

The young man has finally met someone that he really connects with and might have a shot at building a relationship with. This is the real deal. He's nervous, but he's determined to see it through. He showers, dresses up nice, fusses with his hair to get it to look just right, and sets off.

It's getting dark and he makes his way to the appointed place, certain that he's about to meet the woman of his dreams. Then he sees her! In the distance, a woman stands with her back to him, but she's wearing just what she said she'd be wearing (in some versions, it's a nice dress, in others shorts and a shirt), and seems to be fidgeting nervously.

His heart pounding, he resolves to go through with it and starts toward her. This is it! It's really happening! As he approaches, he calls out to her, using her username, as they'd agreed. She turns around, excited, flashing a big smile.

Her eyes widen.

His eyes widen.

He can hardly breathe and he's at a loss for words. He starts to shake and gets lightheaded. Finally, a single word escapes from his trembling lips: "Mom?!"

The Hook

There are many variations on the classic urban legend of The Hook, but they all involve a young couple in a car. Sometimes, they are driving through a remote area or, more often, they have parked the car on a cliff overlooking town to have some privacy while they make out. They have the radio on, and a news broadcast warns that a dangerous serial killer is on the loose. Everyone should lock their doors and stay safe. The young woman wants to leave, but the young man says they have nothing to worry about. And here is where many different versions of the story pop up.

A popular one has the woman asking to go home after hearing something hit or scrape their car. When they do get back to her house, they notice either scrapes on the back door, or see an actual hook hanging from the door handle.

Alternatively, the young couple hears the warning, and the man brushes it off. She sees something in the trees, so he gets out to check, against her wishes. He sees nothing, but when he comes back to the car, he finds her dead, brutally murdered with hook slashes all over her, or with the hook embedded in her chest.

One variation has the couple driving through the woods when the car breaks down. The man goes for help, again, against the woman's wishes, and she turns on the car radio while waiting for him to come back. She is startled by the sound of something thumping on the roof, and tries to ignore it, but eventually she gets out to have a look. She's greeted by the sight of the killer sitting on the roof, holding the man's severed head with his hook and slamming it repeatedly into the car.

Sometimes she sees her love's body hanging from a tree overhead, his hands scraping against the car roof, or he's hanging dead by his neck and it's his feet bumping against the roof. Some say she leaves to go look for him, and finds his body nailed to a tree. She screams and turns to run, only to slam right into the hook-wielding maniac. Or, she falls asleep waiting, only to wake up and see the killer leering into the window, her boyfriend's severed head in his hand, and the car keys dangling from his hook. And so on.

Now, if these stories all sound like a scene from a Friday the 13th film, you're not wrong. These kinds of serial killer–spiked urban legends are classic and seem to have originated in America in the 1950s, when more and more teenagers were able to own their own cars. These stories (which many kids probably thought were true), served as a warning to behave responsibly and not give into temptation when alone with their boyfriends or girlfriends. After all, in the world of maniac serial killers on the loose, love and lust can be deadly.

The Screaming Ghost of Catherine Howard

atherine Howard, as we've seen (see page 22), was Henry VIII's ill-fated fifth wife. She met him when Henry was with his fourth wife, Anne of Cleves. The match with Anne was purely for political reasons, and Henry had no real interest in her. He'd married her in January 1540, and by July, he had the marriage annulled. But at least he set up Anne with a lovely house in Lewes in southern England, and she lived out the rest of her days in comfort. Catherine Howard would not be so lucky.

Catherine was young and beautiful, and caught the aging king's eye from their first meeting. She was delighted by the prospect of marrying him and becoming queen of England, but there was an issue: Catherine was not "innocent" in the way that a new bride was supposed to be, as she'd already had an affair with a courtier named Francis Dereham.

Henry knew nothing about this at first, and married Catherine only twelve days after the annulment of his marriage to Anne. On the day of their wedding, the king had his powerful minister, Thomas Cromwell, executed for treason. That probably should have been a sign to the new young queen that her new husband didn't think too hard before enacting his royal powers.

Catherine actually discharged her duties as queen well, but in her personal life, she made some poor choices. She took up with a man named Thomas Culpepper, a gentlemen in

king's household, and the two began a love affair. It's possible that Culpepper pressured her into the relationship, as he seems to have been a sexual predator. By the end of 1541, she'd been found out and confessed to affairs with Culpepper, Dereham, and a third man named Henry Manox. The king was overcome with heartbreak and a sense of betrayal, and in those days, a queen's adultery meant only one thing: execution. On February 13, one day before Valentine's Day, Catherine was executed by beheading at the Tower of London.

Her sad story doesn't end there. There have been persistent reports of hearing the young queen's screams in Hampton Court, where she was arrested. She'd tried to escape her captors' grasp, but her attempts to flee were futile. The so-called Haunted Gallery is alleged to be the place her ghost returns to, forever reliving the terrible moment when she knew her fate was sealed. It's a creepy image, except there's a problem: her original apartments no longer exist, and she would not have used the gallery as an exit anyway. So, why then would her terrified ghost haunt this section of the palace?

Who knows? Perhaps ghosts have their own logic, which is inscrutable to the living. Perhaps Catherine's spirit does linger at least some of the time in the Haunted Gallery, screaming as she is repeatedly dragged off to her doom.

Emily's Bridge in Stowe, Vermont

Emily's Bridge, near Stowe in northern Vermont, is like many of the state's picturesque covered bridges. It's a short bridge, only about 50 feet, and so might not look all that special. However, it's the oldest surviving covered bridge in the United States, and a specific legend is attached to it, of heartbreak, loss, and a ghost.

The bridge was built in 1844, and the story goes that at some point afterward, a young woman named Emily agreed to meet her beloved there. They had planned to elope, and arranged to meet at a certain time to slip away together. No doubt excited, Emily waited on the bridge, eager to begin her new life with this young man, only for him to never arrive. Stricken with disbelief and grief, Emily didn't bother to try to find or confront him. Instead, she found a rope and hanged herself from the rafters of the covered bridge.

Of course, that should have been the end of this sad story, but Emily's spirit couldn't move on. Death changed her from a loving young woman to a spirit filled with hatred, so much so that she would appear from time to time and attack unwary travelers who crossed the bridge. Now manifesting as an apparition with long, sharp nails, she struck out at carriages (and later, cars), and even people, leaving nasty scratches.

All of this would be terrifying to the bravest who attempt to cross the bridge at night, but, of course, there is more to Emily's haunting. There are several versions of the story, some saying she was thrown from a horse and died, or was

murdered by a jealous lover. It turns out that the whole story was invented by a local woman named Nancy Wolfe Stead, who wanted to scare off kids from partying nearby at night and annoying her and her neighbors. This strategy backfired, as more and more people wanted to see the bridge where Emily had died, and maybe catch a glimpse of the horrifyingly clawed ghost herself. So it turns out Emily never existed, and her tragic death in a love story going terribly wrong is just another of so many similar legends around the world.

And yet people who've visited the bridge late at night have insisted that they have experienced some very strange things, ranging from ghostly lights to disembodied voices. Some recall seeing the figure of a young woman standing in the murky distance. Some have even claimed to find scratches on their cars.

Is it possible that belief in the legends of a place can give it the power to bring about some of our worst fears? Has Emily been created simply because enough people have believed in her? Only the bridge knows for sure!

Stony Hollow Road in Iowa

Stony Hollow Road has a reputation for being the most haunted road in Iowa. Located outside the town of Burlington near the Illinois-Iowa border, Stony Hollow Road has been the subject of many a creepy ghost story over the years. This rural road looks normal during the day, but at night, things start to go "bump," at least according to some who have experienced the unexplained while traveling along it.

There is a point on Stony Hollow where a cliff rises up on one side of the road, and it was here that, in the 1800s, a tragic death occurred. A young woman named Lucinda was engaged to be married to a man she was devoted to. The two had arranged to meet at this very spot, but while Lucinda made sure to be there on time, her fiancé was nowhere to be seen. As time wore on, she got more and more worried. For whatever reason, Lucinda became convinced that he had jilted her and run off with another woman.

Overcome by grief, she climbed to the top of the cliff and threw herself off, falling to a tragic, gruesome death. And then the tragedy only worsened—it turned out that the man hadn't run off with anyone. He had simply been late, because his cart had gotten stuck in some mud farther down the road. Lucinda had killed herself over nothing.

Because of this pointless death, her spirit couldn't rest in peace, doomed to haunt this stretch of road, appearing to naïve travelers in the dead of night. Many have claimed to have seen the ghostly form of a woman up on the cliff or at the roadside, but

usually, Lucinda's spirit won't show up unless summoned. To do that, someone must call out her name three times in a row.

If someone does this, the would-be ghost hunter might catch a glimpse of her, on the cliff or nearby. However, this is a dangerous game, for if Lucinda shows up and she lays a rose at the feet of the summoner, it means they will die the next day.

That's a pretty big risk to take, but, of course, it hasn't stopped many curious people from going to Stony Hollow Road and pressing their luck in the hopes of seeing something supernatural. Such a glimpse, while extraordinary, doesn't seem worth it—she clearly is a bit impetuous in matters of life and death.

Seguin Island Lighthouse in Maine

Lighthouses are a natural setting for paranormal activity. They are already lonely, spooky places, set aside from the rest of the world, and need people with a hardy personality to tend them. This particular tale is set at Seguin Island Lighthouse (also known as Seguin Light), Maine's second-oldest lighthouse, built in 1795–96 with the approval of George Washington. It sits on Seguin Island, a remote and desolate place off the coast of central Maine.

The story goes that in the late 1800s, a new keeper was appointed to the job of manning the lighthouse and set off to the island with his new wife. As you might imagine, the young lady didn't take well to life on a small, desolate island. She was bored and frustrated, with nothing to do, no friends, the endless stretch of the Atlantic Ocean to the south, and uninhabited stretches of Maine coastline to the north.

Her husband was sympathetic, but wasn't a regular companion, as he was busy with his lighthouse work. His duties also meant that they couldn't just take a boat to the mainland anytime they wanted. He came up with the idea of ordering a piano for her to relieve her boredom and entertain them both. Getting such a large instrument to the island wasn't easy, but after a few attempts, the piano was finally delivered. The wife was very happy with the instrument, but there was a problem. She couldn't play without sheet music, and only one piece of sheet music had been included with the piano, a simple song by American composer Scott Joplin. It wasn't much, but it was something.

There wouldn't be a chance to bring over more sheet music, since winter was setting in and ice was forming atop the waters surrounding the island. As it would be too dangerous to cross to the mainland, they were stuck there for the winter. With no chance of getting any more music, she sat down, learned the Joplin tune, and played it over, and over, and over again.

Now, if you hear or see anything too often, it will start to make you insane, and this song was no exception. Her husband tolerated it at first, but soon it became annoying, then infuriating, and finally, it started to drive him mad. Stuck together in on an icebound island, with nothing to do and only one song playing endlessly, both of them probably lost it.

Eventually, the lighthouse keeper snapped and he did something terrible. He took an axe, and hacked the piano to pieces. When his wife screamed at him for doing it, he turned the axe on her. Likely full of regret, he killed himself with the same axe. When a supply boat come to the island a few weeks later, the sailors found the grisly scene.

Ever after, some who have visited Seguin Light have said that they heard a ghostly piano playing in the night, sometimes coming from the lighthouse, sometimes just echoing over the water.

William Axtell and the Hidden Chamber

Yes, this entry sounds like a book title, but the tale is a tragic ghost story in the classic Gothic tradition. In the early 1800s, an army colonel named William Axtell bought Melrose Hall in Flatbush, a neighborhood in Brooklyn. It was a nice, if strange, home, and Axtell was eager to set up residence there. Inside, there were odd halls, twisty staircases, weirdly shaped rooms, and hidden passages. All of which suited William perfectly. You see, he was moving into the house with his fiancée, a sophisticated woman, but William wasn't in love with her. He was in love with her sister, Alva (in some versions, she's named Isabella), and he had devised a way to allow Alva to live with him, without the poor fiancée ever knowing.

One of the house's many features was a large, hidden room upstairs. There, he set up Alva in lavish comfort. The catch was that no one could know she was there, and she couldn't leave the room if anyone else was around. Only one other person knew of Alva's presence: an elderly slave named Miranda. Yes, William was a slave owner, as if he wasn't already terrible enough.

He visited Alva as often as he could, and she seemed content with this weird arrangement. (Even stranger: Why did her sister never wonder where she was?)

At some point, William had to leave on an extended business trip (or a military campaign), and he told Alva that she should leave too, for her own safety. Alva refused, insisting

that Miranda would take care of her needs. William reluctantly agreed and left, but in his absence, Miranda became ill and died. Now, Alva had no one to bring her food. You would think that she would sneak out, but in some versions of the story, she was locked in, and rather than cry out for help, she simply wasted away and died. William came back some months later and found her dead. Legends say that at a welcoming reception for William, her angry ghost appeared, frightening everyone, and making William feel so guilty that he killed himself.

Alva's spirit was said to wander the halls of Melrose, freer than before, but still unable to leave the building. In 1835, a lawyer named James Mowat bought the house, and he and his wife, Anna Cora, moved in. She was a famed actress and later novelist who became fascinated with the house and its ghosts (there were other ghosts residing in the hall, too). She was the one who named the building "Melrose Hall," and she later confirmed that she had seen Alva's ghost, although, as a novelist she very likely added poetic license to the descriptions of her home, if not outright invented a lot of it.

These days, Melrose Hall is long gone, but perhaps Alva's ghost haunts the apartments that now stand on the site, still trapped there as she was in life ...

Kuchisake-onna ("Slit-Mouthed Woman")

Japan has no shortage of terrifying ghosts, which often take the form of young women who were wronged in life and now eternally seek vengeance. Kuchisake-onna, the tragic ghost in this entry, is most definitely one of these, and she is particularly horrifying since she met her death in a terrible way and seeks to do the same to others.

The legend tells of a young woman who suffered mutilation at the hands of her jealous husband. Some versions say that she was the wife of a samurai who was always off fighting in battles. She grew lonely and began to have an affair with one or more men in their hometown. Eventually, the husband heard about her infidelity, and in a fit of rage he sliced the corners of her mouth open from ear to ear with his razor-sharp sword. This horrific attack left her so injured that she soon bled to death. Another version of the legend says that she was mutilated by a woman performing surgery on her who was jealous of her beauty. In either case, the dead woman was not through with this world.

She now roams the world, looking for people to suffer as she did. She is a spirit of vengeance, called an *onryō* in Japanese. She travels about with a cloth mask over her face and carries some kind of sharp instrument in one hand, a knife, a sword, or even a pair of scissors. You can already see where this is going ...

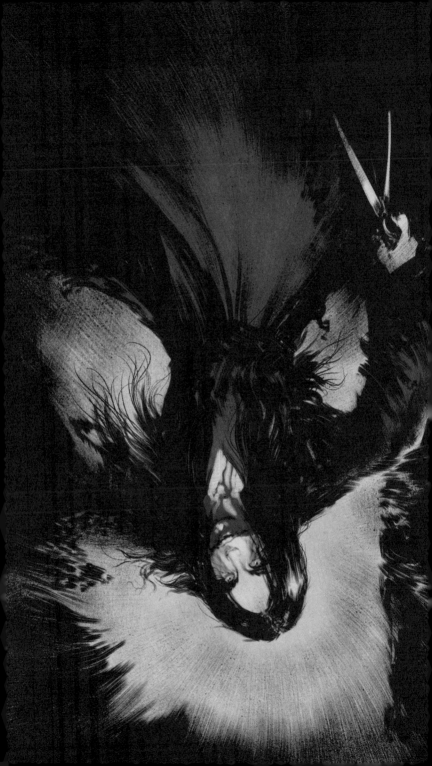

She will approach an unsuspecting victim and ask them, "Am I beautiful?" If the person says "No," she will kill them on the spot, usually by stabbing them or slashing their throat. If they say "Yes," she will pull off her mask to reveal her sliced-up face (her mouth is sometimes said to be full of sharp teeth) and ask, "Even now?" If her victim says "No," she will kill them. If they shriek or cry out in any way, she will kill them. If the person somehow manages to say "Yes," she will slice open their mouths from ear to ear, the same as was done to her, leaving them to bleed to death.

What, if anything, can the victim do to escape such a horrible fate? There are several things, actually. Sometimes answering "Yes" to both questions will make her leave the person alone, though she might show up at their house later to finish what she started. Another answer, weirdly, is to tell her that you're late to an appointment. She will often simply bow and apologize; she's polite at least! A third tactic is to answer that she is average in appearance, which will confuse her, and hopefully give the would-be victim a chance to run away. One can also throw money or hard candies at her, and she will stop to pick them up.

This strange tale of a woman wronged by a lover might date back to the seventeenth century, but it probably really came about in the 1970s, an urban legend that some people took to heart.

La Sayona
("The Sackcloth Woman")

J apan is not the only country with vengeful ghosts. From Venezuela, there is La Sayona, a a particularly disturbing spirit, driven by rage and a misunderstanding. As is often the case with such legends, there are several different versions of this story. In most of them, a young woman, sometimes named Casilda, lived happily with her husband and their infant child. All seemed well, but one day, while she was bathing in the river, she noticed a man watching her. She angrily told him to go away, but he surprised her by saying that he had come to warn her.

He said that her husband was being unfaithful to her, and even worse, he was having an affair with Casilda's own mother! She didn't believe it, but raced back to her mother's house, where she found her husband sleeping, holding their baby. Not knowing why he would be there, she flew into a rage, assuming that what the stranger told her was true (we never find out if it was or not).

Driven mad with rage, she set the house on fire, took up a machete, and killed her mother, slitting open her belly. Before the older woman died, she cursed her daughter, telling Casilda that she would never have any peace after death, and would become a ghost that would seek to punish men who had actually done wrong. Her mother spoke truly. Casilda died not long afterward, and she was condemned to haunt the world of the living as La Sayona.

Various stories say that she appears as a woman with long black hair and a white robe (hence the name "Sackcloth Woman"), though she may also wear a black cloak with a hood over the robe. She can also take the form of a wolf. Another gruesome version says that she hides her face under a hood, but those men unfortunate enough to catch a glimpse of her face will see only a skull with fangs.

She appears to men who are unfaithful to their wives, or may be considering it. If she judges them to be guilty, she will attack them. Sometimes her victims are lucky, and escape death, but other times, she will tear them apart with her horrific fangs, leaving their mutilated bodies as a warning to other men who might be tempted to cheat.

In some versions, she appears to men as a beautiful temptress and tries to get them to follow her into the wilderness. If they refuse, she might judge them worthy and let them live, but if they are tempted and do follow her, hoping for more than just a kiss or two, she will reveal her true form, let out a terrifying cry, and tear them apart.

La Sayona will go on forever, trying to lure men to their doom, to make up for her own terrible crimes, and avenge men who actually have done what she thought her husband did to her.

Murders
Most Foul

The hurt and pain of love are as intense as the joy and bliss, and when the pain becomes too much, it can push people over the edge, causing them to commit acts like trying to murder their romantic rivals. When that happens, everything from poison and pistols to axes and swords can be brought in to get the job done. Sadly, sometimes these murderers get off scot-free, as you'll see in some of these entries. Unfortunately, when it comes to love, sometimes crime does pay.

Gesualdo's Crimes of Passion

Carlo Gesualdo (1566–1613) was an Italian nobleman known mainly for two things: writing wonderful, if rather odd, music, and committing brutal murders. He was the Prince of Venosa and Count of Conza, and he also wrote madrigals and played the lute. His music is still widely studied and appreciated in early music scenes and college music classes.

In 1586, he married his first cousin (a common practice among the upper classes in those days), Donna Maria d'Avalos. As was often the case in these types of marriages, it wasn't a love match, and within two years, she was having an affair with another nobleman, Fabrizio Carafa, who was the Duke of Andria.

The two managed to keep the affair secret for a long time, but it all came out in 1590 at the Palazzo San Severo in Naples. Gesualdo had been out hunting for a few days, but came home early. Maybe he was tired, or maybe he finally suspected something to be afoot at home. When he returned to the palazzo, he found them, shall we say, in the middle of their amorous activities.

Gesualdo was furious and decided to hand out punishment right then and there. Helped by some loyal servants (even though they presumably had kept the whole thing secret from him), he forced Fabrizio to put on Donna's nightshirt and then stabbed both of them several times with his sword, before finally shooting Fabrizio in the head. He came back a second time and mutilated the corpses, just to be sure that the two of them were truly dead.

The next day, officials examined the crime scene, but determined that Gesualdo had done nothing wrong. This was because, as a nobleman, Gesualdo was immune to prosecution for pretty much any crime; he had a literal "get out of jail free" card. So unfortunately, he got away with it. However, he knew that the families of the victims might come looking for revenge, so he fled Naples and hid out for a while.

Meanwhile, lurid stories began to circulate about the crime. People said that Donna and Fabrizio had an infant child, whom Gesualdo also murdered. Other rumors said that Gesualdo cut off their private parts and displayed the bodies publicly, and even murdered Donna's father when he came after Gesualdo. None of these accusations seem to be true, but Gesualdo did need bodyguards. He also suffered from mental health issues later in life. He does seem to have been tormented by guilt, and eventually had himself beaten every day to drive out "demons." The lyrics of his strange musical pieces seem to reflect his state of mind, and when he died, rumors started up that his second wife had murdered him. Maybe he met with some justice after all?

Cruel Colonel García Martí

St. Augustine, Florida, is the oldest European-built city in the United States, and harbors some dark secrets. Founded in 1565, it has seen more than its share of bloodshed over its long history. This is especially true of its famed military fort, the Castillo de San Marcos, built in 1672. In addition to the usual violence and intrigue seen at such a place, the fort wasn't immune from problems arising over matters of the heart.

In 1763, at the end of the Seven Years' War, Spain gave up control of St. Augustine to the British, in exchange for a part of Cuba, dividing up territory as colonial powers often did. The situation changed again when the United States was born. The young America returned the city and fort to Spain, and soon, a certain Colonel Garcia Marti arrived on the scene, taking up a post at the castillo with his beautiful young wife, Dolores, in 1784.

The colonel took his work seriously, to the point that he neglected his wife, and she grew frustrated and lonely. Relief came in the form of Garcia's handsome young assistant, Captain Manuel Abela. Dolores was drawn to him, and the two embarked on an affair that grew into genuine love. They were also both very popular with the soldiers stationed at the fort. All of which Garcia seemed not to notice, though that would soon change, when Dolores outed herself.

She had a liking for an unusual and high-quality perfume, and one could usually tell when she was nearby. It happened that

once after she'd been with Manuel, he was in the presence of Garcia, who smelled her perfume on him; he'd forgotten to wash it off, apparently. Garcia immediately began to suspect that something was up. Consumed with jealousy, he decided to take matters into his own hands.

Over the next few days, the soldiers noticed that both Dolores and Manuel were gone. Garcia said that his wife was unwell, and had sailed to Mexico (some versions say Spain) to recover and receive treatment, while Manuel was on a special mission in Cuba. These seemed like good explanations, but as time wore on, it became obvious that neither of them would return. Eventually, Florida became a part of the United States, and about fifty years later, a soldier noticed something unusual about the dungeon. Investigating, he found a hidden chamber behind a thin wall. Inside were two skeletons, and he smelled a very nice perfume in the air. Were these the bodies of Dolores and Manuel? No one was certain, but it seems likely that in a fit of rage, Garcia walled them up in here, a scene straight out of Edgar Allan Poe.

Ever since, there have been people who have claimed to smell perfume late at night in the fort, or see shapes and lights near this cruel prison. The victims of a ghastly crime, for which Garcia was never punished, Dolores and Manuel might now dwell forever together in the fort where they died.

Christiana Edmunds, the Chocolate Cream Killer

Who doesn't love chocolate? Few people, but after reading this story you might think twice about eating it again. Chocolate is the favorite sweet treat for Valentine's Day, and for pretty much any other day of the year, but for the poor victims living in Brighton, England, in the 1870s, chocolate was deadly.

The subject of this tale, Christiana Edmunds, was born in Kent in 1828, and grew up in a wealthy family, who saw to it that she received a good education. Still, there always seemed to be something a bit off about her, and a doctor diagnosed her with "hysteria" in the late 1850s. Bear in mind that this was an often sexist, catch-all diagnosis. However, it seems that Christiana was definitely troubled, and while living with her mother in the late 1860s, she began an affair with a married man, a doctor named Charles Beard. Christiana seems to have wanted the wife out of the way, so she offered Mrs. Beard a chocolate cream that she'd poisoned. The wife became very sick, but didn't die. Beard would later say that he suspected Christiana was the culprit, but he didn't have proof, and plus, being a typical Victorian, he didn't want his dirty little secret to be made public.

In any case, the incident seemed to help Christiana develop a taste for poisoning. By 1871, she started acquiring chocolate creams, poisoning them with strychnine, and then having a local vendor, John Maynard, sell them. She obtained the poison from a local chemist, saying that she needed it to kill stray cats. But it wasn't cats on her mind, it was people. She even tried

to hide her activities by sending a couple of boys to buy the poison for her.

As a result of her awful activities, several people became ill from eating the chocolates, but at first, no one died, and no one linked the chocolates to these incidents. In June of 1871, a young boy, Sidney Barker, ate one of the chocolates and died. The coroner was able to link his death to the chocolate from the shop, but thought the poisoning was accidental.

Christiana then started sending her poisoned chocolates to unsuspecting recipients, including Mrs. Beard, who again became very sick. It was now clear that someone was poisoning people with chocolate, but Christiana tried to deflect suspicion by mailing some of them to herself, claiming that she had been targeted, presumably by Maynard. Finally, Dr. Beard did the right thing and told the police about his suspicions, but denied that anything had ever happened between him and Christiana. Her evil plan fell apart quickly, and she was arrested, tried, and sentenced to death, although her sentence was eventually reduced to life in prison. She lived out the rest of her days at an insane asylum, dying in 1907.

We'll never know what drove her to use the world tastiest treat to try to kill random people, but it probably put the people of Brighton off Valentine's Day chocolate for a long time.

The Mad Dentist of Wynyard Square

A dental surgeon branded with this wonderfully morbid tabloid moniker caused a sensation in Sydney, Australia, in the mid-1860s. Henry Louis Bertrand originally had come from England, and trained as a dentist in London, and perhaps Paris. After his mother moved to Australia, where she married another dentist, Henry decided to come on down and establish himself there as well. Upon his arrival, he put a rather ridiculous ad in the newspaper, claiming to have been a surgeon dentist "To the Imperial Court of France," which was not even remotely true.

Henry's fib must have worked, because he soon had a thriving practice at Wynyard Square, and married a woman named Jane King. Of course, since this is a book about dark love and passion, it won't be any surprise that Henry soon met another woman, Ellen Kinder, after saying "I do" and began an affair with her. Ellen was married to a banker named Henry Kinder. He had come to Sydney from New Zealand because of financial troubles, and because Ellen had been having an affair with another man there as well. Henry Kinder had taken up drinking in response, so it's safe to assume that Ellen was pretty unhappy with how everything had worked out.

In any case, Henry Bertrand became enamored enough with Ellen that he decided that they needed to get rid of the other Henry. On October 2, 1865, Henry and Jane called for a doctor to come to the Kinders' home, claiming that Henry Kinder had been drunk and shot himself in front of them. He took

four days to die. The death was ruled a suicide at first, but investigators soon grew suspicious, and when police exhumed Kinder's body, they found evidence of poison still in his stomach, suggesting Kinder had been given poison and then shot to make it look like a suicide.

The story got even stranger when the investigation revealed that Henry Bertram had bought a pistol while disguised in his wife's clothing. Further, newspapers delighted in reporting that Henry had pressured his wife into sharing their bed with Ellen, which shocked the prudish sensibilities of the time. Henry and Jane were eventually charged with murder, while Ellen was charged with being an accomplice. The charges against both women were eventually dropped, due to lack of evidence.

Henry Bertrand, however, was not so lucky. There was enough evidence to send him to trial, because he'd foolishly recorded many of his deeds in a private diary, and his sister would later testify that he had bragged about getting away with it. Henry was found guilty and sentenced to death. The sentence was then reduced to life in prison, and he spent time in various prisons and an insane asylum. In 1894, he was released and deported back to England. Henry went right back to being a dentist, though he didn't kill anyone else as far we know, and lived on until 1924, outliving all the others involved. He didn't pay the ultimate penalty for his crime of love and lust, but his reputation as the Mad Dentist has gone down in infamy.

Mary Cecilia Rogers

J ohn Anderson's cigar shop on Liberty Street in New York had quite a boom in customers during the late 1830s. This was due to a certain employee, Mary Cecilia Rogers (c. 1820–41), who charmed all of the gentlemen that came into the shop. Her admirers lined up to have the chance to chat with her as they bought their cigars. Unfortunately, Mary was soon to be a murder victim, bound up with a possible love gone wrong. The case has never been solved, even though many, including Edgar Allan Poe, tried.

Before her murder, Mary mysteriously disappeared for a few days in 1838, according to the *Sun* newspaper, and there were rumors that she had killed herself. She later turned up alive and well, and it's possible that the *Sun* made up the story to help sell papers. By 1841, Mary was happily engaged to a man named Daniel Payne. On July 25, 1841, she told her mother and Payne that she was going to visit some relatives in New Jersey and would be back the next day. She never returned. On July 28, a group of men noticed a body floating in the Hudson River near Hoboken, New Jersey, and rowed out to retrieve it. It was Mary. The body showed signs of attack, and right away, many suspected that Daniel Payne was the murderer, even though he had a good alibi.

A tavern owner, Frederica Loss, said that in August she'd seen Mary in the company of another man at her establishment, and later heard screaming from the woods. Her sons had found some of Mary's clothes in those woods, where they'd been for some time. It seemed like Mary had been abducted and murdered, but no leads for a suspect turned up. Then in October,

Daniel went on a drinking binge that took him to the site of where her body had been found. He fell onto a bench and died of a laudanum overdose, leaving behind a handwritten note: "To the World—Here I am on the very spot. May God forgive me for my misspent life."

Was this a confession of murder? Did he kill himself because of a broken heart?

Edgar Allan Poe became so interested in the mystery that he wrote the short story "The Mystery of Marie Rogêt," which set the crime in Paris. Using fiction, he tried to work out the details of the culprit, but even though he came up with his own conclusions, his readers would have to work out the answer to the real murder.

The story took another twist. In November, Frederica Loss was accidentally shot by one of her sons, and on her deathbed, she confessed that she knew the man with Mary, a doctor who she might have contacted to terminate an unwanted pregnancy. The operation failed and Mary died, and the doctor dumped her body in the river. The problem was that this didn't fit with all the evidence. Was Frederica lying? Covering up for someone else? We might never know. To this day, the mystery of the popular, pretty, and flirty young woman working in the cigar shop remains unsolved.

The Murder
at Cherry Hill

I n the mid-1820s, a young man named Jesse Strang decided
to abandon his wife because he thought she was being
unfaithful to him. Leaving his home just north of New York
City, he moved about aimlessly for a bit, before taking up work
in Albany, New York. Assuming the name Joseph Orton, he
was able to secure work with the prestigious Van Rensselaer
family, at their historic house, Cherry Hill. While there, he met
Elsie Van Rensselaer, who took a liking to him, even though
she was already married to a man named John Whipple.

Elsie was known to have loud outbursts of anger, but Jesse
liked her anyway, and he reasoned that her behavior was
because she was unhappy with her husband. That evaluation
seemed on point, because they started having an affair, and
soon Elsie was talking about killing John so she and Jesse
could run off together.

While Jesse wanted to be with Elsie, he wasn't too keen on
murder, but she talked him into putting arsenic in John's
tea. This attempt failed, and John, suspecting something
was up, decided to keep a loaded gun nearby in case
someone came for him. Jesse tried to spread rumors that
someone was out to kill John, to remove suspicion from
himself and make it seem like he was worried. If he'd let it
go there, he might have gotten away with it, but Elsie was
determined to have her husband out of her life. She got
John's gun and gave it to Jesse. She told him to shoot John,
and, unfortunately, he relented.

One night in May 1827, Jesse was able to shoot and kill John. He immediately fled the scene and went to a nearby store to "prove" that he was nowhere nearby when the crime happened. He even returned to assist the doctor examining John's body. Despite these deceptions, it wasn't long before suspicion began to fall on him and Elsie. They'd had to buy the arsenic, for example, and many people had seen them together.

The police detained Jesse, and, thinking that he might get a lighter sentence if he admitted it, he confessed to the crime. At his trial, he blamed Elsie for spurring him on, thinking that if she could be charged, her powerful family would intervene and save them both. He even asked his lawyer to plant false papers at Cherry Hill incriminating Elsie (the lawyer wisely refused). This plan failed because since Jesse had pulled the trigger, he was the one responsible for the murder. The jury took only about fifteen minutes to come back with a guilty verdict. Elsie was also tried, but amazingly, she was found not guilty of aiding and abetting him, due to a lack of evidence. She went free, and Jesse was hanged.

The restless sprits of all three are said to wander now in Cherry Hill, doomed forever to be in each other's company. In the end, it seems like Jesse's wife was lucky.

Thomas Montgomery and the Dangers of the Internet

The internet has always attracted fraudsters, con artists, and criminals who assume fake identities and involve themselves in shady dealings, folks who are always looking to prey on the vulnerable. And little leaves someone more vulnerable than an aching heart.

While the following story has the elements of a good urban legend, it is in fact true, and the news reported on it at the time.

Back in 2005, when the internet had a bit more of a Wild West feel to it, a 46-year-old man named Thomas Montgomery started messing around on the web. He was married and a father, but that apparently wasn't enough for him to overcome temptation. Maybe it was a midlife crisis; maybe he was just being foolish. Thomas met someone going by the name Jessi, who said she was 18, and went by the screen name "Talhotblond." That should have been the first sign that something was a bit off.

The two traded photos, letters, and even chatted on the phone, but Thomas knew he wouldn't be attractive to a barely legal teenager, especially if she was "hot," so he sent her photos of himself when he was a young man in the Marines. He lied and said he was about to be deployed to Iraq, a convenient excuse should she want to meet him any time soon. That way, he could keep up his online flirtations and not have to face any

consequences. Except, of course, the consequences then came knocking at his door, so to speak.

Thomas became more and more obsessed with the young lady, and their communications grew more frequent. It might have kept going, but one of Thomas's teenage daughters found one of Jessi's messages and alerted her mom, who was, of course, furious. Jessi realized that the man she thought was a handsome young Marine had been lying to her the whole time. She broke things off with Thomas, and then started messaging an actual young man named Brian Barrett. The problem was that Brian was a co-worker of Thomas and used the same chat room, so it wasn't long before Thomas found out about them.

Thomas became ever more jealous of Jessi and Brian's burgeoning relationship, especially since he knew Brian in real life. When he heard that Brian was going to drive to West Virginia to meet Jessi in person, Thomas flipped out. He took his military rifle and shot Brian in the parking lot of their workplace. He was arrested, and one of the main concerns the police had was to make sure that he hadn't gone and killed Jessi, too. They went to her home, but another surprise awaited them.

The woman claiming to be Jessi was actually named Mary Shieler. She was about Thomas's age, and had been using photos of her daughter Jessi to meet men on the internet. The real Jessi knew nothing about it. Mary was never charged with any crime, because at the time, pretending to be someone else on the internet wasn't a crime, or at least it wasn't something the law knew how to deal with. Hopefully, she learned her lesson.

Unusual Customs around the World

Every culture has its own rituals, beliefs, and practices concerning romance. Even though humans are all pretty similar, the ways we express ourselves about sensitive topics such as love vary quite a lot around the globe. Here are just a few examples of how people think about weddings in different cultures as well as a brief discussion about why some countries have decided to ban Valentine's Day altogether. While dictators and thought police might try to control the heart and emotions, and all the dangers they can bring, they will never succeed, meaning the lore of love will continue to be filled with everything from the beautiful and inspirational to the strange, tragic, and even horrific for a long time to come.

Rotten Food, Fish Guts, and Worse: An Old Scottish Wedding Custom

People traditionally throw things at weddings: rice at the bride and groom as they're leaving, or the bridal bouquet to a group of young, hopeful women. In northeast Scotland, the act of throwing things occasionally gets a whole lot messier for spouses-to-be, as an old folk custom known as "the blackening" still sometimes takes place.

At some point before the wedding, one or both of the couple will be "abducted" by their friends and subjected to what can only be described as torture. They'll be taken somewhere and then doused with all sorts of garbage, mainly rotten food. They might first have molasses smeared on them to make them sticky, and then all kinds of truly gross things will be tossed at them: rotten eggs, fish or fish guts, sour milk, dog food, and so on. And this is supposed fun!

Sometimes, the friends get carried away, and not only the soon-to-be bride and groom get attacked, but also the best man and the bridesmaids. It's all taken in stride, and (usually) there are no hard feelings.

But why do people do this and more importantly, allow it to be done to them? Well, it's said to bring good luck to the happy couple, the idea being that if they can put up with something so awful at the start of their marriage they'll pull

through as a couple. Think of it as a kind of marital baptism by fire, only with stinky fish guts. It also represents an event that they can't control, unlike every other aspect of their wedding. If they can cope with the unexpected early on, that bodes well for their future.

It's also a way to bring the community together, since all their friends, families, and neighbors can get in on the plot to capture the couple, arrange when and where to do it, and decide what disgusting things they can toss at them. So this strange ritual can bring everyone closer together. Of course, sometimes the attackers can get carried away, and unintended injuries can happen, but in general, it ends up being a good, if messy, time for everyone.

This unusual custom seems to have begun as a pre-wedding cleansing ritual for brides, where their feet would be covered in soot from a chimney and then washed to symbolize their transition to a new life. As time when on, this custom evolved into the more vigorous and elaborate "blackening," with not just the feet getting covered, and not just with ash. Still, why fish guts?

The custom could also be a way for the couple and the community to do something unusual, even odd, for themselves, in the face of so much commercialization around weddings and every other celebration. They can put a unique Scottish touch on the whole getting married business that is unique to their region. Given how revolting blackening is, it will probably stay that way.

Valentine's Day Bans

Valentine's Day brings up mixed feeling for a lot of people. Some see it as nothing more than a cynical plot conceived by candy and flower companies to sell a lot of products. Other people think that it unfairly forces romance down our throats. Still more worry about the message: If you have to set aside a day to celebrate romantic love, then what are you doing on the other 364 days of the year?

Those are valid concerns, and many people don't celebrate the day, whether they're single or taken. But what about actual bans on Valentine's Day? There are several countries, or parts of countries, around the world that don't look kindly on February 14, with reasons ranging from it being "morally corrupting" to being a crass commercialization of love (they might have a point with the latter).

Here are a few places where Valentine's Day is not welcome:

Saudi Arabia: To be fair, Saudi Arabia has amended their laws, and since 2018, some Valentine's Day celebrations are now permitted. Prior to that, the day was considered contrary to their culture and religious practices, and anyone caught selling cards or candy on February 14 could be arrested, fined, or even jailed.

Uzbekistan: Celebration of the day is technically legal, but since 2012 the Ministry of Education's Department of Enlightenment and the Promotion of Values has discouraged it. Instead, they want people to celebrate the birthday of Babur, a Mughal emperor and descendant of Genghis Khan. This decree wasn't so much targeting Valentine's Day in particular, but any holiday that the department considered to be foreign to Uzbek culture.

Iran: Since 2011, Iran has banned Valentine's Day and all of its practices due to its associations with Western culture and immorality. To replace Valentine's, a much older holiday, Sepandārmazgān, has been resurrected in recent decades. Dating back to the days of the ancient Persian Empire, Sepandārmazgān is a celebration of friendship, love, and women, and men were expected to give them high praise and lavish gifts upon them. Since this holiday has its roots in Persian culture, the authorities seem more willing to tolerate it. Another ancient festival that honors love and friendship, Mehregan, is celebrated in Iran in October.

Belgorod, Russia: This city near the Ukrainian border decided to issue its own ban on Valentine's Day in 2011, though the holiday is celebrated elsewhere in Russia. The deputy governor said that if they were to have Valentine's Day, they might as well also have a "Vodka Day," where everyone presumably drinks themselves silly.

Other countries that don't look kindly on Valentine's Day, most often for its so-called "corrupting influences," include Pakistan, Afghanistan, Indonesia, Brunei, and Malaysia, where officials have gone so far as call the day a "gateway to disaster."

Thailand's Coffin Weddings

A wedding day must surely be one of the most exciting and stressful days in one's life, a day of celebration and promise, but also of big plans and outlandish expenses. We imagine groups of happy people toasting, dancing, cutting cake, and having the time of their lives. But what happens to all that fun if you have to spend a part of your wedding day in a coffin?

In 2015, Valentine's Day fell on the same day as Māgha Pūjā Day, an important Buddhist holiday celebrated in Southeast Asia. On that day, ten engaged couples went to the Wat Takhian Buddhist temple in northwest Bangkok to get married in an unusual ceremony. Each couple took turns making offerings to the monks and the temple. Then, with both the bride and groom holding bouquets of flowers, they lay down in a coffin large enough to fit two people, the inside of which was decorated in bright pink.

The monks then laid a large white sheet over the couple, like a shroud, symbolizing the deaths of their previous lives. The monks began chants that were normally reserved for funerals, as if the couple were dead. When they completed this chanting, the monks offered up blessings for a new life together and removed the shroud.

This ritual was believed to dispel bad luck for the new couples. They would be able to enjoy a life of love, happiness, prosperity, and be free from anything that had plagued either of them in the past. The monks performed this ceremony for all ten couples and then sent them on their way.

The abbot, Phra Kru Samu Sa-ngob Kittkayo, explained that this unusual ritual was a new practice that they'd never done before, but several couples liked the idea and wanted to "die" so that they could begin their new lives together. The ceremony also served as something of a somber reminder of the Buddhist philosophy that as all things are subject to change nothing lasts forever—including a happy marriage. Eventually, one or the other partner will die, and the survivor will experience the pain and suffering that comes from loss. Indeed, much of Buddhist teaching is about easing suffering and finding true peace.

The ceremony was meant to be a one-time event, but many people wanted to be married in the same way, including some gay couples, who the temple married even though a full marriage equality law has not yet passed in Thailand (though it's expected to become law soon). In Thailand, at least, mingling death with the start of a new life together seems to be gaining popularity!

China's Ghost Weddings

When it comes to marriage customs, the ghost wedding is an ancient ceremony found in several cultures around the world. It's especially common in China, where it's a tradition dating back more than 2,000 years. The ceremony is what you would think it is, only there is more to the ritual. A ghost wedding involves the marriage of two dead people or, in some cases, one living person and one dead person. So, what is the purpose behind these ceremonies?

The answer has to do with cultural expectations, as well as Chinese philosophy. There is an abiding belief that all things need to be in union with their opposite, as shown in the famous yin-yang symbol. Because of this, when anyone who is unmarried dies, there is a fear that the person's soul will be unhappy in the afterlife unless it can be joined with a companion. To remedy this, the family members of the dead person will sometimes seek out someone else of the opposite sex who also died unmarried, and then, with that family's blessing, join the two in a symbolic marriage ceremony so that they can be together in death. Obviously, this kind of ritual is intended for the family members, and, like a funeral, it is meant as a way of honoring the dead. On the more macabre side, the bride's bones will be dug up and reinterred with those of her new husband, so that they can be together forever in this world as well as the next.

In some cases, people have claimed that the deceased reached out to them and requested a spouse. The dead might contact the living through dreams, or even make a relative sick until they hold a séance and discover the true cause of the illness.

Once the family pledges to marry the dead family member, the spirit relents, and the sickness goes away.

In China, there was a long-standing cultural belief that having an unwed daughter brought shame on the family, so if she died unwed, this was a chance to restore the family's honor, as well as give her spirit some peace.

In more recent decades, especially in Southeast Asia, there have been controversial marriages between a living and a dead person. In some cases, it has involved a woman marrying the man whom she intended to marry, but who was tragically taken from her. She could then adopt a child and carry on his family's name. There have also been stories of grave robbing: in Shanxi province in 2015, the corpses of fourteen women were stolen and sold to families who needed dead brides for their weddings. Unfortunately, there are even reports of murder, where someone is killed so that their body can be sold for marriage purposes. Of course, this is illegal, and the Chinese government has tried to crack down on it, but in more rural areas, the sinister practice of selling corpses for ghost weddings may continue.

About the Author

Tim Rayborn has a life-long interest in the unusual, the strange, the bizarre, and the rather creepy. He has written several books on these topics, including *The Scary Book of Christmas Lore*, *The Big Book of Paranormal*, *A History of the End of the World*, and *Beethoven's Skull*, among many others. He's written nearly fifty books and more than thirty magazine articles on subjects such as music, the arts, general knowledge, fantasy fiction, the paranormal, and history of all kinds.

He is planning to write more books, whether anyone wants him to or not. He lived in England for several years and studied at the University of Leeds for his PhD, which means he likes to pretend that he knows what he's talking about.

He's also an almost-famous musician who plays many unusual instruments from all over the world that most people have never heard of and usually can't pronounce. He has appeared on more than forty recordings, and his musical wanderings and tours have taken him across the US, all over Europe, Canada, and Australia, and to such romantic locations as Umbrian medieval towns, Marrakech, Vienna, Renaissance chateaux, medieval churches, and high school gymnasiums.

He currently lives in rainy Washington State with many books, recordings, and instruments.

www.timrayborn.com

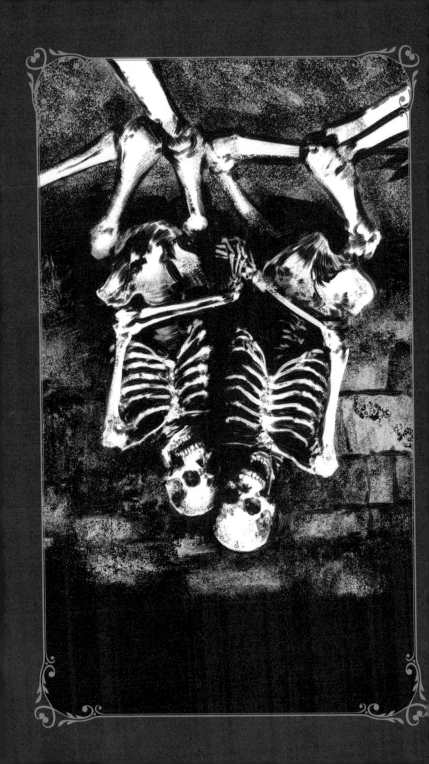

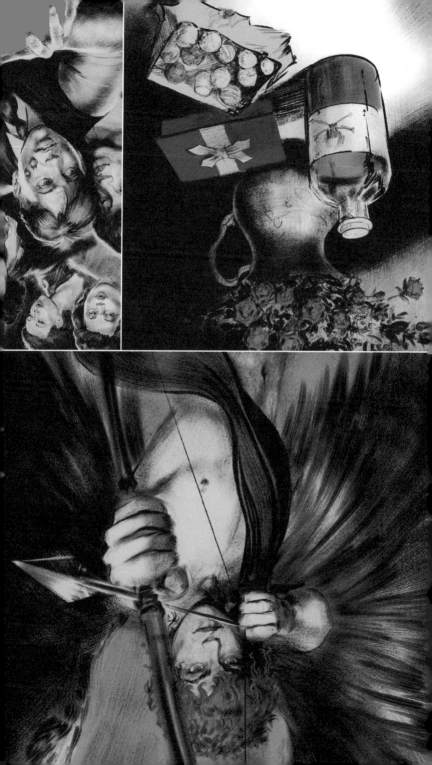